For Mum
I know you would have got this

Your wings already exist.
All you have to do is fly.

1

AFTER

March

I know exactly what you'd say if you were sitting next to me.

The journey of a thousand miles begins with a single step.

Not your words – they're Lao Tzu's. You loved old wisdom – the way it held true, even hundreds of years later. And you would have loved this journey: the wide, open road ahead of us, the ever-changing landscape, your imagination sparking off in a hundred different directions. Poring excitedly over spread-out maps, you'd have made lists of places to check out, while I'd be thinking about getting my nails done and wondering how many outfits I could cram into a small suitcase.

But adventures were your life-blood – you told me your boyhood tales of climbing and wild camping, gazing at seascapes and skyscapes, riding waves, harnessing the wind. The beaten track wasn't for you. *There are a million other paths, Cassidy,* you'd say to me. *The same old is never going to take you anywhere new.* It was one of a hundred reasons I fell in love with you.

Setting off into the unknown was your best kind of adventure. *Leaving space for the unexpected*, you always told me, *because that's where the magic happens...*

I was cool with that, even though I'm more of a busy airport and crowded flight kind of girl. After all, there'd still be shops and bars and restaurants – everyone knows France is full of them.

Sitting next to me in your faded jeans, a long-sleeved T-shirt under your soft grey jumper, your eyes would have danced as you laughed at me. *Paris, maybe, babe. But not where we're going.*

I'd have given you a sideways look, because there was no way there wouldn't be at least one bar. France was on our list of places to see – you knew about the image I had. Us, sitting outside a bistro with painted shutters and pots of geraniums, elegantly sipping wine and watching the world go by. Rural France was just the beginning. Beyond lay Paris, Bordeaux, the Cote d'Azur; then across the mountains into Spain where there'd be beaches and music and heady nights of dancing under the stars with you.

Holidays are the best of times. Remember that one I was going on with Ellie, the day you and I met? But if we were planning this together, I wouldn't have cared about bars or restaurants, or the clothes crammed into my suitcase. I would have gone anywhere in the world with just the clothes on my back, as long you were with me.

2

BEFORE

January, last year

'Come on, Casey!' Sweeping her long red hair over one shoulder, Ellie was getting agitated.

'We have loads of time,' I told her. While my friend liked to arrive hours early, I preferred to leave it till the last minute, rather than spend hours in a crowded departure lounge.

'We don't,' Ellie said firmly. 'You know I want to go to the duty-free shop. And I need books...'

'You won't have time to read, Ell. We'll be too busy.'

'Not that busy... And I'll be keeping a firm eye on you, Casey Cassidy. I still can't believe you snogged that guy on New Year's Eve.'

I shook my head, regretting for the umpteenth time that I'd told her. 'You don't have to announce it to the entire airport! And I can't believe it either.' It had been a terrible party and a sleazy guy – there's nothing like seeing in another year to make you look at your life.

But actually, there was nothing wrong with my life. I had the job I loved in a primary school, my home in my sister Polly's house, great friends. I had this dream, too, that one day I'd fall in love with the right man, someone with whom I'd have a big, happy, noisy family. Wasn't that what life was about?

As we hurried through Gatwick airport, Ellie threaded her arm through mine. 'I can't wait for us to get there! Do you know how long I've wanted to do this?'

'I think so,' I reminded her. 'You may have mentioned it at least fifty times – and that's since Christmas.' Ellie's wanderlust was a standing joke between us.

'OK,' she said good-naturedly. It took a lot to rile my friend. 'It's just that January is the most depressing month. And work is so bloody full on. Don't you ever want to stop the treadmill and get off?'

While I was a teacher, Ellie worked for a digital marketing agency. 'Ellie! We're young. There's plenty of time for a quiet life when we're old and wrinkly. Besides, it's never going to happen. There's always too much to do and not enough time!'

'Way too much, if you ask me.' She shook her head. 'I need different, Casey. I want to be zen. Learn yoga. Meditate. Watch sunsets. Let the peace and quiet soak into me.'

'I don't think Morocco will be that kind of peaceful.' At least, I was hoping not. I'd been picturing bustling souks, calls to prayer, and plenty of life. Crowded bars, maybe some harmless flirting if the opportunity presented itself. 'And not that kind of warm, either – not for watching sunsets. Not in January.'

'Then I'll wear a big scarf and a jumper.' Ellie gave me a withering look. 'It's my quest on this holiday to find peace and sunshine.'

As we reached security, she detached her arm from mine, before getting her phone out and scrolling through it for her boarding pass. Fishing in my pocket, I felt for mine, folded where I always put it, inside my passport. I preferred a printed version. Besides, the screen on my phone was cracked and I wasn't taking any chances. Trying the other pocket, I frowned. 'Ell, wait. I can't find my passport.'

Crouching down, I unzipped my cabin bag and started going through my clothes. But as I sat in the middle of the airport, frantically going through my pockets, there was no sign of it. 'Fuck.' Sitting among my jumble of clothes, I stared at Ellie. 'I've only done the stupidest thing.'

'You'd better be kidding.' A look of panic crossed her face. 'We don't have time for this, Casey. We should be through security by now. They're about to start boarding our flight.'

But as I sat there, my heart was sinking. 'It isn't here.' I'd left my passport at home. I wasn't going anywhere.

'Fuck.' Ellie looked stricken. 'I can't go without you.'

'You have to,' I said miserably. 'I'm so sorry, Ell. I've really ballsed this up. There's no point both of us missing the flight.'

Glancing at the departure board, she looked torn. 'Oh fuck, Casey. What do I do?'

I looked at her. 'You'd better hurry – or you'll miss it.'

'I can't go without you.' She hesitated. 'I'll stay. We'll both change our flights.'

I shook my head. 'No way. I'll try, but what if there aren't any? You can't miss this, Ellie. You've been looking forward to it for ages.'

'I suppose you're right.' Sounding reluctant, she leaned down and kissed me on the cheek. 'But if I'm going to make it, I need to run.' Picking up her bag, she started jogging towards security, turning briefly to call back to me. 'Let me know which flight you'll be on! And I'll check out a bar for tomorrow night...'

As she disappeared through security, I started squashing everything back into my case, jamming it shut and forcing the zip to close. Then as I got up and started heading for the exit, a feeling of wretchedness descended over me. What an idiot I'd been, not checking I had my passport with me.

As my self-pity grew, behind me I could hear a man's voice calling out. 'Hey, wait...' Footsteps seemed to gather pace, then someone fell into step beside me, holding out something that looked like my makeup bag. I looked at it in surprise. 'What the...'

'You left it in the terminal. At least, I guess it's yours.' The man sounded bemused.

Taking it, I unzipped it. Yep, definitely my Benefit makeup and Clarins skin serum, none of which was cheap. Turning, I took in the body attached to the hand, then the face, meeting eyes the colour of the ocean, sparkling slightly as they looked at me.

'Thanks.' Clamping it under my arm, I turned away. How dare he look amused. Nothing about any of this was remotely funny.

He didn't take the hint. Walking beside me, he glanced at my case. 'Been somewhere nice?'

'Not really.' I felt myself scowl.

'Oh. What was it? A business trip?'

In my flowery orange tunic and flared jeans, did I really look like I'd been on a business trip? 'If you must know, I was going away with my friend. But I left my passport at home, so while she's about to board a flight to Marrakech, I'm staying here in crappy old England.'

'Oh.' The amusement left his face. 'That's a bummer.'

'Actually, it's worse than a bummer. I'm going to try to change my flight, but because it's the school holidays, the fares will be exorbitant. So... you can see why I'm pissed off.' Getting a hold of myself, I turned to look at him again. Suddenly I was mortified that I'd spoken to a stranger that way – particularly a stranger who'd run after me with a pink makeup bag covered in fluffy kittens. 'I'm so sorry. You've been nothing but kind. It just isn't a good moment. I'll sort it. Thanks for picking up my makeup bag.'

Walking faster, I headed for the exit.

3

AFTER

March

That day, that meeting, was the beginning of us. A moment that was to define the rest of my life in ways I could never have dreamed of. Packing a few last things, I try not to think too much. Looking around what used to be our bedroom, I pick up the old jumper of yours you were going to throw out, when I hear Ellie let herself in.

I go downstairs, carrying the bags. 'Hi.' I drop them by the door.

'Hey...' Her green eyes look worriedly into mine. 'How's it going?'

'OK.' I shrug. 'I'm just wondering what I've forgotten. We both know how that one goes.' *I'm good at forgetting things, as you know. Jackets, purses – even passports.*

'Passport?' Ellie says, on cue.

I nod towards the table where my car keys are positioned on top of it. 'Not taking any chances.'

'What about the rest of Ben's stuff?'

'There isn't much,' I say shortly. 'Most of it's at his parents' house.'

'Well, that's something.' Ellie sounds relieved, then the anxious look is back. 'I know it's good you're getting away – and Kevin says the house is really peaceful. But at the same time, I kind of wish you weren't.'

Kevin's the friend who came up with the idea of going away for a while, before telling me he had a friend who owned just the place. And though I'm not sure how I feel about peaceful, something has to change. Swallowing the lump in my throat, I try to smile. 'All I know is, right now, I can't stay here, Ells.' Not while I'm still waiting, the knot in my stomach tightening, hoping any moment you'll walk back in. 'But you know me. I'm good on my own. And before you know it, I'll be back.'

'What I'd like to say to him.' Ellie's voice is mutinous.

'Don't, Ell.' There'll be a time for recriminations, but it isn't now. I glance at the clock, at the irrepressible constant of time – steadily moving forward when you'd do anything to make it stop. 'You know how good I am at being late.'

Ellie picks up one of my bags. 'So, come on! You have a ferry to catch!'

Outside, I lock up the house and load my bags into my car, before saying goodbye to Ellie, while battling sudden, fleeting doubts telling me I shouldn't be doing this.

'You need to go.' Reading my mind, Ellie hugs me again. 'Keep me posted! And don't drive too fast... and...'

'I won't.' I hug her back, breathing in her familiar perfume, already missing her.

Getting into my car, I check again that I have my passport. Starting the engine, I pull out, glancing in the rearview mirror to see Ellie still standing there. Lowering the window, I stick my hand out, tooting once.

It's exciting, babe. An adventure!

The words startle me. It's exactly what you'd say if you were sitting next to me. I grip the steering wheel more tightly. The last thing I need is my mind playing tricks. You see, I've been holding on to this dream that I'll hear the sound of your key in the lock, you calling out as you come in, telling me there's been a terrible mistake, your blue eyes earnest. *Will I forgive you?*

For once, I wish the clichés were true. But there isn't always a reason why things happen. As for the great healer that time's supposed to be, I could wait a thousand years but every moment of every day, I will miss you.

* * *

I drive on autopilot as the rush hour maelstrom carries me to the outskirts of Portsmouth. Following the signs for the port, I imagine the other drivers on their way home to their happy, uncomplicated lives. Before you and I met, that's how mine was. I had a job I loved, my friends, and OK, a chaotic social life, but it was fun. I was happy, Ben. Then we met and for a while, I was even happier.

My hands tighten on the steering wheel. We should have been doing this together, but sometimes life takes unexpected twists. Things happen that rock you out of your world. That's what's brought me to the docks in Portsmouth on a damp March evening to catch the overnight ferry – another of those firsts I measure my life by now. My first trip away without you.

4

BEFORE

January, last year

'Hey!' the guy called after me. 'Wait! I might be able to help.'

Overtaking a group of Chinese tourists wheeling enormous suitcases, I started to walk faster. I was the one who'd left my passport at home. I didn't need some man I'd never met before offering to help me. But before I could reach the exit, he'd caught me up again.

I frowned. 'I don't think so.'

He fell into step beside me. 'I mean it – with that flight.' He paused. 'I'm Ben, by the way.'

I slowed down slightly and my frown deepened. Help me with that flight? Was that a euphemism that even I hadn't heard of? 'What do you mean?' I asked suspiciously.

'Well, I have a friend who works for one of the airlines. It may come to nothing, but there's nothing to lose by giving her a call and asking.' He was remarkably unfazed given how narked I was.

Oh. Right. I got it. A girlfriend. So why was he chatting me up?

'Why don't I buy you a coffee?' He paused again, before adding more pointedly, 'If you're not in too much of a hurry? And I'll call my friend.'

I hesitated, still not sure why a total stranger would go out of his way for me. But as I looked at him, there was just something about him. Against my better judgement, I felt myself waver. 'OK.'

He nodded towards the coffee bar by the exit. 'How about there?'

Reaching the table, I pulled out a chair, suddenly grateful to be sitting down.

Ben stood there. 'How d'you like your coffee?'

'Black. Thanks.'

As he walked away, I opened a message from Ellie.

I've just boarded. Hope you're OK. Let me know when you've booked a flight xxx

After messaging her that I was already working on it, I logged in to the airport Wi-Fi and started googling flights to Marrakech tomorrow, but as I scrolled through the availability, my heart was sinking. There was only one flight that had seats left and the price was ludicrous.

Seeing Ben come back, I put my phone down. 'I've checked tomorrow's flights. The prices are outrageous.' I tried to mask my disappointment, but I was gutted. 'I guess I'm going to be staying at home.'

'All is not lost – yet.' Putting the tray down, he sat opposite me and passed me one of the cups before getting his phone out. After scrolling through his contacts, he made a call. 'Hi. Look, I wanted to ask you a favour. I'm with a friend who's just missed her flight to Marrakech. She's checked to see what's available tomorrow, but the prices are crazy. It's a long shot, but you know you got me that cheap flight to New York last summer? I just wondered if there was any chance you could help.'

All the time he was speaking, his eyes were lingering on me. Then putting his hand over the phone, he muttered, 'I don't even know your name.'

'Casey Cassidy.'

'Casey Cassidy,' Ben repeated into his phone. Then, 'Yes, she's a friend.' His eyes were still fixed on mine.

As he spoke, I shook myself. What on earth was happening to me? I didn't need a stranger sorting my problems out. He was quiet again, then those deep blue eyes swivelled back to mine. 'She's asking if you have a valid UK passport.'

As I nodded, I suddenly forgot about the missed flight, about Ellie going to Marrakech without me. Logic had gone out of the window. Instead, as I looked at him, I knew I'd met someone special. Watching him speak, I took in the faded tan, the faint scar on his jaw, the well-worn cotton shirt under a distressed jacket, the way he listened, because these days, so many people don't.

He put his mobile down. 'Well.' He looked pleased. 'Lexie's booking you on a flight tomorrow. You'll be on standby, but she checked the loads and there are five spare seats. With any luck, you'll be in one of them.'

Opening and closing my mouth, I managed to stop myself saying 'fuck' in the nick of time. 'Thank you. So much.' I shook my head, dumbfounded. 'I can't believe you've done this. Please say thank you to Lexie. How much do I owe her? Or you?'

He looked evasive. 'It's very little – and I'll sort it out with her. She owed me a favour. She's going to send me your booking details so that I can forward them to you – if you give me your email?' He looked at me questioningly. 'All you need to do is add your passenger information. Then check in back here at six tomorrow morning. If it doesn't work out, they refund the ticket. All in all, there's nothing to lose.'

I stared at him, still not sure why he was doing this. 'You've saved my holiday. Honestly, I can't thank you enough for this.'

'Well, let's hope there's a seat.' His face lit up in a smile that reached his eyes. 'But all in a day's work. You're welcome.' He hesitated. 'Do you need a lift anywhere?'

Suddenly I remembered the missing passport I still needed to retrieve. 'What time is it now?'

He glanced at his very nice chunky watch that was clearly expensive, but not ostentatious. 'Nearly five.'

I tried to think. 'I guess I'll get a cab home, then another back here for six tomorrow morning...' Except Ellie and I had already looked into the cost and they were about sixty pounds each way. As it all stacked up, I could feel my heart sinking again. On my teacher's wage, on top of the holiday itself, I hadn't budgeted for two taxi fares.

'Where's home?'

'West Sussex. Near Chichester.'

'Ah.' He paused. 'I could give you a lift if you like. And I'm about halfway between the two, if that's any help? In Midhurst,' he added. Then seeing my face, he held up both his hands. 'Listen, I have a spare room and if it would help, you're welcome to have it for the night. And I'm a perfectly decent law-abiding citizen. Why don't you text your friend? Tell her where you're going. And that I'm dropping you back here in the morning to catch your flight.'

This was getting weirder by the minute. I stared at him for a moment, losing myself in his beautiful eyes. I'd only just met him, but the same instincts that generally warned me off men were telling me to trust him. Then common sense kicked in. This was going way too fast. 'You've been so kind, and I don't want to seem ungrateful, but we've known each other, what – forty minutes?' I looked at him pointedly.

He looked mortified. 'You're absolutely right. Why don't you find yourself a hotel for the night? Then... I'm happy to drive you home to pick up your passport. And if you don't have any plans, maybe on the way back I could take you out for dinner?'

Of course I didn't have plans. I was supposed to be on a plane, remember? But the offer of a lift was hard to turn down. And dinner with him, I could definitely cope with. 'That would be really nice.' My heart fluttered as I held his gaze. 'I might just look at hotels first.' Picking up my phone, I brought up one of the comparison websites, where there was a room that cost a fraction of two taxi rides. 'There's a room at the Premier Inn. Right next to the North Terminal.' Booking it before someone else did, I instantly felt better.

Ben was already ahead of me. 'If you like, I could take you over there now, so that you could check in to your room and leave your suitcase?'

'Can I just text a friend?' Truth was, I was too used to good-looking men turning out to be complete losers. Ben, however, was fast proving to be the exception to the rule. 'But if you really don't mind, thank you.'

Knowing Ellie would soon be airborne, I texted Suki.

Very weird, Sukes. Forgot my passport. Still at the airport, about to get in a strange man's car to go and get it. He's a nice strange man obvs. Just so you know in case I'm wrong xxx

As we walked towards the car park, the darkness was broken every so often by the lights of a low-flying aircraft on its final approach. Ben's car was a big, shiny Hyundai hybrid which, as he unlocked it, he was already apologising about. 'It's useful for work. Plus I like climbing and surfing, and I can throw everything I need in the back.'

Wondering what work was and why he was apologising, I watched him lift my case in, suspicious again. 'So, you haven't told me why you were here today.' Dropping off a girlfriend, maybe?

'I gave my parents a lift. They're off to the Caribbean for a month. Since Dad retired, they like to make the most of the chance to travel.' He sounded envious. 'You said the Premier Inn, didn't you?'

I nodded. 'Next to the North Terminal.' I paused. The idea of a shower and a change of clothes was growing more appealing with each passing minute. But suddenly it seemed an unnecessary detour when I was coming back later on. 'This is silly. We don't need to go there first.' Aware of how much I was putting him out, I shook my head. 'I've already taken up too much of your time. It's enough that you're giving me a lift home. You can drop me. I can work it out from there.'

He hesitated. 'I don't mind. I don't have anything planned this evening – I'd kept the day free to see my parents off. And the hotel is only a few minutes away.'

Feeling torn, I hesitated. 'I feel terrible about putting you to so much trouble. But you know, it would be really good to sort my case out. When I was looking for my passport, I just squashed everything back in. It will only take me five minutes – if you're sure.'

'It's no problem. Really.'

Sitting back, as he started driving, I was silent, slightly mesmerised by a kind of warmth coming from him, the fresh scent of his cologne.

'Where in Chichester do you live?'

'Not far from the theatre. It's actually my sister's house, but she lives in the States.' Pulling up outside the hotel, we got out. As he lifted out my case, I made a mental note of the vehicle registration to text Suki.

'I'll go and park. Shall I see you in reception when you're ready? No rush,' he added. 'I'll get a coffee.'

'Thanks.' Doing my best to look nonchalant, I wheeled my case towards the tinted glass doors of the hotel, in which I could see Ben's reflection as he stood by his car. Then they opened to let me through, before closing behind me. When I glanced back, I felt a smile flicker on my lips as I saw him still standing there, watching me.

After checking in at reception, I got in the lift. It was all too bizarre. Firstly, I'd never missed a flight before; not ever, always timing it to perfection for minimal hanging around. Then, secondly, abandoning my precious makeup bag on the airport floor. I'd never done anything like that either. How many people would have walked straight past it? But Ben hadn't. He'd picked it up and come after me.

As I closed the door into my room, I had a sudden reality check. What if this guy was some kind of psychopath? All this might be an act he'd honed – underneath, he might be completely different. As I took a deep breath, I had a feeling he wasn't, but the sleazy guy on New Year's Eve had left me questioning my judgement. After texting Suki the registration number, she got straight back to me.

Don't do anything I wouldn't!! xx

Slightly relieved, I opened my suitcase, perusing the crumpled contents, hastily hanging some of them up, before jumping into the shower. Brushing my hair into a slightly more restrained state of unruliness, I touched up my makeup before pulling out one of the dresses destined for Morocco. If I was going out for dinner with a good-looking guy, I wasn't going in my airport-weary jeans. Pulling on black leggings and the boots I'd been wearing earlier, I checked my reflection. Not perfect, but it would do.

Less than ten minutes later, I walked coolly across reception to where Ben was engrossed in reading something on his mobile. 'Hi.'

'Hey.' Looking up, his eyes flickered over me. 'You look nice.'

'Thanks.' I raised my eyebrows. 'This was the least creased item of my holiday wardrobe.'

There was a look of approval in his eyes as he got up. 'Shall we go and find your passport?'

As we walked, I couldn't stop thinking. How was it I'd known this guy less than an hour? It felt so effortless between us.

As he drove, he told me he'd booked a table in a pub for later just outside Crawley. 'I should have asked what kind of food you like.'

'I'm almost vegan,' I told him. 'But don't worry, I'm not evangelical.'

'I'm much the same – for all kinds of reasons.' Without elaborating, he changed the subject. 'So, your sister lives in the States?'

'Yes. In New York. She has a high-flying job with a bank. She moved there two years ago – it was only supposed to be for six months, but she loves it. I don't think she has any plans to come back.'

'And how about you?' He sounded curious.

'Oh, I'm not like Polly.' I wasn't being self-deprecating, it was true. 'She's massively clever and wears designer clothes, and has the next ten years of her life mapped out. While I... I'm not really like that. I'm a teacher – in a primary school, which means a class of twenty-two seven-

year-olds are entrusted into my care. And I'm not very organised.' But I hardly needed to tell him that.

'Wow.' Ben sounded astonished. 'I can't imagine ever coping with that many kids.'

'That's what I used to think, but they're great. Some of them are really sure of themselves and others are quite shy... and it can be hard work, but I love it. Even though it's the reason why I have to go on holiday at the most expensive times of year...' I grimaced.

'You're lucky – that you love your job.' I was aware of Ben's eyes flickering sideways towards me.

'I am.' Then I paused, curious, because Ben's swanky car must have cost a fortune. 'What about you?'

'Well... I used to have a soul-destroying job working in advertising. Actually, that's not quite right. I worked in London for one of the big agencies and for the first few years, I loved it. But...' He hesitated. 'I suppose I got disillusioned. All that money going into promoting products that were ethically questionable... It came down to my conscience, in the end. Quite simply, I didn't want to be a part of it.'

'Oh?' I was curious. An advertising geek with morals? 'So what did you do after that?'

'I took off for a year, with my surfboard. I went to Bali, then Sri Lanka. Had the best time of my entire life.'

I was bemused. 'But you came back.'

'Yes.' He was silent for a moment. 'But with a different view about life. That trip completely opened my eyes, I suppose you'd say. I'd forgotten what a big world it was. Out there, I met so many people who live the simplest of lives. They have so little compared to us, but they're happy. It got me thinking. So...' He took a deep breath. 'After getting the necessary qualifications, a year ago I set up a business with Jez, a mate, filming – using drones. It can be anything from promotional films, to evidence of planning being flouted or industrial pollution...'

I was impressed. 'So you could go anywhere.'

'That's the idea. At this stage, I take whatever work comes my way.

But this is just the first step. What I want to do is focus on the environment.'

'Wow.' I was intrigued. 'So you actually fly the drones yourselves?'

'We do.' It was too dark to see his face, but from his voice, I could tell he was smiling. 'It satisfies my compulsion to be outside and not stuck in the same place all the time. So far, it's really good.'

On the outskirts of Chichester, I glanced at the clock, thinking of Ellie. In an hour from now, she'd be touching down in Morocco. 'It's the third exit.'

He turned onto the roundabout. 'Last time I was here was for the Festival of Speed.'

'It goes mental around here when that's on.' I shook my head, thinking of the thousands of people who flocked from miles away. 'But not really my thing.'

'So what is your thing?' He sounded amused.

'If you really want to know...' I wondered how I was telling him all this. 'It's music, cooking, dancing – preferably barefoot, under a night sky, somewhere hot... Bars that are buzzing with life, drinking wine with friends... And cats – I love cats. But mostly it's about hanging out with the people I love. Enjoying life. I guess I'm basically a happy person.' It was a philosophy I'd adopted. 'You turn right here. Keep going. It's up the far end.' As we got there, I pointed to a parking space close to Polly's house. 'Why don't you stop here while I nip inside? I won't be a minute.' I crossed my fingers, hoping that my passport was where I thought it was.

He pulled over, and my key was in my hand as I leapt out. Going inside, I flicked on the light, and glanced across at the table at the foot of the stairs where my passport was exactly as I left it this morning – it seemed unbelievable that it was only this morning. Stuffing it in my pocket, I went back out, locking the door behind me.

'I am an idiot,' I said as I got in the car. But in a whirl of excitement about going away, I'd been distracted.

'Easily done.' He looked at me. 'So, how about dinner?'

* * *

Ben had picked a cosy pub with a log fire and, assailed by the scent of hot food as we walked inside, suddenly I realised how hungry I was. Sitting at a corner table with a glass of red wine, I was starting to enjoy myself.

'What are you having?' Ben was studying the menu. 'Sorry. I thought there'd be more for vegans.'

'No, it's great.' Reassuring him, I scanned the options. 'The tagine, I think.'

After ordering two tagines, he poured me another glass of wine. 'So how long have you and Ellie been friends?'

'Since we were six.' I sipped my wine, a soft, fruity red. 'On my first day at school, she rescued me. My family had just moved. Everyone else in my class knew each other and had their little gangs. I was this shy kid with sticky-out teeth that Ellie couldn't stop staring at, while she had hair the colour of a carrot. It was the beginning of a beautiful friendship.' As I proceeded to tell him how, when I was a child, my parents had moved to Devon, he listened intently. 'My mum...' Sighing, I hesitated. 'I love my mum, but she always knows what's best for me – even now.' I rolled my eyes.

He nodded. 'Funny, isn't it? I know people like that – they like to believe they're right and anyone who disagrees is missing something.'

'Exactly!' I exclaimed. 'My dad is endlessly patient. He just accepts that's the way she is...' I felt a sudden pang of remorse. 'I'm really sorry about earlier.'

He looked surprised. 'Sorry?'

'I was quite rude to you – when you found my makeup bag.' I watched his face. 'I'm not normally like that.'

'Don't worry about it! You'd just missed your flight.' He smiled. 'So, this holiday with Ellie...' He looked slightly awkward. 'You said it was a girls' holiday? I guess what I'm asking is...' He hesitated. 'Are you seeing anyone?'

Taken unawares by his directness, I almost choked on my wine. 'Um.

Not especially.' I had a history of unhappy endings, meaning I had very self-protective instincts, which was why I'd been surprised I felt I could trust Ben. 'I really like my independence,' I said carefully. 'There are many scoundrels out there. Let's just say I've found that out the hard way and I'm extremely careful about avoiding them.'

'Ha.' Ben's eyes were teasing. 'Should I take it from that you don't think I'm one of them – a scoundrel, I mean?'

'Maybe. Not yet, at least.' Not yet, at least? What was I thinking? 'But that is always the problem. Most men...' Feeling slightly pissed, I wagged my finger at him. 'They're very good at pretending to be something they're not. When it suits them. In my experience,' I added.

'Not guilty.' He held up his hands. 'Not as far as I know, anyway. There was a girl...'

'Not airport girl,' I said quickly. 'The one you said owed you a favour?'

Confusion flickered across his face before he shook his head. 'Oh no. She's a friend of a mate. The girl I'm talking about... Her name's Olivia.' He paused briefly. 'Lovely girl. But it was all about her. She wasn't really interested in what I – or anyone else – might feel, about anything. The bottom line is she was wrong – for me, at least.' His eyes met mine. 'And once you know that, what's the point?'

'I couldn't agree more.' It was one of the reasons I'd been single for over a year. As I gazed into those ocean-coloured eyes, for a moment, neither of us spoke. If you knew when it was wrong with someone, could you know just as instinctively when it was right?

As we carried on talking, I found out more about Ben. How he felt when he quit his advertising job; then how his grandparents had left him some money, which was how he bought his first drone and paid for his training. But as I soon discovered, there was far more to him. How he couldn't bear the lies and dishonesty of people in power, nor cruelty to any living creature. But what got to him most was what humankind was doing to this planet; how the more time went by, the more driven he was to use his work to expose what he saw as wrong. Now and then, some-

thing distant flickered in his eyes, as if he was back in Bali or Sri Lanka, but as he cracked a joke and laughed, it would vanish.

As we walked out to his car, I shivered in the night air. Then I forgot all about the cold as I felt his arm go around my shoulders. On the way back to the hotel, chill-out music played from the speakers, as I thought about how weird today had been; about how the unlikeliest of circumstances had brought us together as if it were meant to happen – made doubly weird, because I didn't believe in fate or synchronicity or any such things.

Reaching the hotel, Ben slowed down, stopping outside. 'Well?' He looked at me quizzically.

'I don't normally do this.' I paused, looking at him warily, knowing I was putting my fiercely protected heart on the line. 'And I know we've only just met, but I don't really want to say goodbye. Not yet.'

'Me neither.' He glanced towards the hotel. 'How about we get a coffee?'

'That would be nice,' I said quietly.

Putting the car in gear, he drove on and turned into the car park. Finding a parking space, we got out and as we walked towards the hotel entrance, his hand found mine. As the glass doors opened then closed behind us, he glanced towards the bar. 'How about a nightcap?'

Emboldened by the wine from earlier, I took a deep breath. I mean, how often did I meet a good-looking guy who was actually nice? 'Why don't you have one? You could stay, if you like.' I couldn't believe I was saying this. 'I have two beds, by the way. Just in case you were getting the wrong idea...' I broke off. However I put it, it sounded wrong. 'I'm really not suggesting anything. But you have done such a lot of driving today and it is quite late... and it is nice, just talking...'

'It is.' A smile slowly spread across his face as he took my hand again. 'Why don't you find a seat? I'll order us drinks.'

5

March

When Ben and I met, it was just over a year since my last relationship ended – with Colin the bastard, as Ellie had christened him, a title he'd earned many times over. No man was worth what I'd put myself through. Not only had I wasted two years of my life, my self-esteem had been shredded. But it was why, when Ben and I met, I was wary.

While I wait to board the ferry, I stare uneasily through the window. Maybe there's a reason my relationships don't last. Maybe I'm destined to be alone. Noticing the darkening clouds, I imagine the weather worsening, even a storm. It would be fine for you, Ben Summer. You like waves and ships and being at the mercy of the elements. I, however, will be seasick.

I imagine Ellie's no-nonsense tones. *Concentrate on the pesky seagulls. Or the other drivers, off to their fancy holiday homes without a care in the world. Look at that fat middle-aged Brit standing next to his swanky Mercedes and the much-younger wife who looks pissed off with him.*

So I watch the seagulls, the ominous sky, the first spots of rain on the windscreen, the queue edging forwards as a song comes on the radio. 'Sunrise'. So many times you've watched me dance, moments woven into the melody, so that now, as I listen, it brings them back, memories of heady, sunbeam days of love and laughter; the pure joyousness I felt at finding you.

Switch it off and stop wallowing. Ellie's voice again. As the traffic in front of me starts to move, I turn the radio off and follow the car ahead, up the ramp. Manoeuvring my car into the tiny space I'm marshalled towards, I get out and go to find my cabin.

* * *

As the ferry's engine starts to rumble, I reach for the bottle of wine I packed, pouring some into the glass I added at the last minute. Then as the ferry pulls out, I gaze through the window, counting down the twinkling lights. Closing my eyes, I can't help myself, as suddenly I'm in another world, one with you in it.

Cheers, Cassidy. As England disappears into the darkness, you raise your glass and clink it against mine. *Finish your drink and we'll go outside! Come on... It'll stop you feeling seasick...*

You wouldn't have taken no for an answer, persuading me out on deck in the rain, me clinging on to you while we're buffeted by cold air and sea spray, before heading back to our little world within a world for a few hours, our fates resting in someone else's hands.

Great, isn't it?

Easy for you to say, buster. Don't forget, the seasickness pills never work and it will be you holding my hair back while I throw up.

When I open my eyes again, the cabin is empty, the sea smooth as the ferry ploughs on through the darkness. Pouring another glass of wine, I cast my mind back. This time last year, I'd known you three dizzying, electrifying months that had shown me that when you met the right person, it was the easiest thing in the world to fall in love.

But instead of learning from the past, I'd made the same mistakes all over again, never imagining that a year later I would be on a ferry headed for France, without you.

As the alcohol starts to circulate through my veins, a tear rolls down my face, the feelings I've buried beginning to float to the surface. The unfairness, my anger, an aching yearning for you, followed by the inconsolable sadness of losing you.

Thinking of the house I've left behind, suddenly I'm homesick for its sash windows, the pillar-box red front door, the neatly trimmed box hedge edging the path that was your idea; the clashing spring flowers that were mine. A house that for a while, was filled with love.

Lulled by the motion of the ferry, I sleep intermittently in the imagined warmth of your arms, waking much later to another coastline, watching its spangled lights through the spray hitting the windows. You would have seen it as an omen that after leaving a rainy England, the sun rises in a cloudless sky. *It's a sign*, you would have joked, nudging my elbow, because you knew I didn't believe in signs. Suddenly I'm angry with you. *This benign universe you believe in that gives us signs we're on the right track, where is it when I need it most?*

* * *

As the ferry docks, I go to my car. It's a glorious morning; the air cool, the sky an opalescent blue. I watch Mercedes man, impatiently glancing at his oversized watch, his wife looking as unhappy as she did last night. Then I think about calling Ellie, but she'll be getting ready for another day at work. Ellie and I tell each other everything. She was the first person I told about you when, a day later, I eventually reached Morocco.

6

BEFORE

January, last year

In the terminal the following morning and finally in possession of a boarding pass, I was still deep in conversation with Ben.

'I really do have to go,' I said at last, checking for the twentieth time that I had my passport. 'Otherwise, it'll be a replay of yesterday.'

Ben's eyes were fixed on me, his hand still in mine. 'Can I call you when you're back?'

I gazed back at him. 'I haven't put you off?' As we stood there, both of us were silent for a moment. Then on impulse, I reached up and kissed him.

For a few heart-stopping seconds, the world faded around us. Lost in the moment, all I was aware of were his lips against mine, how familiar he felt. Suddenly I remembered my flight. Reluctantly I pulled away, picking up my bag as our eyes met again. 'Thank you – for rescuing me. For dinner. For everything.'

'You're welcome.' His voice was soft. 'Have a great time.'

'I guess I'll be seeing you.' I lingered a moment longer, then forced myself to turn away. Heading towards security, I briefly looked back,

blowing him another kiss; trying to look nonchalant. Underneath, floating on cloud nine.

Making the flight with five minutes to spare before the gate was closed, I settled in seat 2A with no one beside me. One of the perks of travelling standby it seemed, was that the more expensive seats got left till last.

After the aircraft taxied out and took off, I watched the ground fall away, warmth filling me as I remembered our kiss. Would Ben call me when I got back? I smiled to myself. I wanted so much to believe he would.

7
AFTER

March

As I drive through France, drawn-out kilometres pass that wouldn't have fazed you. In your faded jeans and crumpled shirt, you'd be enthusiastically pointing out place names you recognised, laughing as I swore at other drivers. Damn you, Ben Summer. You should be here – if only to help with the frigging driving.

I glance at my satnav, and my heart sinks. It feels like I've been driving forever and there's still two hundred kilometres to go. Stopping at a motorway service station for a caffeine hit, I check my phone. Seeing two missed calls, instinctively my heart misses a beat, imagining you calling. But they're from Ellie and my sister, Polly.

After calling Polly and leaving a message, I try Ellie.

She answers straight away. 'Hey! How's it going?'

'Slowly. It's a flipping big country, Ells.' I try to sound bright.

'Don't fall asleep at the wheel,' she warns.

'Don't worry. I've topped up on coffee and Red Bull. I'm not going to be able to sleep for at least a week.'

'Is it sunny?'

'Actually, it is.' I glance at the sky that's still the same cloudless blue as when the ferry docked this morning. 'Not that warm, though.'

'You left at a good time. It's pissing down here. Hasn't stopped.'

I imagine the grey skies, grey streets, grey everything, the way it's been all winter. It was another reason to leave. 'Sounds crap, Ell. I wish you could come to France.'

'I wish, too...' She sounds wistful. 'Shit. I've just noticed the time. I have to go – I have a horrible meeting to go to. Listen, drive carefully, won't you? And call me when you get there?'

Turning off my phone, I rejoin the traffic on the motorway; the last kilometres counting down agonisingly slowly. The only channels on the radio, mindless French Euro pop, and my only company, your imagined enthusiasm.

Look how the landscape is changing the further south we get! The Cypress trees – like you get in Tuscany, babe... And the colour of the houses...

As more kilometres pass, I feel a flicker of irritation. If you were here, we would have broken the journey with a romantic night in a hotel. But you're not, so I keep driving, blindly following my satnav's robotic voice, determined I'm getting there, no matter what it takes.

At last, I leave the motorway and the pace changes, the roads growing quieter as I pass through a succession of sleepy towns. Eventually I turn up a narrow lane and, a minute or so later, my satnav tells me I've arrived at my destination.

I pull into the driveway and turn the engine off. As I stare at the small house set back from the lane, instead of elation that I'm here, exhaustion hits me like a brick as I hear your voice – loud, excited.

Come on! Don't you want to see the house?

Getting out, I stand there taking in the silence. You'd be enthusiastically striding ahead looking up at the tall trees, their branches stark against the pale, windblown sky, all of them timeless things. But as I follow your invisible footsteps, dismay fills me. A million miles from the quaint, rustic charm I'd imagined, the house is plain and squat. Built from stone, the paint on its shutters is blistered, while beyond is an overgrown garden.

Around the back, fallen branches block the way to the door.

Nothing a chainsaw can't fix, you'd have said, before heading off to search one of the outbuildings.

But I don't have a clue what to do with a chainsaw and as I stand there, for the first time, I'm wondering if you were right. If signs really do exist, that these branches are trying to keep me out; slowly realising, I should never have come here.

It's too soon to cut myself off from everything familiar. I should be at home, cocooned in the comfort of my friends and family. But as I think of the life I've left in Sussex, an unwanted feeling of claustrophobia comes over me, because I don't want to be there, either. And that's the root of my problem. I don't want to be anywhere without you.

8

BEFORE

January, last year

Those first hours in Morocco, I was preoccupied, as I started to harbour doubts that Ben would call. So far, I'd kept what happened to myself but as, now and then, Ellie glanced at me, I knew she'd guessed there was something I wasn't telling her.

Sitting in a cocktail bar set back from the beach, I was on my second Marrakech Mule when my phone buzzed with a text. I tried to read it without Ellie noticing but, of course, I failed.

She watched suspiciously. 'Who's that from?'

'Oh. That would be Ben...' I tried to look nonchalant. 'Hot guy who took me out for dinner last night.'

Her eyes like saucers, her mouth opened and closed like a goldfish. 'You're kidding, aren't you? And if you're not, why don't I know about this?'

A smile crept across my face. 'I was going to tell you, Ell. I tell you everything.'

'Just not this, apparently.' She shot me a look.

'So, I'm telling you now.' I had another sip of my cocktail. 'It was kind of weird. After you went off through security, I threw everything back in my case. Then as I was walking out of the airport, he came running after me.'

She looked disbelieving. 'Why?'

'I'd left my makeup bag on the floor when I was looking for my passport. He picked it up. I ended up telling him what happened. He bought me a coffee, then he found me the flight.' I watched Ellie's eyes grow wider. 'After that, he drove me home – my passport was on the table at the bottom of the stairs. Duh.' I rolled my eyes. 'Then he took me out to dinner.'

'Fuck.' Ellie looked astonished. 'But he could have been stringing you a line. He could have been seeing off a girlfriend, not his parents... Luring you out for dinner when he was planning to kidnap you for his own nefarious purposes. He could even have been stalking you and stole your makeup bag when you weren't looking – as an excuse,' she added, her imagination running away with her.

'Suki knew where I was – I texted her. Anyway, what is the matter with you?' I stared at her. 'You're the one who believes in love and romance and happily ever after. I'm supposed to be the cynical one.'

Ellie didn't look impressed. 'He's called Ben?'

'Yes.' I tried to swallow my pride. 'And he's just texted me. Look.' I passed her my phone.

Hi, hope you got there without any more hitches! Have fun with Ellie x.

'He knows about me? And an x?' Ellie looked amazed.

'I kissed him, Ell.' I gazed into her eyes, before adding hastily, 'Not that night...' I shook my head at her disapproving look. 'He spent the night in my hotel room... But nothing happened. I swear. You know how untrusting I am... or normally am. Anyway, this morning...' I frowned. Was it really only this morning? 'He came with me to the airport to see *me off.' I told her how, as we stood in departures, I hadn't been able to resist kissing him. How it felt like the most natural thing in the world, all the time watching her eyes grow rounder.*

'I don't believe this.' She looked dazed. 'I mean, you truly are the least trusting woman I know, and here you are, looking like a love-struck teenager.'

'I know. Mad, isn't it!' Jolted back down to earth, I was silent for a moment, contemplating that probably I was certifiable. I looked at Ellie more soberly. 'I still can't quite believe it.'

'Hadn't you better text him back?' She passed my phone back. 'And then, Casey Cassidy, I want to know what else went on. After dinner, the rest of that evening, the fact that he was still there the next morning, because I'm not sure I believe you that nothing happened.' She paused. 'And then I want to know why it's taken you so long to tell me!'

I texted Ben.

I'm here! Thank you again. So much. For everything. x

Pressing send, I looked up at Ellie. 'There isn't much to tell. OK...' A broad grin spread itself across my face. 'Of course I was going to tell you! There's something about him, Ell. We talked, most of the night – about everything.' It was true. My eyes had closed for an hour at most, but in that most uninspiring of hotel rooms, as we began to share our life stories, a kind of magic had stolen over us.

9

March

A bird sings loudly from a nearby tree as I stare at the house again. This is insane, I tell myself. I can't stay here. Then I reassure myself. *It's a stop gap, OK? It doesn't have to be any more than that.*

Climbing over the branches blocking the steps onto the terrace, I swear loudly when my sweater catches, but when I reach the door, the key is under the doormat where I was told it would be. Unlocking it and going inside, I shiver. The house is bone-numbingly cold, the kind that comes from being empty too long. Switching on a light, it is at least clean, a hint of furniture polish in the air as I look around an L-shaped kitchen with wide floorboards and a high, beamed ceiling.

At one end, there's a wooden table and chairs; at the other, two sofas, pulled up close to a wood burning stove. I take in the pile of neatly stacked logs. If you were here, you'd already be lighting a fire and piling the stove with firewood while I'd unpack the French bread and wine we would have stopped for on the way.

When I investigate the door leading off the kitchen, I find myself in a small hallway where there's a huge bookcase and the staircase. Going back out to my car to bring in the rest of my stuff, I try to summon your sense of adventure.

That wood burner's great, babe. It'll heat the house in no time. And there are no streetlights! It'll be a proper dark sky out here... Imagine the stars. And in the morning, there'll be no traffic noise, just birdsong...

You've always loved a log fire – I'm a central heating kind of girl. And dark skies are only romantic when you have someone to share them with. Coming in with the last of my stuff, I drop it on the floor by the table. Crouching down next to the fireplace, I manage to coax a fire into life as I send a prayer of thanks into the ether for the supermarket I passed – and for the fact that wine is so cheap.

After locking the door and closing the curtains, I search the kitchen for a corkscrew. Pouring some wine, I huddle beside the wood burner, cradling my glass in both hands as I summon your face, craving the fleeting comfort it brings before it triggers the memory of another fire, a May bank holiday weekend when we camped on the beach. Sitting on a blanket, we drank cold beer and ate the food you'd cooked. I remember the sound of the waves breaking; how, later, we lie back on the sand together, in the darkness, counting myriad stars.

It's one of many memories crafted from sea air and starlit skies. Had I imagined our happiness? Our love? The wine is a cheap red that could be smoother, but it takes the edge off my heartache. Draining the glass, I pour another and unzip one of my bags to pull out your old sweater. It's dark blue, bobbled from age and worn through at the elbows, but as I drape it over my shoulders, my mind swirls with a hundred memories as I breathe in the scent of you.

* * *

I awake to the sound of birds singing, opening my eyes to find pale light filtering through the curtains, as I slowly remember where I am.

Slightly hungover and wearing yesterday's clothes, I force myself off the sofa. Filling the kettle, I switch it on before opening the door and stepping outside. On the terrace, for the first time I get a sense of how remote this place is. There are no houses in sight, just gently sloping hills coloured the green haze of spring, while far away in the distance are mountain peaks.

I try to see it through your eyes, to wonder at the beauty, but for me, it's too empty, too silent. Last night's unease is back, because I've never faced so much time in such isolation. As I stand there, the silence is broken as my mobile buzzes.

It's Ellie. 'Hi. How are you? How was your first night?'

'Very quiet,' I tell her. 'I lit the fire and drank some wine. Sorry I didn't call you. I fell asleep on the couch.'

'You must have been exhausted.' She pauses. 'So, what's it like?'

'Small. Not exactly modern. Two bedrooms – one for you.' I tell her how from the terrace, I can see the mountains. 'It's OK. Just so frigging quiet, Ell.' Unbelievably so, after England.

'Is it too quiet?' Ellie sounds anxious.

'I don't know yet. If it is, I guess I'll move on.' One of fate's cruel twists that I only have to think about myself now.

'So, what are you doing today?'

'I'm not sure.' I consider the day that lies ahead. 'Unpacking. Maybe reading. Drinking wine. Sleeping.'

'It's going to feel odd, Casey – until you settle in,' Ellie says quietly. 'Just take it easy, OK? And please eat something.'

'I will. Don't worry about me, Ell. Shouldn't you be going to work?'

'Don't remind me.' She pauses. 'It's really weird – you not being here.'

'I know, but I'll be back before you know it.' I try to joke.

'If you want to talk, call me.' Ellie sounds worried again. 'Any time, day or night, do you promise?'

'Thanks. But please don't worry,' I repeat. 'I'll be OK.'

After she's gone, I imagine Ellie caught in stop start traffic, the empty day stretching ahead of me suddenly endless, realising I've just been keeping going, putting one foot in front of the other; everyone telling me I'm strong and brave. But the reality is I'm not.

In the kitchen, I pick out a green mug with daisies on it from one of the cupboards, my eyes singling out a dark blue one I'd choose for you. My phone buzzes again, but seeing my mother's face on the screen, I let it go to voicemail, imagining you shaking your head at me.

She's your mum, Casey. It isn't her fault that you're so different to each other.

Remembering I'd promised to let her know I'd got here safely, I send her a text.

Hi Mum, I'm here and I'm OK. I'll call you soon xx

But you're right. And there are reasons, but I can't think about them now. Taking my coffee back to the sofa, I lie down, closing my eyes, my heart aching as I imagine you next to me; knowing I'd give anything to wind the clock back to the beginning of us.

10

BEFORE

January, last year

Morocco was beautiful, mystical, awesome in every way, with vivid sunsets and the best cocktails. Ellie found the zen she was seeking with a bunch of like-minded yogis, while I wandered through the souk and bartered with the stall holders. Meanwhile, Ben was always hovering at the back of my mind. But a few days after we got home, when I still hadn't heard from him, I was beginning to wonder if yet again, I'd got it wrong and he'd changed his mind.

By the time he called me, my defences were back in place.

'How was your holiday?' His voice was warm, just as I remembered.

'Good, thank you,' I was slightly cagey. After all, it had taken him three days to get in touch. 'The sun shone, we found some bars, did a bit of shopping, met some cool people...'

'Great.' He sounded slightly taken aback. 'I thought I'd give you a few days to settle back into normal life, but...' He hesitated. 'Are you busy on Saturday night? Or do you fancy having dinner?'

'Dinner would be nice.' Nice? What was I thinking? But I was being cautious, I reminded myself.

'Great. I'll pick you up at seven thirty.'

* * *

The restaurant was in Chichester, near the canal. It was a chilly night, our breath freezing in small clouds as we walked across the car park. After opening the door, I liked the way Ben stood back to let me walk in first. And it was a cool place. Gazing around, I took in the warehouse-style interior with bare wood and exposed brickwork, the hum of voices.

After being shown to a table near the window, we sat down on chairs upholstered in clashing colours. I looked at Ben. *'I love this.'*

He looked pleased. *'Great, isn't it? A client of mine owns it. I've never been here before – but I'm assured the vegan food is good.'* Ben opened the wine list. *'Wine?'*

'Please. Red?'

We ordered and soon a waitress was pouring a couple of glasses. Ben raised his. *'Cheers!'*

'Cheers.' The wine tasted delicious. *'You know... I wouldn't have blamed you if you'd accidentally on purpose lost my mobile number. I really put you out of your way that day at the airport.'*

He shrugged. *'It was fine! Anyway, I learned something.'* His eyes were dancing. *'When it comes to passports, always check!'*

Smiling back, I was nodding. *'I'm not usually so disorganised.'* I stopped myself. *'Actually, that's probably not quite true. I mean, I'm organised at work, but the rest of the time, not so.'*

There was the same glint of amusement in his eyes I'd seen that day at the airport. *'For the record, I'm quite glad that you leave things in the wrong places. Otherwise, we might never have met.'*

I breathed in sharply. *'I was wondering about that.'* I looked at him. *'Or maybe we would have – some other way.'* I was silent for a moment, because it wasn't the kind of thing I'd normally say. 'Not that I really believe in these things, but we'll never know, will we?'

After giving me a quizzical look, he turned his attention to the menu. Doing the same, I saw that he was right and it was an amazing menu. We agreed on a couple of sharing platters, and then he picked up his drink. 'I'm really glad you're here.'

Taking a deep breath, I held his gaze. 'So am I.'

By now, the wine had seen off any remaining reticence I had. Over dinner, we talked nonstop; me telling him about Morocco, before moving on to our friends, work, families, places we both knew, places we wanted each other to know. It was nearly midnight by the time we left, and as we walked out towards his car, he put his arm around me.

'I've had a really good time. Thank you.'

'So have I.' As we reached the car, I watched his eyes drift skyward.

'Wow.' His voice was quiet. 'It's so rare you see a proper night sky around here. Incredible, isn't it?'

I followed his gaze. 'It really is.' Out of the sky's inky depths, what seemed like millions of stars were twinkling down on us. As I stood there, I felt his arms go around me. Then seconds later, he was kissing me.

* * *

After driving me home, he walked me to the door. Kissing me again on my own doorstep – OK, Polly's doorstep – somehow made it all the more real. Either that or it was the wine making my head spin. But after watching him drive away, as I closed the door, a warm glow was filling me.

Lying in bed that night, I couldn't sleep. Instead, my head was still spinning as I relived the evening; from the food to the conversation to the stars, the kiss, until much later, eventually my eyes closed.

But the next morning when I awakened, my doubts were back. Instead of my usual Sunday routine of a morning at the gym followed by a long lunch with my friends, Ben had suggested a walk in the country. Already worrying that it was too much, too soon, I called Ellie.

'Hi! How did it go last night?' She sounded excited. 'Don't tell me, he's there, isn't he? Oh my God! This is so...'

'He's not here, Ell.' I interrupted her. 'Last night was really great, but...'

'But what?'

'We're supposed to be meeting up today. Just for a walk and a pub lunch. It's just...' I hesitated. 'I'm scared, Ell. Of stuffing this up. Scared of getting hurt again.' I knew how it went. How one minute life was bright and full of promise; the next, decimated.

'If it was me, I'd talk to him.' Ellie's voice was gentle. 'At least, tell him what happened with Colin.'

'I can't! He'll think I'm an idiot.'

'You don't have to tell him you fell for a narcissist who treated you like a piece of—'

'So what exactly do I tell him?' I said more pointedly.

'That you were with this total dickhead guy who asked you to marry him, but then you found out he was cheating on you. Tell him everything, Casey. If he's going to be in your life, you need to trust him.'

I wasn't so sure. 'I don't know. Anyway, Sundays are when we all get together.'

'There will always be another Sunday.' Ellie sounded frustrated. 'If you like him...'

As she spoke, there was a knock at the door. 'He's here, Ell. I have to go.'

Opening the door, I couldn't ignore the way my heart fluttered as my eyes met his. 'Hi.'

'Hey.' His face lit up, then as he looked at me, he frowned. 'Is something wrong?'

I sighed. 'You'd better come in.'

Following me in, he stood in my sitting room. 'You're having second thoughts, aren't you?'

Taking a deep breath, I knew I had to tell him why I was wary. 'I suppose there's something I need to explain. It's about the last guy I dated... He really hurt me – he was seeing other girls.' I hesitated. 'Of course, I'm over it, now. God, I'm so over it. But...' I paused for another breath. 'It wasn't a good time. And the thing is, I really love my life – as it is. I wasn't expecting to meet anyone and I don't want to risk getting hurt again...' I was gabbling and there was more I wasn't saying. But if it was too much and he walked away, so be it.

After listening, he nodded. 'Maybe it isn't the right time – sometimes, it just isn't.' There was regret in his voice.

But as I stood there looking at him, I knew that wasn't what I wanted. 'Can we just take it really slowly? Get to know each other a bit? That way, we'll have a better idea of whether it would work or not?'

For a moment, I thought I'd put him off. No one likes to feel they can't be trusted – unless you happened to be Colin the bastard or some other such scumbag, who wouldn't have cared.

But he nodded. 'If that's what you want, then sure.' He paused. 'So, what shall we do about today?'

I looked at him again. I wanted to spend time with him. I'd be lying if I pretended otherwise. 'Can you give me five minutes?'

Ten minutes later we went out to his car. As we headed into the Sussex countryside, I was already feeling better. I liked that he'd listened and he hadn't taken it personally; that he seemed to understand.

As we tramped across fields in the cold sunlight, I started to wonder what I'd been worrying about. By the time we reached the pub, our hands were cold and our boots were caked in mud. But inside I glowed with happiness.

* * *

More days passed and I couldn't deny there was an ease between us that could have been years in the making. But I should have known that eventually the topic of conversation would wind its way back to Colin.

'You never told me what really happened with the last guy you were seeing.' Ben looked curious.

'I'm supposed to tell you about my murky past in here?' Half kidding, I glanced around the pub he'd taken me to. 'His name was Colin. He was very charming.' I paused. 'We'd been together for a couple of years when he proposed.'

Ben looked startled. 'You left that bit out.'

'Well, considering what followed, it's not surprising.' I shrugged. 'He wanted to keep our engagement a secret – until we'd set a date. But he started missing my calls and changing our plans at the last minute. Then I saw him in a pub with another girl. It was blatantly obvious the girl was more than just a friend. I was devastated. It took months for me to start getting over him.' I paused. 'And I felt stupid – for not seeing through him. I was twenty-five when I met him – old enough to have known better.'

I'd been watching Ben's eyes as he listened. 'What a jerk. But it's his loss,' he said softly. 'He'll never find anyone else quite like you.'

Feeling my heart warm, I breathed out slowly. There was more I'd get around to telling him, but not until I was sure I could trust him.

* * *

Meanwhile, my chaotic world was taking on structure. In the past, where I'd crammed my spare time with friends, shopping, the gym, girls' nights were still there, just more planned; shopping shoehorned in whenever there was time instead of taking up leisurely Saturday afternoons, leaving me time to spend with Ben.

It meant life was busier, but I never questioned it until Ben commented.

'Don't you ever slow down?'

'Not that often.' I smiled brightly at him. 'Something always comes up – you must know what I mean.'

He frowned slightly. 'I guess. But I do take time out – just to chill. Read. Go for walks.'

I was silent for a moment. I couldn't remember the last time I'd taken *time out. Even in Morocco, while Ellie sat on the beach with her eyes closed, meditating, I'd been pacing along the high-water mark, impatient to get on to the next thing. It was true I didn't stop. But I didn't want to.*

Then one Friday early evening, a couple of hours before we'd arranged to meet, he called me. 'Casey? Do you mind if we take a rain check? Only something's come up.'

11

March

That's how we were in the beginning. Me caught in my old life, never stopping to catch my breath; you in the shortest time sparking change, a never-ending wave that's still rippling through it.

After putting it off, I decide to call my mother.

'Holsworthy 59111.' She's the only person I know who still answers reciting their phone number.

'Hi, Mum. It's me.'

'Casey! Thank goodness, I've been so worried about you. Now, tell me. What is the house like? And have you met your neighbours? Now, I've been—'

I try to get a word in. 'I did text you, Mum. The house is OK. And I'm OK. Really I am.'

'I'm glad to hear it. I'm sure Gina will be, too.'

My mother is in touch with Ben's mum? I'm not sure how that

makes me feel. But before I can say anything, she goes on. 'She said you'd probably be wanting some time on your own, but I had to make sure you'd arrived safely and the house was nice and—'

'The house is fine, Mum,' I say patiently.

'Good. Now, once you get back, I thought—'

Alarm bells start to ring. 'Mum, I've only just got here. I haven't decided when I'm coming back.'

She sounds huffy. 'I thought—'

'How's Dad?' I interrupt again. 'And Polly?'

'Your father is fine. He's outside in his shed.'

It explains why she's on my case now, while he isn't there to censor her. Hearing a car coming up the lane, I seize my chance. 'Mum, I have to go. There's someone outside.'

'I do hope you're being careful, Casey. I mean, a young woman your age, going away on her own...'

It's like I'm fifteen, rather than twenty-nine. 'I've got to go. Bye, Mum.' The car passes, the sound of its engine already fading as I end the call, trying not to feel irritated. Encapsulated in that one call is the essence of my relationship with my mother. After everything I've been through, not once did she really ask me how I am.

But that's how she is. Hiding behind the same bright smile no matter what's going on. She's always been the same – she hasn't changed. But in the last few months, I have.

* * *

With nothing I have to do, I potter. Make coffee. Sit on the sofa. Get up and go outside. Make more coffee. Walk around, unable to concentrate, until the silence is broken when Polly returns my call.

'Hi, sis. It's me. How's it going?' Polly sounds like she looks – solid, black-haired, unflappable – a bit like Nessa in *Gavin and Stacey*.

'OK.' I shrug.

'Just OK?' Polly sounds slightly anxious. 'You are eating, aren't you? Not going to starve yourself in some tragic gesture like when you and that arsehole Colin split up?' It's how Polly talks, after years of honing it in her escalating attempts to shock our mother.

'No, Poll. I'm just sad.'

'So what's the place like?'

'Quiet. No traffic. No neighbours.'

'Shit. Bit like home, then.' Polly sounds alarmed.

'Quieter,' I tell her. 'Like Devon without the cows and if all the cars had blown up.'

'Shit,' she says again. 'But there must be bars. Everyone knows France is full of them. And wine...' She sounds envious.

'No bars as yet. But yes. The one consolation is the wine.'

'Are you sure it's where you want to be? You could come to New York. I'll buy you a ticket. It would do you good – a dose of late nights and city life.'

'I'll think about it.' It's a generous offer, and she means well, but Polly's life is non-stop and right now, I'm not sure I'm up for that.

'It must be hard,' she says gently. 'But you'll be OK. Us Cassidys are tough, right?'

Polly's right. We are. But even tough can reach a breaking point.

After Polly's call, my phone buzzes yet again with a call from Suki. Not able to face talking to anyone else, this time I let it go to voicemail.

Taking another mug of coffee outside, thoughts of you fill my mind as I consider that maybe I got you wrong; that in a sliding-doors moment, fate made a massive blunder that day at the airport; that I was never intended to miss my flight. As you walked past security, I would have been out of your sight; a flicky ponytail and the rear view of a denim jacket all there was to see of me, had you even glanced my way. One year on, I'd still be the girl I used to be. For a moment I ponder if that would be a good thing.

As I gaze at the mountains, their jagged peaks seem somehow a metaphor for my life, as I contemplate that maybe it's no accident I've ended up here. Suddenly I'm hungry for one of our conversations about how simple life can be.

Everyone talks about advances and scientific breakthroughs. They call it progress – but no one talks about its true cost – to human nature, to our environment, even our quality of life. Only somewhere like this can you truly imagine a different life.

It bothered you that people have lost sight of what's important. I'd have reminded you how not everyone wants to live out in the sticks – me included. You'd have shaken your head, before going on, because it was more than that.

Life's too fast, babe. We've lost out by cramming too much into each day; by not slowing down, taking the time to really look at the world around us.

It's a conversation we've had many times. Me saying how we don't all want to keep chickens and dig up the earth to plant vegetables – some of us don't even have a garden. Take Polly in New York or Ellie in her flat. How I, for one, wouldn't know where to start. You telling me I'm missing the point.

We've gone too far, Casey, that's the problem. While we took our eyes off the ball, the political machine took over. Take factory farms. No one noticed them silently creeping in. But suddenly, they were everywhere, vast structures escalating the scale of animal suffering, all kept conveniently out of sight and justified in the name of cheap food. It takes years, if not longer, to undo something like that.

You opened my eyes about what matters in this world, cruelty being another of your bugbears, one we shared, whether towards people or animals.

We seem to believe it's our right to impose suffering on other living creatures – all neatly validated by the 'facts' we're fed, our acceptance of the so-called 'standards', which we're told are humane but are abysmal. But not enough of us care – about the people who suffer or the discrimina-

tion that exists, let alone the billions of animals who only see daylight on their way to the slaughterhouse.

Concerns that had driven you relentlessly, along with a whole long list of human attributes you couldn't bear, among them arrogance and entitlement.

When you look at politicians, they're playing a game, aren't they? One that perpetuates the status quo, because it suits their egos – and bank accounts. We forget our place, don't we? How miraculous it is that we even exist? When we're like ants on a spinning rock, that if it shifted a mile closer or further from the sun, would wipe us out, just like that.

I'd watch your thoughts spiralling out of control, before turning towards you, calling in one of my tried and practised means of shutting you up. Taking your face gently in my hands, I'd gaze into the depths of your eyes that could look so troubled. You and your passionate desire for a kinder, more compassionate world. My coffee forgotten, I imagine kissing you.

Even this far from home, I still miss you every day. *Why did this have to happen?* I keep asking myself questions. *Why me, why this, why now?* Couldn't my life have been straightforward, even for a year or two? Calm and undisrupted, so that I could have done what everyone else does and get on with my life; be happy, like I was before you and I met.

Is that what you really want? It's like you're sitting next to me. *The same old life you've always had? Working, having fun with your friends, planning the next holiday, on repeat, year in, year out? Don't you want more?*

I'm narked. There was nothing wrong with that life. It's the same life most people live. And yes, I know now, there is more. But don't you get it? What I crave is for this relentless seesawing of emotions to stop – even for a moment, so that I can catch my breath, while I work out what I want to do next.

Maybe you need to take time to just be. It's peaceful here.

Too frigging peaceful – you know how hard I find that, I flash back. Especially now.

Maybe you need to ask yourself what this is really about.

You, Ben. Frigging leaving the way you did. It takes time to get over something like that.

This time, you hesitate. *Babe... I think we both know it's about more than that.*

Go away. I don't want to hear any more. Enough.

* * *

After what passes for dinner, I call Ellie again.

She picks up straight away. 'Hey, how's it going?'

'OK.' On hearing her voice, I suddenly miss her terribly. 'I feel weird, Ell. I have all this time and I don't really know what to do with myself. Sorry. It hasn't been the best day.'

'Oh, Casey...' Her voice is warm. 'This was always going to be tough. Look, why don't I take a few days off and come over?'

'It's OK, Ell. I'll get through it.' She's been my rock. But I don't want her to come here while I'm feeling like this. 'It's just one of those really shit days.' Then I remember. 'Suki called. I didn't pick up, though.' When my friends have been so great, suddenly I feel guilty. 'I just didn't feel like talking. Can you send her my love when you see her?'

'Sure.' She's silent for a moment. 'Have you spoken to your mum?'

'Yes.' My voice is subdued. 'She was talking about when I go home – she doesn't get why I've come here.'

'I don't suppose she does.' Ellie pauses, before adding more quietly. 'How about Gina? Have you heard from her?'

At the mention of Gina's name, resentment fills me. Ben's mum, she knew more than I did, kept things from me, things I should have known. 'No,' I say shortly.

'You know, it might help to talk to her.' As Ellie pauses, I know there's more she wants to say, but today at least, she doesn't go there. 'I had an idea. Have you thought about writing it all down? A cathartic outpouring of how you and Ben met and what went wrong... Writing about it might be good for you.'

I'm silent. I used to dream that one day, I'd write a book. I'd just never hit on the right idea. But writing about Ben isn't going to help me stop thinking about him.

'Casey? You still there?'

'I was thinking. It would be a pretty crap book.'

'It wouldn't. Think how many people would relate to it. I mean, everyone goes through break-ups. But it doesn't have to be a book for anyone else. Write it for you.'

'Maybe.'

Ellie's quiet for a moment. 'You need to give yourself time. Your life has changed – in a way you weren't expecting. Your mind has to find a place for that.'

'Thanks, Ell.' I swallow. 'For listening. And for always being there... Love you.'

'Love you too.' She pauses. 'Call me any time, Case.'

After she's gone, I sit there for a while, thinking about what she said about Gina – feeling my anger rise again – and about giving it time; more days, weeks, months carried along on this tidal wave that feels like it will drown me.

Waves you'd surf, Ben, when I don't know how to.

12

BEFORE

February, last year

After he'd cancelled our date, I didn't hear from Ben for several days. I wanted to know why he'd gone silent. But also, I found myself missing him.

It was towards the end of the following week, when he called me. 'Hi.' There was no hint of anything wrong in his voice.

'Hi.' I was hesitant. 'How are things?'

'Yeah, good.' He paused. 'Listen, about last week...'

I interrupted him. 'Honestly, it's fine. I've been really busy,' I added defensively.

'OK.' He was quiet for a moment. 'It's just that something came up at short notice and I don't think I explained very well. But maybe it was just as well, if you've been so busy.'

Completely wrong-footed, I could feel myself going around in circles. I took a deep breath. 'Look, how about we meet up and talk?'

We arranged to meet at a pub near Goodwood. In my favourite jeans *and a long silky T-shirt, as I put on some makeup, I was already deciding what to say to Ben. I was going to be honest and let him know what I wanted – feeling my way as I worked out whether he wanted the same, or not.*

As I pulled into the car park, my heart flip-flopped when I saw his car. Getting out, I walked towards the pub, too late in considering that maybe this was over before it started. If so, screw him, I told myself. I'd be perfectly fine on my own.

Inside, he was sitting by the bar with a drink. But he'd clearly picked up something wasn't right, and as I walked over, his eyes were anxious.

'Hey.' He made no attempt to kiss me.

'Hi.' Keeping my voice breezy, I glanced at his almost full pint. 'Can I get you another?'

'Let me get this. What would you like?'

'A gin and tonic, please.' I stood there as he ordered it and paid.

'Shall we sit over there?' He pointed to a table away from everyone else.

I nodded. 'OK.'

We wandered over in silence. Sitting down, I had a sip of my drink. 'Ben?' I said, at exactly the same time as he said, 'It's...'

'You first.' Ben sat back, his eyes studying me.

'I'm not really sure what's happened. To be honest, it was when you cancelled last weekend and didn't say why... I guessed you were having second thoughts.'

'Ah.' He was quiet for a moment. 'Jez and I got this last-minute assignment. When I called you, he was in his car, waiting outside. And the whole time we were away, I didn't have a mobile signal – we were in some remote part of the Yorkshire Dales. I'm sorry. I should have told you.'

No mobile signal – for a whole week? But I remembered what Devon could be like. If they'd been in the wilds of Yorkshire, it sounded plausible. Too much so? The trouble was, it had triggered the same feelings of insecurity I'd had when Colin the bastard let me down. Still suspicious, I folded my arms. So why hadn't he got in touch when he got back?

But in his next breath, he answered my question. 'Then the afternoon I got home, I called you.'

I exhaled slowly. It was my choice as to whether I believed him or not. If I didn't, there was no point going on with this.

His face creased into a smile. 'Look, I should have found somewhere I could call you from.' He paused. 'So... should we pretend last week never happened?'

I hesitated. It seemed a little too convenient. But as I looked at him, his eyes were sincere. 'OK.'

* * *

So far, Ben had yet to meet my friends, but that was about to change. It was the first Saturday in February and we were on our way to a party at Suki's house.

'I can't wait for you to meet everyone.' I was ridiculously excited about it, as well as seeing Suki, whose parties were always a bit bonkers. 'And I probably should warn you about Kevin.'

'Kevin?' Ben's eyebrows went up and down. 'Why?'

I hesitated. It was no secret among my friends that Kevin had a major crush on me. 'He's a nice guy but he'll probably witter on about his latest trip to Machu Picchu or some hippy colony in the south of Spain. You'll see what I'm getting at.' Not wanting to dwell on him, I changed the subject. 'As for Suki, you'll know her the moment you clap eyes on her. Think Taylor Swift – except Suki has the kind of voice that shatters windowpanes. She cannot sing,' I added, because I'd heard her try and it was painful. 'It's left here. Then the first right.'

After parking near the large, detached house that Suki shared with her banker boyfriend, we got out. As we stood there, the air was crisp, the pavement glistening with frost.

'Freezing, isn't it?' Ben pulled his jacket around him. 'So which house?'

I nodded across the road, where you couldn't miss it. 'The one with flashing lights and music.' Suki had it all worked out. She invited the neighbours she liked, and didn't care if those she didn't complained about the noise – she had friends in the local police and was very good at generous apologies. Kissing Ben on the cheek, I took his hand, pulling him across the road, hesitating at the door for only a second. 'Ready for this?'

Before I could ring the bell, the door was flung open by a whirlwind with gorgeous red hair and dressed in black. 'Casey!'

'Ellie,' I mouthed to Ben. Clearly pissed, she flung her arms around me, then pulled away and did the same to him. 'Ell, meet Ben.'

'Hi, Ellie!' He grinned. 'Good to meet you!'

Standing back, as Ellie weighed him up, I watched a smile dawn across her face as this time she kissed him on the cheek, winking at me. 'It's good to meet you, too. Now come on in and have a drink. Suki's been making cocktails!'

I gave Ben a warning look. Suki's cocktails were renowned for being lethal. I turned to Ellie. 'Lead the way.'

In the kitchen, there were a dozen or so people in various states of disrepair, including Suki's boyfriend. 'Dave!' Tottering over, I hugged him. 'I want you to meet Ben.'

As I introduced them, Suki appeared. 'Casey! Darling!' In high heels and a tight red dress, she looked like a supermodel. Kissing me on both cheeks, her eyes swivelled around and stopped on Ben briefly, before glancing questioningly back towards me.

'The guy you texted me about?'

I nodded. 'Suki. This is Ben.'

And in the middle of this merry madhouse, Ben just took it in his stride – these slightly inebriated people he'd never met before, the lethal cocktails and loud music, the curious looks of my friends, even Suki, at her most flamboyant and more like Taylor Swift than ever. Leaving him in conversation with Dave, I crept back to Ellie. 'So? What do you think?'

'He is bloody lovely. Really bloody lovely.' She drained her glass. 'In *fact...' More pissed than I'd realised, she hunted for the word. 'Actually, really bloody sexy, Case. If he wasn't with you...'*

'Stop right there,' I warned. 'I'm getting you some water.' Going to the kitchen, I rinsed out her glass and filled it up, then took it back to her. 'You should be pacing yourself. We both know what Suki's cocktails are like.'

'Maybe I'd better just have wine.' A picture of innocence, she handed me her empty glass.

'Come with me.' I led her back to where Ben was still talking to Dave, loving every second of this evening, my heart warming as I watched my friends welcome him into our little fold.

Two cocktails later, music thumping in our ears, I spotted Kevin. 'Kevin,' I nudged Ben. 'Over there.'

I suppose, looking back, I was a bit pissed too. Plus, it was a test. Kevin was at best, different and at worst, annoying, but he had a kind heart and when I'd been at my lowest, he'd been good for my ego, no question. Tonight, in worn jeans and a rock and roll T-shirt, he was surrounded by a small throng who seemed to be hanging on his words, which if I knew Kevin were imbued with hippy dippy leanings towards peace and love, man. These were usually helped along by whatever hallucinogenic substance was his current predilection and which, judging from the darkness of his eyes, had already happened. My cue to blunder in and shatter the ambience.

'Brainwashing a few more followers, Jesus?' Going over, I planted a kiss on one of his cheeks.

His face lit up. 'Casey Cassidy. What the bloody hell are you doing here?'

I rolled my eyes. 'You know me! Never one to miss a party!'

Surveying his band of followers, Kevin looked apologetic. 'Excuse me guys. She doesn't know it yet, but this is the woman I'm going to marry.'

Until that point, our banter had been typical. But marry? Glancing frantically at Ben, I grabbed his arm, holding on for dear life as he saved me for the second time. 'Kevin,' I said firmly. 'I want you to meet Ben.'

As Kevin looked at Ben, then back to me, a look I couldn't read flickered in his eyes. But then a beaming smile spread across his face. 'Good to meet you, man. Any friend of Casey's is good by me.'

There was a look of relief on Ben's face. 'Good to meet you too.' He glanced at me. 'Casey's told me all about you.'

As Kevin shot me a look, I bit back my laughter. But weirdest of all was how that moment turned out to be the beginning of a beautiful – albeit brief – friendship, between two of the nicest people I'd ever known.

13

April

Alone, I find myself questioning the ways of your so-called universe – how we're no longer together when I thought we would be, always. After all, we were soulmates. Written in the stars.

But stuff happens. You just have to deal with it. You have no choice.

But that's the trouble because I don't want to frigging deal with it. I want the fun, buzz, laughter of my old life back. As my eyes fill with tears, I notice the small black cat that's been hanging around, just as my mobile buzzes and Kevin's face appears on the screen.

Surprised, I pick it up. 'Hi, Kev.'

'Hey, Cassidy. How's it going?'

'OK.' I try to swallow the lump in my throat.

'Ah, you're sounding like you're probably not.'

The kindness in his voice makes it worse. 'I am...' My voice wavers. 'Mostly. You caught me at a bad time.'

'Having a moment, huh? I'm guessing you have lots of those.

Tough times, Cassidy.' He pauses. 'You been out and about much? Found any cute French bars?'

'Not really. Just getting used to being here.' I pull myself together. 'You didn't tell me how frigging quiet it is, Kev. Your voice on the phone is about as noisy as today is going to get.'

'I'm not noisy, Cassidy.' But his indignation is fake.

'That's my point,' I tell him. 'It's so quiet around here. And on the subject of being laidback, how did you get to be so zen, because I could really do with some of that.'

'All part of my mysterious allure,' he drawls. 'I didn't know you'd noticed.'

There's a flirty tone in his voice, one I'm not sure I want to hear. 'I'm being serious, Kev.'

There's a pause. 'Life.' His voice softens. 'The stuff that happens to us all. I guess you either fight it – or you go with it. When it comes to things we can't do anything about, there's no point stressing about them. After all, there's only one certainty in this life.'

'Yeah?'

'Yeah. You can't count on anything staying the same.' He changes the subject. 'Anyway, I just wanted to check you're OK – when you're not having a moment, that is.'

Another tear rolls down my cheek. 'Thanks, Kev.'

After the call ends, I sit there, thinking about what he said, remembering as I wipe my face again that, since coming here, I haven't thanked him for finding me this house.

It was one of those serendipitous events, I imagine you saying. *Like when you and I met – the right place coming up at the right time.*

But it isn't the right place, I mutter at you. And if it was the right frigging time, you would have been here too. You know I hate too much quiet.

You're displaced and angry. But someone like you doesn't hate.

You're right, I don't hate the house. It's the circumstances that have brought me here. In truth, I'm grateful. The house belongs to a friend of Kevin's – Antigua – no one else would have a friend named after a Caribbean island. She'd allegedly inherited it, but prefers city life to rural France. Back in England, I'd known I had to do something. There's a limit to even the most devoted friend's capacity to go over and over the same old – and I knew I'd fast been approaching it.

* * *

Driven by my rapidly diminishing stock of wine, I venture out to the local supermarket. I buy enough for a couple of weeks; adding crisps, fruit and baguettes, and as an afterthought, a bag of cat food. Then, on my way home I take a wrong turning, which happens to be fortuitous, because in the middle of beautiful nowhere, I find a bar.

Close up, it's unassuming, a big old house set back from the road. In front are wooden tables, while above the door is a simple sign, *le bar,* with a menu chalked on a board – not exactly buzzing but a welcome sign of life.

Noting where it is for another time, I drive back to the house. When I go inside, the cat blinks lazily from the sofa.

'Hey. How did you get in?' As I step towards it, it gets to its feet. I back away. 'OK. I have something for you.' Opening the bag of cat food, I tip some into a bowl, but as I put it down the cat scarpers.

Leaving the bowl outside, I go back in. With nothing to distract me, my head is all over the place. I wipe away the tear that rolls down my cheek. There are things I can't let go of. Things that shouldn't have happened. Things I can't change, because it's too late.

Part of coming here was to have time to come to terms with what happened between us. But spending too much time in my head isn't helping anything and in search of a distraction, I check out the bookcase. As I scan the shelves of French and English titles, one in particular catches my eye. The brown cover is blank, and as I open it and turn the pages, I realise it's a diary.

I hesitate – diaries are private, but then I think of my own, hidden where no one would ever find them. If this one was personal, the writer would hardly have filed it in a shelf of paperbacks.

Curling up on the sofa, I start reading.

1st January

I've spent too much of my life in a job I don't love, in a part of the world that isn't doing it for me, in relationships that don't last. So, I've made some decisions. If I want my life to change, I have to do things differently. Which starts with me – the way I think, the choices I make. It's why I've come away to this quiet corner of the world, to take stock.

For the next year, I'm working remotely. I've taken a cut in pay, but I'm OK with that. I'm not so worried about money right now; it's more the fundamentals I need to think about.

What do I want from life? How do I want to live? What's important to me? I'm hoping, away from everything in my old life, I'll find some answers.

In one page, I'm drawn in. Bizarrely, the diary could almost be describing me. Curious to know more, I read on.

7th January

So far, I'm embracing the remoteness, the howl of the wind when it picks up, even the rain leaking in around the window frames. And in between, there's this vast, far-reaching quiet, broken only by the creak of floorboards or the crackle of flames when the fire is lit.

Though a few days in, it was definitely a relief when I

stumbled across the bar. Thank fuck for a sign of life around here, not that I wanted to immerse myself in it, but it was good to know it was there.

Hard to pass up a local bar. And I wasn't expecting too much from a place hidden away up a country lane, but I've started going there, most days, to drink a glass of wine or two and watch a microcosm of how life is for the generations of hard-working farmers, second-home owners, and proprietors of vineyards that live around here.

Once or twice, I've noticed a woman. Julia – according to the conversations I've eavesdropped on between her and the ubiquitous ladies-who-lunch who usually accompany her. A second-home owner I'm guessing – though given the time of year, it's equally possible she lives here.

There's a restlessness about her, in her body language, in those luminous eyes constantly on the move. The first woman I've noticed in a long time, but I didn't come here to meet someone, I need to remember that. Draining my glass, I walked out.

12th January
Julia's stuck in my head. No harm in that, I've told myself. As long as that's all it is. The next time I went into the bar, as I waited to pay, I turned and there she was, standing beside me.

Up close, her skin was smooth, her eyes fringed with long lashes. As her perfume reached me, I felt a frisson of something. So much for not wanting to meet someone. It doesn't matter what you tell yourself – these things have a way of happening in their own sweet time, like it has before, but that's a whole other story.

Julia's French is good, but when she first spoke, I could tell she's English. Anyway, her clothes had already given her away. Boyfriend jeans and a loose-fitting top that hung off one of her tanned shoulders. As we fell into conversation, I told her I was visiting – for about a year. It turned out I was right about her living here. They moved ten years ago from Paris, she told me, leaving me wondering who 'they' were.

As her eyes held mine, my question was answered – I looked at her wedding ring. Noticing me look, she covered it with her hands. A fleeting look of sadness crossed her face as, for a moment, she didn't speak. Then pinning on a smile and wishing me au revoir, she turned back to her friends.

I wonder if the bar is the same bar I found. Closing the diary, I'm struck by how much it resonates. Like me, the writer had come here to take time out. But it was the line about meeting someone, how these things happen whether or not you're ready for them, because that's how it was when you and I met.

The afternoon brings a deluge of rain that leaks in around the windows just like I read in the diary. As I run from room to room, with towels to mop up the water, there's a crash of thunder and, with a simultaneous flash of lightning, the lights go out.

For a moment, my heart races. Then anger rises in me; at this house, the elements, but most of all at you, because if you hadn't left, I wouldn't have come here.

Lighting a candle, I text Ellie.

Motherfucker of a storm going on here, rain coming in through the windows. I am so mad at Ben right now, I can't tell you.

A few minutes later, she texts back.

Mad is good. Shut the windows?

Of course they're shut!!! Shit. Just remembered left my bedroom window open. Be right back.

Running upstairs, I slam the window shut. But when I come back down and pick up my phone, there's no signal. Guessing the storm has knocked out the already inadequate internet, I pour myself a large glass of wine. Lighting a candle and putting more wood on the fire, I huddle into your sweater and carry on reading.

January 17th

Didn't see Julia there for the next few days. Then yesterday when I went in, she was sitting alone at a small table. I noticed the sun's rays through the window catching the auburn lights in her hair, but instead of laughter in her eyes, there were tears. I walked towards her, glancing at an empty chair opposite her.

I hesitated. I'd no idea what was going on with her – plus there was the not-so-small matter of the wedding ring she was wearing. Then I thought, what the hell. Quite simply, she looked like someone who needed company.

After buying her another cognac, we started talking. More like old friends than strangers, the way it happens sometimes, whether it's because you're kindred spirits or just both know how it feels when your world falls apart. As days go, Julia's had been a shit one. Enough that she necked the cognac and ordered another.

Being the responsible, decent guy I am, I tried suggesting she should slow down a little. Her answer was she hadn't had nearly enough to numb the raw, aching feeling in her gut when she thought about her life, her marriage, about the happiness that was missing. Only the small stuff, then. I tried to persuade her that even the most shit days pass. I wasn't expecting her answer: 'Not always.'

I ineloquently tried to cheer her up, quoting Frida Kahlo. You know the one: I tried to drown my sorrows, but the bastards learned to swim… But she had an answer to that, too.

Apparently, hers were Olympic fucking gold medallists. Whatever she tried, there was no stopping them.

Clearly her sense of humour was still there – but I was sensing this was more than a fit of the blues. Then in her next breath, she surprised me, telling me about everything good in her life. Her children, her home, how lucky she was... which made her feel even worse that she wasn't happy. Her kids were twelve and eighteen – they meant the world to her.

She didn't mention her husband, just told me a part of her was empty. Something fundamental was missing in her life – had been for years. Something she'd worked out might be love.

As I listened, it cut to the core of me, because believe me, I know in every cell of my body how that feels. Plus, it had to be far worse to be married and know it was missing. She was so drunk she'd probably never remember anything I said. So, putting my battle-scarred heart on the line, I told her. It was how I felt, too. How I was missing someone who could see me with all my imperfections. Someone who would love me, no matter what.

Draining her glass, Julia's eyes filled with tears. Getting up, she wobbled to the bar for another cognac and came back with the bottle. I knew it wasn't going to help, but short of brute force, I couldn't stop her. Nor was it my place to, because I got it. When we're consumed with pain, all any of us want is to make the world go away.

My hands are shaking as I put the diary down. I've thought so much about how that feels – the need to make the pain stop; the numbing beauty of alcohol that's only transient, because the next morning, whatever you were hiding from hasn't gone.

20th January

Thinking about my conversation with Julia, I'm slightly mystified. It was clear as day her marriage was in trouble, but she hadn't given any indication why. I've seen her since and we had a glass of wine together. Her mood had lifted – or so it seemed. We laughed about one or two things, but as we sat at a table, she told me more about where her unhappiness stems from.

Her husband was having an affair. And as if that wasn't bad enough... He'd been screwing another woman for a year – and Julia had no idea. Moreover, he blamed it on her. Apparently, she was cold and distant, and a man needed love from somewhere – at least, that was his excuse.

I knew the French could be pretty laissez-faire when it came to extra-marital sex, but there was no question, Julia's husband is a shit. When I asked her if it was still going on, she hesitated. Then she told me she wasn't devastated or heartbroken the way she ought to feel if she loved him. Her terrible, gut-wrenching sadness was for her children.

They'd never know how a united family felt. Did I know how unhappy that made her feel? Seeing tears in her eyes, I tried to tell her that her husband's behaviour wasn't her fault. It was his choice, that they were two very separate things. But he'd screwed with her head too, that much was obvious. When I asked her if she was leaving him, she said 'I can't'.

I was dumbfounded. She had choices that might seem daunting, impossibly shitty ones, but she didn't have to stay, not if she didn't want to. She could make a new home; give her children everything she wanted for them. It might not be ideal, but why live with a man who was cheating on her?

She told me I didn't understand. That all she could do was lead this hideous charade of a life. He refused to agree to a divorce, and there was nothing she could do about it; a thousand words I couldn't read in her eyes as she fell silent.

My heart fills with sympathy for Julia. But as I stare at the pages, one word stands out as an uncomfortable feeling comes over me.

Choices. It denotes taking responsibility for your actions, including your mistakes, when so often it's easier to blame anyone or anything other than yourself. It's a word I don't want to think about – too close to home – because there are times we all fuck up and make the wrong choice.

As the candle flickers, then goes out, I find some music. But instead of soothing, I've clicked on the soundtrack of our life together and as it starts to play, memories come flooding into my mind.

If only we could talk, Ben.

If only I could have done something different.

Too many if onlys, and all too late.

14

BEFORE

April, last year

As the weeks passed, a relaxed familiarity grew between us and I found myself drifting into what Ben and I wanted to do together. Movies, take-aways, long walks, seeing friends; cooking and drinking wine, talking into the early hours about everything and nothing.

At last, I met Ben's business partner, Jez, and his wife, Lisa. I was nervous – after all, they'd known him much longer than I had.

'They're over there.' As we walked into the bar, Ben nodded towards a couple sitting at one of the tables. When he saw us, the man's face broke into a smile. 'Hey, mate.' Ben hugged his friend, then as his wife stood up, kissed her on the cheek, before turning to me. 'Jez, Lisa, this is Casey.'

'Hi.' Lisa had warm eyes and long curly hair. Holding out her arms, she hugged me.

'Hello.' Jez was as tall as Ben. 'Good to meet you – at last!' He glanced at Ben. 'What are you guys drinking?'

'I'll come over with you.' Ben turned to me. 'Wine?'

As I nodded, Lisa leaned forward conspiratorially. 'I'm so glad you're here. Those two when they get together...' She glanced towards them at the bar. 'Let's just say, they always have so much to talk about.'

Following her gaze, I watched Ben talking while Jez listened intently and Lisa touched my hand. 'So, tell me how you met. Ben never gives anything away!'

I smile. 'Well, as it happens, that's quite a good story...' I told her about the day at the airport.

'He really is one of the good ones.' Her eyes sparkled. 'And just so you know, these last weeks, I've never known him so happy.'

* * *

With winter behind us, an unseasonably warm spring arrived, the trees bursting into life, flowers blooming early, while the sun was warm enough that on Easter Saturday, we headed for the coast. Sitting on a blanket, lulled by the sound of seagulls and the waves breaking on the shingle, I was watching Ben kite-surf, the wind carrying him airborne as my eyes settled on a pebble, glinting slightly. Reaching to pick it up, I saw a seam of crystals sparkling as the sun caught it.

When Ben came back, I showed it to him.

Taking it from me, he scrutinised it. 'It's quartz.' His skin was pink, his eyes glowing with exhilaration, as he handed it back. I put the pebble safely in my pocket to take home, as he stripped off his wetsuit and showered me with cold water. 'We need to get you a wetsuit, babe. You have to try this.'

'No way. Not in the English Channel. It's freezing, Ben! Somewhere hotter, maybe.' For now, I was perfectly happy just watching him.

* * *

I placed the pebble on the windowsill in my bedroom, where I'd see it every morning. Meanwhile, as my life slowly shifted to merge with Ben's, I could feel myself changing too, though so far, true to my old commitment-phobic self, what was happening between us remained unspoken. But I knew I wasn't the same girl any more. What I didn't know was how to explain to Ben how different this felt. As it happened, it didn't matter, because he did.

'You know, don't you, when it's right?' Lying in bed one night, his dark blue eyes were close enough that I could make out small hazel flecks. 'I've never known anything like this, Casey. It's like...' He hesitated. 'It's like you get everything about me. I don't have to pretend anything, because whoever I am, you're OK with that.' Looking slightly uncertain, he broke off. 'You're not freaked out, are you?'

Reaching out, I gently touched his cheek. 'That's the thing. I should be, completely. I've been trying to work out why I'm not...' It was my turn to hesitate, wanting to tell him how, forever, there'd been a Ben-sized hole in my life, which had vanished the day he walked into it. 'I've thought so many times, how easily we might never have met.' I shook my head. 'In fact, you could argue, we weren't meant to. If I'd remembered my passport, our paths would never have crossed...' I looked at him, wondering if fate really did exist. 'Weird, isn't it? But being together... it feels so right.'

It summed it up. It didn't matter that we'd only known each other three months. There was nothing contrived or awkward between us. From the start, there never had been.

'You know, you seem different...' Ben hesitated. 'In a good way,' he added quickly.

Pushing myself up on my elbows, I looked down at him. 'This better be a really good kind of way.'

'It is.' He held my gaze. 'It's like you've slowed down – well, your life has.' He paused. 'So what was it?' he asked softly, 'that meant you could never stand still?'

'Habit, I guess.' It was the first thing that came into my head. There

were reasons I didn't like spending too much time in my own company, but I didn't want to spoil this most perfect of moments. As Ben kissed me again, I closed my eyes, pushing the thought away. It was as though all that existed was the two of us.

April

After reading the string of messages Ellie left last night during the storm, I text her a reply.

Sorry, signal knocked out. Shit internet in rural France xxx

When I go outside, the air is fresh and the pale, watery sky is streaked with wisps of high cloud. Noticing the cat's food bowl is empty, as I pick it up, the cat appears. Gazing mistrustfully at me, seconds later, it's joined by another, smaller but painfully thin, ginger cat.

I look from one to the other. 'Food?'

* * *

On my way back from the shop, I pass the bar, where a couple of small, battered Peugeots have been abandoned at the roadside. Thinking of the bar mentioned in the diary, I pull over and get out.

Beside the door, the menu has been chalked on the board and as I go inside, I take in the sparse interior, with scrubbed wooden tables; the aroma of caramelised onions coming from the kitchen.

'Bonjour!' A woman's voice comes from behind the bar.

As I walk over, I notice she looks about my age. 'Bonjour.'

'Ah, English?' She raises an eyebrow at me.

I glance at my clothes. Like the guy wrote in the diary, you can tell – no self-respecting French woman would go out dressed in the tattered jeans and shapeless sweater I pulled on this morning. I nod. 'Could I have a glass of wine please?'

'Sure. At the bar? Or do you want a table?' She gestures towards the almost empty restaurant.

'Here is fine.' I pull myself up onto one of the bar stools, watching as she gets a glass.

'What would you like?' She looks at me with interest.

'Red, please. Just a small glass.'

Getting a bottle, she pours me a generous amount with a flourish, before replacing the cork. Her eyes meet mine again. '*Santé.*'

'*Santé.*' As I raise my glass, she's already writing on a notepad, the simplicity of the bar seemingly incongruous with her mahogany-coloured hair in a sleek ponytail, and her neatly pressed shirt over immaculate jeans.

My eyes scan round for anyone who might be Julia or one of her friends, but the only customers are a group of weathered farmers. Sipping my wine, I imagine you here. The two of us sitting outside, tanned, wearing sunglasses and drinking chilled wine as we plan our next adventure.

'*Madame?*' The voice from behind the bar jolts me out of my daydream. '*Quatre euros.*'

'Sorry.' I fish in my pocket for change, putting a couple of coins on the bar, suddenly wanting to get out of there. Drinking the rest of my wine quickly, the woman watches as I place my glass on the bar.

'Do you know about the market?' Her dark eyes appraise me. 'On Saturday mornings, in the car park outside – if you're still here? Only small, but it's nice. You should come.'

I used to love markets, whiling away hours perusing colourful stalls in search of a bargain. But that was before. Already on my feet, I nod. 'Thanks.'

Hurrying back to my car, I take a deep breath. It's insane that ordering a drink in a bar can feel like a milestone, but it's what I have to do now. Do these things we planned to do together, without you.

* * *

In the solitude of what's become home, the breeze reaches me through the open window as, with a mug of tea, I sit at the kitchen table. Seeing the diary, I open it and carry on reading.

25th January

Talking to Julia left me with a problem. While my head was telling me to step back and let her sort it out herself, she seemed naïve, somehow. Either she didn't know a good lawyer, or there was more going on than she was saying.

I know people can be complicated; that most of us only share what we want others to see. And I didn't want to pry – we all have our secrets, but I didn't doubt her distress was genuine and she seemed to want to talk. So, I've been back to the bar several times, hoping she'll be there, but every time, there's been no sign of her.

29th January

Today I ran into Julia while I was shopping. Fraught, anxious, I barely recognised her at first. When I called out her name, she spun around, a look of panic crossing her face when she saw me; her eyes darting about as though she was terrified someone might see us.

I didn't get why she was so agitated. After all, there was nothing wrong with talking. But there was no calming her down. Intent on berating herself for getting drunk that time, she said she'd talked far too much when what she really had to do was just get on with things.

When I asked if she'd sorted things, she told me I didn't understand. Whatever I might think, she didn't have choices. Whatever was going on, no way could she leave her husband. I started to wonder what kind of man he was. I mean, I already had a pretty good idea, but I'd never seen Julia so frightened. There had to be something going on she hadn't told me about.

I tried to get her to agree to meet at the bar, but she didn't answer. Instead, the strangest look crossed her face as she walked away. I watched as she got into her brand new Range Rover and drove off, trapped in a web of her own making, but I knew how that felt. It was the whole reason I'd come here, to escape the past, hoping freedom and happiness wouldn't be too far behind. Isn't that what we all aspire to? The kind of stress-free existence we spend our whole lives dreaming of; where we are not dictated to by anyone else, least of all a faithless partner.

I wonder how much Julia really wants to be free of her husband. The way I see it, she's so used to his betrayal and her own unhappiness, they've both become completely normal to her. Distracted, I stop reading as my phone buzzes with a text – a missed call from my mother. Even here, hundreds of miles away, she wants to reel me back in.

She's your mother. Your voice is crystal clear. *After what you've been through, surely you can understand she's terrified of losing you?*

Don't you think, every hour of every day, I'm aware of that?

Then ask yourself. Is it her you're angry with, or you?

It feels like a step too far, because the deepest scars don't heal – and you know about what happened; you know I haven't, never will, forgive myself. And I will never get over the pain of losing you. It's the flip side of loving you.

16

BEFORE

May, last year

Having known how it felt when life fell apart, I wasn't prepared for such happiness, until eventually I worked it out. Maybe this was how it should be; that they were simply opposite ends of the human experience.

'Do you believe in predestiny?' I asked Ellie one day.

'I don't know.' A frown flickered across her face. 'But when I look at you and Ben, I do wonder.'

'I never used to. But now, I'm not so sure.' I paused, thinking. 'There are so many reasons why Ben and I should never have met.' Taking a breath, I went on, because I'd been thinking more and more about it. 'I mean, it's the timing. And apart from the whole thing about my passport, there are so many ways out of the terminal building. He happened to walk by at the exact moment I was there. The airport was crowded, too.'

Ellie was staring at me. 'You've never said anything like this before.'

'I know.' I sighed. 'But nothing like this has ever happened before.'

She shook her head. 'You know, I used to think you and Kevin would end up together.'

'Kevin?' We'd always been friends. I remembered what he said at Suki's party, about how I was the woman he was going to marry. But he'd been kidding – hadn't he? 'We're mates, but we could never be more than that.'

'I know that now, obviously.' She hesitated. 'But...' She hesitated again. 'If you and Ben really were predestined, shouldn't there be some kind of cosmic reason?'

I was silent. I knew how motivated Ben was, but was ours the kind of love that could change the world in some small way? I didn't have the answer.

'Have you told him about Jenna?' Ellie's voice broke into my thoughts.

As I thought about her, there was a lump in my throat. I shook my head. 'Not yet.'

'Don't you think he'd want to know? I mean, I would, if it was me.'

'I know.' As I thought about her, I felt the familiar knot in my stomach. Talking about Jenna always did this; it brought back emotions I kept deeply buried, emotions I didn't know how to deal with.

'I know it's hard, Case. I mean, I know how much you miss her.' Ellie's voice was quiet. 'But it might help if you talked about her.'

I was silent for a moment. 'I will tell him, Ell – when the time is right.' Tears blurred my eyes, but the truth was nothing helped, just as nothing would bring Jenna back. As familiar guilt returned, I did what I always did. I suppressed it.

17

AFTER

May

I take the diary outside, wanting to know more about Julia. Moving a chair into the shade, I carry on reading.

5th February

Yesterday, to my surprise, I saw Julia at the bar, walking in as though she hadn't a care in the world. It was only close up I could see the despair in her eyes, the pallor of her skin under her makeup.

After ordering her a Coke and a beer for me, we went over to one of the tables. As she sipped her drink, her hands were shaking. I gave her a minute, then asked her how she was. Getting better, she told me, at pretending. At hiding the truth from everyone, that inside, she was dying.

I didn't get it, and I told her so. Her husband was unfaithful, she didn't love him, she'd already said she wanted to leave, but she seemed inexplicably bound to him.

Watching her eyes fill with tears, my heart went out to her. None of this made sense – I had to be missing something. In her next breath she told me what it was.

When Julia told me she was ill, I felt my stomach churn. A tear snaked its way down her cheek as she tried to put it into words. She was unstable. How it went way beyond what you might call mood swings. Some days, she could reach the giddiest heights – they were incredible days, when anything, everything seemed possible. But they were feelings she couldn't trust, because she'd found out the hard way. Joy and mania were shades of the same colour. So close, she couldn't tell which was which.

Her voice dropped to a whisper as she went on. When she felt good, it was the most unbelievable feeling. Time she held on to every precious second of, because at any moment she knew she'd come crashing down.

Silent, I took her hand, as she described what always followed when the mania stopped. How it would slingshot her into the total opposite; like falling from the height of a glorious summer into the coldest, darkest hell that went on forever. Those days... I felt her hand shake in mine. She couldn't get out of bed, let alone be a mother. People thought she was weak – that she should snap out of it. Her voice was bitter. They had no idea.

In short, Julia was bipolar. A madness gripped her brain, spinning her around at warp speed without a brake pedal, before pitching her into the abyss – at least, that was how it felt. As if that wasn't enough, her husband used it against her. Told her she wasn't a fit mother. Her children needed someone who was calm and level. Shaking her head, her eyes were filled with despair as she said, he's right.

Right now, she was neither one nor the other, waiting for the next dip, not sure when it was coming. It was less of a problem than it used to be – there was a drug she took that helped. But her husband would still use it against her – he had a lawyer who would say anything.

She was frantic, she told me. Stuck. Didn't have the strength to take him on. But more than that, she couldn't risk hurting her children. They came first. They always would, no matter the cost to herself.

I swallow as I put the diary down. Going to the kitchen, I pour myself a glass of water. Taking it outside, I gaze across the garden. The mountains are lilac tonight, the sky a swirl of purple which as I watch the sun set, fades to navy blue shot with stars. Standing there, I suddenly realise that unlike Julia, I do have choices. Feeling the faintest stirring of change starting, this time the voice that comes to me is mine.

This pain you hold on to... maybe it's time to let it go.
You have the whole of the rest of your life, Casey Cassidy.
Just imagine if you could do something amazing with it.

* * *

The feeling stays with me the following morning when at last I find a rusty handsaw and deal with the fallen branches in front of the terrace. It takes an hour of sawing, but as I pull them away, I'm euphoric.

After showering and pulling on clean clothes, I'm still thinking about the diary as I make a mug of coffee and text Ellie.

Hello Ell, how are you? Decided I need a plan. Started by sawing down a tree xxx

Hi. That's great!! The plan I mean. What is it? The tree??xxx

Have climbed over it since I got here. The plan – no details, but deciding I need one feels like a start. I have choices, Ell xxx

Yay, because you do! A plan is v good. Keep me posted

After Ellie signs off with a line of heart emojis, I take my coffee over to the sofa and pick up the diary.

10th February

Two days ago, Julia came over here. As she walked through the door, the house seemed filled with light. Our time together has come to mean more to me than I'd realised, as we drank wine and talked the whole afternoon. She'd been thinking, she told me. Trying to believe in a different kind of future, imagining living in a smaller house, with her children, a garden, a dog, a couple of cats. She'd been looking online and found the perfect place, not far from a river. In her mind, she'd even furnished it.

I was relieved to see her optimism; that there was no sign of the dip she was dreading. Taking her hand, I told her she could do this. That she could find someone to be on standby for the difficult days, but she was ahead of me on that one. She had a friend who'd promised to help. She'd also found herself a lawyer. They were meeting at the end of this week. After, she was seeing her doctor.

Watching her talk, I was awestruck. I knew what it had taken for her to reach this point. She was doing the right thing, I told her. But suddenly she was anxious again. Was she being selfish? Thinking of herself instead of everyone else?

Getting up, she came over to me. Then very slowly, for the first time, she kissed me. I kissed her back. I couldn't stop myself. I mean, she's gorgeous. A Titian-haired temptress, with fire and passion. My kind of woman – at least, she could be.

If it was complicated before, now it's complicated multiplied

because I can't stop thinking about her. When I'm not working, I've been sitting outside, listening to twittering birds and looking at snowy mountain peaks, and thinking about Julia; asking myself a question that everyone should ask themselves.

Am I happy?

What does happiness mean to me? I know I don't laugh the way I used to, feel ridiculous giddy excitement or wild optimism. But I'm getting older. Things happen. People change.

Going back, I re-read the line about seizing moments, feeling it tap into something in me. It's what I used to do, not just seize them, but fill them until they were overflowing. But since losing you, that's changed.

Studying the diary, I wonder who this man is, what happened to bring him here. It's like you used to say, how everyone you met had their own story. This diary is part of the writer's. The makeup bag you picked up at the airport that day – that was part of mine.

18

May, last year

'You guys will end up married one day, I'm sure of it.' Ellie sounded oddly matter of fact.

I looked at her, shocked. I was a free spirit. The kind of girl who ran thousands of miles if anyone mentioned the m-word – Ellie knew that. Yes, I loved being with Ben, but I'd seen the sparkiest relationships dwindle into apathy after exchanging vows. Uncertainty kept things hot. 'Don't say that, Ellie Richardson! It's only been four months,' I reminded her. 'Anyway, when everything is perfect, why on earth would we want to get married?'

'You will.' Giving me a knowing look, my friend sank into the other end of the voluptuous purple sofa that dominated her living room. 'Everyone does. It's about timing. I don't think it makes any difference how long you've known someone. You just know when it's right, don't you? Anyway, I'd put money on it. You and Ben will be the first of us.'

'No way.' But a feeling of warmth was blossoming inside me. I was *thinking of the conversation we'd just had – about how this was different, for both of us. The idea of marrying Ben didn't hold the horror factor it should have. It felt exciting.*

Anyway, there was plenty of time to think about marriage. We were young, the rest of our lives stretching ahead of us. Leaning back on my end of the sofa, I rested my feet on Ellie's lap and lifted up my empty glass. 'More wine, Ell.'

'Has he mentioned it?'

'No!' Picking up a cushion, I hurled it in the general direction of her head. 'I'll tell you, when – if – he asks.'

'Ha! You said when! But you've met his parents, right?' Leaning forward, Ellie's hair fell across her face as she topped up my glass.

'Yes! But that means nothing. It was Sunday lunch. Ben just happens to like cooking and they only live a few miles away.'

'It won't be long,' Ellie said calmly. 'Mark my words, Casey Cassidy. Honestly. Sometimes I think I know you better than you know yourself.'

Sipping my wine, I was silent, imagining sharing life with Ben, spending years, decades, as we grew older together, weathering the ups and downs, excitement filling me again, the last of my defensive barriers melting away. But then another thought struck me. If I felt like this about Ben, it wasn't right to be keeping things from him. I couldn't go on putting it off. I had to talk to him about Jenna.

19

May

When Saturday arrives, there isn't a cloud in the sky. Pulling on clean, unripped jeans and a faded sweatshirt, I add a hint of makeup for the first time since coming here.

The roads are quiet, the low sun sparkling through the hedgerows. When I reach the bar, the market is underway, three or four cars parked at the roadside. Pulling over behind them, I get out.

Wandering over to the small number of stalls in the car park, I imagine you here. *This is great, babe,* you'd have enthused beside me. *OK, so not what you were expecting, but it's proper locally grown food... A real slice of rural French life.*

Bit frigging quiet, I'd have said to you. Markets are supposed to be vibrant and bustling, with clothes, handmade soaps and candles, artisan jewellery, not this handful of local producers selling seasonal food, which at this time of year amounts to potatoes and kale, neither of which I'm a fan of. Ignoring the vegetables, I buy some eggs of varying colours, then as I'm heading back to my car, I hear someone call out.

'Hey!'

The English word makes me turn around as I recognise the woman from the bar walking towards me. 'Hi. Thanks for the tip off.' I wave the box at her. 'I got some eggs.'

'It's quiet today. There are usually more people.' She sounds apologetic. 'Do you have time for coffee?'

I hesitate for a moment, torn between the appeal of her company and not wanting to explain why I've come here. But then I find myself nodding. 'Why not?'

Following her into the bar, I see a small group of old men huddled around a table over their coffee cups. Calling out in French to the man behind the bar, she heads towards a table near the back. 'We can sit here.'

Pulling out a chair for me as she sits down, her eyes are bright. 'It's nice to have an excuse to be on this side of things for once – and to have someone else to talk to. I'm Sylvie.'

'I'm Casey.' I sit opposite her. 'This is your place?'

'My family's. That's Marco, my brother.' She nods towards the guy behind the bar. 'I never thought I'd be here at my age, but you know... Life – shit – happens. So here I am.' Unperturbed, she sits back. 'So, what brings you to this part of France?'

I'm not sure where to start. 'A bit like you. Life. Shit.'

As her brother brings our coffees over, her face breaks into a smile. 'OK. My shit? A lazy, lying, cheating bastard of a husband. I stuck it for five years, before one night I asked myself what I was doing with my life. I didn't much like the answer I got. So, the next day I packed my stuff and came back here – about a year ago.'

'Wow.' I stare at her. 'I'm sorry.'

She shakes her head. 'I'm not. It should have happened a lot sooner. I can't believe how stupid I was to stay with him so long.

Five years! What a waste! Life is quiet here, but I have my own space – here, upstairs. And I'm free of him. Your shit? Much the same?'

'Not really.' I smile sadly at her.

A look of confusion crosses her face. 'But you are alone, yes? Why?'

'I was with someone, but it didn't work out...' I start to tell her how we met. 'It was a coincidence really. I was supposed to be going on holiday with my friend, Ellie...' I go on to tell her the story, at least the airport part.

'I'm not sure I believe in coincidence.' Sylvie shrugs. 'Sometimes I think fate takes a hand. What happened next?'

I tell her how glorious it was – and how it didn't last. Then taking a deep breath, I tell her how you left me.

She listens intently. 'That is real shit.' Her voice is sympathetic. 'So you've come here – what for, a holiday?'

I shake my head. 'I've been here since March – a friend of a friend has a house about ten minutes away.' I explain where it is. 'I don't think anyone's lived in it for some time. I didn't plan to stay long, but I'm really not in a hurry to go back.'

Sylvie nods. 'Many places around here are empty. Young people move away to find work – like me. Unlike me, most of them don't come back,' she says, rolling her eyes. 'I think I know your friend's house. Little house with brown shutters? I've seen an English car parked outside – a red one?' When I nod, she goes on. 'My cousin Louis has a farm over that way.'

'I haven't met your cousin – to be honest, I haven't met anyone.'

'Life is quiet here.' She shrugs. 'And apart from this bar, there isn't anywhere to go. But a surprising number of people live in houses like yours, hidden away.' She looks curious. 'What did you do before you came here?'

'I was a teacher. I taught seven- and eight-year-olds. Maybe I'll go back to it – I don't know yet.'

Sylvie looks thoughtful. 'You know, there are often families around here looking for English tutors. People come here and put notices up. You should look.' Turning, I follow her gaze to a large board near the door with several notes pinned to it, as she looks hopeful. 'Please tell me you can cook? I could really use some help.'

'I have a great pasta recipe but that's about it.'

She shakes her head. 'I will find someone. But think about teaching, yes?' Her eyes fix on mine. 'We should have dinner one evening. Drink too much wine and talk about life.'

I find myself smiling at my unexpected friend. 'I'd really like that.'

*　*　*

As I drive back to the house, I think about Sylvie's suggestion. The money would be useful and teaching would give me something else to think about. Hadn't I been hoping the way forward would somehow reveal itself? Maybe this was the first step. Almost immediately, I snap myself out of it. *Since when did you get so passive?*

But when I get back, I forget about teaching. When I reach the door, instead of two cats waiting to be fed, there are three.

'This has to stop,' I tell the black cat. 'One of you, two at most... that's fine. But...' As he flicks his tail at me, I study the newest, a kitten with huge eyes and thick fur. I crouch down, and as cats number one and two back away, the kitten comes and rubs his head against me.

*　*　*

When I go back to the bar a couple of days later, Sylvie and I have lunch.

'Have you decided how long you're going to stay? Or what you'll do when you leave? Will you go back to England? I need to stop asking so many questions!' Sipping her wine, she pulls a face. 'This is not good. I will get a different one.'

'It's fine,' I tell her. 'It's nicer than most of the stuff I buy.'

Getting up, she frowns. 'Then I should teach you because this one definitely is not good.' Taking the bottle and our glasses to where her brother is behind the bar, she's back in no time with replacements. 'You were saying?'

'I wasn't. Other than not wanting to go back to the UK, I haven't really thought much further than that.'

'You're planning to stay here?' She looks mildly horrified.

'No. I just haven't decided where next.'

As a waitress brings our omelettes and a basket of bread, Sylvie looks at me thoughtfully. 'I've been thinking about the house where you are staying. I drive past it often – and you are right. It's been empty for quite a while – but I'm sure before that, a man was there.'

Thinking of the diary, my ears prick up. 'Did you meet him?'

She nods. 'We spoke once or twice. He was English and always alone. He used to sit on his own with a glass of wine or beer. But I didn't find out his name.'

'I'd love to know who he was.' The omelette is deep yellow, embedded with sliced girolles. 'This is amazing.'

'The eggs are from my cousin's chickens.' Sylvie carries on eating. 'Someone else running away would be my guess – the guy, I mean. He had that look.'

'What look?'

She shrugs. 'Closed. Giving off stay away vibes. You know.'

I decide to tell her about the diary. 'I'm guessing it was written by a man who was staying in my house. Maybe it was him.'

'You're reading someone's diary?' Sylvie looks shocked.

I shake my head at her. 'If something was private, you wouldn't leave it in a bookcase. It's more like a kind of love story – so far, at least.'

Sylvie raises one of her eyebrows. 'If it's the same guy, I don't remember seeing him with anyone.'

I shrug. 'Maybe you wouldn't have. She was married.' I change the subject. 'So, what about you? Are you staying indefinitely?'

Sylvie looks horrified. 'God, no. I have told myself I'll stay for the summer to help Marco, but after that... I want to go somewhere very different to here. I've spent too long in the same places – and I want warm winters.'

'So do I.' It was what Ben and I had talked about.

Putting down her fork, Sylvie's eyes meet mine. 'You should do it. Travelling alone is liberating. You're free to go wherever you want, without worrying about pleasing anyone else.'

Back then, I'd pictured fancy hotels, sandy beaches, funky bars. But this time, I imagine myself in unfamiliar, wild places, where the sea is vast and open, the thought igniting something in me until I see the empty space next to me, where you should be.

There's a lump in my throat as I look at Sylvie. 'Maybe I will. When the time is right.'

Reaching across the table, her hand rests on one of my arms. 'Of course. It's too soon,' she says. 'But I promise you, it won't always feel like this.'

20

BEFORE

May, last year

It preyed on my mind that I needed to talk to Ben, but I knew it wouldn't be easy. Talking about Jenna never was.

As I stood at the cooker, stirring what I hoped would be an unforgettable meal – for all the right reasons rather than the wrong ones – I heard Ben come in, then felt his arms around me.

He spoke softly. 'Can I get you a drink?'

'Please! Wine? There's a bottle of white in the fridge.'

Letting me go, he found a couple of Polly's rather expensive glasses and the bottle. Turning down the gas, I took the glass he held out.

'Cheers.' He raised his glass.

'Cheers.' Raising my glass, I was suddenly nervous. 'Ben? I need to talk to you about something.'

'Yes?' Frowning slightly, he sat at the table. 'Is something wrong?'

'No,' I blurted. Then, 'Actually, yes.' Going over to the table, my heart was starting to race as I sat opposite him. 'It's something I've wanted to *tell you for ages. But I don't find it easy to talk about.' My face felt hot. 'It's about my sister.'*

'Polly?'

Staring at the table, I shook my head. 'We have another sister.' My voice wavered. 'Her name was Jenna.' I watched his face as he took in the past tense. 'She was younger than me – by three years. Anyway, one day...' As I spoke, tears blurred my eyes. 'She was walking to catch the school bus. It was the same as any other morning. Except that morning... a speeding car...' Choked, I broke off. 'It veered off the road.' I couldn't stop the tears pouring down my face. 'It killed her.'

Ben looked shocked. 'Casey, that's so awful...'

'It was.' My voice shook. 'Especially for my parents.' Losing Jenna shattered all our lives, turning us overnight into a tragic family who were different for the worst possible reason.

'It must have been terrible for all of you,' Ben said gently. 'How old was she?'

'Twelve...' Guilt swamped me as I broke off. 'Everyone loved her. She was pretty and talented... She had everything to live for, Ben...' I sobbed. 'It shouldn't have happened.'

'Oh babe...' Ben sounded upset. 'I wish I'd known.'

'I'm so sorry,' I mumbled. 'I wasn't deliberately keeping it from you. I just find it really hard to talk about.'

'That wasn't what I meant.' Ben was quiet. 'I meant I wish I'd known so that I understood what you'd been through. I completely get why you don't talk about it.'

As he spoke, I felt the smallest weight lift. 'I have a photo.' Getting up, I wiped my face with a tissue before going over to one of the drawers where I kept one of the few photos I had of me, Polly and Jenna. It seemed an impossibly long time ago. I put the photo in front of Ben.

'She looks a bit like you.' He was silent for a moment. 'I can't imagine how it must have felt.' His voice was husky. 'For all of you.'

I couldn't speak. The thing was I'd never forgotten how it felt; how suddenly our lives changed forever; how devastated my parents were.

How it need never have happened, how guilty I felt. Grief had engulfed me, its pain overshadowing everything else so that all I could do was lock it away.

Noticing smoke pouring from the saucepan, I ran to the cooker where the curry had blackened. 'It's ruined. I'm sorry…' It felt like the last straw as my tears overwhelmed me.

'It doesn't matter. We'll get a takeaway.'

As Ben's arms went around me, a mixture of emotions surged through me. Relief that he knew; that he understood why I hadn't told him before. But there was guilt too, because it was only part of the story and even now, I hadn't told him everything.

21

May

As the days grow longer, change becomes more tangible – in the opening of my eyes to the beauty around me, in my fledgling friendship with Sylvie, enough that I can believe that there will be new horizons I've yet to glimpse. But the question, *what next?* remains unanswered.

One day... Your spark will come back... And you'll shine the way you always did, Casey Cassidy.

It's true, I realise. Since coming here, I've become aware of a part of me that's missing, that I need to find. The Casey Cassidy you met who was ready to take on the world with you, with her sense of adventure and the reckless streak that meant I took a chance the day you found my makeup bag and came after me; when I looked into the depths of your warm, blue eyes and my life shifted somewhere there was no coming back from.

You said it was like that for you, too. A kind of knowing you couldn't rationalise, but unlike me, you believed in the mysterious workings of the universe. It wasn't a mistake that we were in the same place that day. It was destiny, fate, whatever you wanted to call it, at play.

That just about sums it up, Ben Summer – your knack of making me question just about every frigging thing in my life, from getting hammered in bars on Friday nights to pondering the greater meaning of almost anything. But there's still one bit I can't figure and never will. Why you left me.

* * *

One morning, as I walk into the bar, Sylvie waves a piece of paper at me.

'I have found you a job!' She lowers her voice. 'I took it off the board before anyone else saw it.'

I look at her, slightly shocked that it's happened so quickly. 'What is it?'

'A family who live near Samatan – it's a town, about twenty minutes away. You don't seem very pleased.' She looks at me impatiently. 'This is the phone number.' She hands me the piece of paper. 'I've already told them you'll contact them.'

* * *

When I get home, I call the number and speak to a woman called Nathalie – which is how I come to be driving to the small hamlet of Sabaillan the next morning, looking for a house called Cap du Bosc.

At the end of a long track, Cap du Bosc is pale and unassuming as it comes into sight, with a wooden front door and white shutters, but the view from the garden towards the mountains takes my breath away. As I walk towards the door, it opens before I get there.

A woman about my age comes out. 'You must be Casey! I'm Nathalie!'

'Hi!' My eyes are pulled back towards the mountains.

She follows my gaze. 'Incredible, aren't they? Come on in. We'll have a chat – then you can meet Brad.'

I follow her into a wide hallway with a stone floor and pale walls, then into a huge kitchen where glass doors are slid back, leaving it open onto the garden.

'Have a seat.' Nathalie gestures towards the long wooden table. 'Would you like a drink?'

'No thanks.' As I sit down, I'm too busy looking around this stunning room, with its big American-style fridge and vast work surfaces, the huge worn sofa at one end, a freestanding wood burning stove in one of the corners.

'OK.' Nathalie sits opposite me. Her hair is slightly wavy, her brown eyes bright. 'I'll tell you a little about Brad.' She pauses. 'He's thirteen. For various reasons, he's missed a lot of school – health reasons,' she says vaguely. 'I've been here six months, so I only know part of the story.' She takes in my look of confusion. 'I should have said. I'm not Brad's mother. I'm the housekeeper.'

'Where are his parents?'

'His father is away – a lot. And his mother died. He has an older brother who's at uni, who'll be spending the summer with friends in London.' She lowers her voice. 'Since his mother died, Brad's been at school in England. Most of his friends are there – he's only back for half-term. But you can see...' She shrugs. 'It really isn't how the summer should be for a boy of his age.' Hearing footsteps, she glances towards the door. 'That will be him.' She calls out. 'Brad? Casey's here.'

The door swings open and a boy comes in. Tall for his age, he's wearing a funky T-shirt and oversized shorts. I look at his face, trying to hide my shock. There's something about him that reminds me of Ben.

* * *

After deciding to begin with two mornings a week, as I drive home, I work it out. It was the same closed look that uncannily resembled Ben's when his thoughts were somewhere else. It makes me think all is not right in Brad's world.

On the outskirts of Samatan, I detour through the town, where a market is underway – but unlike the one at Sylvie's bar, this one fills a couple of streets. I park up and then wander through the stalls, gazing at the clothes, splashing out on faded denim shorts and a strappy T-shirt, picking up some street food for later. By the time I get home, the sun is at its peak. Leaving my shopping on the table and getting a beer from the fridge, I sit outside.

The heat is lethargic, the garden alive with the sound of bees. Closing my eyes, I conjure your face.

It's your time, babe, you say quietly. *To think, rest, heal. Then one day, when you're ready, to dream new dreams.*

Sadness sweeps over me, shattering the peace as nostalgia hits full on. We had so much to look forward to, Ben. We shared such great dreams. And it's all gone.

Then out of the blue I'm jolted further back. To another morning, when I'm fifteen, bunking off school on my way to a friend's house when a screech of brakes reaches my ears, followed by the thud from an impact, a name screamed on the wind.

My eyes spring open, my hands tremble as I sit there, a sick feeling in the pit of my stomach, the same emotions hitting me as back then, when my childhood was severed.

Needing to hear a familiar voice, I get my phone to call Ellie, but in one of those telepathic moments that exist between friends, she calls me first.

'Hi! How's things?'

'It's a weird day, Ell. I'd literally just picked up my phone to call you.'

'You mean sad weird?'

'Yes.' My voice wobbles. 'My brain's doing that thing where it piles everything up until it feels like my head will explode.' I take a shaky breath. 'But I have a job.'

'Wow.' She sounds surprised. 'That's great! I didn't know you were looking.'

'I wasn't. It's only two mornings a week. Tutoring – I couldn't go on doing nothing every day. I start in the summer holidays. And I've found a bar, with a very French owner called Sylvie. She's really nice – she found me the job. Then just when I was starting to believe things might be OK, it's all hit me again.' My voice wavers. 'I have these questions, Ell. Questions I don't have answers to.' A tear rolls down my face. 'But I can tell you that the mountains are pretty. When the sun sets, they're pink. The fields are filled with wildflowers. And I have some cats.'

'*Cats?*'

'Three, Ell. It started off with one, but he's brought others with him.'

'Don't they have homes?'

'I don't think so. I feed them. I like them being around.'

'It sounds beautiful...' Ellie sounds wistful. 'And it's great about your job. Even the cats... You're in the right place, aren't you?' She's silent for a moment. 'At least, for now.'

'Maybe.' I swallow the lump in my throat. 'Feeling like this... It seems endless.' I'm talking about the sadness, the sense of loss, but she knows. She's been there every step of the way with me. 'I can't imagine ever feeling happy again.'

'I know.' Her voice is quiet. 'But keep hanging on, because you will, Casey. And it will get easier. You'll get there.'

I wipe my face. 'Anyway, let's talk about you. How is everything?'

'Oh, I'm good...' She sounds vague. 'Same old. I need a break – that's partly why I called. Can I come and see you?'

'Come any time.' I feel my heart lift. 'Apart from the mornings I work, I don't have plans.'

'Yay!' She sounds excited. 'I'll book some time off and let you know. Erm... have you talked to your mum or Polly?'

'Not for a while.' I've kept putting it off, but Ellie knows how my mum is.

'You know she worries about you?'

'I know.' Polly and I haven't spoken in a while either, but she's like my mother. Scratches slightly deeper beneath the surface, but no more than that. 'It's OK, Ell. We do talk – but you know how it is.'

'You need them, Case. And they care.' Then she sounds horrified. 'Shit. I didn't realise what time it is. I have to go. Listen, I'll look at flights and message you.'

After she's gone, I sit there for a moment, suddenly feeling cut off. Then I pick up my phone again, waiting as it rings a few times before my mother answers.

'Hi, Mum. It's me.'

'Casey! How are you? Now, I was just talking to Marjorie about you. I've been so worried, with you so far away and—'

'You don't need to worry, Mum.' I try to sound bright. 'I'm OK. I have a job, actually. Only part-time, but I'm teaching English.'

'A job?' My mother sounds shocked. 'I hope you haven't signed a contract. Surely it's time to think about coming back?'

I hedge. 'How are you? And Dad?'

'Your father's fine and I'm... Well, I've been getting migraines again, but the doctor's put me on a new medication. Marjorie says...' She's off again, listing inconsequential snippets about people I barely know, after which she hands the phone to my dad.

'Hello, sweetheart. How's it going over there?'

At the sound of his voice, tears prick my eyes. 'Hi Dad. It's OK. Quiet.'

'You're not too lonely then?' He says it gently.

'Sometimes.' My voice wavers. 'But that isn't a bad thing. And I'm not really alone. Some cats have moved in.'

He chuckles. 'Know a soft touch when they see one, don't they?'

'It really is OK, Dad. It feels like where I need to be – for now.' I try to sound brighter. 'And there are good things. I have a part-time job, tutoring.'

'Good for you.' His voice is husky. 'And you take your time. There's nothing to rush back for – and don't let anyone tell you otherwise.' He's talking about my mother. 'I know it must be tough.' He pauses. 'Not surprising there are ups and downs. But you'll be OK, you do know that, don't you?'

'I know.' The lump in my throat is back. 'Thanks, Dad.'

As I end the call, homesickness washes over me, my finger hovering over the screen. It would be so easy to call them back and tell them I'm coming home – I could be packed and out of here in an hour if I wanted to. But as the kitten rubs against me, I know that for all the safety it would offer, it would be a step back, when what I need to do is keep edging forward.

* * *

Later, installed on the sofa, a glass of wine in my hand, I pick up the diary to read the next update on diary-man and Julia.

5th March

Julia's dilemma is as old as humanity, driven by the essence of what it means to be a mother, versus her own personal freedom. Sacrificing her happiness because she believed it was in the interests of her children. Against my better judgement, when she came to the house again, I asked her in.

Taking the bottle of wine she was clutching, I found a corkscrew and opened it while Julia talked, rapidly, without pausing for breath. Her husband had shown her what his lawyer had written about her illness. He had records of her appointments, the medication she was on, as well as every frigging date she hadn't been right, as he liked to put it. She was shaking as she went on. If she left, he wasn't going to let her see her children.

Wondering if this was the start of another fall into the abyss, sadness filled me. Then anger. These were Julia's children too. Her husband couldn't get away with this.

But there was panic in her eyes. If he convinced everyone she was mad, she would get a few hours a week of supervised visits. The rest of the time, they'd live with him.

Passing her a glass of wine, I tried to persuade her she needed a professional assessment; that no judge was going to listen to her husband's bent lawyer over a psychiatrist. And what he was doing was bullying her.

Apparently, her lawyer had said the same. But she was frightened. Terrified that she was risking losing her children. She could only see one way forward, and that was to stay, until they'd grown up. It was only another six years. Six years that sounded like forever.

Her hands were shaking as she drank some of her wine, her voice trembling as she went on. Then I think of you. Her eyes gazed into mine. We hardly knew each other, but she had this feeling about us – the same feeling she'd had, right from the start. I was taken aback – it was quick. Then I felt my heart turn a somersault. It seemed incredible that she felt like that – about me. For a moment she was calm. She knew it was complicated – and part of her was frightened to go there, but she felt safe when we were together. Like she was free to be herself, whatever that happened to be, because I was on her side and didn't judge.

That I could be that person to her blew me away. Going over, I put my arms around her. Pulling her gently close, so that I could see the curl of her eyelashes, the curve of her mouth, breathe in the trace of her perfume. I wanted her to know how beautiful she is, to believe she could be free to live the life she deserves, not this half-life with her two-faced husband.

It seems like one of the universe's miracles that when you meet all kinds of people, now and then, something special happens. As I gazed at Julia, I couldn't resist those beautiful eyes. Or her lips. This time, it was me who kissed her. A kiss that went on and on, one that I didn't want to end and nor did she.

6th March

I didn't sleep last night. I couldn't stop thinking about how Julia's husband was holding her prisoner. I thought about going to her place to talk to him, but he was a step ahead of me. This morning there was a knock at my door. It was him.

He was aggression personified as he told me his wife had enough problems without being encouraged in her delusions by some imbecile of a man who didn't know her.

Folding my arms, I stared back at him. Who did this guy think he was? But here was my chance to stand up for Julia. It wasn't up to him who she spoke to. She deserved someone who listened. And it was pretty bloody clear she wasn't happy.

Glaring at me, he told me Julia wasn't capable of being happy. That every now and then, she went a little wild. That her medication needed adjusting; that I was simply another imbecile who had been taken in by her.

I was quietly seething. He was a jerk. I told him what I thought, that she knew he was cheating on her and she wanted a divorce, one that she was perfectly entitled to.

Looking at me like I was dirt, he told me to give it a week, a month, six months... That Julia didn't know what she wanted. Then in the biggest lie of all so far, he said he'd tried to help her, just like he was trying to keep things together for their children's sakes. All he wanted was for them to be a family.

I was gobsmacked. Did this guy actually believe his own bullshit? Since when did cheating cohabit with happy family life? But when I challenged him, he was furious. What was going on in his life was none of my fucking business.

I told him he wasn't making sense. That shagging someone else wasn't the best way to keep your family together. That Julia deserved to be treated with respect; that the way I saw it, he was a selfish bastard who wanted the best of both worlds.

I told him to get the fuck off my doorstep. For a moment I thought he was going to punch me. But as he stormed off, I decided this was ridiculous. Whatever I feel for Julia, getting embroiled in this mess wasn't going to help anyone. Whatever there might be between us, first, she needed to leave this asshole. Afterwards, that would be a whole other thing. Meanwhile, I needed to sort out my own life. Until then, I was in no position to help anyone else.

Putting the diary down, I'm lost in thought. We all have our ideas about how life is supposed to be; how in a just world, love should triumph over adversity. But sometimes, it doesn't. It can be messy, complicated; can take boundless courage to share the truth the way Julia did, because if I've learned anything from the past, it's that it would have been far easier for her to hide it.

As I'm sitting here, the kitten climbs onto my lap. Stroking it, I listen to it purr as unwanted memories start flooding back, because we both had secrets, didn't we, Ben? All those times I'd known you were keeping something from me, when we'd pledged to always be honest with each other and agreed relationships were based on trust.

We failed. I failed – that's the truth. And it hurts, *so frigging much*... We should have been honest with each other. I should have listened to you, instead of hearing what I wanted to hear. It would have been so much easier for both of us.

22

June, last year

As Ben's birthday came closer, I racked my brains for ideas for his present. After hours of searching, when at last I found it, I knew straight away he'd love it.

'Give me a clue, Cassidy.' There was a look of boyish excitement on Ben's face. 'All you've said is pack your toothbrush. I need more to go on than that.'

'You'll have to wait, I'm afraid.' I tossed my hair over my shoulders, determined not to give it away.

'What else do I need?' He looked hopeful.

'Nothing.' I shrugged. 'Maybe a rope ladder. Or binoculars...' I added, enjoying the look of confusion on his face.

It had come down to a choice between a night of five-star luxury cocooned behind thousand-year-old castle walls, or being close to nature and slumming it. I'd known immediately which he'd prefer.

Changing into a pair of ripped denim shorts, I twisted my hair and *clipped it on top of my head, then spritzing myself with perfume, found my sunglasses. As I went downstairs, I was trying to think what we needed.*

'I have my toothbrush.' He waved it at me.

'Cool.' Going over, I kissed him. 'Shall we go?'

As I drove, Ben quizzed me. 'Come on. Give me something, Cassidy. We can't be camping. There's nothing in the back of the car.'

'How do you know?' I glanced sideways at him.

'While you were changing, I checked.' He sounded amused. 'So I'm guessing a hotel somewhere?'

'In these shorts?' I rolled my eyes. 'I'm not saying, so you may as well give up.'

Putting some music on, I drove on, away from the town until we were deep in the Sussex countryside. An hour later, we were almost there. 'Close your eyes, Ben. No peeking.'

As the lane wound on through tall pine trees, either side, banks of cow parsley shimmered in the sunlight. Reaching a lake, I slowed down and parked, sitting there for a moment, taking in the dappled shade of the trees, the water glistening in the sunlight. 'OK. You can open them.'

I watched Ben blink, before a broad grin settled across his face. 'So we are camping! This is fantastic, babe!'

'Not exactly...' I opened the car door and got out. 'Come with me.'

Following the directions I'd committed to memory, I walked towards the lake. 'I think we go this way.' I found the narrow path that continued along its edge towards a huge chestnut tree. 'OK. I think we're here.'

Ben glanced uncertainly up into its branches. 'Um, you mean this tree is it?'

'Yes.' Behind the tree, narrow steps spiralled into the branches and as we started up them, the tree house came fully into view. With a pitch roof and weathered by the elements, it looked as though it had always been there. Reaching the top of the steps, I opened the door.

'Oh, wow.' Ben stood there. 'This is awesome, Cassidy.'

None of the photos of the treehouse had done it justice. Left unpainted, the space was dominated by a huge bed with soft white pillows, while the front was open; a diaphanous floor length curtain floating in the breeze. Far from slumming it, this was the most rustic luxury I'd ever seen. Going over, Ben stepped out onto the narrow balcony. 'Come out here, babe.'

Going to join him, I could just make out the lake glistening below, while around us were sounds of nature – songbirds, water fowl, bees; the softest breeze rustling the leaves. It was like a fairy tale. Becoming even more so as Ben turned and kissed me.

Leaving him in the shade, I went to find the champagne that had been left for us in an ice bucket. Opening it, I poured it into two flutes I'd found in what passed for a minuscule kitchen.

Taking them back outside, I gave one of them to Ben. 'Happy birthday.'

Being here was everything I'd hoped for – and more. Venturing back down the spiral staircase, we sat for hours at the edge of the lake, watching birds swoop down to catch insects while dragonflies skimmed across the water. Then after a barbecue, we watched the sun sink lower, the sky darkening as millions of stars came into view.

Ben gazed at the sky. 'Shooting stars,' he said quietly. 'Look.'

'Wow,' I breathed, straining my eyes to pick out pinpricks of light whizzing through the darkness. Were they one of Ben's signs?

I was still looking up at the stars, when I heard him say, 'Casey?'

'Um.' Transfixed, I didn't move.

'Babe?'

I turned to look at him. His eyes were glowing as he reached out to take one of my hands. His voice fell quiet as he spoke the words. 'I'm falling in love with you.'

In that moment, in the stillness of the night, I could actually feel what love was. It was mirrored in our eyes, its presence tangible around us, more real than I'd ever believed possible. 'I love you, too,' I whispered.

* * *

The following morning, when I woke up, Ben was already sitting on the veranda, a blanket draped around his shoulders. Slipping out of bed, I went to join him.

'Hi.' I wriggled under the blanket next to him. 'You're up early.'

'It was the birds.' He spoke quietly. 'I love that you can't hear anything else. Apart from you snoring,' he teased.

'Hey. I don't snore.' I nestled against him.

'It was what I loved when I was away – how the noise of life disappeared. I just wish...' He hesitated.

'What?' I watched his face.

He was silent for a moment. 'I wish everything could stay – like it is, right now, in this moment. That nothing will happen to change it.'

As he spoke, I felt my skin prickle. 'It won't, Ben. Not if we don't let it.' Turning towards him, I kissed him. 'Let's do that. Not let anything get in the way of us.'

His head rested against mine as, for a moment, he didn't speak. 'This is the best present.' His eyes gazed into mine. 'Not just the tree house – I mean, it's epic,' he paused. 'But so is knowing you love me.'

'Ditto,' I said softly. 'I think there's a kettle in there.' I glanced back inside. 'Would you like coffee?'

I put together a tray of the fruit and pastries that had been left for us, taking them and the coffee back outside. As romantic moments went, I wouldn't have changed a thing. It was perfect.

23

June

As summer settles over this small part of France, your birthday comes and goes. The first without you.

Remember the shooting stars? When we got home, I'd looked them up. They foretold change; I remember telling you. And they were lucky. They could signify endings too, but that didn't apply to me and you. We were just starting out, weren't we?

Outside, I sit on the edge of the terrace. Last year, the isolation of the tree house had been perfect for one night. But since coming here, I've come to appreciate solitude. Started to understand what you so often talked about – how it's only in the quiet moments that you can hear what is so easily drowned out – your subconscious mind, the universe you used to talk about, nature's heartbeat.

And it isn't just you I'm sad about. I feel the same sorrow you felt about the way life has become, about our abuse of this beautiful world and what lives in it; the way we're destroying habitats and species. Feel the same grief. I discovered it has a name. Solastalgia –

a collective despair felt by people around the world; a form of homesickness for an environment that doesn't exist any more.

* * *

My tutoring job is brought forward when, after being off sick from school, Brad comes back to France before the end of term.

'So, Brad...' I look at the boy sitting opposite me. 'Why don't you tell me a bit about you? Have you any idea what you might like to do – when you finish school?'

Avoiding my eyes, he shrugs. 'I don't know.'

I try again. 'Which subjects are you most interested in?' I pause. 'Do you like science, for example? Or books?' When he's quiet, I change tack. 'You're at school in England, aren't you? You must really miss your friends.'

Looking surprised, he nods.

'Do any of them come and stay?'

Brad shrugs. 'Not this year.' A light flickers in his eyes, before going out. 'I did want to be a doctor. But I don't know.'

'What changed your mind?'

'I've missed too much school.' He looks defeated. 'And my grades aren't good enough.'

'Who says?'

'My teachers – and my dad.'

'OK.' I sit back, looking at him. 'You're thirteen?'

'Yeah,' he mumbles.

'Right. Well, the way I see it you have a choice.' As I speak, he looks at me with interest. 'You can give up now and settle for something that maybe you don't really want, or you can go for it. You have enough time, Brad. Do you have any of your schoolbooks here? And your grades?' Suddenly I have his attention. When he nods, I go on. 'Can we look at them?'

It soon becomes apparent that his grades only slipped when he missed a lot of school. Identifying where we need to start, we spend the morning working out a plan.

* * *

As I get in my car to drive home, I'm thinking about Brad's teachers and his father, and everyone like them, who instead of encouraging, puncture people's dreams. It enrages me that anyone would do that to someone Brad's age, because when you take away hope, you kill something.

As I turn into my lane, my phone buzzes with a text from Ellie.

Is next week OK? Tuesday? Xxx

Yes! Can't wait to see you xxx

When I get back, the kitten is by the door, waiting for me. When I scoop him up, he purrs noisily. Just then, my mum calls again, under the guise of checking I'm OK, but it soon becomes apparent that in her not-so-subtle way, she's trying to persuade me to move back to Devon.

'It really does seem the most sensible idea, Casey. Now, I bumped into Lesley Williams this morning. You must remember Lesley... You were at school together. Such a nice girl, I always thought. I told her all about you.'

Sitting down, I feel my heart sink. Lesley was a bitch. 'Mum, please don't talk about me to strangers. Surely you remember she was horrible to me.'

'Really, Casey. It wouldn't hurt you to say something nice for once.' My mother sounds shocked. 'She was actually very concerned.'

I bet she was. If I know Lesley, she'd have been soaking up every titbit she could prise out of my mother, so she could gossip about me. 'Mum. I can't come back. Not yet.'

'So when?' she asks accusingly. 'When are you coming back?'

Uncertainty settles over me. 'I don't know.'

'What you're really saying is, you don't want to.' She sounds hurt. 'It's this job of yours, isn't it? I knew it was a bad idea.'

I pause, knowing that she has my best interests at heart. But I know what Polly would say. *That's shit, Casey. It's her best interests. She's probably already sniffed out that nice Devon farmer she always wanted to fix you up with.* 'It's nothing to do with my job,' I say at last. 'And it isn't that I'm not grateful, Mum. But I'm where I need to be.' Knowing as I speak it's the first time I've actually said that to her.

'You've been away for weeks, Casey.' She sounds huffy. 'It really is time you came home.' She stops abruptly. 'What's that noise?'

'A kitten.' I glance down at the kitten curled up on my lap, still purring. 'It's very sweet.'

'You can't start collecting pets. What's going to happen when you leave?'

'I'm not leaving, Mum. Not yet.' Though she may have a point about collecting cats. But even from hundreds of miles away, her verbal demands leave me feeling trapped in a way I can't deal with. 'I'm sorry, I have to go. I'll call you soon.'

Before she can say anything else, I end the call, relief flowing over me. Holding the kitten, I go outside and take a deep breath, letting the peacefulness soak into me. The air is still, lethargic, the sunset painting the mountains a soft, ice-cream pink just as I've described to Ellie.

In the silence, the smallest sounds are audible – crickets, birds, the wings of a hummingbird moth. You and I used to share silences like this, inhabit the same quiet moments. Memories that are bitter-sweet, laced with sadness.

24

BEFORE

June, last year

'There's something I wanted to talk to you about.' Sitting opposite me at a table in an Italian restaurant, Ben looked uncharacteristically awkward.

'So ask away.' Sitting back, all of a sudden, I was guarded. He sounded serious. Surely he wasn't about to dump me? I watched his face, suddenly anxious.

He hesitated. 'I was thinking... Actually, I've been thinking about this for a while.'

Growing more defensive by the second, I folded my arms.

Reaching across the table for one of my hands, his eyes held mine. 'What if we moved in together?'

As my mouth dropped open, I felt my heart miss a beat. OMG. Did he actually just say that or did I imagine it? 'Um, me live with you?' I said stupidly. When we spent most of our time at his, it wouldn't make sense for him to move to Polly's. A thrill of excitement went through me as I *pretended to think. 'Well...' My voice was intentionally casual. 'I suppose, on the plus side we spend so much time travelling between each other's houses... and your place is nearer to the school. But...' I wanted to, so much, but we'd only known each other five months and a part of me was holding back.*

'But?' Ben looked surprised. 'But what?'

'Nothing,' I said hastily, knowing I was ruining a beautiful moment. 'Honestly.'

'No good, Casey.' He was shaking his head. 'Tell me!'

I hesitated again. 'OK. If you insist.' Gazing at him, I prepared to bare my soul. 'I don't want things to change between us. I've seen it happen to other people. I want us to stay like we are – for however long we're together, Ben. I don't want us to become one of those sad couples who've stopped trying and deep inside are shrivelled and miserable, and who should probably have split up years ago. I want my heart to always miss a beat when I think of you, to be excited when we plan things...' Suddenly worried I sounded ridiculous, I broke off. This felt high-risk, especially for me. 'I've said too much, haven't I?'

'You haven't.' Ben's eyes were earnest. 'It's like we said in the tree house. If we're together, we can make it whatever we want it to be. We're not other people – we don't have to fall into the same traps they do. We're us.'

My eyes stared back into his as I realised the magnitude of what I was facing. This was commitment without the 'm' word, but no less about trust, loyalty – and risk. Was I ready? But I knew I couldn't lose him. It was early days, but that was irrelevant when you felt the way we did. Seized with recklessness, the last of my objections melted away as the broadest of smiles spread across my face. 'You're right! Let's do this!'

* * *

The first person I told was Ellie, who shrieked with joy and flung her arms around me. 'Yay! I'm so happy for you! I told you, didn't I?'

'We're shacking up, not getting hitched,' I reminded her. 'But yes, it's brilliant!'

'When are you moving in? You must have a party to celebrate!' Her eyes were bright with excitement.

'This weekend. One thing at a time, Ell!'

The second person I told was my sister, Polly, in the States. 'Guess what, sis?' I said when she answered. 'You're getting your house back. Ben wants me to move in.'

'Wow.' She sounded genuinely dumbstruck. 'When? Why?'

My sister and she's asking why? 'I think possibly because he loves me, Poll,' I said quietly. Wasn't it obvious?

Less than five minutes later, my mum called. 'Polly tells me you're moving in with someone. Are you sure you know what you're doing?' She sounded most put out.

No, Mum. I'm following my wayward, reckless heart. It's called living. 'He's a nice guy, Mum. And I've known him a few months, now.' Happiness making me generous-hearted. 'You'll really like him. I'll bring him down to meet you and Dad.'

'Well, it can't be this weekend. I'm helping out at the WI craft fair. But I can manage the one after. Sunday lunch? You could always stay, I suppose.' Sounding doubtful, I knew she'd already be worrying about sleeping arrangements.

'Don't worry. We probably won't stay, Mum. But thanks. I'll ask him.'

The following Saturday, I gathered together my possessions, cramming them into both our cars before driving to Ben's. We celebrated that night with Mexican food and cold beer at the table in the back garden, then spent the night curled in each other's arms.

I floated through our first week together, high on happiness, my feet barely touching the ground. Then on Sunday morning, we set off early for my parents' house. On the way, I tried to prepare Ben. 'My mother...' I hesitated. 'She means well... It's just that... I suppose she doesn't always say things very kindly. Not that she isn't kind.' For a moment, loyalty overriding honesty.

'I'm sure it will be fine,' Ben looked slightly amused.

I didn't reply – he didn't know my mother. There was something else I needed him to know, too. 'About Jenna... We don't really talk about her – just so you know.'

'It's OK.' Ben glanced at me. 'You don't have to worry.'

'I know.' But I didn't know how to explain that every time I went home, in the weirdest way it was as though nothing had changed; that any moment, Jenna would come dancing back in, exactly as she was when we lost her.

* * *

But Ben meeting my parents was always going to be fine. Mum initially sized him up with one of her typical frowns, but when he smiled and shook her hand, called her Mrs Cassidy and gave her the bunch of flowers we'd bought her, she was won over. Dad, of course, was just Dad. Gentle and patient, with never a bad word to say about anyone, shaking Ben's hand, genuinely pleased to meet him.

I'd wondered how it would be, bringing Ben to my childhood home that was cluttered with a lifetime of memories, but it felt effortless. I pinned on a smile. 'Would you like a tour?'

As I showed Ben around, he looked envious. 'You're so lucky to have this. Dad got moved around so much with his job, nowhere was home for long.'

'Yeah, but this is Devon, remember?' If he wanted sympathy, he wasn't getting it from me. 'While you were seeing the world, I was here.'

I watched his eyes rest on a framed photo of me, Polly and Jenna, his hand tightening around mine for a few seconds. Meanwhile, Mum had cooked one of her spectacular roasts, even stretching to a nut roast for me and Ben, while the dining room table was set with the best silver and the china that usually only came out for Christmas. When Mum went out to the kitchen, I glanced at Ben. 'I hope you feel honoured.' I nodded towards the nut roast. 'She never bothers when it's just me.'

Beside me, Dad cleared his throat, just as Mum came back in carrying a vegetable dish. She beamed at Ben. 'More parsnips?'

25

June

We moved fast, didn't we Ben? Was it too fast? Like when you asked me to move in, you'd streaked ahead, waiting surprised, excited seconds as I caught up.

Such happy days, babe. The best.

My heart twists, because they were. The brightest of crystalline memories, that I'm frightened will melt like shards of ice.

They'll always be there, babe. And in time, there'll be more, just as brilliant.

Even if there are, these will always be the most precious, Ben.

* * *

The next time I arrive in Sabaillan, I find the front door open. In the kitchen, Brad's pouring a glass of orange juice.

'Hey.' He looks brighter than last time.

'Hi. Is Nathalie around?'

'She's gone to the shops.' He raises the orange juice carton. 'D'you want some?'

'Thanks.' I watch him get another glass. 'So, do you have an idea what you'd like to do today?'

Passing me the glass, he nods. 'I'll show you.'

I follow him into the study, where two chairs are pulled up at a big desk.

'After the last time you were here, I thought about what you said – about not giving up. I mean, if I want to be a doctor, I should try, shouldn't I? To get the grades I need?'

'Definitely.' I pause. 'We're starting with maths, aren't we?' Seeing his face, I add, 'Maths really isn't so bad. And if we get that up to speed, we can move on to science?'

Seeing a face light up with understanding is what I love most about teaching. Brad is smart and focused. By the end of the morning, I'm quietly angry. Whoever told him to lower his sights got it so wrong.

On the way out, I see Nathalie. 'He's great,' I tell her. 'He's working really hard and he's motivated. He just needs encouragement.'

'I agree. Unfortunately, his father has his own ideas. Wants him to follow in his footsteps.' She shakes her head. 'He works for a large corporation...' She breaks off as Brad reappears. 'There you are! Shall we have lunch?'

* * *

Back home in the afternoon, I take the diary outside onto the terrace.

15th April
  After Julia's husband came to see me, I stepped back. I had

to. I couldn't get drawn into the wreckage of their marriage. When I texted her to explain, she called me, begging me to meet her. I knew she was hurting, but I stood my ground. It broke my heart. Whoever was right or wrong, there was stuff the two of them needed to sort out and it was better they did that without me.

If I was here for long enough, I guessed our paths would cross again – next week, next month – who knows? Or maybe it isn't meant to be – which leaves me where? Beneath these endless depths of sky, the earth beneath my feet, as spring arrives, alone. And maybe that's no bad thing. I have time to think in a way you can't when other people are around, which when I think about it is the whole reason I came here.

It's taken time to work it out, but it's exactly how I feel. I really am where I need to be. And it isn't so bad being alone. I text Ellie:

I've been getting it so wrong, I've been seeing this house as somewhere I don't want to be, instead of as what I need Xx

As she texts me back a line of heart emojis, I'm drawn back to the diary.

6th May
I'm signing out for a bit. Can't write about it now – I'll explain later.

That's all it says. Disappointed, when I flick through the following pages, I'm relieved to find more entries later in the year. But with Ellie about to arrive, I put it to one side. Tidying the house and picking some flowers from the garden, I place them in a jug on the kitchen table. Then the next day, after doing a shop, I go to meet her.

After the rural lanes I've become used to, the volume of traffic is terrifying. Once or twice, a vehicle swerves too close to me, a sudden reminder of your accident. I remember too clearly how mangled your car was, how you so nearly died. I remember you saying how quickly it happened. As the traffic streams past, I don't want to think about it. Pushing the thought from my head somehow, I reach Toulouse and navigate my way to one of the short-term car parks before heading inside the terminal towards the arrival zone, where only a few minutes later, the automatic doors open and my friend walks through.

'Casey!' Pulling her case, Ellie runs towards me, flinging her arms around me. 'God, I've missed you!'

'I've missed you too!' As we stand there hugging each other, I've never been so pleased to see her. Suddenly aware we're in the way of other passengers, I grab her suitcase and link my arm through hers. 'Let's get out of here.'

As we drive, Ellie chatters animatedly, twisting strands of her long red hair. 'I am so glad to get away from work. Last month, we lost one of our biggest contracts and everyone's blaming everyone else. Oh, and I saw Suki the other day – a few of us went round for her birthday. Everyone sends their love. You won't believe this but she's stopped drinking... I'm thinking she might be pregnant – I mean, Suki not drinking? Can you imagine? Anyway...' She goes on, filling me in on more gossip, but then she goes quiet.

Keeping my eyes on the road, I nudge her elbow. 'And the bit you're not telling me?'

She glances sideways at me. 'Casey Cassidy, how do you do that? I was going to save it for that first glass of wine when we get to your place.'

'You're forgetting I know you better than anyone.'

'OK.' There's excitement in her voice. 'I've met a guy.'

Something about the way she says it gives me a feeling that this one is different. 'Just another guy, right?'

'He's really nice, and I'll tell you more, but it can wait! I want to hear about France! What we're going to do while I'm here – and what you've been doing since you got here.'

'The truth? Until recently, I wasn't doing a lot.' Fully aware of how boring that sounds, I tell her about the ugly tree and the peeling paint on the shutters, the changing colours of the distant mountain peaks and the miles of emptiness. 'But then I met Sylvie – I'll take you to her bar – and through her, I have my job. And I've found a diary, Ell. I'm not sure whose it is – but I've been reading it. There are so many parallels with how I'm feeling. It's really weird.'

'You shouldn't read someone's diary!' Ellie sounds astonished.

'That's what Sylvie said.' I shrug. 'It was in the bookcase. And if you didn't want anyone to read it, you'd hide it. At least, I would.' As we leave the motorway, the traffic thins out. 'OK. This is much more like where I'm living. Empty towns, open fields, miles and miles of trees – with the odd crazy driver. Another half an hour and we'll be home.'

When we eventually arrive at the house, she stares at it for a moment, then stifles a giggle. 'I kind of had this image in my head of decaying elegance... Sorry.' She glanced at me.

'No need to apologise. I'm not in the least offended.' I get out of the car. 'It's a bit of a hobbit house. When I got here, I very nearly didn't stay. But back then, nothing would have been right.'

Looking at me, she's quiet. 'Is it right? Now, I mean?'

'For now.' It's another of those instinctive answers. 'But I've always known I wouldn't stay here long.' Ignoring her quizzical look, I get her suitcase out of the back. 'Come on. I'll show you around.'

It takes all of a few minutes to show her the basic French kitchen, the sofas pulled up close to the wood burner, the two bedrooms squashed under the eaves, while I try to see it through Ellie's eyes. Shabby, simple, but comfortable.

'It's cute, Casey. Cosy.' She turns to me. 'If I were you, I wouldn't want to leave.'

Is she mad? 'As far as I know, I can stay as long as I want.' I pause. 'But I'll stay until I decide where I'm going next.'

'Wow.' Ellie's voice is quiet. 'So you're really not planning to come back.'

'To England?' I'm as perplexed as she is. 'It's weird, Ell. But it doesn't feel right. It's like earlier, when you asked me if I was going to stay here. That doesn't feel right, either. They're gut feelings.' I shrug. 'I'm learning to trust them.'

After she follows me downstairs into the kitchen, I get two wine glasses from one of the cupboards, then get a bottle of white from the fridge. Pouring it into the glasses, I pass one to Ellie and sit opposite her. Raising my glass, I clink it against hers. 'I am so happy you're here.' I gaze at my friend. 'It's the longest we've ever gone without seeing each other.'

'Cheers,' she says quietly. 'It is, isn't it?'

'OK. Now you have your glass of wine, I want to know everything.' I give her a look. 'Especially about this man.'

A smile crosses her face. 'His name is Jim!' I take in the familiar light in her eyes. 'So, we met at this horrendous corporate day – you know, where they talk about vile company mantras and buzz words and all that shit?'

I pretend to stick two fingers down my throat. 'When?'

'The end of February.' A shadow crosses her face. 'I wanted to tell you, but... Casey, I couldn't. After what happened with Ben, it felt like the worst time in the world for me to meet someone.' She pauses. 'And it was too soon to know if it would last.'

'It's quick, isn't it, Ell?' The words are out before I can stop them.

'No quicker than you and Ben,' she says quietly. 'You just know, don't you?'

'Yes.' My voice is sober. 'But there was also a whole lot I didn't know, remember?'

She grimaces. 'You wouldn't have believed that corporate day. It was dreadful and everyone was taking it so seriously. I was trying not to laugh at all the bullshit, when all of a sudden, I caught Jim looking at me. It was obvious he was thinking exactly the same. I held it together until the coffee break.' She shakes her head. 'Anyway, we chatted over coffee. Then at lunch, we got talking properly. It turns out he hates the corporate world so much he's quitting his job and setting up on his own.'

My ears prick up. 'Wow! Doing what?'

'Well... he's decided he wants a complete change – and he wants to buy some land. He was going to look for a smallholding in Wales, but this is the exciting bit... A friend of his moved to France a couple of years ago, with his family – to the Dordogne. They've never looked back. He says everything is better here – not just property prices, but the lifestyle, the weather... as you obviously know. So, to cut a long story short, Jim has decided to do the same. He's been looking for a place not too far from his friend's – with enough land to grow veg, keep chickens, that sort of stuff.'

Taken aback, I gaze at Ellie, wondering why she looks so happy about it. 'But what about you? You have your job – and your flat. Your entire life is in the UK.'

Ellie's eyes sparkle at me. 'OK, so this is the best bit! When he first mentioned it, he asked if I'd come over for weekends. But then he asked if I'd move with him. So of course, I said yes!' She goes on more soberly. 'I don't want to waste more years of my life in a job I can't stand. After the shit at work, it was a no brainer. So, I've handed in my notice and my flat is on the market...'

'Oh my God. This is amazing!' I stare at her, incredulous. 'You're my best friend, Ellie. How do I not know any of this?'

She looks anxious. 'After everything you've been through, it wasn't something I could tell you over the phone. It would have felt so insensitive.'

'I could never think that about you.' There's a lump in my

throat, because Ellie's the most caring, supportive friend. 'You deserve this. I'm really happy for you.' I raise my glass. 'To you and Jim. And all your dreams.' My smile is bright, but I hear my voice waver, hating myself because this is Ellie's moment.

'Oh, Casey.' Ellie looks stricken. 'I'm so sorry. I know it's still early days for you.'

'I'm OK, Ell.' I pick up my glass. 'I keep hoping that one day I'll wake up and I'll feel better. And some days, I do.' Pulling myself together, I force a smile. 'But this is about you – and it's such great news. What you said about it being the worst time in the world to meet someone, it really isn't. It's the perfect time. It proves that life – and love – go on.'

'Oh Casey...' Ellie leans forwards and strokes my hair over my shoulder. 'You know, I think it is starting to get better. In small ways... I can see it in you.' Looking into my eyes, she frowns. 'Have I said the wrong thing?'

Feeling a tear roll down my cheek, I wipe it away. Ellie's the only person in the world I can say this to. 'I can feel it, too – but a part of me doesn't want to. I want to hurt, Ellie.' My voice is husky. 'Desperately, for the rest of my life, because if it stops, it will mean I'm over Ben.'

Coming over, Ellie puts her arms around me. 'Listen,' she says quietly. 'No matter what you do or who you're with, it will never take away how much you loved Ben. Nothing can. But you have to stop beating yourself up.'

As Ellie touches on the core of what I don't want to face, it's too much. *'It shouldn't have happened.'* Suddenly sobs are erupting from me as everything I've repressed comes to the surface. *'I ought to have known it was coming. I should have seen how he was feeling...'* And as all the should-haves and ought-to-haves pour out of me, I collapse into my friend's arms. Strong arms that hold me, while a storm of emotions rages through me.

* * *

Eventually, much later, it ebbs away. My face buried in her shoulder; I mumble into her hair. 'I'm so sorry, Ell.' Her perfume is comforting. 'I didn't mean to do this to you.'

'It's what friends are for... and it's OK.' As Ellie holds me, I realise how long it is since I've had any physical contact with anyone.

'Can I stay here? For a bit?' As I lean against her, more tears flood down my cheeks, as I give in to the pain of losing you.

* * *

My tears are cathartic; healing tears that leave me lighter and calmer the next morning as I show Ellie around outside.

'God, I love this heat.' Stretching her arms above her head, she gazes up at the sky. 'Doesn't it make a difference?'

'I know. I've already forgotten what English summers are like.' It's a dream of a day, with soft, warm air, the leaves rustling in the lightest of breezes.

'It's a gorgeous garden,' she says unexpectedly.

'You think? I do like the wildness, but the house is still ugly.' In my newfound appreciation for my surroundings, I catch myself. 'I really have to stop saying that.'

'You know, I quite like it.' She glances back at it. 'I bet it's a house with a story.' Ellie threads my arm through hers. 'Come on. Let's see what you have out there.'

'Now just hold on a minute.' I hang back. 'Since when do you know anything about gardens?'

'Since Jim – I'm learning. Bet you couldn't have pictured me being a *Gardener's World* addict, but I want a huge veggie garden and tons of flowers, so I need to learn about growing them.'

I stare at her incredulously. 'Who are you and what have you done with my friend?'

'Come on, Casey.' There's an edge of bossiness in Ellie's voice. Taking the steps down from the terrace, we follow the line of the hedge. 'Maybe you should learn too. See these little white flowers? These will be blackberries by September.' She glances at me apologetically. 'If you're still here... except I'm guessing you won't be.'

'No,' I say shortly.

'The grass needs cutting. I can do it, if you like! Do you have a mower?'

Ellie enthusiastic about mowing grass? 'No idea. There's a barn with stuff in it, but I haven't looked.'

'I'll check it out.' Dancing ahead of me, she points at the trees that earlier in the year were laden with blossom. 'These will be apples – or maybe plums. And these...' Looking at a sprawl of bare canes growing out of some weeds, she sounds like an excited child. 'You have raspberries, Casey!'

Which is all very well, but if I want raspberries, I can buy them in the supermarket.

But Ellie seems bewitched. 'This is what I want.' Standing still, she gazes across the fields towards the mountains. 'Remember when we went to Morocco? I was craving peace and quiet, just like this.'

If it's true that some people come into your life when you need them most, Ellie is warm sunlight – but at her strongest far too early in the morning. 'Get your sorry ass into gear, Casey Cassidy. I didn't come all this way to watch you lounge around till midday and drink yourself stupid.'

'I'm not,' I protest, but I'm in the mood for strong coffee, not pointless physical exercise. 'I work now, remember? Go without me. Or better still, let's go to Sylvie's.'

She ignores my protest. 'You work two mornings – it doesn't count. It's a beautiful day. There must be some epic walks around here. Where are your trainers?'

'I don't know. In one of my bags?' I thought I was doing all right, but under Ellie's scrutiny, I'm not so sure.

Glaring at me, Ellie goes upstairs, as for the first time since she arrived here, your voice comes to me.

She's right. It's gorgeous out there. And you're doing OK, babe. But you know what? You could do better...

As the rummaging sounds stop, Ellie comes back down, a look of disapproval on her face as she chucks my trainers in the direction of my feet. 'I can't believe you haven't unpacked. Anyway, put those on.' She nods towards my shoes.

Not daring to argue, I do as she tells me. And as we walk up the lane, the sunlight is pretty, the chorus of birdsong at its most spectacular. 'When I was first here, I didn't like any of this,' I admit to Ellie.

'I know. But you didn't want to like anything,' she says pointedly.

'I think I was shell-shocked. It was the empty space and lack of shops – a bit like Devon. I was gathering a list of resentments – until the Lesley Williams moment.'

'The what?' Ellie stares at me.

'Lesley Williams – in our class. Cocky, mouthy cow, remember?' I watch the look of recognition dawn on Ellie's face. 'Anyway, my mum bumped into her recently and in her own words, "told Lesley all about me." I was furious at the time, but I should be grateful really, because Mum was trying to persuade me to go home, and all of a sudden, I realised what a terrible idea it was.'

'Lesley Williams of all people – how could I forget her?' Ellie shakes her head in disbelief. 'How is your mum?'

'She's OK. Same as ever. She dreams of matching me up with a Devon farmer. She thinks she knows what's best for me.' I shrug. 'The only time she didn't was when Ben was around.'

'She worries about you.' Ellie glances at me. 'She called me a couple of weeks ago. Asked if I'd try to persuade you to move back to Devon. I did try to explain to her, that it was up to you and you had to figure out your own way.'

'Since when did you get so wise?' I'm only half-joking though. 'But thanks, Ell.'

'She didn't say a lot after that. Have you thought about inviting her to visit?'

'Can you honestly imagine?' I picture my mother dealing with the basic kitchen as well as her daughter's alcohol consumption. 'It's not her kind of place and in all honesty, we'd probably drive each other mad.' But I want to know more about Ellie's plans. 'Tell me more about you and Jim. What kind of houses have you been looking at?'

A smile breaks out across her face. 'Well, originally, he found a two-bed place with ten acres, but now that I'm selling my flat and coming with him, we're looking for somewhere that could be a business for both of us. A bigger house – with gites or a B and B – something like that – with land.' There's excitement in her voice. 'I can't wait, Casey. I can't imagine anything better than waking up to the kind of peace and quiet you have here.' Ellie pauses, gazing across the fields. 'Away from the rat race and traffic, it's like you can really breathe.'

'Just so long as you know, there are no shops,' I warn her. 'No hurried Saturday afternoons looking for perfect sexy dresses and heels. And no lovely pubs for Sunday lunch.'

She shrugs. 'Honestly? I'm not fussed. I have drawers of clothes I've only worn once or twice. I'm ready for something different.'

I arch an eyebrow towards her. 'It's certainly different. Just make sure you stay stocked up on wine, my friend, because the supermarkets close on Sundays. It's like the dark ages.' I pause. 'But the quiet here, it's definitely addictive.'

Further up the lane, we stop and look across the valley. Amidst the fields are huge barns I've never noticed before.

'What are those?' Shielding her eyes from the sun, Ellie looks at them too.

'Factory farms,' I say quietly, taking in the silos beside the huge metal structures and the lorries for animal transportation. 'Probably pigs.'

'In this heat?' Ellie looks horrified. 'They must be cooked alive in there.'

'Yes. Ben loathed them.' I stare at them, knowing how vile these places are. 'Every year, billions of animals are raised like this.'

* * *

In the evening, I cook properly for the first time since arriving here. Only pasta, but a tried and tested recipe I know Ellie loves.

Afterwards, slumped on a cushion on the floor, Ellie's face is thoughtful as she leans back against the sofa. 'Have you any idea where you might like to go when you leave here?'

I shake my head. 'Maybe south – somewhere closer to the sea, but I'm not sure where exactly.'

She looks interested. 'In France?'

'I've been thinking about Spain... but I don't know. Right now, I can't make any far-reaching decisions, so I'm going with the flow. When the time is right and the place is right, I guess I'll know.' But I can see from Ellie's face, she's worried about me. 'It's different for you, Ell,' I say gently. 'You and Jim, buying your lovely big French place, making it your home... and it will be a wonderful home, because you're together. But I don't have that. Right now, nowhere is home. I'm sure, one day, it'll be different and there'll be somewhere I'll want to settle.' I shrug. 'But at the moment, there isn't. And I still have a lot of stuff to get my head around.' Then I pause, before I tell her, 'Sometimes, it's like I hear his voice.'

She looks startled. 'Whose – Ben's?'

I nod. 'It's almost like we have these conversations. It started the day I left England. Sometimes he's giving me a pep talk. Other times, it's about life and stuff. In a strange way, it's comforting.' Folding my arms around myself, my eyes well up. 'I'm not mad, I promise you.'

'I know you're not.' Her voice is sympathetic. 'Your house in Sussex, Case... Have you thought any more about what you're going to do with it?'

Part of my reluctance to make decisions is the enormity of them, the house being a case in point. 'To be honest, I've been putting it off. I think I wanted to know I had the option of going back.' I think of all the memories it holds. 'Right now, I can't bear the thought of walking through the door. But I suppose I need to think about selling it.'

Ellie's silent for a moment. 'Don't you think it's too soon? Further down the line, you might change your mind. I'm sure you could easily rent it out.'

'Possibly.' But it would still be there, the biggest reminder of everything I've lost, a link to my old life, when more and more, I want freedom. 'If I sell it, I'll have choices.'

'Well, you won't have to do it on your own.' She picks up her wine glass. 'I'll help you. And I'm sure your parents will, too.'

'Thank you.' Relief floods through me. 'It might be better without my parents.' My mother would only go on about me moving back to Devon. Picturing the familiar walls of our home, I think of the life we shared that went on inside them. Selling feels like pulling away my safety net.

26

BEFORE

June, last year

'I like them.' Four hours later, on our way home from Ben's first encounter with my parents, I didn't think he was talking about my mother's parsnips.

'I'm glad. They're not bad,' I said. 'As parents go. I'm afraid Mum's always wanted me to move back and meet a nice North Devon farmer, produce dozens of grandchildren and live happily ever after... It's her dream. She still doesn't think I can look after myself. But even though you're not from North Devon, I think my parents really liked you.'

A Polly-esque text from my sister that evening confirmed it.

They really like him, sis. Think the Devon farmer's out of the picture.
Thank fuck.

* * *

After Ben's initiation into my family, our days of living together began, as slowly I started adding feminine touches to the house. Scented candles, my soft white bed linen, the ornate lamp I'd brought back from the holiday with Ellie in Morocco. Ben looked pleased. 'It's your home too, babe. Honestly, do what you like with it.'

'Don't worry.' I reassured him. 'I won't paint the walls pink without running it by you first.'

I didn't, of course, but in the end, he opted for the funky curtains that went with his sofa, and a battered mirror we found one weekend at an antiques market. With my assorted china mixed with his, and big vases of flowers, it soon felt like my kind of place too.

'It's great we like the same things,' I said happily.

'I guess.' Ben looked slightly mystified. 'It's only stuff though, babe.'

'Yes, but it's our stuff,' I gazed at him. 'Looks cool in here, don't you think?'

'It's different.' He looked around the bedroom. 'But I like it much better with you here.'

Winding my arms around his neck, I snuggled against the warmth of him. I'd always thought home was a house. But I'd learned something else since moving in here. Home was with this man, wherever that was, wherever life happened to take us.

27

June

'Casey?' In the dim light from the wood burner, Ellie's voice brings me back to the present. 'Are you OK?'

'Yes.' Inside me, there's an aching sadness. 'I was thinking about when I moved in with Ben. Probably not a good idea,' I try to joke, swallowing the lump in my throat.

Coming over and sitting next to me, Ellie puts an arm around my shoulders. 'I haven't said this before, but Ben's left you with so much pain. Do you know how mad at him that makes me feel?'

'That isn't fair.' I shrug her arm off. 'You don't understand what was going through his mind. Even I didn't.' And that's what hurts most. That Ben wouldn't let me in. I turn to my friend. 'Ell? Have you heard of solastalgia?'

Ellie frowns. 'No.'

'It's the grief people feel when their environment is altered, typically by climate change. Indigenous peoples are worst affected because their lives are so connected to the natural world. Climate change has forced huge shifts in the way they live, causing a very real feeling of homesickness because their way of life doesn't exist any more.'

'I'd no idea.' Ellie's voice is quiet.

'Most people don't. And it isn't just a way of life that's threatened. It's their life skills, the passing on of centuries of wisdom and knowledge. It means they feel a profound sense of loss.'

I've read about eco-grief too, the pain people suffer in response to the loss of species, environments, habitats; things that are all happening globally. An image of your face comes to me, but this time it isn't love your eyes are filled with, it's the torment I so often saw, because all of these things haunted you.

'Remember how passionate Ben was about environmental issues?' As Ellie nods, I go on. 'There was so much he couldn't stomach, all of it caused by human beings. Take those factory farms we saw earlier... All he could see was the suffering of the animals inside. It kept him awake at night. Hung over him, constantly.' A sigh comes from me. 'He found it agonising, because he couldn't imagine any of it changing. I used to look at him and think he was taking on the pain of the planet.' A tear rolls down my cheek.

'He should have cared more about what he was doing to you,' my friend points out quietly. 'And you have to think of your life, now.'

She's right. Your voice comes to me. *It is about you, now. About what you want from the rest of your life.*

Sighing, I rest my head in my hands, wishing you could both understand, it isn't that simple.

* * *

The next day, when I get back from a morning with Brad, to my amazement Ellie's found a mower and cut the grass.

'Looks really good, doesn't it?' She surveys it proudly.

'It does.' I'm astonished at how tidy it looks. 'Thanks, Ell. As a reward, I'm treating you to lunch at Sylvie's.'

* * *

'I like it,' Ellie says as I pull up outside the bar.

'Good – because it's the only one for miles,' I tell her.

As we go in, Sylvie's busy behind the bar, in jeans and a red top, her glossy hair twisted up and clipped at the back of her head.

'Casey!' Her eyes light up when she sees us. 'How are you?'

As I introduce my newest friend to my oldest, Sylvie puts a couple of wine glasses on the bar. 'Can I get you both a drink?'

'Can we have a carafe of the house white? And lunch please?'

'Sure. It's cassoulet – not your thing. But I can get you salad, French bread, mayonnaise – if you leave it with me.'

'Sounds perfect.'

'Sit over there, by the window. It says reserved, but I can move them somewhere else.' Sylvie winks at me.

Away from the bar, the table has a view onto the garden. Picking up her glass, Ellie sips her wine.

'This is lovely.'

'It is,' I tell her. 'You see my problem?'

'I'm beginning to. You know, I'm looking forward to this – when Jim and I move. Nice wine, simple food...' She stops talking as Sylvie comes over with fresh bread and homemade mayonnaise.

'The rest won't be long. How is the wine?'

'Wonderful. I was thinking of taking Ellie to the market at Samatan.'

'That's a very good idea. We have one here.' She turns to Ellie. 'But Casey doesn't really buy fresh food. You should talk to her about it.' Giving me a stern look, Sylvie turns to go back to the kitchen.

I shake my head. 'Don't mind Sylvie, it's just her way.'

'I like her.' Ellie frowned. 'You are eating, aren't you?'

'Of course.' I change the subject. 'As markets go,' I say to Ellie, 'the one here is tiny. We're talking three stalls, selling eggs, tomatoes, muddy lettuces... In winter, there are potatoes. Samatan, however, has clothes and street food...'

I break off as Sylvie reappears with the rest of our lunch, placing it on the table with a flourish. '*Bon appétit!*'

* * *

After taking Ellie to Samatan and wandering among the colourful stalls, we spend a leisurely afternoon at a lake beach. But her visit ends too soon. The following day when I drop her at the airport, I make her promise to come back before I leave.

'I'll try, but if not, you must come and stay with me and Jim.' She pauses. 'Let me know what you decide about your house.'

I nod. 'I just need to be sure.' For a moment I gaze into her green eyes, then reach to stroke the familiar red hair. 'I'm sorry for being so all over the place. But I'm so pleased you've met Jim and it's all working out for you. You're going to be so happy.'

'Thank you...' Her smile is wistful. 'You will be too – you know that, don't you?'

As we hug each other tightly, I almost believe her.

Letting go of me, she picks up her bags. 'I meant what I said – about helping you sort everything.'

I nod. 'I know. Look, can I give you my key?' Fumbling with my key ring, I slip off the front door key. 'Would you mind going over there? Just to make sure it hasn't caught fire or anything.'

'Sure.' She puts the key in her bag. 'I have to go.'

After she hugs me one last time, I let her go, watching her walk away before turning to blow a kiss; waiting until her red hair fades into the terminal building. Walking slowly back to my car, I battle with the ticket machine, then leave the airport and join the madness of the motorway, suddenly feeling very alone.

For fuck's sake. Stop wallowing in self-pity, I tell myself. *Where's the old Casey Cassidy gone, because it's about bloody time you brought her back.*

But in my next breath, I answer my own question. *I met the love of my life. Then I lost him. Stick that where the sun don't shine.*

Merging with the traffic, I switch on the radio. It's not my kind of thing – an upbeat, rocky pop song. But instead of cruising quietly, I turn up the volume and put my foot down hard, a rush of adrenaline flooding through me as I swerve into the fast lane.

I arrive home just before sunset. In the garden, the air is still, the warm light reflecting off the mountain peaks. As the dusk song of a lone bird reaches me, nothing moves, and for a moment, I stop thinking about what I've lost. When I have friends, family, these beautiful surroundings, my life is rich in so many ways. Closing my eyes, I revel in the peacefulness.

28

June, last year

'You been to Greece, Cassidy?' As Ben looked at me, his eyes were alight with excitement.

I liked the way he'd lapsed into calling me by my surname, the way my friends did. 'Once. I was about thirteen. We stayed in a hotel near the sea and I had a crush on one of the waiters.' I glanced at him, curious. Was he planning something? 'Why?' Getting up, I went and peered over his shoulder at his laptop, but before I got there, he closed it.

'No reason.'

'Don't believe you.' I slipped my arms around him. 'What are you planning?'

'Go away.' But laughter was dancing in his eyes.

'Not until you tell me.'

'There's nothing to tell.' Closing his laptop, he stood up. 'Tea?'

I followed him into the kitchen. 'That is quite random – asking me about Greece.'

Filling the kettle, he stood with his back to me. 'You break up in what, two weeks?'

'Yes.' I stood there.

'Well...' He turned around. 'I've been asked to go and do some filming.' Opening one of the cupboards, he got the teabags out.

I stared at him. 'Who by?'

'A company that runs luxury yacht holidays. I know boats aren't really your thing but...'

He had to be kidding, right? I interrupted. 'I absolutely love luxury yachts, Ben. Love them,' I repeated.

'Oh.' His face fell. 'I've already told them. I didn't think you'd want to come.'

'What?' I couldn't believe what I was hearing. 'You're joking.' I watched as his eyes twinkled. 'You're winding me up, aren't you? You'd better be, babe...'

'Of course I am!' His face lit up as he went on, filled with enthusiasm. 'It's a brilliant gig, Casey. These yachts are state of the art. They charter them out for holidays and they want me to film for a few days – while you lie on the deck and sunbathe.'

* * *

Though I'd always loved the winding down of another school year, this time it couldn't happen fast enough. But the days whizzed by and after some last-minute shopping for a couple of bikinis and a new beach dress, Ben and I were packed and ready.

'I can't believe it was nearly six months ago that we were last here.' At Gatwick airport, as we walked towards security, it didn't seem possible that in such a short time, so much had changed.

Stopping suddenly, Ben turned to look at me. 'I can't believe I didn't ask you. You do have it with you, don't you?'

Removing my passport from my pocket with a flourish, I waved it at him. 'I checked at least six times.' I smiled at him.

In what seemed like no time we were through security, then a short walk later, boarding the plane.

'I think this is us.' Ben checked the numbers above the seats.

Still near the front of the plane, I stared at the wider seats. 'But this is business class.'

'Yeah.' He lifted his bag into the overhead locker. 'That's right. I hadn't realised till they emailed the tickets. Great, isn't it?'

'Very cool.' I was impressed. Sitting down in the seat nearest the window, I suddenly felt grateful – for being here with Ben, and the prospect of a glorious week in Greece stretching ahead of us.

'This is amazing.' I reached for Ben's hand. 'Honestly.'

He grinned. 'It's pretty good, isn't it?'

Behind him a stewardess appeared, carrying a tray of glasses. 'Champagne, sir?'

'Thanks.' Taking a couple, Ben passed one to me before raising his. 'Here's to Greece, Cassidy.' He paused, before adding softly, 'And to us.'

* * *

It was the beginning of five days that felt out of this world, not least because the Greece you saw from the water seemed a million miles from the crowded holiday resorts. The sea was the clearest turquoise, while we discovered empty beaches of glittering sand, mooring in a different harbour each night, trying out restaurants and local food. And during the day, I lay on the deck, lulled by the motion of the sea, more relaxed than I'd known it was possible to be.

Now and then a view would take me back to our family holiday all those years ago. Polly uber-sophisticated in a halter neck swimsuit, me a gawky kid with all this hair I couldn't do a thing with. Jenna, still a little girl with gappy teeth, shrieking excitedly. Memories made no less happy by the Greek waiter I fancied who barely noticed me.

The highlight of our week was a pod of wild dolphins, unexpectedly appearing and putting on a show it seemed, just for us. Sitting on the deck, we watched their lithe bodies arching out of the sea, before eventually they disappeared towards the sunset.

'I could do this again.' Lying on our luxurious bed that night, I gazed at Ben.

'It's great, isn't it?' His hands were folded behind his head. 'I'm glad you like being at sea, babe.'

'I love it.' I mean, this was the life, wasn't it?

'We should do it again. Though maybe next time, something simpler.'

I frowned slightly. 'What do you mean?'

'Well...' He paused. 'Don't get me wrong. This is amazing – but I was thinking a single berth yacht, just you and me. Kind of like camping on the water.' He glanced at me. 'It's so beautiful here. It's not like we'd need much. We could fend for ourselves for a week. Drop into places where you get to see what Greek life is really like. What do you think?'

'What – more than we have been?'

Ben frowned. 'We've seen the high-end side of tourism, babe. Real life in Greece is tough. A lot of people who live here have very little.'

I hadn't thought of it like that before, but a small boat with just the two of us would be magical. 'It's a great idea.' When you had surroundings like this, what else did you need? Noticing Ben was silent, I turned towards him. 'Are you OK?'

For a moment he didn't speak. 'Yeah. Just thinking. This yacht, this client... I mean, don't get me wrong, this is a great contract and it pays the bills, but when you think how much a week on this boat costs... and what that money could do for people who don't have any, I don't know... it just seems ridiculous.'

I frowned. I'd made a conscious decision in the years since losing my sister to search for the good in life. When you never knew what lay ahead, you had to make the most of what the present moment held. 'That's life, Ben. There will always be people with less or more than you. It doesn't mean it's wrong to enjoy this.'

For a moment, he was quiet. 'You're right. And I am enjoying it! The coast, the dolphins, having you here...' But he said it too quickly. As he put *his arms around me, I knew there was more he wasn't saying. 'I just get carried away in my head.'*

I could see the sense in what he was saying, but it wasn't going to stop me making the most of these luxurious surroundings. 'It so happens I have a cure for that.' Leaning towards him, I kissed him.

29

AFTER

July

On the boat in Greece, I had my first, most fleeting glimpse of what troubled you, before you hid it and I forgot, my attention turning instead to the clear water, the next cocktail, my increasingly golden tan.

Back then, I'd seen what I wanted to see; what suited my vision of us, of you, my brave warrior man blazing your way through an unjust world. But alone under an intense French sun, I have a clarity that wasn't there before, because I hadn't known about the grief you carried, that was every bit as real as mine is now. So many times, I told you I loved you, *no matter what*. And I did. But when there were warning signs, instead of turning away, it's my biggest regret I didn't ask you.

* * *

As the drive to Sabaillan grows familiar, Brad's confidence builds.

'You know, if you keep working like this, you're not going to have any problems with your exams.'

'Really?' His face lights up in a way that warms my heart. 'Awesome.'

'Walk in the park,' I tell him, high-fiving him. 'And it's you that's awesome.'

One morning, he surprises me. 'Which subjects do you find most interesting?'

'Me? Wow.' I frown, thinking. 'If you'd asked me a couple of years ago, I'd have said English and art. But now... I'd say geography, biology, anthropology, climatology...' I look at him. 'I want to learn more about them. Given what we're doing to this planet, I think we all should.'

'Yeah.' He's quiet for a moment. 'My dad works for a global investment company. He doesn't talk about it but I've seen a list of what they invest in – all linked to deforestation. I don't know how they get away with it.' His face looks mutinous.

'It's good that you know, Brad. And that you care. But there's so much that's wrong,' I say sadly. 'The plastic in the oceans, pollution, intensive farms and animal welfare... The list goes on.' I pause, because I don't want to overwhelm him, then because I know it's what you would have wanted, I steel myself to tell Brad about you. 'The reason I've learned about these things is because of a man I knew. His name was Ben. He cared so much about this world. Sometimes, I think, too much.' I force myself to go on, because this is what your legacy means. 'He was afflicted by something called solastalgia. It's a kind of grief, for a world that used to exist before our destruction of it got out of control.' I pause. 'He would have loved that you are passionate, Brad. I always told him the world needed people like him. Change is starting, but it's going to take time. I think it needs your generation even more.'

'I hate the farms.' A cloud crossed Brad's face. 'Do you know about the pig farms around here?'

I think of the barns I saw with Ellie. 'I'm aware of them.'

'A friend of my dad's owns one. He has all these barns – really massive ones. I went into one once. I wasn't supposed to, but I could hear this noise coming from inside... Afterwards, I wished I hadn't. It was horrible.'

'Sows in cages?'

'Yeah.' He nods. 'They couldn't even move. I can't believe how cruel it is. But it was the piglets. They were so small and it was so hot in there. It stank. I watched this guy go in. When he came out, he was pushing a wheelbarrow full of dead ones.'

I feel sick. 'We have a choice, don't we, whether or not to support this kind of farming. If more of us choose not to buy meat that comes from farms like that, they will have to change.'

He nods. 'They need to, don't they?'

'I think so.' I pause. 'You will be a great doctor, Brad. I know you will.'

He looks surprised. 'Thanks.'

* * *

Now and then, when I arrive at Cap du Bosc, Brad's face looks overcast, but by the time I leave, it's invariably lifted. One day, on the way out, I catch Nathalie.

'I'm curious... What do you know about his mother?'

She looks troubled. 'Not much – just that she died in a tragic accident.'

Driving home, I think about the future Brad's generation will be taking on, how there isn't unlimited time to reverse the damage we're causing to this planet. The human race can't go on putting it off.

A new sense of urgency fills me. It shouldn't be down to another generation to sort out the mess they've inherited. While you can't force people to change, you can educate, about the ways we shop and consume. And it begins with each and every one of us, in whatever way we can, however small that is, so that over time, together, we can make a difference.

At home, I open my laptop, bringing up the list of websites you'd bookmarked for me. They're about all kinds of global issues – climate change, the hidden victims of war, political oppression, organisations dedicated to animal welfare; all of them voices that are too often ignored.

Right on cue, the kitten jumps onto my lap and starts purring, before my phone buzzes.

It's Polly. 'Hey, you. How's it going?'

'Not bad.' I pause. 'It's still quiet. But I've found a cool bar and Ellie came out to visit. And I have a teaching job – two mornings a week. I've decided I'm staying here, at least for now.'

'I'm glad you've had company.' Polly sounds relieved.

'Yeah, me too. She's met a man and they're getting a place together – in France.'

'Why France?' She sounds mystified.

'Property is cheap here, Poll. And the countryside is lovely... She's ready for a change.'

'Wow.' Polly's silent for a moment. 'I've had Mum on the phone. You do know, don't you, that she's trying to orchestrate your life from the wilds of Devon?'

'I know,' I say miserably. 'She's been talking to Lesley Williams, telling her all about me.'

'What's the matter with her?' Polly sounds exasperated. 'You're a grown-up – and Lesley Williams is a monster. Doesn't she get that?'

'I cut her short,' I say quietly. 'I didn't want to be mean, but she still seems to think that she can fix everything – and she can't.'

'No.' When Polly goes quiet, I know she's thinking of Jenna. But as always, neither of us mentions her. 'That's our mother.'

'So how's New York?' I change the subject.

'Crazy. Big. Fast... If I could get away, I'd come and see you, but work is flat-out. You do know you're welcome here, don't you? Any time. Have you thought any more about that ticket?'

'I have. And thanks, Poll.' As the kitten stretches out one of its paws, I don't hesitate. 'But right now, where I need to be is here.'

30

BEFORE

July, last year

It was a lazy Sunday morning, the curtains moving in the warm breeze whispering through the open window; a day that as I opened my eyes was already overflowing with happiness.

'So, you don't mind giving up your precious independence?' Lying in bed, Ben was teasing me.

'I haven't given it up.' I puffed myself out with fake indignance. 'All I've done is let you in, babe. You should feel deeply honoured to be sharing this beautiful and precious thing with me.'

'I know. And I am.' He sounded amused. 'But you're happy, aren't you? Tell me you're happy! Come on. I want to hear you say it!' He started to tickle me, and my laugh turned into an unflattering snort, before he kissed me, one of those kisses that went on and on, that I never wanted to pull away from.

It was nearly midday by the time we made it downstairs. While I bustled around frying mushrooms and making toast, I felt Ben behind me.

Gently he turned me around to face him. As he took my hands, his eyes were serious. 'Marry me, Casey. I know we've only known each other six months, but it's like you're a part of me. I can't imagine being without you.'

Oh my God. As I looked into those dark eyes, my heart missed a beat. He wasn't kidding. He was proposing.

Incredulous, I stood there as he went on, his eyes searching mine. 'I want to share every moment we have together. I want to love you always. To explore this amazing world with you. I want us to have children together...'

As it sank in, it wasn't shock I felt. Instead, I was blown away, seeing the future opening up in front of me. One where Ben and I would be together – always, because I couldn't imagine anything else, either. Touching a finger to his lips, tears of happiness filled my eyes as I shook my head. 'Stop. The children line...' But I didn't mean it. Thinking of the family we'd have, I pulled him close, whispering in his ear. 'Yes. A million times. Yes.'

He'd even chosen a ring. A beautiful, very grown-up solitaire diamond that fitted perfectly. The very act of sliding it onto my finger seemed to catapult me into the next level of my life – grown-up life, with a husband, then maybe in the not-too-distant future, children. I knew the time was right, too, otherwise I would have been running for the hills. But the truth was I'd never been happier.

After announcing our engagement, I discovered privacy went out of the window. Suddenly my mum and Ben's mum, Gina, were new best friends, comparing bridesmaids' dresses and wedding flower ideas, discussing dates, venues and menus without even consulting me or Ben. Having been summoned to join them for one of their confabs, I'd made my escape as soon as I could, calling Ben the minute I was out of their earshot.

'Babe. They're both getting far too carried away. They're talking white doves and eight bridesmaids and the full shebang. What do you think about eloping?'

But we couldn't have done that to them. The only way was to present our mothers with a fait accompli that they'd both approve of, except that like privacy, spontaneity is impossible where weddings are concerned. People plan years in advance. Arranging one at short notice is nigh on impossible.

After calling several registry offices and getting nowhere, it was Ellie who presented a solution. 'My aunt has just opened a guesthouse in Cornwall. Would you like me to call her?'

'Could you?' Picturing rolling green hills and the turquoise Cornish sea, I felt a flicker of excitement. 'Ben and I have to do something. Our mothers are taking over. All we want is to have our wedding and get on with the rest of our lives.' Seeing Ellie's face, my face turned hot as I realised my faux pas. 'Oh my God. Ell? I can't believe I haven't asked. You will be my bridesmaid, won't you? I only want one – and it absolutely has to be you.'

Her cheeks clashed with her hair as she flung her arms around me. 'I'd love to!' Her eyes were bright as she beamed at me. 'Shall I call my aunt?'

I nodded. 'Yes! Please! Can you do it now?' Collapsing onto her sofa, my excitement was building as she hooked her long red hair behind her ears before making the call. After talking for a few minutes, she put her hand over the phone.

'She has plenty of availability – but the only hitch is you'll need to find a registrar. She has contacts and she's offered to phone around – if you'd like her to?'

'Could she?' Suddenly I felt properly excited. 'We can fit the timing around them if we need to.' My mind was flitting all over the place. 'I need to talk to Ben about dates. Can you ask her to let us know as soon as she finds one?'

* * *

By some miracle, Ellie's aunt found us a registrar who was free on the last day of August. After provisionally booking the date, all I had to do was break the news to my mother.

Opening her mouth and shutting it again, I knew she was disappointed. 'Oh, Casey. I really wish you hadn't done this without discussing it with me. Gina and I have spent hours making plans. We'd even thought about some dates, maybe next Easter. I've found a very nice marquee that we could have put up in the garden... Such a lovely time of year and it gives us plenty of time to make sure everything is exactly as we want it to be...'

'I know. But Mum,' I reminded her gently, 'it's mine and Ben's wedding. We don't want to wait that long and a big fancy do with billions of people isn't what we had in mind. We want a lovely party with our families there, and our closest friends, but that's all.'

Setting her jaw, she shook her head. 'It isn't how things were done in my day.'

'But that's my point,' I persisted. 'It isn't your day, Mum. It's mine and Ben's.'

After persuading her we'd still need to decide on flowers and a menu, I showed her photos of the guesthouse with its tropical gardens and path leading down to the beach, and she soon came round. Then when I told her about asking Ellie to be my bridesmaid, she softened slightly, more so when I suggested the three of us should go shopping together. Three that turned into four, when Gina joined us.

After going into the first bridal shop, I found out the reason why they ply you with lovely chilled prosecco; it's incredible the number of terrible dresses you will agree to try after that second glass. I lost count of how many I squeezed into over that day, but it was exactly as it was when I met Ben. When I slipped on what was to become my dress, I knew immediately I'd found the one.

My intuition was confirmed by the silence that greeted me as I stepped out of the changing room, then again, by the tears in both mothers' eyes.

'Fuck me.' Even Ellie was untypically short of words. 'Casey, you look... stupendous.'

In truth, that dress made me feel like a bad-ass ice queen. A pale sky-blue, it was deceptively feminine and pretty, with tiny iridescent stones stitched to the bodice and poufy layers of tulle, but it clung to my curves and made my very average boobs look positively magnificent.

I'd been fully prepared for a lecture about how wedding dresses were supposed to be white, but no one even mentioned the colour. 'Your turn now.' I turned to Ellie, dragging her over to a rail where there were dresses in every colour of the rainbow. 'What do you think?'

Surprising both of us, she went for a faded turquoise with pink embroidery. 'With bouquets of orange roses?' my mum suggested hopefully, clearly buying in to our non-colour-scheme.

I grinned at Ellie. 'Sounds perfect!'

31

AFTER

July

I watch the days lengthen, feel the sun's warmth on my skin, hear the bird song become louder; your voice growing slowly quieter as I dread the day it's gone forever. So, I bring you back. I will always do that, Ben. Pull out one of those gossamer-thread memories of you. That day you took me to meet your parents; your dad the same gentle amiable man I've come to know since – it was hard to believe that he had some high-ranking post in the military – and your mum, warm, yet guarded. The day I moved in with you that felt like coming home; the universe I'd never taken much notice of before suddenly lavishly abundant.

I remember your whisper. *There is magic in your heart, Casey Cassidy.* The joyousness I felt that you saw something in me no one else had. It happened so quickly, didn't it? The two of us swept along by an unstoppable force; you grasping happiness, holding on tight, worried if you didn't, it would escape you.

With my neat and tidy, blinkered vision of how life was meant to be, I had my own definition of what happiness was. I hadn't wanted anything to change. It makes me wonder what it was about me you loved, when in many ways, I was so different to you.

I imagine your air of mock-exasperation. *Were you so different? Under the carefree, happy-go-lucky Casey Cassidy I fell in love with, there's another side to you. One who cares just as much as I did.*

Of course I care. You changed me, Ben, from the original material girl to living out of a couple of bags in rural France. I don't even know where home is any more. What's even stranger is, I don't even mind.

So why are you still hanging on to the house in Midhurst?

Our home was important, I flash back at you. It was supposed to be somewhere to bring our children up; that was a sanctuary. Somewhere to sell when the time was right, to put our money into something bigger.

Going inside, I need to distract myself from these bizarre conversations we keep having. Pouring myself a glass of wine, I pick up the diary for the first time in ages and take it outside.

As I sit at the table, the black cat hops onto the chair next to me as I start reading.

7th June

So much for stepping back. These last weeks have been tumultuous, like I'm caught in the eye of a storm. I've seen every side of Julia, from meek, powerless, persuasive, to raging aggressive temptress.

Then yesterday, she came round here again. She didn't understand what had changed between us. She thought we were friends. I told her we are. Then I told her I'd had a visit from her husband, that I didn't buy his act about keeping the family together. If he meant it, he wouldn't be having an affair. When I told her he'd warned me off, her frightened look came back. She couldn't believe he knew about us – not that there's much to know.

I told her how I felt – that she was a beautiful woman, how if things were different... but they weren't. She was married to a man she couldn't leave. In the here and now, I wasn't looking for a fling. If I was going to be with someone, I wanted more.

She pleaded with me to let her stay. Told me she needed me, that I made her feel strong. In that moment, it would have been so easy to sweep her into my arms; to be her knight in shining armour. To tell myself we'd work it out. After all, love conquers all. But I stopped myself, because sometimes it doesn't. If she wasn't leaving her marriage, there was no place for me in her life.

Shocked, she stalked off to her car. I didn't go after her. If nothing was going to change, I owed it to myself to let her go.

My heart goes out to diary-man. All he wanted was to help Julia. But he couldn't, and I know how that feels. I used to think love conquers all – and sometimes it does, but not always – or maybe not in the way you think it will. Putting the diary down, I wander across the terrace. The air is soporific, the light across the garden hazy; catching dozens of white butterflies fluttering above the grasses.

But tonight, not even the diary can distract me as our house comes into my mind. There's no point keeping it. I know I can't go back, but it's my last tangible link to you. Selling is going to feel like breaking it.

* * *

This morning, as I'm making coffee, sunbeams pierce through the open window, taking me back to another day, in my old life, where I'd been watching sunlight streaking through our kitchen window. You'd been sitting at the table, your head resting in your hands.

Unable to reach into that dark, distant world of yours, I'd been desperate, my heart breaking for you.

Suddenly I'm acknowledging what I never could before, and that's how hard it was for me, too: the way each morning, I'd wake up, not knowing whether it would be another day of your suffering, of enduring the pain visible in your eyes that I could do nothing to soothe.

Guilt crashes over me that I can even think like this. My suffering was a walk in the park compared to yours. I never wanted to lose you. I love you, the way I did on our wedding day, from the wildest, deepest part of my soul. Every minute of every day, if I could, I'd bring you back; just as I'd do whatever it took to help you.

32

BEFORE

August, last year

Amidst the excitement and euphoria of wedding planning, a single cloud loomed, threatening to blot out the sun. It wasn't the time to be keeping secrets from Ben – I knew that.

He came in one evening, a slightly anxious look on his face. 'Hey, are you OK?'

It should have been my cue to tell him, but I couldn't. 'I'm great.' Reaching up, I kissed him.

'You're sure?' He took my hands.

'Of course I'm sure.' Gazing at him, I frowned.

He paused. 'It's just I keep getting the feeling something isn't right – like... I don't know, but maybe there's something you're not telling me?'

Ben had this way of picking up on how I was feeling, but as he watched me, I couldn't speak.

'What is it, Casey?' His voice was anxious. 'You're worrying me. Please, whatever it is, tell me.'

The palms of my hands felt sweaty. 'Let's sit down.' Going over to the table, I forced myself to take a shaky breath as Ben sat opposite me. 'It's...' I broke off. 'It's to do with Jenna.'

As Ben frowned, my hands started to tremble. 'Before... when I told you she died, I didn't tell you everything.' I was trying to hold myself together. 'You see, every day, she and I used to walk to get the school bus together.' My eyes were hot with tears. 'That morning, I'd decided to bunk off school and go to a friend's house. Jenna was really upset. Some of the other kids had been giving her a hard time and if I was there, they left her alone. But in the end, she went on her own.' Tears rolled down my cheeks. 'I knew she was worried. Jenna had this way of standing out – she was the pretty, smart girl who got top grades... Plenty of the girls at school couldn't stand that.' I wiped my face, still haunted by the memory of how selfish I'd been. 'If we hadn't argued, if I'd been there, if she'd been there a few seconds earlier... She'd still be here. It's my fault, Ben. And I've never forgiven myself...'

As my words tailed off, sobs racked my body. It was why I tried so hard to wear a smile, be happy-go-lucky Casey, hiding the guilty, selfish Casey that lay beneath. With our wedding coming up, he needed to know the truth about me.

'Oh, babe...' There was anguish in Ben's voice as he reached for one of my hands. 'It wasn't your fault. Just think. If you had been there, the car might have hit both of you... It was a terrible, tragic accident. You have to stop blaming yourself.'

'But it was my fault,' I sobbed.

'Listen.' Ben's voice was firm, his hand tightening around mine. 'It was the car that killed Jenna. It was nothing to do with you.'

But after keeping it to myself all this time, it was like taking the lid off a Pandora's Box. Not only had I been lying to Ben, I wasn't the person he thought I was. 'I envied her, Ben. How awful is that? Because she was the pretty one. She wanted to be a teacher.' It was the reason that, after she died, I became almost obsessive about it. 'Mum doted on her. She even had the prettiest name...' I broke off, sobbing. I *was a terrible person, who'd let not just her sister, but her whole family, down.*

I felt Ben's arm go around me. 'And all this time, you've been carrying this. Oh, babe...'

Still crying, I rested my head in my hands. I felt stripped bare, vulnerable, horrible. I'd no idea what Ben was thinking. But he knew the truth now. Not only was I the reason my sister died, I'd been jealous of her.

'Do your parents know any of this?' Ben's voice was gentle.

I shook my head. 'I can't talk to them about her – not after everything they've been through.'

'Maybe you should. It might help them, too.'

But I knew what losing her had done to them. I wasn't going to be the one to dredge it up.

'Casey... listen. There's no way your parents will think it's your fault. Your guilt is because you're here and she isn't, but you have to stop punishing yourself. If it had been Polly who'd bunked off school that day instead of walking to the bus with Jenna, would you be blaming her?'

As I stared at the table, I felt the smallest of weights begin to lift. 'No.'

'And I bet you'd give anything in the world to have her back.'

'I would,' I said tearfully. 'Anything.'

'So there you go.' Ben reached forward to wipe away my tears. 'I've never known how it is to lose a brother or sister. But the best thing you can do to honour her memory is really live – fully and wholeheartedly.'

* * *

That Ben knew what I'd always thought of as my terrible secret, and loved me anyway, brought us closer than ever. For the first time, I began to consider that maybe it wasn't my fault; that the worst, most tragic accidents simply happen.

I knew it was the real reason my life had always been frenetic. Quite simply, I couldn't bear time alone with myself. But I had no more secrets –

Ben now knew everything. And it was just as well – our wedding day was rapidly drawing closer.

Rather than a formal wedding, we wanted a party and the guest-house had a large terrace overlooking the sea, which was where our reception was to be. Ellie had shown me photos of the palm trees in the garden and I had scoured the internet, gathering ideas for decorating it.

'Bunting and flowers – on the terrace. What d'you think?' Going over to where Ben was sitting, I showed him a photo.

'Love it, babe. I've been thinking about music.' Ben was making a list. 'I was wondering about Spanish guitar for the ceremony. Listen to this.'

As he played a piece of music, I closed my eyes. Soft and atmospheric, it seemed to hold the essence of summer. Leaning down, I kissed him. 'Love it.'

Meanwhile, gifts started arriving, including one from Ben's parents, a large, simply framed painting of a Cornish beach.

'Wow.' Ben stared at it.

'It's stunning.' The sunlight was perfectly reflected in the water, as were the multiple shades of blue and green. Looking at it more closely, suddenly I realised it was even more poignant. 'It's our beach, babe. Where we're getting married.'

After hanging the painting above our fireplace, time seemed to speed up. With my hen night in the hands of Ellie and Suki, I wasn't sure what to expect but, in the end, they surprised me with a weekend at a spa for just the three of us. My only regret was Polly being too caught up in work to be able to join us.

'This is blissful,' I said to them, as we sat in a whirlpool, jets of water pummelling the muscles in my legs. 'You want to know what I was expecting?'

'A boozy weekend with loads of girls.' Suki stretched a lithe, tanned leg above the water, as Ellie shot her a warning look. 'There may, however, be a teeny surprise at the end of this.'

After a weekend of pampering, my muscles were unknotted, my face line free, my nails manicured. Totally blissed out, Suki's teeny surprise was a full-on meal with the rest of our friends, complete with her trade-mark cocktails. By the time I made it home the following day, I felt terrible.

'Don't ask,' I said to Ben as I walked into the kitchen. 'The spa was lovely. My skin is velvet smooth and my body has been mercilessly pummelled. But as we both know, anything to do with Suki was always going to be messy. We were at hers last night and she made cocktails.' Going over to the sink, I filled a glass with water. 'How was yours?'

'Predictably laddish – gallons of beer and a stripper. But don't worry, babe. I controlled myself.' He glanced at me. 'Don't you think you'd be better off in bed?'

'Do I look that bad?' Going out of the kitchen, I glanced at my reflection in the mirror in our hallway, grimacing.

If life was about light and shade, joy and sadness, I knew this time was one of the brightest; our family and friends, even the so-called universe Ben believed in, showering us with love and happiness.

33

AFTER

August

When I arrive at Cap du Bosc one morning, Nathalie catches me as I get out of my car.

'I don't know what's happened, but I can't get him away from his books.'

'Oh? Is he OK?'

She rolls her eyes. 'He is intense, I think you say. I have never seen him so focused. He's in the study. He's been there since breakfast.'

Following her inside, I carry on further up the hallway, knocking on the door to the study before pushing it open. 'Morning. How's it going?'

Brad looks up. 'Hi. Good.'

'Looks like you're working hard.' Going over, I sit on the chair next to him.

He nods. 'I've been reading all this stuff about climate change and pollution – and food.' He frowns. 'I've never thought about it before but so much food is processed. And I don't get why everything has to be wrapped in plastic.'

'I agree – but a lot of people don't question it. We live in the age of convenience foods – and not everyone knows how to cook. They probably don't read the labels on the packaging – while other people can only afford whatever's cheapest.'

'More people need to think about it.' Brad shakes his head.

'Absolutely.' I pause. 'But you can't force them. It is frustrating – and we could talk about this for hours.' I look at him. 'Do you have anything in mind for today?'

He nods slowly. 'Kind of a mixture – of geography and anthropology?'

'Wow.' I'm taken by surprise. 'Sure.'

What follows isn't strictly academic. We talk about climatology and ocean currents, and densely populated regions; looking at how the oceans and marine life are being affected by pollution and global warming. I watch Brad's growing passion, realising this is how it starts – with conversation and education, followed by conscious choice and action as the message spreads. Your message, Ben. Still out there, reaching people.

Back home, I think about this time last year, days that were filled with excitement and wedding plans; with tweaking final details that had taken on undue importance, because I wanted our day to be perfect. A lump lodges in my throat as I think of you, taking it all in your stride – calm, tanned, glowing with happiness.

Beautiful, precious memories that I will always cherish... Wanting to distract myself, I pick up the diary.

29th June

So, this thing with Julia isn't to be. But if I'm going to bare my soul, at least on these pages, I have to be honest, because there's a bit I've been leaving out. I've kind of been running away. You see, there's this other girl. I've known her for a while now. She's sassy and funny, with a smile that can light a whole room up. Man, does she make my head spin.

But she's with someone else – the best ones always are. It's why I kind of hoped things might work out with Julia – after all, there's someone for everyone, or so they say. I suppose I want to believe there's a reason this has happened. That it's teaching me something, maybe shifting me onto another path. This was meant to be a year to sort my life out, after all.

Maybe diary-man was meant to be with the first girl. Maybe that's why he had to meet Julia, to help him figure it out. But for a while I forget about the diary. With the end of August approaching, the biggest of firsts looms closer. The one that was always going to be hardest. Our first wedding anniversary.

As I wake up on what should have been the most joyous of days, already I'm wishing it was over. Taking my coffee outside, a myriad dandelion clocks sparkle in the morning sunlight. This time last year was everything it should have been. A celebration of love, happiness, family; the precious things in life. I remember packing your car, my dress entrusted to Ellie so that you wouldn't see it. Your mum coming round, how touched I felt when she fastened her pearl and gold bracelet around my wrist – my something borrowed.

The most joyous memories come flooding back. Ellie and I getting up early to walk along the coast path. Picking wildflowers to decorate the cake. Putting on my beautiful dress. The tiny bird perched on the bedroom windowsill, watching Ellie pin a rose in my hair. The streak of teal blue behind Ellie's long black eyelashes. The perfume I wore that will always take me back, because scent is so evocative. My mum, basking in her role as mother of the bride; my dad, quietly proud in his best suit, his orange rose buttonhole slipped sideways; Polly, all the way from New York. Everyone who meant the world to us waiting to share our day. That moment I saw you standing there, I thought my heart would burst.

34

August, last year

At the end of August, we headed en mass for Cornwall, where even I had to admit, it felt like a benevolent universe was looking out for us. Ellie's aunt's guesthouse was even more stunning in real life, while a ridge of high pressure meant blue skies all the way.

'You awake, Cassidy?' Ellie's voice came from the other bed. 'This is it, you know! The big day!' She sat up. 'You're getting married!'

Opening my eyes, remembering where I was, excitement filled me. I stretched my arms above my head. 'I really am!' I picked up my phone to check the time. 'It's only seven. Fancy a walk before anyone else is up?'

Pulling on shorts and T-shirts, we crept out and headed for the coast path. It was already warm, the air soft and salt-scented. Standing there for a moment, I gazed out at a sea of the deepest blue, thinking of Jenna for a moment.

As my eyes met Ellie's, she could tell. 'Today is about you and Ben,' she said softly, taking my hand. 'And you are bloody lucky with the *weather, Cassidy. It wouldn't be quite the same with a force eight blowing.'*

But nothing could have spoiled this day for us. Letting go of my hand, Ellie started walking. 'Come on! We need flowers.'

After picking bunches of delicate wildflowers, we headed back, leaving them with the cake and hurrying upstairs. After mugs of coffee, Ellie triumphantly produced a bottle of champagne, but I sipped it slowly. I wanted a clear head – I didn't want to miss anything.

In my dress, with my hair loosely pinned up, at last I was ready. Ellie's eyes were bright as she gazed at me. 'You look incredible, Cassidy.'

I felt my heart swell with love as I thought of Ben, but then another thought struck me. 'You won't be able to call me Cassidy after today.'

She raised one of her eyebrows. 'It's still your name. Have you considered keeping it?'

'Not really.' I had – for a split second, but no longer than that. I'd wanted the world to know I was married to Ben.

* * *

After a civil ceremony in the shade of the terrace, beneath flower garlands Ellie and I had hung the previous day, Ben and I exchanged another set of vows we'd written ourselves, on the beach, just as we'd dreamed of doing, with the softest of breezes ruffling our hair, and standing inches from the gently lapping sea we both loved. With Ben's hand in one of mine, my bouquet of orange roses in the other, the sun dazzled my eyes as I breathed in glorious, perfect moments to keep forever.

I couldn't have imagined a more blissful day, with our families and closest friends, the delicious food and wine, my mother's cake decorated with the flowers Ellie and I had picked. As I looked around, I wasn't taking any of it for granted. I knew how lucky we were. That in my wildest dreams, life didn't get any better than this.

I waited for my happiness to fade, but it didn't. With it being all rather last minute, Ben and I had decided to stay in Cornwall for our honeymoon, renting an old fisherman's cottage in a sheltered cove. Walking under the sun, we gazed at sea birds and waves, breathing crystal clear air, my happiness knowing no bounds, while in the evenings, we found country pubs or bought takeaways to eat on the beach, watching the brilliant sunset colours reflected in the water.

It was happiness that seemed endless – until four days later, when the heatwave abruptly ended and a violent storm struck. Overnight, the benign sea turned to a churning, eddying swell. Staying inside, we lit a log fire, listened to the rain lashing against the windows, and cooked sizzling seafood which we ate with chilled wine.

As evening fell, we played music and danced by candlelight. 'I love you,' I thought I heard Ben say in my ear, as he held me close against him. 'No matter what happens, I'll always love you.'

My head resting blissfully against his chest, I closed my eyes, feeling our bodies sway with the music. 'I love you, too,' I murmured back to him, our love a blanket enfolding both of us.

When I awoke the next morning, the storm had passed and a weak sun was filtering through the gap in the curtains. I lay there for only a few seconds before I realised that beside me, the bed was empty. Ben had gone.

35

AFTER

September

With our wedding anniversary behind me, I'm ready to deal with the house. As I start looking at flights to Gatwick, Sylvie unexpectedly turns up.

'Casey? Hello?'

'Hi.'

Hearing an unfamiliar voice, the kitten appears, staring at Sylvie with wide eyes.

'Oh. This is cute.' Reaching down, she strokes his head.

'There are two others – they come and go. I've been feeding them.'

She shakes her head. 'You will have twenty if you keep doing that. I swear there's a cat grapevine around here. Anyway, I brought you these.' She hands me the bunch of flowers she's carrying. 'There is orange blossom and sweet william, I think you call them.

And fern. It's for magic, if you believe in such things.' Rolling her eyes to indicate she doesn't.

'They're lovely.' I bury my nose in the flowers.

She shrugs. 'They grow in hedges. Like weeds. I came round because I haven't seen you in the bar. I wondered if you were OK.'

I hesitate. 'It hasn't been the best time. Yesterday would have been our first wedding anniversary.'

'Oh, Casey.' She looks sympathetic. 'That's so sad. Are you OK?'

I nod. 'I'm about to book a flight back to the UK. I'm selling the house.'

'Wow. So much happening.' Sylvie looks surprised. 'Are you busy tonight? Of course you're not. Come for dinner. We need to catch up.'

* * *

After she's gone, I put the flowers in water, then text Ellie.

About the house… Definitely selling. Can you let me know when's best for you? xxx

She gets straight back to me.

The end of next week or the one after. Jim and I are hoping to see his parents. Can I get back to you? xxx

I arrive at Sylvie's just after 6pm. It's the first time I've seen the large apartment above the bar that's her home. It's surprisingly light and cool, with wide floorboards and hefty beams holding up the high ceiling, the kitchen dominated by a long table and a huge, faded velvet sofa.

'Thank you.' She takes the bottle of wine I give her, glancing briefly at the label. 'I have a bottle in the fridge. Would you like some?'

Opening it, she pours it into two glasses then passes one to me. '*Santé.*'

'*Santé.*' The wine is cold and crisp. 'This is lovely.'

'Good. Why don't you sit?' She nods towards the table. 'While I cook.'

Pulling out a chair, I sit at the huge table and watch her.

'OK.' She goes to the fridge again. 'Here. Aioli.' She puts a small dish on the table, with another of mixed olives, adding a baguette on a wooden board. 'Help yourself.' She turns back to the cooker. 'So, tell me about the house – you've decided, then?'

'I think so.' I pause to pick out an olive. 'I've been hanging on to it, but I can't imagine living there again. Ellie suggested renting it out. But I would still know it's there and I don't want that.'

'Renting would pay your mortgage, no?' Sylvie pours a sauce into the sizzling saucepan, releasing a cloud of steam.

I shake my head. 'I don't want to feel tied. In a weird way, I think it's holding me back.'

'I understand.' Sylvie looks sympathetic. 'It will be good to do it. But sad, too. Try to remember... we keep what's important in here.' Sylvie touches one of her hands to her heart. 'And in our memories. Stuff...' She shrugs. 'Too much isn't good. It weighs us down. Everything I had in Paris, I left behind. It belongs to another lifetime.' Waving a tea towel to clear the steam, Sylvie goes on. 'Paris was very different. Crazy; my lazy bum of a husband drank too much, so, of course, we argued more... I love the city but I wouldn't go back.' She sounds remarkably unbothered. Glancing at my glass, she puts the bottle on the table. 'Have some more.'

I top up both our glasses. 'So, we both have to decide where we go next!'

'Yes.' She pauses. 'It's exciting! An adventure!' She shrugs. 'I keep asking myself, why not? And there is no reason.' Bringing over a bowl of thinly sliced salad, she places it on the table, followed by another. 'It's tofu – the sauce is sesame and garlic. I've made it before – I hope you like it.'

Breathing in the Eastern flavours, I'm suddenly hungry. 'It smells amazing.'

'I love cooking. I wish we could sell more in the bar, but the locals like traditional food. If I gave them tofu, for instance... You can imagine, can't you!' Shaking her head, she sits opposite me, glancing at the table, a look of satisfaction on her face as she passes me a serving spoon.

'Thanks.' I take some of the food. 'Ben loved exploring. He had this thing about not planning too much, so that you left space for the unexpected to happen. I never got it before, but I do now. When I think about the way we met,' I shake my head. 'A few seconds were all it would have taken for our paths not to cross. Yet against the odds, they did.'

'Yes.' She picks up her glass. 'It was like that with my husband – I missed a train by a few seconds. If I'd caught it...' She shrugs. 'I can't tell you how much I wish I had caught that fucking train!'

I almost choke on my food. 'That bad?'

'Worse. Sometimes I really don't understand myself. I don't know what I saw in him. Big, soulful eyes, charm... good sex.' She shakes her head. 'But I learned from him – about what I don't want. So now, I am very happy on my own.' She sips some of her wine. 'A toast to this ridiculous life!'

Raising my glass, I clink it against hers. She has no idea how much I need this.

* * *

A couple of hours later, slumped onto her giant sofa, Sylvie's quite pissed.

'I want to know what you are going to do with your life, Casey

Cassidy. I like your name. It's very... interesting. You are interesting. Anyway, my question. About your life.'

'Well...'

Holding up a hand, she interrupts. 'Wait. I have this red wine I have to open. Keep your story a minute.'

I shake my head. 'I'm driving, Sylvie.'

'You can sleep here, on this sofa.' Retrieving a bottle and two clean glasses with surprising speed, she's back in seconds. 'Talk,' she orders, pouring the wine. 'Where will you go?'

'I don't know. Maybe Spain...' The idea keeps coming back to me. 'But I haven't decided. Like you said yourself,' I remind her. 'When it comes to next week, next month, who knows?'

'I suppose it depends what you want.' Sitting back, she watches me.

'OK. What I want? Somewhere warm, near the sea – with more life – and I never thought I'd say this, but I want calm, too. And I want to do something.' The wine has loosened the logjam of thoughts in my head. 'Ben always wanted to make a difference in the world. He supported all these causes – to do with the environment, climate change, cruelty, exploitation, animal welfare. But it interested both of us.' I try the red wine. 'This is so nice, Sylvie.'

'It's a very good one. Just now...' She frowns. 'What you said about Ben and how he cared about the world... If you are the same, maybe that's where you should start.'

'Exactly. Since I started helping Brad—'

'The boy you are teaching?'

I nod. 'We've been talking about so many things. In between my visits, he's been doing all this reading. It's amazing.' I broke off. 'Just one conversation sparked his interest.'

After more of Sylvie's red wine, I take her up on her offer. But as I lie on her sofa under the soft blanket she gives me, my mind is whirring. It isn't enough to stay still any more, or to keep going over the same old. I need to find a way to make a difference.

* * *

It's early in the morning when I creep out without disturbing Sylvie and make my way home. After a shower, I get into my floral pyjama bottoms with a kaftan pulled over the top, a pair of your old slipper socks on my feet, as your voice chimes in my ear. *Nice look, Cassidy.*

But after talking to Sylvie last night, I'm still preoccupied and as I take some aspirin for my thumping headache, the winds of change seem to be picking up speed as I try to work out where to start.

With whatever fires you, babe. Follow your heart. Find other people who feel the same.

Your voice is free and light, the way it was when we met. As I stand on the terrace, my mind empties, then a flow of thought begins. Hurrying inside, I open my laptop. Months have passed since I've been able to bring myself to look at your Twitter feed. This morning, as I do, I steel myself for more of the abuse that used to torment you. But apart from one or two offensive messages, the Twitterverse has swamped you with love. As I read them, tears fill my eyes. I'm about to add my own tweet, wanting to thank all these people for their kindness, when my mobile buzzes and Kevin's face flashes up on the screen.

'Hey, dude. How's it going?' His voice is warm.

'Hi Kev. Not too bad. How about you?'

'Yeah, great. Just thought I'd catch up and see how you are. Been up to much?'

'Well, I've found a bar and made a new friend. And I have a job – two mornings a week. I'm on the way to figuring out what comes next.'

'Yeah? That's good to hear, Cassidy. You going to tell me about it?'

'Not yet. But I will.' I pause. 'I'm going to sell the house.'

'I wondered about that.' He speaks more quietly. 'So you're not moving back?'

'Not for a while, at least. But I don't want to be tied. There are too many memories there, Kev. I don't think it could ever be my home again.'

'No, sure.' He's silent for a moment. 'I really get that.'

I change the subject. 'Oh, I forgot to say, Ellie's been over.' Then I realise, he probably doesn't know. 'You know she's met a guy? They're looking for a place to buy, here in France.'

'I've met him.' Kevin sounds cagey. 'We were at Suki's a couple of weeks ago. He's a nice guy, Cassidy. You'll like him.'

Imagining my old friends gathering at Suki's, envy washes over me.

He goes on. 'They seem really happy. But apart from Ellie and Jim, everyone's doing the same old... which is fine. I guess it all depends what you want from life. What I'm trying to say is you're not missing anything.'

'Thanks Kev.' It doesn't stop the pang of homesickness I feel. 'So how about you? What have you been up to? Anything exciting? Any women in your life?'

'Work is busy. As for women... Just so you know, I've sworn off them, Cassidy. A hundred per cent. The best ones are always with someone.'

Suddenly I remember the diary. 'I've been meaning to ask you. Do you happen to know who else has stayed here recently?'

'I'm not sure – as far as I know, people come and go.' He hesitates. 'Why?'

'I found a diary in the bookcase and I was wondering who it belonged to.'

'A diary?' There's astonishment in his voice. 'Could be anyone's, Cassidy. I mean, anyone who's stayed.'

'Well, we can narrow it down. The writer is a man.'

'I'm not sure that helps much.' Kevin's silent for a moment. 'But he was probably one of Antigua's friends. Have you read any of it?'

'A little,' I confess. 'The guy who wrote it seems interesting. He writes... from the heart.'

'That's what a diary's for, I guess.' Kevin pauses again. 'I guess it will forever remain one of life's unsolved mysteries – unless you want me to ask Antigua?'

'I don't think so.' When she's been so generous, I don't want her to think I'm prying.

'Whatever. Anyway, got to go. Just wanted to make sure you're doing OK over there. Look after yourself.'

After he's gone, I go back to my laptop. Logging in to Ben's Twitter account, I compose a post, then read the latest Tweets from people he used to follow. Twisting my hair back over one of my shoulders, I feel myself frown. It's something Kevin said earlier, about how the best ones are always taken.

Getting up, I go to find the diary, leaning against the worktop as I flick through it until I find what I'm looking for. *She's with someone else – the best ones always are.* It's almost word for word what he said just now.

It's like a light being switched on. The diary's Kevin's.

Suddenly I can't wait to read more.

1st July

Julia turned up here today, desperate, needing to talk. There were dark circles under her eyes – she hadn't slept for days. Wired, her brain was in overdrive with all this stuff she wanted to say to people; to me, too, which was why she'd come here.

I tried to get her to sit down, but it was as though she couldn't hear me – then in her next breath she told me we should be together. How great it would be; that her kids would love me. We'd get a dog – she'd already been to see some puppies in the next village.

Slightly shocked, I passed her a mug. When she saw it wasn't coffee, she was snappy. She didn't want chamomile tea – and she was sick of everyone thinking they knew better than her. For my information, right now, she was living on coffee and no one in the world was going to stop her.

It was another side of Julia – the unstoppable force, cramming her days, her mind constantly on the move. She told me she was changing everything up – not just her marriage. She had a whole new wardrobe, with bright colours, high heels... Think French Riviera, back in the day. She'd made a hair appointment too, for the day after tomorrow. She was going to cut her hair short and have it highlighted. I tried to get her to focus, but pacing around the kitchen, she told me she couldn't stay. She had the lawyer to call, shopping to take care of. Then as she glanced at the clock, suddenly her eyes were stricken. She was late to pick up her children. A sob came from her as she began crying, her hands shaking, mania turning to despair before my eyes. Her boys were the most important thing in the world to her. What kind of mother forgot her children?

It was the first time I'd seen her mood flip. I wanted to stop her, calm her down, but she was too on edge, pausing long enough to kiss me, but even that was hurried. As she ran out to her car, she stumbled on the path. Watching her drive away, I was seriously worried about her. I was guessing this was the end of the high, that at any moment she'd come crashing down. I've no idea if anyone will be there to catch her.

After she'd gone, I sat outside for a while, let the silence permeate into me as I waited for my mind to clear. I've still no idea what's going on here. I can't tell if I'm a fool and this isn't going anywhere – or if I'll regret letting her go, for the rest of my life.

It even reminds me of the way Kevin talks. I remember how he wasn't around much for a while, showing up now and then with the tales of travels I used to joke about. I can't believe I never asked him where he'd been, what he was doing. Caught in my own little bubble, I hadn't stopped to think that life, stuff, happens to all of us.

As evening draws in, I pour a glass of wine and pull a chair to the edge of the terrace. *Cheers, Ben.* I raise my glass in your direction, imagine your reply.

Epic, isn't it?

And it is. Sitting here, I watch the pink-washed mountains turning to lilac, the ice-cream-coloured contrails above valleys filled with mist, a high crescent moon lighting a corner of the sky. It is epic, a dreamscape that's constantly moving, carrying me slowly, unstoppably forwards.

36

BEFORE

September, last year

There was a churning feeling inside me as I leapt out of bed. I had a horrible sense that something was wrong. Pulling on jeans and a cardigan over a T-shirt, I hurried downstairs, calling him again. 'Ben?' My voice echoing through the house as I checked the small sitting room, before I slipped my shoes on and went outside.

'Ben?' My call was drowned by the cries of seagulls as I took the path towards the beach. Then as I looked ahead, I saw him. Further along the cove, he was sitting on a rock. Clambering to join him, a sense of foreboding hung over me. It was as though he was completely unaware that I was there. 'Ben? Babe? You had me worried.'

As he turned to look at me, there was an expression on his face I hadn't seen before. Sitting next to him, I felt my blood run cold. 'What's wrong?' When he didn't answer, I took his hand. 'Talk to me, Ben. You're freaking me out.' I'd never seen him so disconnected, so switched off from me. 'What's going on?'

'I couldn't sleep.' His voice was flat as he stared across the water. 'I came down here as it was getting light and watched a couple of fishing boats go out. The sea is wild out there today. I was thinking how they don't have a choice. How everyone needs money and here, it's the only way they can make any. You should have seen them, Casey. Two old guys who must have been in their seventies. Then two teenagers. Kids. Look at that sea.' He glanced up the channel that joined the sheltered bay to the open water. 'They're risking their lives going out in that.'

I frowned. I'd no idea where this had come from. 'Hey...' I stroked his hand. 'They know what they're doing. It's a way of life around here.'

But he shook his head. 'It's such a bloody unfair world, isn't it? That life can be so tough for some while others have it so easy.' As he turned to look at me, his eyes were haunted. 'It's so wrong.'

He didn't have to tell me. I could see it in the defeated way he sat, as though there was pain, deep inside him. Feeling myself shiver, I pulled my sleeves over my hands to keep them warm, noticing at the same time what little clothing Ben was wearing – a thin T-shirt and shorts. 'Come back to the cottage,' I tried to persuade him. 'You're cold, Ben.' I got up, but he didn't move. 'Ben? Come on. I'll make some coffee.'

'You go.' He let go of my hand. 'I'll join you in a moment.'

As I started to make my way back to the cottage, the strangest feeling hung over me. It was as though Ben was in another world, one I couldn't enter. All of a sudden, my happiness dimmed. I thought I knew him so well, instinctively, to the very bones of him. Yet clearly, I didn't.

Putting the kettle on, I watched the clock. It was another ten minutes before Ben walked in. 'I'm going to have a shower.'

'OK... Would you like scrambled eggs?' Normality, Casey, I was telling myself. Bring him back.

He nodded briefly. 'Thanks.' As he disappeared upstairs, I went to the fridge, listening to the sound of the shower running, knowing I was missing something.

When he came downstairs, I poured us each a mug of coffee, then before I could speak, he hugged me briefly. 'I'm sorry.' As he pulled away, *for a moment the haunted look was back. 'I guess I got lost somewhere in my head. It happens sometimes. I find it really difficult to watch people struggle.'*

I frowned, because I did, too. But I wasn't affected the way he was.

He was silent for a moment. 'Sometimes... when I think about everything that's wrong with this world, all I feel is pain.'

I stared at him. 'Why?' Trying not to let my alarm show, I watched his face.

He shrugged, wrapping his arms tightly around himself. 'It's the suffering that goes on. So much of it, all over the world.' Desperation flickered in his eyes. 'People can't feed their kids or keep a roof over their heads. All the people fleeing from war zones, with nowhere safe to go, no jobs... They have no hope, Casey. That's the very worst bit. We can't imagine how that feels, can we? To not have hope?'

'Come here.' I put my arms around him, feeling the tightness of his body, trying to hide the fear I felt. It was just that he cared, more than most people, I tried to tell myself.

I finished making breakfast. Then a few hours later, Ben's mood started to lift. I watched him closely the rest of the time we were in Cornwall, but his angst seemed to have passed. Back home, we perused our wedding photos while life went on as before, the episode soon forgotten, as I pushed it to the back of my mind.

37

AFTER

September

You used to talk about taking time, living in each moment. So that's what I'm trying to do here. Inhabit each moment of these late summer days. The graceful movement of the sun-bleached grasses; the red-tinged shades of the apples as they ripen, the heady scent of wild honeysuckle.

As I drive to Sabaillan, I take in the previously green landscape that's parched after months without rain; the hedgerows bright with berries – all signs that autumn is coming, affirmed by the return of snow on the tallest mountain peaks.

* * *

With the autumn term about to start, I spend my last mornings with Brad.

'You won't believe the stuff I've found.' Brad brings up a website

I've seen before. 'I was googling plastic pollution. Look at this.' He zooms in on a photo.

'I know where this is.' It's the same part of the world that Ben had planned to expose. Pausing, I take a deep breath. 'Ben was planning to go out to one of the resorts and film it. He was a drone pilot.'

'Did he go?' Brad's eyes study mine.

'No.' Swallowing, I gather myself. 'But someone should. OK. What are we looking at today?'

'Could we go through some old exam papers? For the first hour? Then after...' He hesitates. 'There's something I want to show you.'

* * *

'So where are we going?' Side by side, we walk along a narrow track.

'I went for a walk yesterday – to the pig farm.'

'The one you told me about? I didn't know it was nearby.'

'It's about a half-hour walk. You can't see it from the lane. There's another barn now. It's even worse.'

As we walk in silence, a cold feeling comes over me. 'Did anyone see you?'

'No.' Brad shakes his head. 'Today I want to take photos.'

Suddenly I'm uneasy. 'What are you planning to do with them?'

'I haven't decided. It's this way.'

I follow Brad downhill through some woods, until at the edge, he crouches down. 'Over there,' he whispers. 'Follow me.'

I stare at the barn that's come into view, gagging as a foul stench reaches me. Before I can speak, he runs, his head ducked down, towards a smaller building, as I follow.

'I don't think anyone's about,' he says quietly. 'Quickly. I'll show you what I saw yesterday.'

It isn't just the smell as we get closer; it's the intensity of animal noise that gets to me, drowning out the drone from a tractor as we make our way towards one of the barns.

Like the one I saw with Ellie, it's huge, constructed of metal. In summer, it would be like an oven inside. Checking behind him briefly, Brad slides the door open.

* * *

As we walk back to Brad's house, my mind is filled with images I'll never forget, of filth, overcrowding, obvious suffering, of the confined energy and density of pigs forced to live entire lives like that, as I hear your voice. *This is just one small farm, babe. There are thousands.*

'Did you see their eyes?' Brad looks haunted.

I nod. 'People don't realise, do they? Each of those pigs is a sentient being.'

'More like they don't care,' Brad says angrily.

'Anger isn't going to help,' I say quietly. 'I think it's more that people don't understand.'

* * *

On my way home, needing her no-nonsense company, I head for Sylvie's bar. When I go inside, she kisses me the French way, on both cheeks. In jeans and a white shirt, her dark brown hair hangs loose on her shoulders.

'Could I have a coffee?'

'Sure.' Her eyes study me.

Pulling out a chair at the bar, I watch her grind coffee then make us a cup each. 'I've just seen something really horrible.'

'What?' Placing a cup in front of me, Sylvie frowns.

'A pig farm – over near Sabaillan. It was vile.' Images dance before my face, of the suffering in the pigs' eyes.

'Oh, Casey,' Sylvie looks sad. 'Is this the kind of thing you were talking about? That Ben cared about?'

I nod. 'You know, I've seen photos – but they don't convey the half of it. Until you actually see one, for real, nothing comes near.'

'And you want people to know. To think about it.' She looks at me. 'It's what you have to do, isn't it?'

'Yes.' I looked at her. 'It's a question of finding the right way. But I will.'

'Good for you.' She pauses. 'Have you booked your flight?'

'Not yet.'

'I have the evening off. So, are you busy later?'

'No. Come over!' Fired up by what I saw at the farm, I want some time to think. 'I have a few things to do – and I really need to talk to Ellie and book my flight.'

'OK! You can tell me about your plans.' Sylvie glances at the time. 'I have to get on. We have a late booking of twenty-five people. I'll come over at eight?'

* * *

Back at the house, I call Ellie before booking a flight, then text my parents to let them know I'm coming back for a few days as the little ginger cat turns up. It doesn't look well and for the first time, it lets me stroke it. Finding an old blanket, I make a cat bed on the terrace and put some food down.

After texting Brad to ask him to send me his photos, I start googling intensive farming. Among the websites are images of pig farms similar to what I saw today, as well as many more, equally horrific, of dairy farms.

In a short time, the nature of farming has changed dramatically. Where there used to be green fields, vast, inhumane factories have taken over, while far from being treated as sensitive, feeling creatures, animals are simply a commodity. The rearing of pigs in filthy barns and ripping away of newborn calves from their mothers in dairy farms is devastating enough, but a whole industry of food production has come to rely on it.

Meanwhile, the cruelty that's endemic in the dairy industry is only just coming out. I stare at the photos – of cows crying for their babies; the male calves killed at birth because they have no monetary value, while those that are allowed to live spend their brief lives in a crate set among thousands of other crates, still babies when they're taken to the slaughterhouse.

But it's what Ben used to say that troubles me most. It's how people think. Our acceptance that this happens, our justification of the scale of suffering. When animals are sentient, intelligent creatures, how has it become sanctioned that each year, billions of them are subjected to this?

As I look at the images, I'm aware of a sense of everything around me coming together. Maybe there's a reason why I'm here, first meeting Sylvie, which led me to meet Brad. Then seeing the brutal reality of factory farming for myself, first-hand. I've gone way past being able to ignore it. So, I make you a promise. I'm in this with you Ben, whatever it takes. I'm giving those without one, a voice.

More change reaches into my life, as I have my last morning with Brad.

'When do you leave France?' I ask him.

'The day after tomorrow.' He pauses. 'This is our last lesson, isn't it?'

'It is. So, what are we doing?'

He opens a web page. 'I found this. I wanted to know if you think it's worth me doing it this term – to help my grades.'

Starting to read, I stop. 'I know this site. It's brilliant. If you have enough time, definitely.'

'I'll make time.' In all the time I've known him, he's never sounded so determined.

I look at him. 'This is going to be a really good term, Brad. A new beginning. No matter what anyone else says, you can make it whatever you want it to be.'

Our two hours pass quickly, as they always do. Before I leave, he turns to me. 'Can I ask you something?'

'Of course.'

He frowns slightly. 'When did you know you wanted to be a teacher?'

'I was a bit older than you.' I consider for a moment. 'About fifteen, when my little sister died.'

A look of shock crosses Brad's face.

'She'd always talked about being a teacher – I thought because she couldn't do it, I would. But I loved the idea as much as she had. I wanted to make subjects interesting so that children or teenagers would want to learn.' I pause. 'How long have you wanted to be a doctor?'

He lowered his eyes. 'Since my mum died.'

I watch sadness flicker across his face. 'Is she the reason you missed so much school?'

As he nods, the empty look comes back. 'I really miss her.'

'She'd be really proud of you, Brad. If you were my son, I know I would be.'

His eyes are bright as he looks at me. 'She was ill – for a long time. It's like with your sister – it's why I want to be a doctor.'

For a child to lose their mother is to lose their cornerstone. But grief is different things to different people, changing the way we think and what's important to us. Makes us kinder, more understanding, stronger; ignites a renewed desire to find meaning in this life, as it has for Brad. But it's happening to me, too.

38

October, last year

As autumn went by, early invitations started coming in for Christmas parties. One weekend when Ben was away working, I went to see my parents. My mother was already planning her Christmas, wrestling control away from me as she always did.

'Now, I don't know if they've mentioned it, but we've invited Gina and Mick. I thought that way, you and Ben wouldn't be torn between two places. I thought you and Ben could have your old room and Gina and Mick could have the big spare room. Then, on Boxing Day, I thought...'

Even though it was only October, she had it all planned out. But having got my way about the wedding, I gave in graciously. Ben wouldn't mind what we did and besides, my mum was an exceptional cook. 'Cool, Mum. Why don't I make the Christmas cake?'

Almost dropping her teacup in horror, my mother stared at me. 'Darling, I'm not sure that's such a good idea. I mean, I always make Granny's recipe. It's the same one I've always made, every year.'

'You could give it to me.' I watched her face. Was my newly married status going to her head or had she always been this much of a control freak? I went on. 'She passed it down to you, after all. You never know, I might surprise you.'

* * *

But actually, it was myself I surprised.

'Fuck. Fricking oven. BEN,' I screeched. 'The cake's on fire!'

'What?' He came running into the kitchen, peering at the oven. 'Casey, why is there so much paper in there?'

'You cover the top. It's supposed to stop it burning.' I said plaintively, looking around the kitchen, nodding towards the photocopy of my mum's recipe on the worktop.

'Hasn't worked too well, has it?' His eyes glinted with amusement. 'Here, give me the oven gloves.' Taking them, he turned the oven off, waiting for a moment for the flames to subside, before opening the door.

I looked at the smoking paper, utterly aghast, running my hands through my hair. 'What am I going to do?'

'Maybe we can fix it.' Ben placed the tin on the cake rack.

'It's ruined. And you don't understand. It's my gran's recipe.' I was getting more and more agitated with each word. 'It was supposed to be for Christmas Day. It was going to be perfect... My mother will never let me hear the end of it. You know what she's like.'

'We can scrape the top off.' Taking both my hands, Ben frowned at me. 'It isn't worth getting this upset over. By the time it's covered with marzipan, your mum will never know. And if it isn't salvageable, we'll make another.'

But I was shaking my head. 'You don't know my mother. She'll have her eagle eye on every currant. And it has to be done today. Next weekend, it will be too late. You have to feed it with brandy – it's part of the recipe...' Seeing his face, I broke off.

'Feed?' The corners of his lips twitched.

'Yes. It makes it tastier.' Trying to stop myself smiling, I swatted him with a tea towel. 'Don't. I am very upset about this. It's going to take the rest of the day to make another.'

'Casey, it's just a cake.' But instead of waiting for my reply, he pulled me close to him, then kissed me. 'Can it wait?'

* * *

My birthday arrived. When I woke up, Ben was already awake. 'Happy birthday, babe.' He kissed me. 'I got you something.' He passed me a small, wrapped box.

Carefully unwrapping it, I opened it to find a simple pair of hoop earrings on which a single sparkling stone hung. I stared at them – surely they weren't diamonds?

He was smiling. 'Do you like them?'

'Like them?' I was gobsmacked. 'I love them! Getting them out, I put them on.

'They look great on you.' Getting out of bed, Ben passed me a mirror. 'They're diamonds, by the way.'

As I looked in the mirror, they glittered back at me. 'They're beautiful.'

'You're beautiful,' he said softly.

But it didn't end there. 'I thought we'd go out for dinner, babe. I've booked a table – at Francesco's.'

'Fantastic!' I loved Italian food and on the outskirts of Chichester, Francesco's was one of my favourite places.

That evening I got ready; twisting my hair loosely back to show off my new earrings, putting on a black dress and suede boots. But it wasn't just us going to Francesco's that evening. With Ellie's help, Ben had invited twenty of our friends.

'Surprise!' As we walked in, I couldn't believe it. Turning around, I gazed at Ben. 'You did this?'

He nodded, looking pleased.

'Thank you.' I kissed him. No one had ever thrown me a surprise party before.

'Happy birthday!' Ellie hugged me. 'This was all Ben's idea. You are so bloody lucky, Cassidy.'

My eyes were glittering like my earrings as I swallowed the lump in my throat. 'I know.'

October

Before I leave for the UK, my thirtieth birthday comes and goes. The earrings you gave me are upstairs, in their box in the bottom of one of my bags. I haven't so much as looked at them since coming here. Haven't wanted to remind myself about the happiness I felt, or the moments I questioned it. One of them is stand-out. A moment my heart stopped.

But that's how it works, for all of us, I hear you say. *Normal life, interrupted by heart-stopping moments.*

So frigging wise, Ben. With one gargantuan exception – when it came to yourself.

We're all different. You're straight back at me. *It's about our genes, our experiences, our programming; from our families to our friends to the society we are brought up in... Think about all that noise surrounding us, filling our heads from the moment we're born.*

You were my heart-stopping moment, Ben Summer. In one fell swoop, shattering everything I held precious.

40

October, last year

Autumn arrived, the season of copper leaves and misty days, for walking on the Downs and making plans. Meanwhile, Ben's drone business was growing to the point he had choices to make.

'I've had another couple of enquiries about shoots next year.'

'That's amazing, Ben!' Warmth filled me. With a growing list of happy clients, he deserved to be successful.

'Yeah...' He paused. 'OK. I have an idea I want to run by you.'

I listened as he told me about the film he and Jez were planning to make next year, to help expose the scale of pollution, knowing as he spoke how important this was to him.

'We were thinking about starting in Indonesia.'

I hadn't realised he planned to go so far away. Taken aback, as I opened my mouth to speak, he went on.

'It makes sense to begin with some of the countries I know – after Indonesia, maybe Vietnam – I have contacts and they're also some of the

worst offenders when it comes to polluting the oceans. We're thinking about filming the resorts – then showing the reality of what's going on there. I really think we could do something with that.'

I frowned. 'But if it was going to be seen by a lot of people, wouldn't you need the force of a TV company behind you?'

'I think if we get this right, Kevin knows someone who might be interested. There's a really good chance this could happen, babe.'

It didn't surprise me that Ben had been speaking to Kevin about it. From their first meeting, a slow-burn friendship had started between them.

He went on. 'Don't get me wrong. The shoots around here are great, but you know how my mind works. I need to do something that means more than that.'

'Then you should do this.' I knew this was the chance he'd been waiting for. 'When are you planning on going?'

He shrugged. 'March… maybe April. We'll probably be away for about a month.' He hesitated. 'You don't mind, do you?'

'Of course not.' Understanding how passionately he felt, what else could I say? But for the second time, I was taken aback. A month seemed a long time – and March wasn't far away.

I pushed my misgivings to the back of my mind, as later that afternoon, after lighting the fire, Ben got out his laptop. 'I'll show you where we're thinking of filming.'

Sitting next to him, I was shocked as he brought up images of rivers of plastic, of stunning beaches covered in more of it, when around the next headland, there'd be a high-end luxury tourist resort. 'Those resorts don't care where their plastic ends up.'

'You mean, you're going to name them?'

Ben shrugged. 'That's the plan.'

Suddenly I was worried. 'But you could get in all kinds of trouble.'

'I'll be careful.' Ben brought up his Twitter feed. 'And we're not alone. More and more people are waking up to what we're doing to the world.'

Scrolling down recent posts, he paused. 'The problem will be those who don't want people like us showing up – namely the resort-owners.'

'I don't want you getting arrested,' I said hastily. Then my eyes caught a new message that had just flashed up, long enough for me to see that it was filled with obscenities, before Ben closed it. 'Who was that?'

I watched his jaw tighten as he shook his head. 'No one.'

* * *

It wasn't long before he had booked their flights and had organised a place to stay. 'We're meeting a guy called Lachlan, from Sydney. The plan is he'll join us in Bali and we'll go from there.'

Over the days that followed, Ben was quieter. I put it down to him being preoccupied with this trip. He seemed to be spending an inordinate amount of time researching online. But it wasn't just about pollution. He was looking at the deforestation of the Amazon rainforest and the declining number of species; the human catastrophe of war-driven migration; the unstoppable fires in Western Australia and the destruction of vast swathes of wildlife, taking on the pain of all of them.

I was proud of him. For caring. For taking action when most people didn't. I didn't see the effort it took, the toll it was taking. How hard it was for him to hide the fact that inside, he was crumbling. On the outside, you couldn't see any of that. My lovely Ben was the same as he'd always been.

41

October

The day I fly back to England, Sylvie drives me to Toulouse Airport.

'It's a very quick visit to sort so much.'

'If I need to stay longer, I'll change my flight.' But once the house is cleared, I know I won't want to.

Ignoring the beeps from other drivers, Sylvie drops me near departures. Leaning over, I kiss her cheek. 'Thank you, Sylvie. You won't forget to feed the cats, will you?'

She rolls her eyes. 'You and those cats. They must have managed before you moved in.'

'I know. But the little ginger one isn't well.'

'Don't worry. I will feed them. Good luck,' she says more gently. 'I will think of you. Let me know when you're coming back.'

* * *

As the aircraft takes off, I gaze through the window watching France vanish beneath a layer of cloud that stays with us for the duration of the flight, until just before we land; the autumnal Sussex landscape appears swathed in mist. As I disembark and walk through the terminal building, it's as though I've never been away.

I am lucky that my friends care so much. As I walk through the doors into the arrivals hall, Ellie is there. Hugging her, I notice a guy standing close behind her watching us, a look of amusement on his face.

'You didn't tell me Jim was coming with you,' I mutter in her ear.

Ellie pulls away slightly, her hands resting on my arms as her eyes sparkle into mine. 'I couldn't wait any longer for you to meet each other.' She holds out one of her hands towards him. 'Say hello, you two.'

'Hi.' I take in kind eyes and a warm smile as he kisses my cheek.

'It's great to meet you, Casey.'

'It's good to meet you too. Whatever Ellie's told you about me,' I shake my head. 'Don't believe a word of it. She's a terrible liar.'

Ignoring Ellie's look of outrage, he grins. 'She's only said the nicest things.' He winks, then glances at Ellie. 'Shall we go?'

England seems grey, the roads crowded with a volume of traffic I never used to think twice about. In the front passenger seat, from the way she talks, it's clear Ellie's organised everything. 'I thought tomorrow, we could go to the house together. I've lined up a couple of estate agents to come and value it, but I can always cancel them.' She glances anxiously back at me.

I shake my head. 'No, don't. Thanks, Ell.'

'OK.' She sounds relieved. 'Anyway, tonight, I thought we could eat and drink and just chill out.' Then she can't contain herself. 'I know this isn't a fun trip, but I'm so happy to see you!'

'Ditto.' Leaning forward, I touch her arm. 'So how are your plans, guys? Have you found a place yet?'

Ellie's eyes are shining as she looks over at Jim. 'We think so. I've just accepted an offer on my flat. And we've found a gorgeous old place, with a couple of run down gites. We think we're going to put an offer in.'

I try to sound enthusiastic. 'That's brilliant! Where is it?'

'Believe it or not, it isn't far from where you're staying. About fifty kilometres away. It doesn't have your mountain views, but it's closer to the sea.'

'So what's stopping you?'

'Nothing really.' She looks at Jim again. 'We only decided for sure on the way to pick you up. Jim's going to call the agent as soon as we're home!'

* * *

After we arrive at Ellie's, Jim makes the call and their offer is accepted. We open a bottle of bubbly, and toast their new home. Watching them, I'm reminded of when you and I met; that together, their lives are on a road to somewhere.

I discover Jim is easy company and he adores my friend, while Ellie shines every second she's with him, in a way I've never seen before. Feeling a pang of envy, I smother it. While it may have been for the shortest time, I too, was lucky to have known love like that.

During the evening, Ellie gives me a small present wrapped in brightly coloured paper. 'Sorry it's late... but happy birthday!'

'Thank you.' Removing the paper, I open the box that's revealed. 'Oh, wow, Ellie!' Carefully I take out a bracelet; a single strand of leather to which a tiny silver surfboard is attached.

'Do you like it?' She sounds apprehensive. 'I know Ben loved to surf – and I thought if you wear it, it will make you think of the sea.'

'I love it.' My eyes fill with tears. It's the perfect link between my past and the future. Going over, I hug her. 'Will you help me put it on?'

* * *

During the night, in Ellie's spare room, I sleep fitfully, thinking about our house – our empty bed, my clothes still hanging in the wardrobe; telling myself it'll be fine. That it's just another day that will soon be over. But in the morning, as the cold light of day hits me, I'm filled with dread.

'Are you ready for this?' Ellie looks worried.

'I suppose.' I pause. 'You won't leave me there, will you, Ell?'

'Of course I won't.'

I'm silent for a moment. 'Shall we get it over with?'

In the ten minutes it takes to drive there, Ellie and I are quiet. 'I don't know what I'm going to do with all the stuff.'

She glances at me. 'We'll do it in stages. OK?'

'I'll be more OK when it's over.' As she turns into our old road, my stomach lurches. It looks the same as when I left and, as Ellie parks outside the house, I imagine my old life still exists and I'm coming back from a girls' holiday; that you're inside, cooking lunch, a bottle of wine open on the side. That I've awoken from what was no more than a terrible nightmare.

Taking a deep breath, as I get out, my eyes skim over the tiny front garden that someone's kindly weeded, and the couple of late, open roses beside the red-painted door.

Ellie fiddles with the key and the door opens. Then as I follow her inside, a tangible wall of emotion hits me. Desolation, sorrow, grief, mixed with the faint smell of furniture polish and scented candles, as a wave of nostalgia crashes over me.

'Fuck,' I mutter, as Ellie switches on some lights. It's like I've walked back into the shattered, broken remains of my old life.

Going through to the kitchen, I hear her throw the windows open, before she comes back. 'Are you OK?' Her face looks concerned, her eyes searching mine. 'Do you want to sit down?'

'Can you give me a moment?' Leaving her standing in the hallway, I go into our sitting room. As I look around, the strangest feeling steals over me as I'm assailed by memories. Everything is as I left it. Our wedding photo above the fireplace: me in my beautiful, sexy dress, you handsome in your dark suit. In this surreal world, it seems impossible that it was just over a year ago.

I try to get a hold of myself. *The worst has happened,* I clench my fists. *You've survived. You can do this.*

What comes next is what I've dreaded most, as I make my way up the stairs. I've forgotten how soft the carpet is under my feet, how halfway up, light pours in through the window. At the top, I hesitate before I walk towards our bedroom. Even now, a trace of scent lingers, an amalgamation of fragrance that was unique to us.

Standing in the doorway, I stare at the chest of drawers and wardrobes still filled with our clothes, before my eye is drawn to the stone with the seam of crystals that I found on the beach. Going over, I pick it up as an image of you fills my mind; the last I have of you.

As I stand there, I try to stifle the sob in my throat, resisting the urge to bury my face in one of our pillows. *You weren't supposed to leave me, Ben...* But I'm not expecting you to answer. Knowing I can't do this alone, I go downstairs to find Ellie in the kitchen.

'I'm OK,' I tell her, steeling myself. 'I'm going to start with our clothes. Can you help me?'

* * *

It's what best friends are for. Tears, laughter and rock solid support. Twenty black bags later, the wardrobes and chest of drawers are empty; my clothes ruthlessly edited, the bags labelled by Ellie according to where they're destined for and only two of which I'm keeping. The airing cupboard is next. Sets of neatly folded bed linen I don't want to throw out but can't keep, either. Pulling out a set of soft linen sheets and pillowcases to take back with me, I stare at the rest before turning to Ellie. 'You're going to need stuff, aren't you? Would any of this do? For your gites? Most of it's new.'

'Are you sure? I can always store them for you. You might want them back, later on.'

I shake my head, suddenly decisive. 'I won't. Seriously, whatever you don't want is going to a charity shop.'

'OK. If you're certain...' Thankfully she doesn't push me further. Hesitating only briefly, she carries on writing labels and filling bags.

Gazing around at the sheer quantity of what's here, suddenly I sit on the floor, utterly defeated. This is far too much to sort out in a couple of days. 'Oh Ellie, what am I going to do with it all?

Coming over, she sits down next to me, and I lean my head on her shoulder.

'Jim and I will take the clothes you don't want to a charity shop.' She speaks quietly. 'Maybe we should look at the stuff in your kitchen next, and think about your furniture. Then we'll talk.'

Following her downstairs, I glance into the sitting room again, at the huge comfy sofa. The distressed mirror we bought in a market together, the antique chest, the painting of the Cornish beach, the photos, our collection of books – all pieces of our lives. It seems so final to think about getting rid of them.

Going through to the kitchen, I find Ellie opening cupboards, getting out piles of assorted plates. 'It can all go,' I tell her. Then I see the new ones we'd bought with some of our wedding money. Plain white with an Aztec pattern around the edge that Ben had thought too jazzy and I'd thought wasn't funky enough. 'They can go, too.'

Opening drawers and more cupboards, I pull out an old plate that belonged to my grandmother; oval shaped and hand-painted, it's been in my family for years. 'This is the only one I want to keep.' As I put it to one side, the oddest feeling grips me that I can say this, when everything in this house was part of the life you and I shared. But it's a life that no longer exists.

As I turn around, I catch my grandmother's plate with my elbow, knocking it onto the floor, where it shatters.

* * *

In the sitting room, I sob noisily into the pile of tissues Ellie hands me. 'All this stuff, Ell. I feel so awful. *It brings everything back...*'

'I know.' Ellie puts her arms around me. 'This is the worst, most shit part, OK? But we'll get through it.'

'Thank you... for being here, Ell. I couldn't face any of this without you.' Pulling away, I gaze tearfully at her.

'You don't have to thank me.' Her eyes are sad. 'It's what we do for each other.'

'Yes.' Burying my face in another tissue, I blow my nose noisily.

'I'll make us some tea.'

'There aren't any teabags. I threw everything away.'

But it seems she's thought of everything. 'I know. I brought some.'

I hear her fill the kettle, then the clatter from a cupboard as she finds some mugs. A few minutes later she comes back. 'Here.' She passes me one of them, sits on the sofa next to me, unwraps a bar of chocolate, breaks off a chunk and hands it to me. 'Eat this. I have an idea I'd like to run by you.' Taking the chocolate, I listen as she goes on. 'Jim and I have been talking. Our furniture will fit in the house, but we'll have two gites to furnish as well. There's also a massive barn to store stuff in. What I thought was we can take everything you're not sure about and maybe use some of it, if you're OK with that – at least to start with. Then if further down the line you want anything back, you can have it. The way I see it, it gets both of us out of a hole.'

I stare at the carpet, stunned. 'But... it will cost a fortune to transport it all.'

But Ellie's already shaking her head. 'It won't. Jim's uncle has an international removal company. He'll tie it in with another job, but basically, it will cost us next to nothing.' She pauses. 'Oh. I almost forgot. Any clothes you want to keep, I can store those, too.'

'But...'

'No buts.' Ellie pauses. 'I didn't want to say anything until you'd come back here. I wasn't sure how you were going to feel. I half wondered if you might want to stay for a bit. But that isn't going to happen, is it?'

'No.' I'm speechless, still processing what she's suggested, but in just a few words she's removed what to me are monumental problems. Then I gaze at the wedding photo of me and Ben, swallowing. 'Can I ask you to keep just one more box? Of important things – like that?' I nod towards the photo. 'If you're sure Jim won't mind?'

Her eyes are warm, as she nods. 'He's completely on board with this. It will be fine. What about Ben's drones and kitesurfing gear?'

'They're at his parents' house.' They came after the funeral and asked if there was anything they could do. All over the place, I'd said the first thing that came into my head.

As Ellie sighs, I know what's coming. 'Don't you think you should speak to them?'

'Probably.' But I still can't go there.

'Oh Casey...' Ellie's voice is sympathetic. 'You're going to have to talk to them at some point.'

'Maybe.' I shrug again, shooting her a warning glance. 'Or maybe not.'

Wisely she doesn't push me. With everything resolved by Ellie and Jim, I pack a box of my most treasured possessions – photographs, books, gifts – then remove myself to the quiet of Ellie's car while she shows the estate agents around. When I see them leave, I go to find her. 'So, what now?'

'Nothing.' She takes my hands in hers. 'Everything's labelled, isn't it? Jim and I will sort it all out.' She pauses, looking at me. 'You're done here. You don't ever need to come back.'

The part of me that's torn teeters on the edge. It would be so easy to change my mind. But it's a house that was only my home because Ben was here. Now that he's gone, it isn't.

Closing the door behind me for the last time, I don't allow myself to look back. 'Right.' Ellie's manner is brusque as she starts marching towards her car. 'Jim just texted me. He's suggested a Chinese. What shall I tell him? The usual?'

'Anything.' Ellie knows what I like.

Texting him, she turns to me. 'You need a sodding great drink. We'll stop on the way home and buy some wine.'

* * *

The Chinese food and chilled wine are restorative, but as I lie in bed, I can't staunch the flow of memories, nor do I want to. I remember the first time you invited me to the house. The first meal you cooked for me. The way you made room for my stuff when I moved in. Long evenings together, drinking wine and putting the world to rights.

It feels like it's too early in the morning when Ellie takes me to the station to catch a train to Devon. Watching the landscape streak past, I feel oddly disconnected as I take in the familiar towns and countryside that belong to my old life. It's the strangest feeling, because none of it's any different. The only thing that's changed is me.

It's a fleeting visit, as much as my emotions can handle, though I'm not sure my mother will understand.

'Casey, darling!' She trills too brightly as she opens the door. 'How are you?'

'I'm OK.' I kiss the cheek she proffers. 'Is Dad here?'

'He's in the garden. You're earlier than we expected.'

'The trains were running on time for once.' Dropping my

overnight bag onto the floor, I hang my jacket up. 'And there was a taxi outside the station. I didn't have to wait.'

'You should have called. Your father was going to come and meet you. Cup of tea?' Mum bustles through to the kitchen.

'Or wine?' I add hopefully.

A look of uncertainty crosses her face. 'Really, Casey. I don't know what you've been up to in France, but until the—'

'—sun is over the yard arm...' I finish for her. 'In France, they have wine for breakfast. I don't, by the way. Tea would be lovely.'

'Darling.' My dad walks into the kitchen, fleeting disappointment washing over his face. 'I was going to come and pick you up. How are you?' Same old Dad, the sadness in his eyes because he can guess how I'm feeling. My heart twists as he plants a smacker of a kiss on my cheek.

'Not so bad. Ellie dropped me at the station. She's been helping me sort out the house.'

A mug poised in each hand, my mother freezes. 'What do you mean?'

All the way here, I've prepared myself for what I'd known would be coming. 'I can't keep everything, Mum. It had to happen at some point.' I swallow the lump in my throat. 'Ellie has a new man. He's really nice. They're moving to France, to this big old house with a couple of gites, so she's going to have our furniture – and anything else that might be useful.'

'What about your wedding presents? That lovely painting Gina and Mick gave you?' My mother sounds horrified. 'And the china you bought with your wedding money?'

'I'm keeping the important things, Mum. But it isn't the same any more. It was mine and Ben's stuff.'

My mother's silence speaks volumes, as my dad looks at me. 'I'd say that sounds like a sensible plan, letting Ellie take things. Don't you think, love?' He turns to my mother.

'Actually, I don't.' Her voice is tight. 'Casey's home is here. I wasn't going to say until after lunch, but I've found a lovely little semi on a housing estate on the edge of Barnstaple – she could easily afford it when the house is sold. And there's a very good school close by. I'm sure she could get a job there.'

'Mum.' I stare at her, shocked. She's talking as though I'm not here. 'I never said I was staying. I'm going back to France.'

'When?' Her voice is sharp.

'Tomorrow night. I'm getting a train back to Ellie's, then she's taking me to the airport. My flight's at nine tomorrow evening.'

'I really hoped you'd at least think about it.' Shaking her head, her voice is filled with disapproval.

'Why?' Suddenly I want to know. 'Why does it matter to you so much?'

My mother huffs. 'I wasn't going to say. But if you really want to know, I don't think it's right a woman of your age taking off on her own like this. Nor does Gina.'

At the mention of Ben's mum, my hackles rise. 'Well, I hope you and Gina enjoy your little conversations about me. But it isn't going to make one frigging bit of difference.' Slamming my mug on the table, my tea slops over the edge. Just as I'm about to get up and walk out, I feel Dad's hand on my shoulder.

Taking a deep breath, I look at her. 'I'm sorry, but this doesn't make sense. You didn't mind when Polly went to the States.'

'That's different.' Her lips are pursed, as she says what I knew she'd say. 'She's only there because of work.'

'Your mum worries about you, that's all.' Sitting down, my dad picks up a mug of tea. 'Isn't that right, love?'

Suddenly I feel selfish. When my mother has already lost one daughter, all I've been thinking about is me. Looking at him gratefully, I try to defuse the atmosphere. 'Look. I honestly haven't decided what comes next. I know I can't live in that house again. And I'll have more choices once it's sold. But if there's one thing I do know, it's that there's no hurry to make decisions. There's no reason for me to come back to the UK right now. And it's still early days but I'll work it out.' As my mother opens her mouth to speak, I get in first. 'You have both been so supportive. And I'm so grateful.' I swallow hard. 'But it hasn't been easy coming back. The last time I was here was Christmas.' As I glance from Dad to my mother, my eyes fill with tears. 'I don't want to fight. I want to enjoy seeing you. And...' I pause. 'I'd love you to try and understand.'

* * *

Thankfully my mother backs off. Over one of her roast dinners, I tell them about France, giving them a censored description of the house. Then I show them photos of the house Ellie and Jim are buying. 'Property is so cheap. The weather is good... I can't imagine they'll ever regret moving.'

'Good for them.' My dad sounds approving. 'It's a lot of house, isn't it? I do admire young people who give these things a go.'

'Well, I'm not so sure.' My mother sounds disgruntled. 'What about their families? And careers? And mortgages? They'll never get a foot on the housing ladder here, once they leave.'

'They'll have a tiny mortgage on the French house. But they'll have their own businesses, too. There are two gites and several acres of land.' I smile at Dad, glad to have him as an ally. 'And they're not planning to come back. It's so easy to travel – flights are really cheap. It will work out, Mum,' I say more gently. 'A lot of people find other ways to live. And they're good.'

* * *

Getting into my old bed, I remember the last time I slept here, nestled against the warmth of you. Waking on Christmas morning, when you gave me the necklace I haven't taken off, while I gave you the gift of a week at the eco-retreat.

The sounds and smells of my childhood home elicit more waves of nostalgia, a part of me soaking up the familiarity and comfort that at the same time are mildly claustrophobic. My parents have worked so hard for this, but it's their dream, not mine. And the part of me waking up is hungry for freedom.

* * *

Saying goodbye to my parents tugs at my heartstrings, not least because I don't know how long it will be before I'll see them again. On the train, I gaze blankly out of the window, the journey interrupted when my phone buzzes with a call. Gina's name flashes up on the screen, but I switch my phone off. Pushing any thoughts of her from my mind, I turn my focus back to the passing landscape.

As Ellie drives me to the airport, I'm quiet. 'You haven't said much. Did it go OK?' she asks at last.

'Mum still doesn't understand.' I shrug. 'But it could have been worse. My dad surprised me, though. He really gets what you and Jim are doing. I realised something about Mum, though. She always looks for reasons *why not* to do something. By the way, I haven't asked you what your mum and dad think about you and Jim moving away.'

'They're happy for us, but I think they'd rather we were nearer. I mean, one day, if there are grandchildren...'

My ears prick up. It's the first time she's mentioned having a family, but it isn't surprising. It's what you and I would have wanted, eventually.

Ellie goes on. 'I know I'd want them closer. But they'll only be a short flight away and there'll be plenty of room for them to stay. It will just be different.'

As I'm finding out, different isn't so bad. Before I leave, I want to tell Ellie what I've been thinking. 'Ell, I've been thinking about what to do next. You know Brad, the boy I've been tutoring? We went to an intensive pig farm. It was one of the worst things I've ever seen. But it's made me realise something. I have to find a way to add my voice to what Ben believed in – but in my own way. Maybe through teaching – or writing. That was your idea, by the way.' I look at her.

She's quiet for a moment. 'You know, not so long ago, I'd have tried to talk you out of it. I probably would have thought you were keeping his memory alive or something...' She pauses. 'But I think you should go for it. Live the life *you* want. It doesn't matter what anyone else thinks.'

'Thank you.' A sense of gratitude fills me. She's right, it doesn't – but Ellie's important to me and I want her to understand. As we reach the airport, she drops me outside.

Switching off the engine, she turns to look at me. 'I gave the estate agents my number – I thought it would be easier. But I'll keep you posted.'

'Thanks, Ell.' Getting out, I haul my case from the back of her car. It holds a few of the things I want to keep – my favourite linen sheets, some clothes, and safely cushioned in the midst of them, our wedding photo. Turning to Ellie, I hug her tight. 'Thank you. A million times. For everything you've done. You're the best friend in the whole world.'

'So are you.' She kisses me resoundingly on the cheek. 'Now go. Carry on your adventures!' When she goes on, her voice is quieter. 'You inspire me, Casey Cassidy. I think you always have, right from that first day in school.' She takes one of my hands. 'You're going to be OK, you do know that, don't you?' Her eyes search mine for a moment, before she smiles. 'You know, I can't wait to see what you do next.'

Astonished, my eyes fill with tears. I'd no idea she felt like that. Opening my mouth to say something, Ellie gets in first.

'Don't say anything! Look, I know you like leaving it to the last minute, but if you're going to catch that flight, you have to go!'

'OK.' She lets go of my hand. Picking up my bag, I start dragging my case towards the terminal building, as she calls after me.

'Love you!'

Turning, I take in her familiar smile, calling back, 'Ditto!' Then as I reach the terminal, I blow her a kiss as the electric doors open, before closing behind me. After dropping my case, I head towards security, suddenly remembering how not that long ago, I'd waved Ellie off to Morocco without me. I could never have imagined that I'd meet you that day, just as she wouldn't have had an inkling that a year later, she'd meet Jim.

But who are we to fathom the workings of the universe? The other side of security, I walk towards the departure gate, feeling lighter with each step. Knowing the house is on the market, a weight has lifted. As I board the plane, I know it's as Ellie said, I'm going to be OK. After it taxis out and takes off, and as England disappears beneath a blanket of cloud, another weight slowly falls away.

* * *

In Toulouse, Sylvie's waiting for me. On the way back, she surprises me. 'Your little ginger cat... You are right. She isn't well. She is a *she*, by the way. Marco's wife is a vet so I took her over there. She thinks it's an infection, so they're keeping her there for now.'

All I care about is that the cats are looked after. 'That's really nice of her.' It's starting to worry me what will happen to the cats when I leave here.

After Sylvie drops me home, I'm filled with relief, yet gripped by a new kind of restlessness. It's the sense that time is speeding up, that one by one the obstacles holding me back are falling away, the future inevitably drawing closer.

A text from Ellie a couple of days later only scatters my thoughts further. *There's been an offer.* Only a fraction under the asking price, I'm slightly shocked it's happened so quickly, but I accept it straight away. Then half an hour later, there's another text that astonishes me. From Kevin.

Hey, Cassidy, how r u doing? I'm swinging by your way. Thought I'd call in if you're not busy? X

I'm taken aback. Kevin? Here? Back in recluse mode in my kaftan and floral pyjama bottoms, a pile of maps on the kitchen table and pages of scribbled notes, it isn't the best time. I leave it until the evening to reply.

Hi Kev. This is a surprise. But sure. Pop by. X

Suddenly I think of the diary. Do I tell him I've guessed it's his? Undecided, I move it out of sight. Half an hour goes by, then I hear a motorbike speed up the lane, revving up then stopping just outside. Curtain-twitching, I watch the motorcyclist get off and pull off his helmet – definitely him. With his long fair hair, I'd know him anywhere.

42

BEFORE

October, last year

As the temperature dropped and the nights became mist-clad, I had the strangest sense I couldn't put my finger on. I was blissfully happy, but watching Ben learn more about the injustices in the world, there was no question I was being pulled in with him.

'I wish I could do something.' There was sadness in Ben's eyes as he looked at me.

'You are,' I said quietly. 'There's the film you and Jez are making – and you're talking about it so that people become more aware.'

He shook his head. 'It isn't enough.'

'I know.' I sat down next to him. 'But you're looking at a massive system, Ben – too massive for anything to change overnight. Take factory farming. There's a whole industry built around it. It makes money for a lot of powerful people. None of them want it to change.'

'I know.' A sigh came from him. 'And they're the problem. It's like the bloody politicians who manipulate the press – making sure we only see what they want us to see.' He paused for a moment. 'Haven't you noticed the way a story is headline news one day, only to disappear the next? It isn't because it's gone away. It's either been suppressed or something more shocking has superseded it, but nobody thinks about that.'

'Hey.' Hearing the anger in his voice, I took his hands. 'It isn't all bad. There are more people like us – as well as a generation growing up who care far more than ours does. I really think change is starting.'

He shook his head again. 'Nothing happens quickly enough.'

'I know.' I hated it as much as he did. 'But it's going to take time.'

That Ben's heart was heavy with the issues he felt so passionately about, only illuminated more sharply the magical moments we shared, moments that were uplit with a love that was endless and far-reaching. I knew life was full of contrasts. I understood too, that no single person could change the world.

I tried to remind him that for all that was wrong, there was much that was good, too. Human kindness and compassion were in abundance as far as I could see – as was the desire for a fairer, more just world. But he didn't, couldn't, see it that way.

43

October

It's the first time I've seen Kevin since leaving the UK. As he walks around to the back, I feel oddly awkward as I go to meet him. Hearing him knock, I hesitate before opening the door, thinking of that joke between us – a joke on my part at least – about him fancying me. 'Kevin?' Opening the door, I feign surprise. 'I had no idea you'd be here so soon.'

'So I see!' Glancing at my pyjama-bottoms-kaftan ensemble, he grins. 'Cool get-up, Cassidy!'

I shake my head, then take in his hair sticking out in odd directions. 'Great hairdo, Kev.' I stand back. 'I suppose I should ask you in.'

'That would be nice. And don't sound so reluctant. I come bearing gifts.' As he produces two bottles with a flourish, I'm suddenly pleased to see him.

'You should have given me some warning.' Before I close the door, the kitten scoots in.

'I tried. I guess you didn't get my message. Oh, wow. Who is this guy?'

Reaching down, I stroke its furry head. 'He seems to have decided he lives here. There's another two. One's staying at the vet's, the other's around, but he's really shy.'

'Collecting cats, eh?' Kevin looks amused. 'Does he have a name?'

I shake my head.

'You should think of one. This is a cute house.' Kevin gazes around the room. 'Don't you think?'

'It's grown on me – now I've got used to how quiet it is.'

'It wasn't always like that.' A smile slowly crosses his face. 'It's seen one or two parties in its time.'

'Can I get you some wine?' Suddenly I'm curious about him and Antigua.

'That'd be nice. Red, please.' He notices my half full glass. 'You've already started?'

Glancing at the clock, I find him a glass and pour him some wine. 'It's not exactly early.' I shrug. 'And when in France...' I gesture towards the sofas. 'Want a seat?'

'Thanks.'

Sitting on the floor in front of one of the sofas, I watch him peel off his leather jacket, before taking the glass I hand him. 'Cheers, Cassidy.'

'Cheers.' Raising my glass, I gulp a slug of wine.

He sits on the other sofa. 'So how are you doing?'

Even now, kindness does it every time. 'OK.' I swallow the lump in my throat. 'Up and down.'

He nods slowly. 'Hardly surprising, is it? I mean, you and Ben really were something. Everyone could see that... He was one of the good ones.'

'Yeah...' Everyone who met Ben had liked him. 'I've just been back to England to put our house on the market. Ellie helped me with everything – in fact, she and Jim are taking most of our stuff for their gites.'

He nods again. 'She told me. She also said you've accepted an offer.'

I look at him, surprised. 'You've seen her?'

He shakes his head. 'We speak now and then.' Then he adds, 'Mostly about you.'

'Me? Why?'

'We care, Cassidy. That's all. So, you're not going back to the UK. OK, so what's next?' He gestures towards the kitchen table. 'Is that what the maps are about?'

'Kind of. I'm looking for inspiration.'

'Found any?'

I shake my head. 'Not so far.'

'There's a Toltec word – *mitote*. Means fog in the mind.'

'What?' I frown at him.

'It comes from all the stories we tell ourselves – like about the person we think we should be. You know, like when you're a kid, it matters what your parents think of you; then as you get older, it's your friends who matter, then society, until before you know it, you have this life designed purely to fit with everyone else's expectations, which kind of works – except we lose track of who we really are, underneath. You have to get rid of all that. It fogs your mind. Stops you seeing clearly.'

I stare at him, because it's exactly how it is. 'You're right.'

'It's still there, Cassidy – the old you. Just swamped – by life and stuff that's happened to you. I don't know... A bit like a dragonfly larva at the bottom of a murky pond, if you can leave those muddy depths behind and burst through the surface, you'll be free.'

'You need wings for that, Kev.' There's a lump in my throat again as I top up my glass, then pass him the bottle. 'I'd offer you some food, but you didn't give me a lot of warning. Crisps? Some eggs? I think there's salad but it might be a bit old.'

'You're not exactly selling this.' He chuckles. 'Don't worry. I ate earlier.' He sips his wine. 'So how was it, going back to your old place?'

'Tricky.' I remember how I felt when I walked through the door. 'Too many memories. Like walking back into the wreckage of something.'

'I bet.' Kevin sounds sympathetic. 'Was never going to be easy, was it?'

'I guess not.' I pause. 'I couldn't have done it without Ellie.'

'She wouldn't have let you,' Kevin says gently. 'That's what friends do.'

'Yeah.' I look at him, thinking of the fledgling friendship that began between him and Ben. 'You and Ben, you got on well, didn't you?'

'Amazingly, yes.'

I frown. 'Why amazingly?'

He looks surprised. 'Well, we were very different people – he had his principles while, in comparison, I felt a bit hopeless, if I'm honest. But I admired him – and where he was coming from. We had this one conversation I can remember practically every word of. At that party, on New Year's Eve.'

My eyes fill with tears as I remember spending the evening at a party you hadn't felt like going to. You must have been feeling terrible. It had been a typical rowdy evening with my friends, and once or twice I'd noticed you in the background talking to Kevin.

'I was so selfish that night.' I shake my head. 'I knew he wasn't himself. We shouldn't have gone.'

'It was hardly your fault.' Kevin frowns. 'But I remember thinking something wasn't right. He seemed to want to talk, but at the same time, he was holding back... You know, I genuinely feel so bad, man. I should have taken him back outside and got it out of him.'

'Hang on a minute.' I feel my brows furrow. 'You said take him *back outside*. I didn't even know he was outside. One minute I was dancing with him, the next he was talking to you.'

Kevin's face was sober. 'I'd say he'd been out there for some time. When he came in, he was shivering. I made him a cup of coffee, and then we talked.'

Sitting up straighter, I put my glass down. 'I didn't know any of this. What about?'

He shrugged. 'To start with, he talked about the car accident.'

As it unfolded before your eyes, you'd been convinced your time was up. I remember the state of your car; how I couldn't believe you'd come out of it alive. 'Afterwards, death held no mystery for him. Those were his words.' I look at Kevin.

'Yeah.' Kevin's silent for a moment. 'Most of the time, we don't want to think about it, do we? Death? We're too scared.'

'Ben wasn't.' When you recovered, you'd been invigorated, as if it had reignited your sense of purpose. Now, I can't help wondering if it wasn't a coincidence that only a few weeks later, you were dead.

I think about that veil you described, between this world and the next, the one you were convinced you'd glimpsed through. Maybe it isn't my imagination and it exists. Maybe in the quieter moments, when my mind is still, you find more chinks in the veil, so that I can hear you.

'Anyway,' Kevin goes on, 'mostly he talked about you. He said how lucky he was.'

'You mean that?' I croak. 'You're not bullshitting me, Kev?'

'I'd never do that to you.' He shoots me a look of disbelief. 'We both know how he felt about you. He said he'd been going through a bad patch. Nothing to do with you guys... but he was sorting it out.'

What were you about to sort out? When you spoke to Kevin?

Suddenly my head is spinning. Did you already know you weren't going to be around? 'He'd been taking anti-depressants. But he didn't get on with them.' My voice is low.

'He told me.' Kevin's voice is quiet. 'He said he'd just stopped them. He said it was like they disconnected the most important part of him.'

'But that was the whole point,' I say agitatedly. 'It meant the drugs were actually working. His feelings were destroying him.'

Kevin just looks at me. 'They weren't, Casey.' It's the first time I can remember he hasn't called me Cassidy. 'Not the way Ben saw it.'

I start to sob. '*But he was alive.*'

* * *

I don't remember Kevin coming over and sitting next to me. Instead, it's like when Ellie was staying, my grief multiplied by the wine, by guilt from selling the house, that I hadn't helped you, hadn't tried hard enough to understand – because if I'd done either of those things, you'd still be here.

As my sobs peter out, Kevin's arm stays around my shoulders. At any time in the past, if you'd described this scenario, I would have laughed out loud. Me sitting on the floor with Kevin's arm around me? But I'm just grateful that someone cares enough to come here, to talk about you, to listen. 'I honestly believed he would have done anything for me. Not hurt me. Like this.' My voice is husky.

'Oh, Cassidy...' Kevin looks so sad. 'He never meant to hurt you. And he was thinking about you.'

'It doesn't feel like that.' My eyes fill with more tears.

'You've got it completely wrong. You were the most important person in the world to him.' Removing his arm, he picks up one of my hands. 'What he wanted more than anything was for you to be happy. All he could think about were the cares of this world. The way he saw it, his pain had become your pain.' He pauses, looking at me. 'It's true, isn't it?'

'I suppose it is.' My voice is quiet. As I'd watched you suffer, more and more, I'd been feeling what you were feeling.

'You know, I honestly think he was protecting you.' Kevin's voice is quiet. 'Ellie told me something I didn't know. About you losing your sister.'

I stare at him, shocked. 'When?'

'A couple of months ago. I'm not sure you know how worried she is. She said you'd been through enough when your sister died. I had no idea. I'm really sorry, Cassidy.'

'I don't talk about it. She was only twelve. She was hit by a car when she was walking to school. I should have been with her – but the morning it happened I wasn't. For years, I blamed myself.'

The silence is broken by the crackle of the fire. 'I can't imagine what it must have been like.' Kevin's quiet for a moment. 'I'm guessing losing Ben brings a lot of memories back.'

I nod, my eyes filling with tears again. He's right. I'd been so weighed down by guilt about Jenna, I'm not sure I ever really grieved. But I don't think grief goes, it just becomes a part of you, woven into the fabric of who you become.

He smiles sadly. 'We like to blame ourselves, don't we? It's like we believe we deserve to suffer. Us humans have an addiction to suffering, Cassidy. It's a habit – we stick with the familiar, however miserable it is. For most of us, it's easier than change.' Getting up, he picks up my glass. 'More red?'

'Thanks.' I watch him pour the wine, suddenly realising. 'You've lost someone, haven't you, Kev? Someone important?'

'We all lose people, Cassidy.' Passing me my glass, Kevin sits back on the sofa. 'It's kind of inevitable. I'd better not have too much. I have a motorbike out there.'

'There's a spare room – if you want to stay?'

'OK. That'll be the little room at the top of the stairs with the bats?'

Thinking of Ellie sleeping in that room, I stare at him in horror. 'Bats?'

'Sure!' He looks amused. 'This old house is just an extension of their living space. Thinking about it, I'm pretty sure they breed in the attic. 'Long-eared bats – tiny little creatures with delicate ears that look like petals,' he adds as my jaw drops open. 'Don't worry. If I remember rightly, there's a mesh over your window. Even if it's open, nothing can get in.'

Wondering how he knows about the mesh over the bedroom window, next thing, I'm imagining him and Antigua together. I drain my glass. 'So, my bedroom? You and Antigua...?' I raise a questioning eyebrow towards him.

'Bloody hell. Has that gone already?' Ignoring my question, he picks up the empty wine bottle, looking at it sadly. 'You're a terrible influence. I guess I'd better open us another.'

As he gets up to fetch the other bottle, I'm curious. 'Come on, Kev... There's something you're not telling me. Spill the beans. You've clearly been to this house a few times.'

Glancing towards me, he looks nonchalant. 'Once or twice.'

But I detect a slightly cagey note. 'So, what are Antigua's plans for it?'

'Not sure.' He looks thoughtful. 'It can take years to sell houses in rural France. Last time we talked about it, she wasn't fussed. That was why I asked her if you could have it.' He pauses. 'Have you decided how long you're going to stay?'

'A bit longer.' I frown, thinking. 'After that, I like the idea of moving nearer the sea.' As I speak, I glance at the tiny surfboard on Ellie's bracelet that I haven't taken off. 'I'm hoping the universe will reveal its plan for me at some point.' I joke, tongue in cheek. 'I guess I'll see.'

He refills my glass. 'You'll have to find a home for your kitten.'

'I guess I will.' My gaze drifts to the small body curled up next to me, as I feel a pang.

We carry on talking over a last glass of wine, and then both of us make our way upstairs. Lying in bed, I listen to Kevin clattering around in the spare room while I gaze through the open window at the crescent moon; liking the fact, that if only for tonight, the house has another heartbeat.

* * *

By the time I make it downstairs, Kevin already has coffee on the go. 'Morning.' He glances towards me. 'Hope you don't mind – I made myself at home. I fed the cats, too. The black one wasn't impressed, but the little guy is very cute.'

'He is.' I sit at the kitchen table. 'Did you sleep OK?'

'Blissfully. I'd forgotten how quiet it is here. Here.' He hands me a mug. 'So, how's the job going?'

I've forgotten I'd told him about it. 'It was really good. But Brad, the boy I was tutoring, is back at school in England now. He'd missed a lot of schoolwork, but he caught up really quickly.'

'Cool.' He looks impressed. 'There's something I've never said to you.' Sitting down, he looks hesitant. 'I didn't want to bring back what was a difficult time for you. But it's about the eulogy you gave at Ben's funeral. It was something else, Cassidy. I wanted you to know it's really stuck with me. I happen to know it's stuck with other people, too.'

I'm stunned. To hear him say this, is everything I'd been hoping for when I wrote it. 'Thank you.' I look at Kevin. 'It was the last thing I could do for Ben and it was so important to me.'

'You did him proud, no question.' Reaching across the table, he pats my hand.

'I wanted people to know what was important to him... but there's more I need to do.'

'Ah. This was what you mentioned before?'

I nod. 'I can't let it go. I want to make the facts more available. I've started researching intensive farming methods. I need to work out how I raise awareness.'

'Wow.' A look I can't read crosses his face. 'I wouldn't stress. The way this is going, it'll come to you.'

I look at him with surprise. 'I really hope so.'

He changes the subject. 'Have you seen that photo – at the bottom of the stairs?'

'You mean the woman?'

'Yeah. Her name is Florence Lenoir. She's Antigua's great aunt. Antigua's bent my ear for hours about this place. I know as much as she does.'

'Really? I was right, wasn't I? About you and Antigua?' I cock one of my eyebrows at him.

'Fuck, you're nosey, Cassidy. She's not my type.'

'Why?' I'm enjoying watching Kevin squirm.

'She's too blonde and skinny. Likes partying all night. Can we move on, please?'

It's on the tip of my tongue to ask him what his type is, but I think about the flippant comment at Suki's, about me being the girl he was going to marry. *Oh no, buster. It's way too soon. It will be way too soon for the rest of my life.* I hurriedly change the subject. 'So, what about Florence?'

He takes a slurp of his coffee. 'It's actually a really sad story. Her husband was a soldier in the Second World War. He and some colleagues were saved by a French farmer, who was murdered by the Nazis after someone tipped them off. I don't think Jack ever got over it. He came back here one last time. The farm where the Frenchman hid them was just a few miles from this house. But going back there tipped him over the edge and the poor guy shot himself.'

Chilled all of a sudden, I don't know what to say. 'And Florence?' I manage at last.

'She came over after he died. When Jack was buried in a local churchyard, I think she wanted to stay nearby. I believe she rented this house before eventually buying it. A couple of years later, she married again – to a Frenchman. She spent the rest of her life in France – not in this house, though. The guy she married had a farm near Auch.'

'So she left the house to Antigua?'

'Something like that.' Getting up, he stretches. 'Fancy going out? I'll show you the churchyard, if you like.'

I raise my eyebrows. 'You sure know how to show a girl a good time, Kev.' I think about it. 'Let me have a shower. Then you're on.'

When I come downstairs in jeans and the strappy T-shirt I bought in the market, the kitchen is tidy. Kevin looks at me. 'No kaftan today?'

I shake my head. 'Only for special occasions.'

'Gutted.' He shakes his head. 'Ready, Cassidy?'

When he suggests we take his bike, I pull on the helmet he gives me. It's a long time since I've been on the back of a bike and I've forgotten how exhilarating it is. Actually, I've forgotten how exhilarating feels, or the rush of air as we speed through it. Trusting Kevin knows where he's going as he tears along the lanes, I hold on for dear life.

Slowing down, he stops beside a pair of green gates set into an old stone wall where I pull off my helmet. Opening one of them, Kevin stands back to let me in. Closing it behind me, he nods in the direction of the narrow path. 'It's near the back.'

We walk past the elaborate graves inscribed with names and dates.

'They do it with style, don't they?' Kevin's voice breaks into my thoughts.

'They really do.' Everywhere I look, there are flowers.

At the far end, Kevin stops. 'Here's our man.'

I gaze at the letters etched into the stone. Jonathan Edwards Lenoir. 1921–1945.

'The French always include the mother's maiden name.' Kevin's voice is quiet. 'Jack was short for Jonathan.'

'It's so sad.' Not for the first time, I try to understand what drives someone to take their own life and, thinking of Florence, imagine her waiting for her husband to come home. 'Poor Florence.' I imagine how many times she must have stood where we're standing now; how she must have been feeling. 'Did she change her name when she remarried?'

'Yeah.' He nodded. 'To Blaise.'

I stare at it, silent. You have no grave. Nowhere to mark the fact that you ever existed in this world. Heartbroken, I hadn't told anyone what I was planning when I took your ashes to the top of the South Downs, casting them to a cold, north wind, letting nature decide your final resting place.

44

BEFORE

October, last year

I was in our kitchen creating another culinary masterpiece, my mind miles away, when Ben's face flashed up on my mobile.

I answered straight away. 'Hi, babe. Where are you?'

'Is that Mrs Summer?' The voice was unfamiliar.

'Yes.'

As he spoke, I felt my world turn on its head. 'It's Chichester Police. I'm calling about your husband. He's been in a road accident.'

Panic hit me. 'Where? Is he OK? Oh God, what happened?'

'His car was hit by a van. He's unconscious. He's being taken to Chichester hospital in an ambulance.'

'I'm on my way.' Without waiting for a reply, I hung up, turned off the oven, then grabbed my keys and ran outside.

The drive seemed to take forever. He'll be OK, I kept telling myself. He has to be OK. Almost hitting the car in front, I forced myself to concentrate, willing the traffic to move faster, until at last I turned into the hospital car park.

Abandoning my car, I ran into Accident and Emergency. 'You have my husband here. Benedict Summer. He's been brought in by ambulance.'

'I'll check for you.' The receptionist scrolled down the screen, then nodded. 'I'll find someone to take you to him.'

A minute later, a nurse walked towards me. 'Mrs Summer?'

'Yes. Where's Ben?'

'He's this way.' As she led me to the cubicle where Ben was, she filled me in. 'He has cuts and bruises to his head. He was unconscious when the ambulance arrived, but he's showing signs of coming round.'

My stomach lurched. 'Do you know what happened?'

'I'm afraid I don't.' She nodded to where Ben was.

In the cubicle, Ben was lying on a stretcher, his skin ashen, splattered with blood. 'Ben?' I whispered, gently taking his hand. 'It's me, babe. You've been in an accident – but you're going to be OK.' My heart missed a beat as I watched the slightest flicker of one of his eyelids. 'I'm here,' I tried to sound soothing. 'I'm not going anywhere without you.'

His lips moved slightly, as I thought I heard him try to say my name. 'A van,' he tried to say. 'Didn't stop...' His voice petered out.

'It's OK, babe. Don't try to talk. You're going to be OK.'

* * *

It wasn't long before he was wheeled away to have the glass removed from his face. While I waited, a police officer turned up.

'Mrs Summer? I wanted a word with your husband.'

'He's with the doctors.' I paused. 'Do you know what happened?'

'A witness said the van that hit his car had slowed down then suddenly veered and sped up again. The driver of the van was dead at the scene – it's possible he may have had a heart attack. But the witness said she didn't think there was anything your husband could have done.'

I felt sick. It could just as easily have been Ben who was killed.

'We will need to take a statement from him at some point.'

I nodded. 'Of course. He's only just coming round – he was unconscious when he was brought in. But I'll tell him.'

* * *

Ben was looking more alert when he was brought back sporting a rather impressive bandage.

'You're not going to be working for a while,' I said softly, taking his hands in mine. 'Nor am I. I'm going to stay at home and look after you.'

He attempted a smile that turned into a grimace. 'I'm sorry,' he tried to say.

'I don't think it was your fault, babe. The police were here just now. Seems some guy in a van drove straight into you... I'd better call your mum.'

I watched as he closed his eyes again, then getting up, I headed outside. After telling both our parents what had happened, I came back in to find Ben was asleep.

* * *

I wondered if the accident would mean his trip would be called off. But over the next couple of days, the speed of Ben's recovery astonished me, as did his memory of the accident.

'I wasn't driving particularly fast.' He frowned as he remembered. 'I'd noticed this van heading towards the main road. It slowed down at the junction, but just as I reached it, it accelerated again.'

Maybe it was the fact that he'd narrowly escaped death, but Ben seemed oddly animated. 'It was like it was in slow motion. I couldn't believe it was happening. I don't remember anything after that.'

'What were the chances?' I said slowly. A second sooner or later, Ben would have been unharmed. 'Of you being in front of him at that exact moment?'

'I know.' Ben was quiet. 'I've thought the same.' An odd look crossed his face. 'As it happened, it was like I was on the edge of crossing over. I saw this jagged line, Casey.' His eyes looked intently at me. 'It was up close, right across my field of vision. Then it seemed to open up. I could see light – and people. A couple of them came towards me. One of them held out a hand.' He broke off. 'I really think I glimpsed the other side.'

His words made me uneasy. That he'd come that close to dying had freaked me out. But conversely, in the days after, he seemed energised, filled with a burning desire to make the most of life. 'I was lucky, babe. But it's a sign, isn't it? I'm meant to be here. It wasn't my time.'

Fuelled by the courage of his own convictions, he was driven to another level, not just to fill his days but to make them worth something. 'It's like I know the value of time in a way I never did before,' he tried to explain.

I wondered if that was what a brush with death did to everyone, as very soon it became the new normal. Another side of Ben's multi-faceted personality, and in the strangest of ways, it was a gift to be reminded of how precious life is.

When he wasn't working, he was on social media, tweeting to raise awareness about the issues that meant so much to him – from refugee crises to climate change to animal welfare, lending his voice to speak for those who didn't have one. He was euphoric, as his number of Twitter followers kept growing – driven to a new extreme, unable to rest.

One night, I awoke to find the bed empty and Ben downstairs on the sofa, still typing away on his laptop. 'Hey, babe. It's the middle of the night.' Yawning, I leaned down and kissed him.

'It's amazing how many people are reading what I write. It just shows, doesn't it?' His eyes were bright. 'There are thousands of people, if not tens of thousands, who feel exactly like I do. Surely if we gather our numbers, we have to count for something?'

'Of course you must.' I was resolutely behind him. 'The world needs more people like you, babe. But don't overdo it. You've only just come out of hospital.'

He reached up for one of my hands, pulling me close enough to kiss me. 'You mustn't worry. Really. It's a long time since I've felt this good.'

I lingered. The same causes could leave him in a state of desperate torment. But he was clearly on a roll and eventually I went back to bed. The next morning, when I woke up, I could hear him singing in the shower. As he ate his breakfast, no one would have guessed he'd been up most of the night.

I kept watching for signs that anything was wrong, but narrowly avoiding death had injected Ben with a new lease of life. A cosmic miracle I didn't understand. My bright, optimistic warrior was ready to take on the world again.

45

AFTER

October

Still staring at Jack's grave, I feel Kevin's hand on my shoulder. 'The living need to eat. How about lunch, Cassidy?'

'Sure.' I pause, thinking of Sylvie's bar. 'I know just the place.'

'Where's that, then?'

'It's about ten minutes from the house if you go the back way from the supermarket – and there's a market there on Saturdays. I could probably direct you.'

He nods. 'I think I know it. I mean, it's not like there are many bars around here.'

Closing the gate behind us, we climb back onto Kevin's bike, zipping along more country lanes, as I enjoy the feeling of the air rushing past us.

As Sylvie's bar comes into view, Kevin slows down, then pulls in at the roadside. Slipping off, I take off my helmet, waiting as he does the same.

'Cassidy, this is a great little place.'

I glance towards the door. 'I know Sylvie quite well – she and her brother run it. Come on. I'll introduce you.'

Kevin links his arm through mine. 'This one's on me, by the way.' Reaching the door, he opens it. 'Whatcha going to drink?'

'Beer?'

As I walk in, behind the bar, Sylvie's face lights up. 'Casey! How are you?'

'I'm good! This is Kevin. His friend owns my house. Kevin, Sylvie.'

Glancing towards Kevin, her eyes sparkle with a question as I shake my head at her.

'*Enchantée.*' Taking her hand, Kevin kisses it theatrically.

'Ah.' Recognition dawns on her face. 'You've been here before, haven't you?'

'A couple of times.' Kevin looks surprised. 'I'd no idea I was so memorable.'

'We don't get many visitors.' Frowning slightly, Sylvie's still studying him. 'Now, drinks?'

'Two beers, please. Will you join us?'

'Maybe later, when this lot have gone.' She nods towards the tables of farmers. 'Have a seat. I'll bring them over.'

In no time, she brings our drinks over. 'There is moules or tarte moutarde-tomate today.' She looks at me. 'The tarte?'

'Great,' I say as Kevin nods. 'For both of us.'

'OK. Shouldn't be too long.'

'Thanks.' Opposite me, Kevin raises his glass. 'Cheers, Cassidy. Happy days.'

I look at him quizzically. 'Cheers.'

'There's nothing wrong with happy. You need to get your head around that.'

I give Kevin a look. 'I think we're done talking about me. You still haven't told me what you're doing in France. Where are you going when you leave here?'

'You're chucking me out already?' He pretends to look wounded. 'I'm planning to head south. I was going to hurtle up a few twisty mountain roads and take in some views to die for. Then spend the night somewhere in Catalonia, before heading for the coast. I'm planning on getting to Jávea at some point. But I may go to a few other places on the way.' He shrugs. 'Bit like you. I'll see... Jávea's a nice place. You should think about joining me.'

'Great you have plans, Kev. I'm not quite there yet but I'm going with the flow.' I eye him calmly. 'When the time is right, I'll just wake up one morning, stick a pin in a map, load up my car and be on my way.'

'I'm impressed, Cassidy.' Leaning back, he stretches his arms behind him, just as our food arrives with a serious platter of chips, which Kevin pushes towards me. 'You need some flesh on those bones.'

It's the best food I've eaten since my mum's roast when I was back in England. When our plates are empty, we order coffee and Sylvie joins us.

'The food was really good,' I tell her. 'Especially after a morning on the back of Kevin's bike. Whizzing around churchyards – he knows how to show a girl a good time.'

Seeing Sylvie's puzzled look, Kevin shakes his head. 'She's exaggerating. You must have noticed she does that. English humour. Right, Cassidy?'

'I really don't,' I tell her. 'Once he's gone, you must come over. I'll cook.'

'Yeah, she does a mean bowl of crisps,' Kevin winks at her. 'And you won't run out of wine.'

'Excuse me,' I glare at him. 'But I can cook.'

'I'd love to.' Sylvie's eyes flit between me and Kevin. 'Next week, I have Tuesday off?'

'It's a date.'

'You'll still be here?' She turns to Kevin.

'Nah. I'll be long gone by then.'

Sylvie opens her mouth to speak, but then her brother calls her away. After Kevin insists on paying the bill, we go outside. 'You need to be careful on that bike,' I say to him as he pulls his helmet on. 'I've been nearly run off the road at least twenty times since I got here. It's like the French have something against me.'

Instead of some funny aside, he looks serious. 'I very nearly came off on my way here, actually. Some idiot pulled out in front of me. I swerved just in time.' He's quiet for a moment. 'Makes you think. How quickly it can all be over. But I hardly need to tell you that.' He passes me my helmet. 'Come on. There's something you should see.'

I climb on the back of Kevin's bike, and we set off, this time along lanes I don't recognise that twist around hillsides, then through woodland. Eventually he pulls over in a wide layby and turns the engine off.

Getting off the bike, he takes off his helmet. 'OK, Cassidy. As views go, what d'you think?'

As I take off my helmet, I'm lost for words. It's an awesome view, of my mountains – the same mountains I see from the garden or Cap du Bosc, but clearer; close enough that I can make out the individual trees on the slopes, the layers of rock, the snowfall on the top of the tallest of them.

It's one of those moments in which I'm intensely aware that events out of my control have brought me to this place, where it feels like I'm standing on the edge of another world, of jagged peaks, pine forests, snow. It's the sense of scale, the possibilities of what lies beyond here, at the same time both humbling and breathtaking.

Eventually, I turn around to see that Kevin's still beside his bike, watching me. 'I have to go there,' I tell him.

'I had a feeling you'd like it.'

I hesitate, but only for a moment. Walking back, my mind has never been more sharply focused as I stop a few feet in front of him. 'What d'you think happens when we die, Kev?' I gaze at him. 'Do you think there are places in this world where the veil thins – between life here and whatever's next?'

His smile fades. 'Big questions, Cassidy. Who knows?' His eyes stay locked on mine. 'I'll tell you what I do think – that it's about far more than what most of us fill our shallow little lives with. Stuff happens and you ask yourself why, but all the time, life changes you. Take you.' He pauses, still looking at me. 'I mean, this last year has altered you, hasn't it? I'm sure in more ways than I can guess at, but I bet you anything, it's setting you up for something. What you said last night about going with the flow. It's what you should be doing, because I have a feeling it's taking you somewhere.'

'Thank you.' My voice is husky as I notice the curl of his eyelashes, eyes from which so much kindness radiates. 'For coming to see me. For bringing me here.'

He's silent for a moment. 'What are friends for?' He reaches for my hand. 'Come on. If you're ready, I'll take you home.'

* * *

We get back to the house, but Kevin doesn't come in. 'Time I was off.'

Suddenly needing to know about the diary, I blurt it out. 'Kev... One thing I wanted to ask you...'

As I speak, he stiffens. 'Yeah?'

'The diary, Kev.' I pause. 'Is it yours?'

For a moment, he doesn't speak. 'I had a feeling you were going to ask.' He pauses. 'Guilty as charged. My words Cassidy and you're the only person in the whole damn world to read them. So be kind.'

'It's interesting, Kev,' I say softly. 'It's making me think.'

He doesn't react. 'So where are you up to?'

'Julia's been to see you a couple of times. So has her husband. She's frightened of losing her children. What happened?'

Sadness flickers across his face. 'It's a really tragic story. It's all in there and I'll tell you about it – another time, over a bottle of wine, perhaps.'

'I'll hold you to that.'

He hesitates. 'I don't mind you reading it, by the way - though I'd appreciate you keeping it to yourself.'

'Of course. So...' I pause again. 'It didn't work out?'

'It's a little more complicated as you'll see if you keep reading. You are now the holder of my secrets, Cassidy.'

'You needn't worry. I won't tell.'

'I know you won't. You're one of a few people I trust. But I've gotta go.' He stands there a bit longer. 'So this is *au revoir*... Who knows? Maybe I'll see you across the border.'

'Maybe you will.' Reaching up, I kiss him on the cheek, my lips grazing the softness of his stubble.

Then he looks into my eyes. 'One of these days, you're going to find those wings,' he says quietly. 'I'm proud of you, Cassidy.' Then he hugs me tighter than he ever has, before gently pulling away. 'Don't think you're getting rid of me that easily. I'm going to be on your case, checking you're eating and keeping up the alcohol intake.'

'Thanks, Kev. For everything.'

'Entirely my pleasure.' The characteristic drawl is back as he fastens his jacket and pulls his helmet on.

'I'll be watching the mountains tonight,' I tell him. 'They're pink when the sun goes down. Wave to me?'

'I sure will.' On his bike, he blows a kiss with gloved hands.

'Watch out for lunatic drivers,' I call after him.

'You betcha.'

I watch as he turns his bike, revving it ridiculously before speeding away; staying to listen until the sound fades.

* * *

Evening closes in and the sunset paints the mountains cerise pink, just as I told Kevin it would. Blowing a kiss towards them, I go inside and pour a glass of wine. Then, out of curiosity, I get my phone and google Jávea. Kevin was right. On the coast, it sounds like my kind of place. As I stare at the photos, I remember a lazy weekend when you and I were first together. You'd looked Jávea up online.

Your voice is crystal clear. *There are loads of little coves and it has a vibe. I really like the sound of that.*

So where were you when Kevin was here, I demand.

I was giving you space. Don't change the subject. Go to Jávea, babe. You'll really like it.

Maybe I will. Visit the first place we'd planned to go to together – without you. And after that, I'll go wherever it is that comes next.

* * *

Autumn, the season of burnished leaves, the sweet scent of bonfires. As the apples fall from the trees and the wild birds gather numbers, my kitten becomes more attached to me, but as I read avidly, thirsty to learn more about the imprint of mankind on this world I feel my restlessness grow.

So move on.

Yeah, right. Help me out here, Ben, because I thought I was ready. What I don't understand is why I'm not.

46

BEFORE

November, last year

After his accident, we were blessed with the brightest days, mine and Ben's minds synched, love invigorating us, his life-force seemingly super-charged, our world filled with boundless possibilities.

Even in our quietest moments, life was blissful. As I educated myself about the world Ben cared so much about, I could feel us growing ever closer.

'You haven't done me any favours.' In our kitchen, Ellie was carefully painting her nails a shade of pale grey.

My first reaction was shock. What had I done now? 'What do you mean?'

Looking up at me briefly, she shrugged before turning back to her nails. 'You and Ben... Well, you're a bit of a hard act to follow. I mean, I used to be able to go on dates. Live in the moment... All that jazz...' Examining the nail she'd just painted, she frowned. 'But now... you want to know what I think?'

'What?' I looked at her suspiciously.

'There's no point – in dates, just for the sake of it.' She shrugged again. 'Unless I meet someone and feel the way you feel about Ben, it's not worth the effort.'

'Then I have saved you a whole lot of time, my friend.' Taking care to avoid her newly painted nails, I slid a glass of wine her way. 'Life is far too short for losers, Ell.'

She shook her head. 'I know all that, but it isn't so simple, is it? I mean, there are any number of Colin the bastards out there, who think nothing of cheating. I want to be with someone I trust.'

'Trust alone isn't enough, Ell,' I said more gently. 'And there are good men out there. You'll find him.'

'Yeah, right.' She started on the other hand. 'And I honestly like my life. It's just that sometime in the not-too-distant future, I'd like to have babies. And however old-fashioned it sounds, I'd like them to have a father.'

'It'll happen, Ell. You're too gorgeous and funny not to be swept off your feet by a lovely man.'

'I'm not talking about looks.' She frowned. 'It's that thing the two of you have. The thing that doesn't need words. Like you're telepathic or something... I've watched you read his mind, Casey Cassidy. Don't deny it.' She pulled a face at me. 'Anyway. I want that.'

She was right. There was this thing between us, as Ellie called it, that wasn't about looks; something that lay beneath – at soul level. It wasn't anything I'd ever believed in before, but since Ben and I had been together, I was thinking differently about a whole lot of things. There was the way I hadn't been looking, yet love had burst into my life at a time I'd been least expecting it. And it was good. So good that sometimes I had to pinch myself.

There was nothing I would have changed, other than maybe one day moving to a scaled-up version of the house we had then, maybe on a quieter street, but that was for the future, when hopefully we'd have had kids.

But now and then, Ben surprised me. 'If you didn't have to stay in the UK... If you had the choice of absolutely anywhere in the world, where would you want to live?' Slouched on the sofa cradling a mug of tea, he rested his size twelve feet on the coffee table.

Cross-legged on the floor next to the fire, I humoured him. 'That's easy. Somewhere hot, with a buzz, and very cool bars... And shops...' I tried to think. 'The French Riviera? Or southern Spain?'

Ben shook his head. 'Too many people. One day, you'll be craving peace and quiet. Empty space and a simpler life. You won't want to be surrounded by expats.' He paused, then added mischievously, 'I bet you. Even shopping will lose its gloss. You just wait!'

'No way, not ever.' I threw a cushion at him. 'So ridiculous, babe. Shopping is a bodily function – like breathing and drinking. But OK, smart arse. Seeing as you have it all worked out, give me some ideas.'

'Maybe Portugal,' he said thoughtfully. 'Far enough south, winters would be like spring in the UK, and summers would be heaven...' For a moment, he looked wistful. 'Or if we're talking literally anywhere, how about New Zealand? It's beautiful and unspoilt. As for the coast...'

Slightly alarmed, I frowned. I'd thought he was joking. Not once had we discussed moving to the other side of the world. If that was what he wanted, I wasn't at all sure how I felt about it. I was only marginally reassured as he went on. 'But if you're thinking about Spain, I'd want to check out Jávea.'

I shrugged. 'Never heard of it.'

But Ben was already scrolling through his phone. 'Here.' He held it out.

Reaching to take it, I stared at the photos of blue skies, a clear sea and glorious uncrowded beaches, behind which were tree-covered hills, bars and restaurants. But what about work? Our friends and family? I couldn't imagine leaving them and starting again. If that was what Ben wanted, we had a problem.

'There are loads of little coves.' I noticed a faraway expression in those gorgeous eyes. 'And one of the reviews says there's a vibe. I really like the sound of that.'

Too busy scrolling through the images, I didn't reply. The sea had a hold over Ben, I knew that. Eventually I handed it back to him. 'It looks amazing. We should go on holiday there.'

A holiday I could deal with. Watching him, I still wasn't sure how serious he was. For now, with our jobs and mortgage, it could only be a dream. But uncertainty rumbled inside me. If he was dead set on moving away, I wasn't at all sure where that left us.

47

AFTER

November

I remember that conversation; how back then, my idea of home was our cosy townhouse on a quiet street, working Monday to Friday like everyone else, spending weekends with our friends. Our lives safely contained within the bounds of convention.

But Kevin was right. This last year has changed me, because from where I am now, I don't want any of that.

So what do you want?

I think about what Kevin said, about *mitote* – how our thoughts are clouded by everything we're brought up to believe, the rules we live by, passed down through families, upheld by our schools, society, politics. For some people, they keep life ordered. But my mind is clear and the answer instantly comes to me.

I want freedom.

* * *

The world shifts again when Sylvie comes over. Picking a couple of late roses, I place them in a vase in the middle of the table, while I cook a vegetable curry with paratha and chutney, a recipe Ben used to like.

'So English,' she says dismissively, helping herself to a glass of wine.

'Actually, it's Indian, Sylvie,' I tell her. 'An authentic recipe from someone I used to work with.'

Unimpressed, she passes me a glass. 'I've been thinking about that friend of yours.'

'You mean Kevin?' Surprised, my mind whirls into overdrive. Does Sylvie fancy Kevin? 'What about him?'

'My brother recognised him – from the bar.'

'Really?' My ears prick up. 'Did your brother happen to say if he was with a glamorous hippie blonde girl?' It's the nearest I can get to describing Antigua.

'No. You see, that's the thing.' She shakes her head. 'Apparently he was with an old woman. He's no idea who she was – and around here, everyone knows everyone.'

'Maybe she happened to be visiting the same time Kevin was.' I shrug.

'Maybe.' Sylvie doesn't sound convinced. 'That man likes you – you do know that, don't you?'

'It's harmless flirting. We're just friends.'

'He wants to be more than friends,' Sylvie says matter-of-factly. 'Do you know, he watches you all the time?'

I hesitate. 'I like him, Sylvie. But that's all.'

She gestures dismissively. 'Anyway, never mind Kevin. I have news. I'm going away.'

Shocked, I put my glass down. 'Where? When? How long for?'

'So many questions.' She calmly sips her wine. 'It was after what you said – about going to Spain. I thought, why shouldn't I do the same? So, I'm going to fly to Malaga, hire a car and go exploring. Mountains, sea, maybe I'll look for a job. Who knows?'

'When are you leaving?' I'm slightly awed by her decisiveness.

'On Sunday.'

My jaw drops. 'That's so soon!'

'Five days.' Her eyes light up. 'It's enough time to pack. We must stay in touch. If you get to Spain, we can meet up.'

I imagine meeting up with Sylvie somewhere the winter sun shines, feeling a smile stretch across my face. 'We must do that.'

* * *

As I get into bed, I pick up Kevin's diary, intrigued to know what happened with Julia.

10th August

A day I'll never forget. The call from Julia's husband, asking if I'd seen her. Upset, she'd gone off in her car. If she turned up, he wanted me to keep her here.

A sense of foreboding filled me. From the way he spoke, I guessed they'd had a row. Julia was fragile right now and I knew her husband didn't get it. I tried to call her but she didn't answer. It was an hour later when her car pulled up. I waited for her at the door, watched her hurry towards me, the new hairstyle too harsh, the colour too bright for her skin tone.

Jittery, her voice was shaking as she told me she was going mad; that there were all these voices telling her what to do. Her life was a mess and she had no idea how to sort it.

I tried to get her to come in for a cup of tea, but tea was far from her mind. She was worried about her beautiful, strong, bright children – I remember her eyes as she said that. Her look of torment, because she truly believed she was screwing up their lives.

I tried to tell her things were never as bad as they seemed, but it was the worst thing I could have said. When I reached out and took her hand, she wrenched it away, telling me that if I believed that, I was just like her husband; that neither of us had the faintest idea what was happening to her.

Sobbing, she ran back to her car and got in. I should have gone after her, taken her keys, done anything I could just to stop her. But before I could, she'd driven away.

11 August

I didn't sleep last night. All I could think of was Julia's distress, how her world had imploded, how she'd turned to me, but I'd let her down.

After breakfast, I sat in the corner of the garden where the shade is dappled, among overgrown ferns and a cloud of tall white flowers. As I sat there, I watched a tiny butterfly flutter past, brilliant blue against the green, the seeds from dandelion clocks suspended in the air as though time had stopped. Then my mobile rang.

It was a number I didn't recognise, one of Julia's friends who knew about us. Yesterday, on her way home, Julia had spun her car and hit a tree. She was killed instantly.

Shock hits me. Poor Julia – and poor Kevin. My hunch was right. He knows how it feels to lose someone. Suddenly wanting to talk to him, I call him, but he doesn't pick up so I text him.

I'm so sorry about Julia. So sad, Kev. I wish I'd known xx

He texts back a few minutes later.

Thanks Cassidy, it was really sad, because I'll always believe I could have stopped her xx

I text him back.

Maybe you couldn't have, because sometimes, however much you want to, there's nothing you can do. X

After a few minutes, he responds with a single word.

Yeah x

Reading on, it's a window into Kevin's mind and what he's been through.

20th August
   I drank myself stupid for a week, until I felt so ill, I stopped. That was when I decided, no more of this. It isn't for me to resolve other people's problems. From now on, it's going to be as I planned when this year started. Just me in this quiet house – alone.

29th August
   I didn't go to the funeral, but I found out where Julia had been buried, then paid a visit to the churchyard at Sabaillan. Finding her grave, I laid a single red rose.
   Since being told of Julia's death, I've felt numb. Haven't known what to do. But the answer found me the way it does sometimes. You need to get away from here. A road trip. The Spanish coastline, Barcelona to Valencia, then Mojácar and the Alpujarras. Have an adventure.
   Weird where those words came from, but there's no point hanging around feeling sorry for myself. Life is too short for all that. Tomorrow, I'll empty the fridge and shut the house up again. My blood is up and the empty road is calling. The need for speed and the wind in my hair. For another adventure in another place

that doesn't remind me of Julia. Caution thrown to the wind. This is about escaping. Time for a new beginning...
   But hey, life's full of them.

I must have driven past the churchyard at Sabaillan a dozen times. I wish I'd known. A month lapses before the next entry.

29 September
   I've been away for the rest of the summer... Hidden my broken heart in laughter, beer, new friends, rowdy beach parties. Amazing what you can hide when no one knows you. Among strangers, I could be whoever I wanted to be. And it kind of worked. Enough that I decided I'd take this new persona with me. The guy who still smiles, jokes and drinks a little too much beer, whose heart is full of love and whose suffering has made him kinder; the same heart you'd never guess was laden with guilt.

I gaze at the words I've just read that describe the Kevin I know, the amiable, easy- going guy, who's been the same even after his heart had been broken. It's why he understood how I felt when I lost you, because he'd been there too. Aware of a movement by my feet, I glance down just as the kitten hops onto my lap, but instead of purring, it stares unblinking at me.

So, what about those ghosts of yours?

This time, your voice reaches into the deepest part of my mind, to the blocked out moments and buried hours.

They're going to hold you back until you let them go. Don't you think, maybe, it's time?

No. My instincts again. I'm still not ready. And this is my problem, because I'm not sure I ever will be.

48

December, last year

As December arrived, my excitement stepped up a notch as Ben and I bought a tree and decorated the house. Hanging coloured lights, I lit candles scented with cinnamon and pine, their fragrance infusing each room. I wanted our first Christmas together to be magical, creating more memories that, one day, we would tell our children about.

Towards the end of term, school was manic, with preparations for the nativity in full swing. After the challenge of organising an excitable crowd of seven-year-old shepherds to keep quiet in the wings before walking on stage at exactly the right moment, the star of the show was struggling to remember his lines.

I'd spent a long afternoon gently coaxing them out of him, and when I got back from work, Ben was already home. 'Hi, honey.' Kissing him, I went to the fridge for a bottle of wine. 'You won't believe how crazy today was. The shepherds kept getting their timing wrong and Joseph still doesn't know his lines. I've spent the entire afternoon practising with him

– and the play is tomorrow. I just hope he remembers...' Pausing to pour myself a glass of wine, without turning around, I asked him, 'Would you like a glass?'

'I've got one.'

Something in his voice made me freeze. Turning around, I took in the look on his face. It was a look I'd seen before. He had dark circles under his eyes that I would have sworn hadn't been there this morning. I felt myself go cold. 'What's happened, honey?'

For a moment, he didn't move. Then he clenched his hands together, a look of angst on his face. Suddenly I was frightened. This person in front of me was so far removed from the Ben I knew; it was like looking at a stranger. 'Talk to me, Ben,' I said gently, trying not to show my fear. 'I want to understand. It might help.'

But he shook his head. 'It won't. Nothing can.' There was a huskiness in his voice. Picking up his glass of wine, he downed it in one. Then as he turned to look at me, his eyes glittered with unshed tears. 'It's nothing new. Just the same as before, like in Cornwall.'

'You mean the pain?' I paused. 'Oh, Ben.'

For a moment, he didn't speak. 'It just gets worse.' His voice wavered. 'Everywhere you look, there's so much wrong, Casey. Look at climate change, factory farming, the destruction of the rainforests...' He started rattling off the list I'd heard so many times before. As I watched his thoughts run away with him, the look in his eyes was wretched. 'We're destroying this planet – and each other. And the worst part is people don't care.'

I wanted to hold him, but everything about him was rigid, unyielding. Staring at him, I couldn't understand why I wasn't moved to tears the way he was. 'You're right. It's a cruel world.' And it was, truly cruel, but I didn't – couldn't – feel it the way he did.

He paused, swallowing hard. 'It isn't just the suffering. It's the way we justify what we do. Every day of their lives, billions of farm animals suffer pain we deliberately inflict on them. And why?' He shook his head. 'Because people can get away with it and they don't bloody care.

Pigs are intelligent, like dogs are, but they get crammed into filthy, barren factories where the mothers are caged and the babies' tails are cut off. But guess what? We're told it's OK and people believe that. The dairy industry is every bit as bad. People don't know that newborn calves are wrenched from their mothers. We're talking about sentient beings who form bonds – yet they're treated as commodities, then spend their last moments in terror. As for slaughter being humane...' He shook his head again. *'Do you know how grotesque the use of that word is? I've looked it up. It means caring, kind, gentle, compassionate – when slaughter is none of those things. But people are blind to what's happening. They don't question. They simply believe the lies that get trotted out. While others...'* He seemed to slump in front of me. *'Same old. They don't care.'*

I agreed with everything he was saying. The global scale of animal abuse is a hideous reality of modern food production, but I agreed wholeheartedly with Ben. It didn't make it right. I watched the anguish on his face as he went on.

'What's it going to take for things to change? For the human race to start acting with compassion – towards each other and all living creatures? For kindness to overtake greed? For people to care.' When he looked at me, his eyes were empty. *'The answer is, I don't think it's ever going to happen. We have a society built on exploiting the vulnerable so that the rich get richer. Money is all they care about.'* He attempted a ghost of a smile that didn't fool me for an instant. *'Maybe it's worse because of all the Christmas stuff and the glut of materialism that takes everyone over. I don't know...'* A heavy sigh came from him.

Going over to him, I took his face in both of my hands. *'You're the most caring person I know, Ben. But you can't change the world – none of us can – not on our own.'* There was a churning feeling inside me, as I waited for a lighter aside to come from him, for him to put his arms around me, to say I know you're right, to ask what's for dinner; but there was none of that. Instead, he stood there, completely silent.

I frowned. *'Did something happen today?'*

Slowly he picked up his phone, then scrolled down his Twitter feed, wordlessly showing it to me.

As I scanned the tweets, revulsion filled me. Who were all these people slating him and writing such hateful responses? One in particular caught my eye, from someone who seemed hell-bent on hounding Ben. 'Just who is this @emma_path?' I was seething. 'Everything she tweets is pure garbage. Block her.' When Ben didn't respond, I went on. 'If you don't, I will.'

But he took his phone from me. 'There are others – people with closed minds who only care about themselves. And for as long as there are enough of them, there's no hope.'

'I'm going to tweet her.' Taking his phone back, my fingers were already on the keypad.

'Don't.' Ben's voice was low. 'People like her thrive on antagonism.'

'There are people who care, Ben. And their numbers are growing. More and more people are waking up. Look at the messages of support you get. The like-minded people you find.' But the likes of @emma_path had well and truly got to him.

I waited for it to pass, trying to shield him with love, but over the days that followed, the atmosphere in our home was leaden. I tried to be bright, defuse it with love, support, understanding – but I couldn't reach Ben. As my desperation reached a new level, I came up with the only suggestion I could think of. Even so, I hesitated before voicing it, unsure how he was going to react. 'Have you thought maybe you should talk to someone?'

A look of incredulity crossed his face. 'Jesus. You think I'm losing it, don't you?'

Seeing the strength of his reaction, I backtracked. 'You know me better than that, Ben.' I spoke gently. 'I'm really worried about you, babe. You haven't been yourself for some time. I was trying to think of a way of managing the effect this is having on you.'

'A pill is hardly going to fix what this is about.' His voice was tight. His words stung. 'That's not what I'm saying.'

I watched him try his hardest to rally himself, to put on the face he thought I wanted to see. But a barrier had come between us. As the Christmas bubble well and truly burst, I was more worried than I'd ever been.

It was a turning point in our relationship, as from that moment on, there were two of us wearing masks. Ben trying not to worry me, while I was trying to pretend that nothing had changed; that everything was the same as it had always been.

A couple of days passed, days he spent at home planning his trip for next year, while I worried about the time he was spending alone.

Running out of ideas, I called Jez. 'Ben's really low, Jez. I'm not trying to interfere, but do you think, maybe you could try to talk to him?'

'Sure.' Jez sounded hesitant. 'I'm not sure it'll help, Casey. Ben can be quite private – but I'll try.'

I never found out if they talked – Ben didn't say. But nothing was changing and when I tried again to gently ask him about the terrible pain that hung over him, he got narked.

'Casey, you're turning this into something it isn't. Things get on top of me, I've already told you. But it doesn't help you going on about it.'

This wasn't the Ben I was familiar with. Cold, distant, angry even, it was a side of him I hadn't seen before. But harder still was the way he was shutting me out. I reached for his hand. 'I just want to help you.'

'You can't.' His eyes were empty, his hand limp in mine. 'I just need everyone off my back and I need time – time to let it pass.'

'What if it's not that simple?' I said quietly. 'Maybe you need help, Ben.'

'Look, we've been through this.' He was starting to get angry. 'I need a wife, not a shrink. OK?' Then in his next breath, he said desperately, 'I'm so sorry, Case. I'd never deliberately hurt you.' His words were filled with angst. 'You mean the world to me. I'll sort this. I promise.'

I felt myself caving in. I never could resist the soulful depths of Ben's eyes. 'OK,' I said quietly. 'But please listen. You and I have something really special. I don't want us to fuck it up.'

My words at last seemed to reach him. 'We can't let that happen.' He hesitated briefly. 'I'll make an appointment to see the doctor.'

His arms went around me, pulling me against him, and as he kissed me, I closed my eyes, trying to ignore the way his body felt slack; that his kiss was dry. But it felt like he'd taken the first small step. I was hoping the GP would prescribe something. Either that, or reassure him it was just a blip. We all had days where it seemed the world was against us. And this was my kind, caring, sensitive Ben, I reminded myself, whose broad shoulders carried so much more than the rest of us.

* * *

True to his word, the following evening, he texted me to say he was going to see his GP. Even so, it was late by the time he made it home.

'How did it go?' In the kitchen, I was chopping vegetables for one of my off the wall curries that Ben liked, the smell of spices filling the room.

He shrugged. 'He's given me a prescription for anti-depressants.'

Poised to chop an onion, my hand froze in mid-air. Putting down the knife, I turned around. 'He thinks you're suffering from depression?'

'That's what he said.' Shrugging, he couldn't look at me. 'He's given me a low dose. I told him I'd rather try and get on top of this without them, but he persuaded me to give them a go.' He made no attempt to hide the resentment in his voice.

I'd heard enough about depression to know that it wasn't a matter of pulling yourself together and getting on with it. But surely a diagnosis was positive. At least he could understand why he was feeling so low. 'Have you got them?'

He held up a small packet. Opening it, he got out the leaflet inside, but as he started reading through it, he shook his head. 'I don't know about this.'

'What's worrying you?'

He looked troubled. 'There are side effects. And it's the whole thing about relying on pills. It's like admitting I'm not capable of dealing with things.'

I was silent. I couldn't say what I really thought, which was that Ben wasn't coping. Most likely he'd accuse me of not understanding, again. 'Did you tell the doctor that?'

'Yes.' He shrugged. 'He still said I should give them a go. They help some people.' Implying they are a waste of time for others.

'If you're one of the people they do work for, it could be good.' Surely it was better to try them, rather than carry on feeling so bad.

Ben tried to cut me off. 'Can we talk about something else?'

'I care, Ben. That's all.'

'I know. But please stop worrying. It doesn't help.' This time he spoke more gently, but there was still an edge to his voice. 'Really, babe. I've got this.'

* * *

I wanted so much to believe him. And for a while, it was as though I had the old Ben back, until just before Christmas, when he came back late from a meeting.

'I'm stopping the pills.' His voice was flat. 'All they do is knock me out and blur my vision.'

'Oh.' I felt my stomach lurch. 'Is there a different one you could try?'

'Honestly?' His eyes met mine. 'I don't want my feelings dumbed down. They're part of who I am. I'm going to see how I go without them for a bit.'

Alarm filled me. 'Is that wise? This pain you describe... It's been taking over your life.' It was affecting me, too, though I could hardly add that to his burden. 'I worry about you. All the time.'

'You don't understand.' Ben was rigid. 'No one can, unless they've felt like this.' Going to the fridge, he got out a beer and opened it.

'So, try explaining it to me.' Pulling out a chair, I sat down at the kitchen table.

I waited for him to refuse, but he came and sat down opposite me.

'What's so stupid is that right now, I should be the happiest I've been my entire life. I have you.' He picked up one of my hands, as his voice became husky. 'I have the job I wanted. We had an amazing wedding... We don't have money worries. We can afford to travel. We're so lucky – please don't think I don't know that.' He broke off, staring at the table. 'But instead of overflowing with joy, when I wake up, my body feels like an immoveable weight. Do you know how much effort it takes, just to get out of bed in the morning? It's like I'm swimming through glue, Case. Glue that's flowing in the opposite direction. It's exhausting... I suppose I feel everyone's better than me – and I'm worthless. That's how it seems. I can't laugh. I can't see the beauty in things.' His voice wavered. 'I'm stuck in this dark, dank, joyless, hole of a place without a light. And the worst bit,' he whispered, his eyes glittering, 'is that I can't see the way out of it.'

'Oh, Ben...' Reaching out, I gripped one of his hands as my heart twisted. 'It will change. I love you. We'll get through this.'

'Sometimes I don't think I will.' His jaw was clenched. 'I can't stop the pain.' His voice trembled. 'And I can't bear what it's doing to us.' His eyes were empty as they looked into mine. 'Inside...' He broke off. 'It's like I'm dying.'

As he spoke, fear filled me. I could see it in his eyes – the light switched off, the layers of exhaustion, anguish, pain. 'Was it like this in Cornwall?' I wanted to know.

He shook his head. 'Not quite.'

'If you don't want to take the pills, what next?' I was out of my depth.

'I give it time and hope I feel better.' He raised hollow eyes to look at mine. 'Like you said, let's hope it changes. It always has before.'

A frown flickered across my face. 'You've felt like this before?'

His cheeks were tinged with pink as he looked away. 'Not for a very long time – years. But it was never as bad as this. I thought it had stopped for good. Otherwise, I would have told you.'

Shock hit me, that when I thought we'd known everything about each other, all the time he'd been keeping this from me. 'I wish I'd known,' I said quietly.

He sighed. 'I thought about telling you. But when I met you, it seemed like life was beginning all over again. I wanted to believe it was behind me.'

And I could understand – but he still should have told me. 'Have you talked to your mum?'

'Look, I don't want anyone else to know. OK?' His voice was harsh. 'Even Mum. She'll only worry and keep asking how I am. She can't do anything.' He shook his head again. 'They're ups and downs, that's all. Everyone has them. Mine are just more extreme.'

'OK.' I was only agreeing so as not to upset him further. The strength of his reaction had rattled me. For the first time, I wasn't sure he was being entirely truthful. 'If it doesn't pass, what then?'

'We'll see, shall we?' The edge in his voice was back, warning me not to push him.

'I'm sorry,' I said quietly. 'I want to understand, Ben. I love you.' Getting up, I went over and kissed him gently. 'And what I want is for you to be happy. Whatever that takes.'

A frown crossed his face. 'You're on about me taking pills again.'

'I'm not,' I objected. 'But if you feel so bad, I don't understand why you're so against them.'

But he was already shutting me out. 'Like I said. You can't understand when you've never felt like this.' Getting up, his face was tight. 'I'll think about it. OK?' Turning around, he walked out.

* * *

I started reading about depression and its many manifestations; the lack of hope, the feelings of worthlessness Ben had described. I wanted a window into his world, but one thing I hadn't been prepared for was the distance that was springing up between us; how easily my words would be misconstrued, how if I said something too close to the bone, it became another brick in the wall growing up between us.

It was hard to watch his brilliant world of glittering horizons shrink alarmingly to one where everything was shrouded in darkness. But I wasn't giving up. Love wasn't about walking out at the first sign of a problem. I was with him for the long haul, at his side, no matter what. Determined that somehow, our love would bring the light back into his world.

49

AFTER

December

Those were the times I struggled most, when I felt I was letting you down, when all I wanted was to help you. You were right. I didn't understand. But we let each other down, Ben, because love should mean being honest with each other.

Pulled between the past and my future, I keep reading Kevin's diary.

2nd December

After months away, I eventually came back to the house, but I've already decided I won't stay long. Lighting the logs I'd left in the fireplace, I spent one last night here thinking about everything that happened this year.

Then I got out this diary. I'd given up on it after Julia died, but now that I'm back, there's a whole lot more stuff I want to write about.

So, I'm going to try to put it all down in words – what it means to live, to love, to lose someone; about how quickly our preconceptions of what life's about can be turned upside down. That whatever the bullshit we tell ourselves, there are no certainties, other than the unexpected and change. CHANGE. Writing it in capital letters – it might be uncomfortable, but it's inevitable, essential. It's how we grow as human beings, discover our potential, find our strength – plus without it, everything would forever stay the same. And that would be a pretty fucking boring waste of a life.

I will always remember you, Julia; I'll always adore you and wish we'd had a chance to see if we could have been more. But I will adore other women and love everything about them, too. And one day – I hope – one of them will love me back enough to want to be with me.

There's one more thing I've wanted to do. I bought a red rose plant to remind me of Julia. After digging a hole at the end of the terrace, I've planted it and watered it in, then stood there for a moment, conjuring her face. This one's for you, babe.

I'm going to put this notebook in the bookcase. Then after tidying the house, leaving it ready for the spring when I plan to come back next, I'll pick up my things and draw a line under us.

As I read it again, I feel something shift inside me. I know what I've been through has changed me. Putting the diary down, I think of the red rose Kevin planted for Julia. Since I've been here, I've watched buds grow, before slowly opening and flowering; the petals falling to the ground, withering and dying, before autumn's alchemy transforms them. Life and death in constant motion around us – in the passing of time, the changing seasons, in our hearts as others pass through our lives. Nothing stays still for any of us.

* * *

I take a trip to Sabaillan to drop a book in for Brad, one that Ben loved about our changing world. Finding the house in darkness, I leave it on the doorstep. On the way back, I stop at the churchyard. Small, surrounded by open fields, it doesn't take long to find Julia's grave.

Someone has recently left flowers in Christmas shades of red, near the headstone. But as I stare at it, a shiver runs down my spine.

Julia Mackenzie Stamford, loving mother of Hal and Brad. RIP

Kevin's friend Julia was Brad's mother. Poor Brad, and Hal, losing the mother who loved them so much. As I try to imagine the woman Kevin described as the mother of the teenage boy I've spent this summer time with, I can't believe I didn't know this.

* * *

Christmas looms – my first Christmas without you. Ellie and Jim have invited me to join theirs, but then Polly calls and tells me she's going back to Devon. The pull to see my sister irresistible, I plan to go home.

With the weather colder and the kitten spending most of the day in the house, I worry about leaving him alone over Christmas. But knowing he needs a long-term home, I have an idea.

After calling Nathalie, I drive to Cap du Bosc. Outside the house, one of the trees is illuminated with Christmas lights. I knock at the door, and Nathalie opens it straight away.

'Hi! Come in – I haven't told him. I thought you might like to surprise him.'

Inside, the house smells of cooking. Carrying the box I've brought with me, I knock on the door of the study. 'Brad? Can I come in?'

The door opens. 'Hey!' Brad's eyes are bright. 'I didn't know you were coming.'

'I wanted to surprise you! How was your term?'

'Really good.' His face lights up. 'My grades are up and my teachers are really pleased.'

'That's so great, Brad. Well done, you.' A plaintive meow comes from inside the box. 'For you.' I pass it to him. 'This little guy needs a home. Happy Christmas!'

Brad looks stunned. 'What about my dad?'

'Don't worry! Nathalie's checked it out with him. He's yours – if you want him?'

Slowly he opens the box. 'Oh wow,' Brad whispers. 'He's cute.'

'He is. And he needs a name. I did have one idea...'

'Yeah?'

'Yeah.' A smile flickers on my lips. 'I was thinking about calling him Kevin. But I think you should decide. I'm so glad you're having him. But actually, there's another reason I wanted to see you.'

As we sit on the sofa in the corner of the study, the kitten checks out Brad and explores his new home, and I tell Brad how his mother knew a friend of mine.

'She told my friend so many times how you and your brother were the most important people in the world to her. You were constantly on her mind – she used to talk about you both all the time. She never wanted to leave you. She loved you so much, Brad. I'm sure she would have wanted you to know that.'

I watch a solitary tear snake its way down Brad's cheek, before he turns to me, a look of gratitude in his eyes.

'Yeah. I know. But thank you.'

* * *

Last Christmas feels a lifetime away. I remember how each headline, each news story drove you harder, dragged you lower, fuelling your determination to fight the injustices you saw, letting them bleed you dry until there was nothing left of you.

If I'd known then what I've learned since... It wasn't pills you needed. It was rest, solace, stillness, a recharging of your soul, a shift in your vision. And as much time as it might have taken, be it weeks, months, years, for the world to reveal its beauty to you again.

* * *

Walking into the arrivals hall is like being blasted into a winter wonderland with a huge artificial Christmas tree and smiling people who've flown home for the festive season.

'Casey!' My mum's voice cuts across the background noise.

Glancing around I see my dad first, head and shoulders above most people. Hurrying towards them, I hug him. 'Hi, Dad.'

'Hi sweetheart. It's so good to see you.' His coat smells comfortingly familiar.

'Darling.' My mum kisses my cheek. 'You look far too thin.'

'Right.' Dad takes my case. 'Shall we go?'

We start walking, one of them on either side of me. 'Is Polly back yet?'

'No.' My mother sounds exasperated. 'She was supposed to be here yesterday but now she isn't coming until tomorrow.'

'Something about checking her house,' my dad says soothingly. 'She's flying in tomorrow morning.'

'I think it's more than that.' But instead of coming up with a conspiracy theory about Polly's absence, as we reach the car, my mum sighs huffily. Climbing into the back, I'm silently grateful that my sister's perceived misdemeanours have taken the heat off me – for now, at least. Leaning back, as my dad drives, I gaze out of the window at passing towns. Then as we turn into our road, I'm hit full on with nostalgia. Every house and garden are decorated; trees with coloured lights in driveways, windows lit with fairy lights. Last year, being so worried about you, it had passed me by. For a moment, I wish it was any other year – just not this one.

There are ghosts of Christmases past in my parents' house. As I sit in the kitchen while my mother cooks, she talks nonstop about the neighbours and the Christmas WI market where she's done most of her shopping, with the predictable dig here and there. *I don't suppose they have markets like that in France.*

Dad catches my eye, and I nod as he lifts up the bottle of wine, grateful for small alcoholic mercies. This time last year, you'd been heroically soldiering on, hiding the extent to which you were struggling.

Over supper, I'm aware of my dad glancing at me now and then. He doesn't say anything until my mother goes upstairs.

'You alright, love?' His voice is kind.

Tears prick my eyes as I force a smile. 'Too many ghosts, Dad.'

'I know.' A look of sadness crosses his face. 'I count my blessings, you know. That I have you and Polly.' As he says that, I know he's thinking of Jenna.

* * *

At breakfast in the morning, I persuade my parents to let me go to pick up Polly.

'That's a good idea, love,' my dad says. 'Isn't it?' He turns to my mother. 'It will be nice for the girls to have a bit of a catch-up.'

'Will it?' she says ungraciously. 'I suppose it will give me time to pop over to Marjorie's.'

The roads are busy as I drive to the airport. While I wait for my sister in the arrivals hall, I watch families greet their nearest and dearest, but wish with all my heart I was waiting for you. But then I see my sister. She comes over and hugs me tightly, my eyes filling with tears as I hug her back.

'Hey, are you OK?' She pulls away, looking concerned.

I nod. 'Just really pleased to see you.'

'Me too.' Wheeling her case towards the exit, Polly threads her arm through mine. 'How are they?'

'Mum has the hump because you're a day late. She's gone over to see Marjorie, whoever Marjorie is – no doubt to bend her ear about how unreliable her daughters are! You know what she's like!'

'She'll get over it,' Polly says airily. 'Once she has her cherubs back in the nest, she'll be fluffing around to her heart's content.' She pauses. 'There is plenty of booze, isn't there?'

'Some.' Last night, I did a quick reccy when our parents weren't watching. 'Probably not enough, though. Shall we go shopping?'

* * *

As Polly and I load a supermarket trolley with bottles of wine and other lovely Christmas drinks, I have a flashback to one of our sisterhood collusions – our parents are only moderate drinkers. 'Takes you back, doesn't it?' She grins wickedly. 'I'll hide some of it in my suitcase. We don't want to shock them.'

50

Christmas, last year

As Christmas drew closer, Ben's struggle grew harder. It was in the leaden movement of his limbs, his slumped body, his eyes. Seeing the cloud of hopelessness that weighed him down, I tried to lift it with my brightest smile that held double the wattage, kept my mood upbeat enough for two, defying his demons. If you walked into our home, there was the warmest of welcomes, the tastiest of food to share, bottles of wine waiting to be opened. Now and then, as the shadows left Ben's eyes, I told myself it was working.

But one evening, when he came in, he didn't have to tell me. It was in his face, the heaviness of his sigh, the tortured look in his eyes. Putting a small bag on the kitchen table, he stood there for a moment. 'I've been back to the doctor, babe. He's given me something else.'

Silent, I looked at him. The fact that he'd made an appointment without mentioning it, told me how worried he was. 'A different anti-depressant?' As he nodded, I tried to hide the anxiety rippling through me as I went over and hugged him. His arms were slack as they went around me. Pulling away, I looked at him sympathetically. 'Hopefully this time, they'll help.'

'Maybe.' Going over to the sink, he filled a glass with water, before opening the packet and taking the first pill. 'Here goes.'

My insides twisted with love for him. To watch him like this was heartbreaking.

I was there if he wanted to talk, but I knew if I asked too many questions, I'd push him away. All I could do was love him – and watch him – relief filling me as the shadows appeared to lift.

On Christmas Eve, we loaded up his car and drove to Devon. 'I'm so happy,' I said quietly as we turned onto the motorway, wanting him to know how special this felt. 'Christmas with you. But the best thing...' I hesitated, not wanting to lower the mood. 'Is you feeling better.'

He was silent for a moment. 'I'm OK. Not back to how I'd like to be. But OK.'

It was going to take time, I told myself, ignoring the sense of disquiet inside me. 'Can you imagine, one day, driving down here with our children in the back?' I was picturing Christmases of the future; their high-pitched voices chattering, laced with the excitement of childhood, as they jostled on the back seat.

'There's no rush, is there?' While Ben's voice was bright enough, it was the first time he'd shown any hesitation where children were concerned.

I was taken aback. But it wasn't the time for a confrontational conversation. I changed the subject. 'I hope you're ready for a feast. My mother will have cooked enough for twenty people.'

'How many of us are there?' He sounded mildly amused.

'Eight. Us, my parents, your parents, and my grandparents.' Ben had met my grandparents just the once, at our wedding. Polly was staying in New York.

As I swallowed the lump in my throat, my worries were still there. Polly and I were such different people and it was rare that I missed my sister, but in that moment, I'd have given anything for her to have been joining us.

* * *

It was a wonderful, family Christmas of the only kind I was familiar with: the tree decorated with the same baubles that Polly, Jenna and I had hung over the years with our chubby child fingers, the presents piled underneath, and my mother's endless buzzing around that she thrived on, as she prepared endless plates of Christmas food. But beyond all of that was the philosophy I'd grown up with. With a log fire burning in the grate, the house warm and welcoming, Christmas was about family – and love.

When I gave her the cake I'd set fire to, which Ben had rescued, my mother scrutinised it. He'd persuaded me we didn't need to make another, and covered in layers of marzipan and icing, you'd never have known. After making him swear on his life never to tell her, it looked as though we'd got away with it.

'I must say, that's really quite nice.' She didn't notice as Ben caught my eye and winked.

On Christmas morning, lying in my old bed, waiting for Ben to stir, I gazed around the room, taking in the familiar furniture, pictures and photos, feeling nostalgia wash over me.

Having racked my brains to think of a present for Ben, I'd accidentally stumbled across the perfect gift. After discovering an eco-retreat in southern Spain, I'd paid a donation which entitled him to spend a week there. Entailing working on the land, eating vegan food, the use of their electric bikes, it had leapt out at me as somewhere he'd be surrounded by like-minded people.

Beside me, Ben stirred, then, pulling me towards him, he kissed me. Then he reached down to the floor for something, and handed me a small present wrapped in sparkly paper, tied with a big shiny ribbon. 'Merry Christmas, babe.'

I kissed him. 'Merry Christmas.' I gazed into his eyes, still drowsy from sleep. 'Our first. I have something for you, too.' Reaching down under my side of the bed, I passed him the envelope.

'You go,' he murmured, nodding towards the present I was holding.

Carefully untying the bow, inside the paper was a small box. Opening it and seeing what was inside, I was stunned. 'Ben, it's beautiful.'

Carefully I lifted out the circular pendant within which the branches of a tree were set with tiny sparkling stones. 'I love it.' Sitting up, I put it on.

'It's the tree of life.' Ben spoke quietly. 'It symbolises connectedness – the roots with the earth, the branches with the sky... I'm so pleased you like it.'

I was blown away. It was beautiful, but I loved what it stood for, too. 'It's the most beautiful necklace I've ever worn.' My fingers still playing with it, I nodded towards the envelope. 'Your turn.'

I watched him open it, then slide out the voucher, a quizzical look on his face as he read it. 'There's a piece of paper in there that tells you more. And there's a website. I just thought...' I could feel emotion welling up inside me. 'I thought it would be your kind of thing, with your kind of people, who feel as passionately as you do about the environment.'

He unfolded the piece of paper and started reading. 'This is a great present!'

'I'm so glad you think so.' Putting my arms around him, I pulled him towards me, before kissing him. 'You, lover boy, are going to Sierra Nevada. Not the Californian one,' I added, seeing his look of confusion. 'The one in Spain.'

* * *

The rest of the day, I was aware that Ben was quiet. But no one else appeared to notice and for the most part, it was a happy, slightly chaotic Christmas Day holding all the components I'd grown up with – Christmas carols on the TV, canapés, food, then more food, accompanied by Dad jokes and my slightly dotty grandparents – as I realised that last Christmas, I hadn't even met Ben. It underlined how much could change in just a year.

On Boxing Day, we walked off our lunch on a hike across the Devon countryside, during which I pointed out to Ben all the landmarks that reminded me of my childhood. A lazy evening followed with board games and my dad's sloe gin, while my mother opened boxes of chocolates and served up a platter of cheese, and my Christmas cake. I thought about trying to talk to Gina about Ben, but I knew he wouldn't want me to. The next day, we headed for home.

51

AFTER

Christmas

It's Christmas Eve, and after our parents trundle off to bed, Polly and I crack open the contraband Baileys hidden in her suitcase.

'Cheers.' My sister chinks her glass against mine. 'God, I've forgotten how good this tastes.' Surveying me, she's quiet for a moment. 'So, how are you doing? Really?'

'OK. Trying not to think too much about this time last year.' My voice is flat. 'Being here brings it all back.'

'Of course,' she says quietly. 'So, how's France?'

'It's good.' Cradling my glass in both hands, I frown. 'I never planned to stay there this long.' I pause. 'But I've been using the time to read – about the subjects that Ben was passionate about.'

'Wow.' Polly looks shocked.

'I saw a pig farm, Poll – one of those huge, intensive ones. Since then, I've been educating myself about farming methods. There are so many organisations campaigning for change.' As I speak, my mind is whirring, ideas flooding into my head. 'All the time, more people are waking up to what's wrong in the world. They want change and I can write – press releases or web content – from anywhere.' I stare at my sister, knowing this could work. My next step has come to me effortlessly, as Kevin said it would.

'Fuck.' She looks uncertain.

But, as Ellie said a while ago, it doesn't matter what anyone else thinks. It's my life to choose what I do with it. Ben's legacy was for me as much as anyone else. I open my mouth to say more, but Polly gets there first.

'Go for it – that's what I say. Life is too fucking short not to follow your heart. No regrets about selling your place?'

I shake my head. 'Not one. Ellie's been amazing. She has most of our stuff in the place she and Jim have bought – in France.' I shake my head again. 'I don't even think about any of it. You know me, Poll. I was a supreme shopper back in the day. New dresses, shoes, lipsticks... skincare products, shampoos... Now I live in my pyjama bottoms and my moisturiser is coconut oil. I've hardly bought a thing since moving to France.'

My sister glances at the threadbare leggings I'm wearing. 'How about I take you shopping – in the sales?'

I'm not sure if I even want new clothes. Then I see the look on my sister's face. 'Thanks Poll. I guess some new pyjamas might be nice.'

'You know you're always welcome in New York.' Polly looks hopeful.

I shake my head. 'Thanks, Poll. But right now, I've got used to being on my own. And living in a really quiet place. I kind of like it.'

* * *

On Christmas morning, you're the first thought in my head as I wish I could slip through time's layers back to last year. I love you, Ben. I will always love you. My hands go to the tree of life necklace I've never taken off. Since losing you, it's taken on a whole new meaning, because as well as connectedness, it's symbolic of rebirth; a fresh start and growth – I've always wondered why you didn't tell me that.

Merry Christmas from the other side. Have a great day, babe. I love you, too. Necklace looks good by the way...

You sound happy, peaceful. Hearing my mum downstairs, already busy in the kitchen, the smells of cooking drifting up the stairs, I whisper to you.

I have a plan, babe. A good one. You'd be proud.

When I walk into the kitchen, my mum looks up from the pan she's stirring. 'Happy Christmas, darling! Did you sleep well? I've just boiled the kettle and there's a new packet of coffee in the larder. Now, you couldn't just stir the bread sauce for me, could you? I need to baste the turkey and put the potatoes on.'

As I take over the wooden spoon, without pausing for breath or waiting for answers, she's on to the next thing. 'The sprouts need peeling and I haven't made the cranberry sauce yet. Your father's lighting the fire. I've no idea if Polly's awake. You weren't late last night, were you?'

It's like we're teenagers again. 'No. She's probably still jet-lagged.' I take the pan off the heat, before reaching for the sprouts. 'I'll peel them, if you like.'

I tune out my mother's bright, mindless chatter, until Polly comes downstairs. 'Happy Christmas, y'all.' Coming over, she kisses us both. 'Bucks Fizz, anyone?'

'Please.' Ignoring my mother's huffs of disapproval, Polly manages to spike her orange juice while her back is turned, winking at me. I drink it quickly, then as Polly pours me another, my dad comes in.

'Bit like the old days, isn't it? My girls here together.' Coming over, he gives us both a hug, before looking at our glasses. 'Is there any for your old dad?' After Polly pours him a glass, he raises it. 'Happy Christmas.' His eyes linger on me. 'To all of us.'

I savour the familiarity of our time-honoured rituals and find comfort in the smallest of details; the same lace tablecloth that's come out for Sunday lunch ever since my childhood, the crystal glasses given to my parents as a wedding present, my mother heaping too much food onto our plates, Polly and me surreptitiously topping up our glasses.

'I will never move again,' Polly says theatrically, as we finish eating. 'Seriously. But thanks, Mum. It was a feast.'

'You haven't had that much.' Our mother tries to shovel more pudding onto Polly's plate, but my sister covers it with her hands.

'Mum! Stop.'

Afterwards, we share our presents the way we always have, in the sitting room where the log fire crackles in the grate. Mine are last-minute purchases from the duty-free shop in Toulouse Airport – perfume for my mother and Polly, a bottle of Irish whiskey for my dad.

'Not very exciting,' I apologise. 'There are no gift shops whatsoever where I live.'

Instead of the usual pile of presents, my dad hands Polly and me an envelope each. 'Your mother and I...' He glances at Mum. 'Well, what with both of us not getting any younger and you both flying back to your respective homes, we thought it was the right time to give you this.'

As Polly and I open them, our eyes meet. They are cheques for huge amounts of money. 'Dad?' I look at him quizzically.

'It's not earning any interest and it'll be yours one day anyway,' he says firmly. 'We thought it made more sense for you to have it now.'

* * *

With our parents in bed, as we start on the Baileys again, my phone
buzzes with a text.

Yo, Cassidy. Greetings of the season. Found those wings yet? Hope
you're having a happy day xx

'Kevin,' I say to Polly, as I text him back.

Cheers Kev, Merry Christmas to you too, wherever you are xx

One of her eyebrows lifts. 'Not Kevin who fancies the arse off
you?'

'The same one.' I pause. 'He came to see me a couple of months
ago. He behaved impeccably,' I say warningly. 'He's a really good
friend.'

'Hmm.' Polly looks suspicious. Then she changes the subject.
'Those cheques, sis... It's a lot of money, isn't it? I mean, they might
need it for care, later on.' She frowns. 'You don't think there's something they're not telling us?'

I shake my head. 'I don't think so. I imagine they think they have
enough put away. And no question, it will be useful.' Though for
what exactly, I'm not sure. 'I suppose you get to a point where you
realise none of us go on forever.'

My sister looks at me sharply.

'It's true, isn't it?' I look at her. 'I mean, don't we know that better
than most people? There are no certainties, Poll. Not beyond today.
That's all any of us ever have.' I pause. 'Dad said something before
you got here. He said he counted his blessings that he had the two
of us. I know he was thinking of Jenna.'

'He said that?' But like my parents, Polly doesn't talk about

Jenna. Shaking her head, she glances at our sister's photo, before switching on the TV and settling on a Vic and Bob Christmas Special. In no time, both of us are laughing uncontrollably as I realise it's the first time in almost a year that I haven't felt guilty for enjoying myself.

* * *

I've survived, I tell myself as I lie in bed. I hope you're proud of me.

You have no idea how proud. Your voice is warm. *You should be proud, too. You're one amazing woman, Casey Cassidy.*

Me? The thought brings me up short. Amazing? I don't think so. Maybe it's the Baileys taking effect, but as I close my eyes, I could swear I feel your hand stroking my hair off my face, your lips brushing lightly against mine. Hear your voice again.

You always have been. About time you started believing it.

* * *

After Boxing Day, my restlessness returns as, with Christmas over, my mother seems more determined than ever to pin me down, pushing me to the point I've had enough. Waiting until Dad and Polly pop to the shops, I go to find her. In the kitchen, she's busy preparing yet another meal.

'Mum? Can we talk? I mean, really talk?'

Turning to look at me, she frowns. 'What about?'

'Us,' I say gently. 'Well, me. Can we sit down?'

Looking reluctant, she pulls out one of the chairs at the kitchen table.

I sit down opposite. 'It's just that I get the feeling that whatever I do, it's wrong.' And at twenty-nine, it shouldn't bother me. But it does.

For a moment she doesn't speak. 'If you really want to know, I suppose I'm cross.' Then it all pours out of her. 'Actually, I'm furious.' When she looks at me, I'm shocked to see tears in her eyes. I can count the number of times I've seen my mother cry over the years, on the fingers of one hand. 'What he did to you, Casey. It's ruined everything. You've lost your home, your job; your whole life has fallen apart...'

'Hey, wait up, Mum. I didn't *lose* any of those things. I made choices. I gave them up. The only one I lost was Ben.'

'Well, that was bloody selfish of him,' she snaps. 'Just when everything was so lovely. You would have had children together. Your own perfect little family.' Her voice wobbles. 'All those things that will never happen... because of what he did.'

Part of me is furious with her for calling you selfish. But it's because she doesn't understand. And she feels cheated, too – of the son-in-law she loved, the grandchildren she would have been besotted with.

'Mum. Listen. I felt like that – at the start. But Ben wasn't selfish. He was in pain – every bit as much as someone dying from cancer or having a heart attack. Physical pain, that racked him every hour of every day... There was only one way to make it stop.'

'He seemed fine last Christmas.' She sounded hurt.

'Well, that shows you.' My voice shaking, I fold my arms. 'Just how much he was hiding. From all of us.' Including me, because even I hadn't realised how bad it was.

Wiping her face, Mum goes on, 'I wanted so much for you. You've always been so bright – and clever, even when you were little. I was so proud of you. I still am...' She breaks off, tearful again. 'So proud...'

Her words startle me. She's never said anything like this before. 'I didn't know.'

'And now you've lost everything...' As I watch my mother dissolve into tears, I take in the lines age has drawn on her skin, grief etching them deeper, and for a moment glimpse the world through her eyes. Knowing what she's put into her family – Dad, Polly, me, Jenna before we lost her – I suddenly realise, we are her life.

Leaning forward, I take her hands. 'Mum. I'm OK. I really am. I have you and Dad. And Polly and Ellie. Sylvie in France. My friends.' Only as I'm speaking do I appreciate it's true; that even without you, my life is rich beyond words, but I've been too absorbed by my grief to see that. 'I've never thanked you,' I swallow before I go on. 'For everything you've done for us. You and Dad – you've given us so much.'

For a moment, our eyes meet, only this time her guard is down and it's as equals, not as sparring partners. 'You and Polly are the most important thing in my life.' Her voice wavers as reaching across the table, she takes one of my hands.

'Mum?' I say softly. 'I know we don't talk about her, but I think I know how hard it is for you, since we lost Jenna.' As I say my sister's name, my voice wobbles.

For a moment, another tear glistens in one of her eyes. 'I think about her every day,' she whispers.

'So do I.' I swallow. 'I blame myself, Mum. I should have been there.'

My mother looks shocked. 'Oh Casey... If anyone's to blame, it was me. I was her mother.' She shakes her head sadly. 'I've thought so many times, that if you had been there that day, I might have lost both of you. But I still have you.' Tears roll down her cheeks, her hands tightening around mine. 'And Polly.'

I'm silent for a moment, my emotions threatening to overwhelm me. 'I thought I'd go to the churchyard before I leave. I wondered... Could we maybe go together?'

I watch her rustle the same superhuman strength that's got her through the years since Jenna died, as she pins on a glimmer of a smile. 'I'd like that.' But it's replaced by an anxious look. 'Are you sure you really are all right? I've been so frightened, Casey. I thought you might not want to be here. That you might decide you'd rather be with Ben.'

It's why she's been on at me about moving back. Worried, she's wanted to keep an eye on me. 'You know...' I lower my voice. 'For a while – I won't lie – I did think about it. But I'm not Ben. I want to live my life. It's been a horrible, difficult, bewildering year, but it's like Polly said a while back, us Cassidys are tough.' I blink through my tears. 'And it's all part of life, isn't it?' As I watch my mother, I know it's true. Unless you know how pain feels, you have nothing to illuminate those glorious, sky-soaring moments of happiness.

Sniffing into a tissue, she shakes her head. 'I'm so sorry about that business with Lesley Williams. I felt so stupid. Of course, after you said, I remembered how horrid she was at school. I bumped into her again – just before Christmas. She asked about you.' Raising her eyes to look at mine, there's a look of defiance in them. 'I actually told her to mind her own business! Then I said, Happy Christmas Lesley.' She giggles. 'I was quite proud of myself.'

My eyes widen in shock. Then imagining the look on Lesley Williams' face, I burst out laughing.

She gets up. 'I've a rather nice bottle of champagne in the fridge. I've been saving it for a special occasion. I rather think that might be now...' Then she hesitates. 'I know I don't say it very often. But I love you, Casey.'

It's one of those moments my overflowing heart comes close to bursting. 'I love you too, Mum.'

* * *

The following day, for the first time since Jenna died, the four of us walk to the church together. The roads are quiet, the grass frost-coated, our breath freezing in small clouds as we leave a posy of winter flowers on my sister's grave.

With Christmas over, my family – my wingmen, I've realised, just as you were – take me to the airport, and wave as I disappear through security. Leaving them is hard, but I have the strangest sense I'm coming to a defining moment in my life. One I need to spend alone.

52

BEFORE

New Year's Eve, last year

When New Year's Eve came, I went through my usual ritual of trying on half a dozen dresses, only this year I had Ben to parade in front of, waiting for him to say 'That one', as I watched his eyes light up. But lying on the sofa, he was lost in a book his mum had given him for Christmas, about the state of the planet.

That afternoon, as I stood in front of him in a tight red number with my hair scrunched up in what looked like a giant messy pineapple, he was so engrossed in the book, he didn't notice me. 'We don't have to go tonight.'

'Tonight?' He looked up, his eyes briefly skimming my dress before returning to his book. 'Oh. The party.'

In the past, Ben's eyes would have lingered, before he made a comment about how hot I looked. My feeling of excitement drained away. 'We can have a quiet one, babe. I really don't mind staying in.'

He was silent for a moment. 'No, it's OK. We can go.'

It was obvious his heart wasn't in it, but I couldn't help thinking that maybe it would do him good to have a change of scene, a few drinks, a bit of a laugh with friends. Going back upstairs, I carried on getting ready. When I came down to get a glass of wine, Ben was in the kitchen. Going over to the cupboard, I got out a couple of glasses. 'I was going to open a bottle. Would you like some?'

'No thanks.' He paused, looking slightly awkward. 'Casey? There's something I need to tell you.'

I felt myself freeze.

'I've stopped taking the pills.' He didn't look at me. 'They've been making me dizzy.'

'Oh.' I put the glasses down. 'That's not good. When did you stop?'

'A couple of days ago.' He shrugged. 'But I'm feeling OK.'

Wondering why he'd waited till now to tell me, I tried to quell my feeling of panic. Without medication, it was only a matter of time before the darkness consumed him again. 'Has the dizziness stopped?'

'It's better than it was. I'm going to close my eyes for a bit. I'm tired and it isn't helping.' He headed back to the sitting room.

Following him, I watched him lie back on the sofa. 'I'll get you a pillow.' Going upstairs, I came back down with one from our bedroom, arranging it behind Ben's head before closing the curtains, then leaning down to kiss him.

A couple of hours later, I'd painted my nails, before doing my makeup, although it was still in my mind to cancel if Ben didn't feel like going out. But then I heard his footsteps as he came up the stairs, then into our bedroom.

I looked at him anxiously. The dark circles under his eyes were back. 'Did you manage to sleep, babe?'

'A little.' His eyes lingered. 'You look gorgeous.'

'Thank you.' I gave him a twirl that was half-hearted. 'Listen...' I paused. 'I meant it about staying at home. We can see in the New Year here, just the two of us.'

He shook his head. 'It'll be good to see everyone. I'll just have a quick shower.'

As he went into the bathroom, I was still in two minds. If he wasn't feeling well, I knew the effort it took to hide it. But after a shower, he seemed brighter. Pulling on a new shirt and clean jeans, before rough drying his hair, he turned to me. 'Will I do?'

'Gorgeous.' Reaching up, I kissed him.

* * *

Suki's house was Christmassy, the music lively, the atmosphere sparking with the anticipation of another year starting. I watched Ben closely and as the night went on, he appeared to be enjoying himself. But after dancing with me, then briefly with Ellie, when I next looked around, he'd disappeared.

53

New Year's Eve

The contrast with last New Year's Eve couldn't be more marked. Instead of a rowdy, booze-fuelled party, I sit outside wrapped in a blanket, with a bottle of wine, gazing at the stars, contemplating the meaning of the universe.

Last year, I could never have imagined I'd be spending the biggest night of the year on my own. But in the chilly air, under an inky black sky dotted with stars, I'm oddly calm.

It's the end of the worst year of my entire life. A year I've fought, battled, kicked my way through, cried buckets, and drunk too much wine, but I've come out stronger, hopefully wiser. More important, I've survived.

Close to midnight, Ellie texts me.

Happy New Year! Love you Casey xxx

I text her back. *Ditto,* followed by a line of hearts.

There's a text from Sylvie.

Hola Casey! Feliz año nuevo! See you soon! X

Happy New Year Sylvie! France isn't the same without you! x

It's true. It doesn't matter where you are, it's about the people in your life.

Then there's one from Kevin.

Hey Cassidy, Happy New Year. Hope wherever you are, it's going to be a good one xx

I smile to myself.

I'm sitting on the terrace watching the stars. Happy New Year dude. Where are you? xx

He comes straight back.

In a bar in Spain. Made your mind up where you're headed next?

I pause before replying.

Not yet, but watch this space.

When eventually I go inside, it's half past midnight, meaning I've missed the momentous passing of one year and the start of a new one. But it makes no difference. Each sunrise brings a new day, a fresh start. One year ago, it was all I'd wanted, for both of us. I'd had no idea it wasn't to be.

54

January, last year

Breathless, I'd come running in from my car to beat the rain that had just started.

Dropping my bag on the floor, I took off my jacket, hanging it just inside the front door, slipping off my shoes before heading for the kitchen. 'Ben, honey?'

I hadn't noticed his car, but from his jacket slung over one of the chairs in the kitchen, he'd clearly got home before me. I imagined him upstairs, earphones in, plugged into a current affairs programme on climate change or the crisis in the Yemen. Filling the kettle, my eyes settled on a vase of deep red roses on the table as I smiled to myself. It was the kind of thoughtful, spontaneous gesture that was typical of Ben.

In the sitting room, the Christmas tree was starting to drop its needles. In a couple of days, we'd be taking it down, putting the decorations away for next year. I wondered where we'd be by then? In this house, or somewhere bigger, maybe even with a baby... Going through to the bottom of the stairs, I called up to him again. 'Ben? Would you like some tea?'

Guessing he'd fallen asleep, I made two cups of tea, then took them upstairs. Our bedroom was in darkness as I pushed the door open, Ben's outline just about distinguishable. 'Honey, are you awake?' I whispered, putting down the mugs and switching on the lamp on the bedside table.

Sitting on the bed, as I reached over and touched Ben's arm, it was as though I'd been electric-shocked. Something was terribly wrong. My heart crashing, I stumbled round to the other side of the bed. His eyes closed; he was completely still.

'Ben.' I shook him, terrified. 'BEN, wake up. Wake up. Wake up. Please...' When he didn't respond, I shook him again. 'Ben... open your eyes. Open your eyes... Wake up.' Automatically I jabbed a finger against his neck where I thought his pulse was, before tearing downstairs and grabbing my phone. Dialling 999, I was already running back upstairs again. 'Ambulance.' Seconds that seemed interminable while I waited. 'It's my husband. I can't wake him. I think he may have had a heart attack. Please, please hurry... 24 Cherry Tree Drive, Midhurst.' I gabbled the postcode. 'Please be quick.'

My hand was shaking as I placed it against his skin. Skin that was already losing the familiar warmth of him. In desperation I tugged the pillows from under his head and started CPR. Counting the chest compressions, I stopped after ten to see if he was breathing. Then taking a deep breath, blowing into his mouth, I started compressions again. I was still doing them ten minutes later when the ambulance came.

When the doorbell rang, my legs were shaky as I flew downstairs to let the paramedics in, frantically hurrying back up again before they'd even closed the door behind them. At the top, I waited, wishing they'd move faster. 'Hurry. Please... He's in here.' I pointed towards our bedroom. 'I've been trying to resuscitate him.'

With the paramedics standing over him, our bedroom seemed crowded. As one of them took his pulse, I was beside myself. 'He was fine this morning.' My voice was shaking. 'Please do something.' But my words *were futile because I already knew. There wasn't anything they could do. It was too late.*

'How long has he been like this?'

Beside our bed, I glanced at their faces. 'He was like this when I found him.' My voice was shaky.

Glancing at her colleague, the woman looked at me. 'How long ago?'

'When I came in about half an hour ago.' I shook my head. It didn't seem possible that only half an hour had passed.

'I'm so sorry.' Her eyes were filled with sympathy.

As my body tightened to breaking point, tears flooded my eyes, my mind refusing to take in a reality I wasn't – and never would be – prepared for.

* * *

After Ben's death, days passed in a blur. Flowers started arriving, followed by dozens of cards, while life revolved around planning his funeral. While Ben's parents took care of most things, only two aspects preoccupied me; the deep red roses I wanted on his coffin, because they were the flowers he'd so often bought me, and the words I wanted to speak.

It was the opportunity for Ben's voice to be heard for one last time that kept me going. I wanted to make people understand what it meant to care as much as he had. To realise how much destruction humankind is wreaking on this world. Toiling over a notepad, I tried to find the right words. Ben's words. It would be another matter for me to stand up on the day and read them.

'It's too much.' Ellie looked worried. 'I mean, of course you should write it. But why don't you ask your dad if he'll read it for you?'

I shook my head. 'It feels like the last thing I can do for Ben. It probably sounds silly…' I broke off, my emotions getting the better of me.

'It isn't silly.' Coming over, Ellie hugged me. 'It's going to be an emotional day. I'm only thinking of what you'll be going through.'

'I'm tough.' I managed a faint smile. 'I'll have a plan B. Don't worry, Ell.'

I'd thought about asking someone like Kevin to step in, or Jez, but then the day of the funeral was here. A day that was frozen, frost covering the grass, every twig of every tree as if dusted in icing sugar. Wearing the red coat Ben had loved, over a plain black dress, my unruly hair tamed for once, my makeup minimal, I summoned my strength.

Outside the church, I waited for Ben's coffin to arrive, adding a single red rose to the bouquet on top of it, following, numb, as it was carried inside.

The church was packed and when the time came, as I walked out in front of everyone, you could have heard a pin drop. As I stood there, my nerves were on edge before I told myself what I knew I would tell myself many times over, in the weeks and months to come. When the worst had already happened, I could do this.

'Ben loved this world.' Hearing my voice waver, I took a deep breath. 'The landscape, the people, the possibilities it held.' Lifting my gaze, I looked at the sea of faces, knowing this was my chance to reach them. 'But what he couldn't bear was the suffering. Once you'd seen it, you couldn't un-see it, he used to say. Global warming and climate change are issues he felt passionate about, as are pollution and our abuse of animals in factory farms. He couldn't bear the arrogance of the wealthy and power-ful, or their sense of entitlement.

'But it was about far more than that. What hurt him most was the scale of suffering; the billions of animals intensively, cruelly farmed in the name of cheap meat, and the effects of war on people's lives, leaving them homeless. He couldn't bear to see the vulnerable being ruthlessly exploited, nor the lack of thought that most of us give to any of these things.' Pausing, I took another breath. 'He always said that television doesn't portray the real story, only the sanitised version, or the version politicians want us to see. It riled him the way news reported yesterday doesn't disappear overnight, but the coverage simply stops, because some-thing more shocking comes along. And in a nutshell, that's what we as humans are constantly hardwired to seek. *The more shocking issues that were everything Ben felt compelled to fight against.'* Pausing again, my hands were shaking. *'He wanted to help make the world a better place. One where kindness and compassion take precedence over greed and self-interest. Where cruelty is no longer something we turn a blind eye to. Where people care about each other and this beautiful planet – because most of us don't. Not enough. Which is why nothing changes.'*

I looked at the eyes still fixed on me. 'Benedict Andrew Summer was born thirty years ago. He should have had a brilliant future ahead of him. But instead, he is every bit as much a victim as the causes he campaigned to help. A victim of a system based on selfishness and greed, that doesn't care enough.

'Ben and I shared the happiest days of our lives together. He will be remembered always as someone who truly cared about this world we're slowly destroying, the mess we're leaving behind for future generations. It's a world that has lost someone special. Maybe we all need to think more about how we live and what we're bequeathing to our children. I think that is his legacy. We owe him that much, each and every one of us, to become more aware. To live more consciously.'

I managed to stay calm as I walked back to the pew – probably down to the vodka shot I'd had before leaving the house – with the clicking of my heels echoing through the church, but I'd always been good under the spotlight. It had mattered so much that I didn't let Ben down, and however else I may have failed him, today I didn't think I had. As I sat down next to Dad, there were tears in his eyes.

'Well done, love,' he whispered. 'You did him proud.'

But after the funeral, I was lost. I had a home I didn't want to live in without him. A job I used to love, but now couldn't face. A life that was suddenly empty; everything I used to enjoy now pointless, frivolous, meaningless, while I lived with the oscillating, unpredictable wave that grief is. At a standstill, I'd no idea what came next.

55

AFTER

January

In a million years, I never could have imagined losing you. Afterwards, I'd given the eulogy all I had, wanting my words to stay with people. Opening my laptop, I bring it up on the screen. Each word had been so carefully chosen to make people listen, but as I read it again, it's as if it's for me.

* * *

As the year begins, I start a blog. *Living Consciously.* The first post I write is about pig farms, illustrated with the photos Brad took at the factory farm, contrasting them with others from a local free-range farm. I want people to understand the difference; to realise what their choices mean but, also, to stand up, speak out for what they believe in.

The next will be about the reality of the dairy industry, and the systemic abuse of cows even though they are sentient, loving beings. How for most cows, pretty green fields are no more than a myth. After being confined and continuously exploited – having experienced grief when their newborn calves are taken away, their bodies ultimately becoming exhausted, or when their milk yield drops – their lives come to an end in the slaughterhouse.

As well as using social media, I'll contact the press and groups that campaign about the welfare of intensively farmed animals. Knowing I have a plan gives me a new sense of purpose, as I think of the money from my parents and the sale of our house – enough to give me time to make this work.

It's like you always said: suffering has become normalised, as has hatred, exploitation, abuse. And I understand the despair you felt, because there are people who will never care. But I also believe more of us seek a different way to live, with love, compassion and kindness. Change is starting, the next chapter being written; the message rippling out, one of hope.

Meanwhile, another milestone edges closer. In the last twelve months, I've moved, sold our house, survived our birthdays, anniversaries, Christmas, leading to the big one. A year since I lost you.

Like you've said yourself, it's just time, babe.

It's been a frigging long time. And I'm frightened your voice will fade, then your touch, your face. What if it happens to our love?

It won't. Your voice is unequivocal. *Love can't. It's infinite, timeless, eternal. It will never fade, Cassidy. It'll be there always.*

My eyes fill with tears because there's a question I haven't been able to ask you. One that even now, I can't find the words for. But you've read my mind, the way you often have.

What if you don't want to be alone any more? That's what you're thinking, isn't it?

You're right. What if I fall in love again? It will never be like it was with you, but what if I don't want to spend the rest of my life on my own? As I wipe my face, more tears pour down my cheeks.

It doesn't mean you won't still love me too. But there'll be someone out there who needs your shining light as much as I did. Maybe he's another part of your story. And that's OK.

But I don't want to want anyone else. I want you.

Listen, you need to think about your life and all the chapters yet to be written, wherever they're going to take you. The amazing things you're going to do...

Do you know how heartbreaking it was, I sob, how I felt when I found you?

I was lost in a dark place, babe. This last year, I know it's felt like that for you, too. But it's a good time to think about those plans of yours. What happened will always be part of who you are, but it doesn't have to define you. You know how shit feels, Cassidy. But you're still there, still you, with that brilliant, vibrant light of yours. Go shine it on this world. God knows, it needs it.

So what now?

Don't think. Do the first thing that comes into your head, babe.

Pack.

* * *

During the night, I dream about you, standing next to me as those terrible hours unfold, shielding me with your love from the horror, as in slow motion I relive them. Finding your body, the paramedics arriving. Ellie coming. The moment they took you away.

If I could go back, I wouldn't have done that to you, you tell me. *But I'd have been a shadow blotting out the sun on your every day, all the time chipping away at the beauty of us.*

In my dream, your hand holds mine as I watch us – from a distance, as though we're watching other people. Finding your body, trying to breathe life into you, willing your heart to begin pumping again, all of it futile; knowing deep inside, you had gone.

So, in your last moments, I find you in the darkness and hold you, lifting the unbearable weight from you so that you can rest, smoothing away the dark circles under your eyes, covering your face with kisses, until at last, the pain has gone and you're at peace.

I know it's been hard, you whisper beside me. *It's changed you. I know it has. You're still changing, will go on changing. That's what life is.*

As the girl I am now watches the girl I used to be, still in my dream I turn to you. Softly, I kiss your cheek; whisper, thank you.

56

BEFORE

January, last year

'Why don't you come downstairs?' The paramedic spoke gently.

Shaking, my arms were wrapped around myself. 'I can't.' At Ben's bedside, I crouched down, stroking the face I knew so well, curling my fingers into his thick dark hair, my tears falling on his skin.

'Is there someone we can call? Your parents, maybe?'

'They live in Devon.' Shivering, I could barely get the words out as I laid my cheek against Ben's.

She spoke gently again. 'Would you like us to contact them?'

Suddenly I wanted the solid reassuring presence of my dad. But with him so far away, there was only one person I wanted here. 'Can you call Ellie?' My hands were shaking as I unlocked my phone and found Ellie's number.

As she went out of the room, her voice was low so that I couldn't make out what she was saying. Less than a minute later, she came back. 'She's on her way.'

Sitting on the floor, I took one of my beloved Ben's hands in mine. Already it was cold. 'Wake up, Ben,' I whispered. 'Please wake up...' Tears of desperation poured down my face, my eyes flickering over the shirt he was wearing; one I'd bought him. I watched the dark lashes that didn't flicker, choking back my sobs. Ben couldn't die. He couldn't leave me.

I was vaguely aware of the doorbell ringing, of footsteps on the stairs, then more footsteps as they came back up.

'Mrs Summer?'

It was a man's voice. Turning my tear-stained face to see who it was, I took in the policeman standing in the doorway. I frowned. Why was he here?

'It's procedure,' one of the paramedics told me. 'When there's an unexpected death at home, we have to call the police.'

The doorbell rang again. She glanced at me. 'It might be your friend.'

As she went out, I heard the sound of the front door being opened before someone came running up. Then Ellie's voice. 'Casey?'

In the doorway, my friend's eyes were wide with shock. Getting to my feet, I went over and collapsed into her arms.

* * *

In the kitchen, one of the paramedics made us strong sweet tea while, sitting next to me, Ellie held my hands. 'When did you find him?'

'When I got back from work.' Staring at the table, I was numb.

'Mrs Summer,' As the police officer told me they were going to move Ben's body, the room started to spin. Getting up, Ellie grabbed my hand. 'Let them be, Casey. They know what they're doing.'

'But they're taking him.' Panic filled me.

'He can't stay here.' Holding my hands, there were tears in her eyes.

All my instincts were telling me to run upstairs, to climb into bed next to Ben, fold my body around his. Gripping her hands, I heard the door being opened again, then murmured voices, the unmistakable sound of something being carried upstairs. Imagining Ben being slid onto a *stretcher, before being brought down and taken out to the ambulance, it was too much. Closing my eyes, pulling my hands from Ellie's, I clamped them over my ears.*

A few minutes later, Ellie gently lifted my hands away. 'Casey? It's OK. They've gone.'

'Where've they taken him?' At the thought of Ben's body being taken away by strangers, I felt sick.

'To the hospital. They need to find out what happened.' She paused.

'It must have been his heart.' I was clutching at straws. 'How else could it have happened so quickly?'

'I'm going to call your mum.' Taking over, Ellie scrolled down my contacts and found my parents' number. But my brain was still taking everything in. Ben had gone. My parents, his parents; they would be devastated.

'I need to tell Gina.' Waves of grief were pouring over me, my body starting to shake again at the thought of telling her.

'I'll ask your mum to call her.'

Taking my phone with her into the sitting room, I could still hear her. 'Hi. It's Ellie. I'm with Casey. I'm using her phone.' She paused for a moment. 'Actually, no. Things aren't OK. It's Ben.' There was another pause.

Unable to bear listening to her tell my parents, I opened the back door and stepped outside. The air was cold, the neighbouring houses cosy behind drawn curtains, the scent of wood smoke coming from somewhere. Gazing up, I looked at the stars. Is that where Ben was now? Out there, somewhere?

As I went back inside, Ellie was still talking. Then she came into the kitchen, holding my phone out towards me. 'Your mum wants a word.'

'Mum?' My voice cracked. Tears were pouring down my face. 'I came back from work...'

'Oh Casey... I'm so sorry... You two were so happy...' She broke off. 'Your father wants to talk to you.' There was a scuffling sound as she handed the phone over.

'Hello?'

At the sound of my dad's voice, my tears spilled over, running down my cheeks. 'Hello Dad...' My voice broke.

'I'm so sorry, sweetheart. So sorry.' He sounded terribly upset. 'We'll get going as soon as we can.'

'Yes.' Tears streamed down my face.

'We'll see you later.' His voice cracked. 'Your mum's going to call Gina. Is that OK?'

As my phone slipped from my fingers, Ellie grabbed it. 'Hello?' She paused. 'OK. I'll tell her.' She paused again. 'Try not to worry too much. I'll call the school, then I'll take her home with me.'

Putting my phone down, Ellie looked at me. 'Do you have the number for the school? Then we'll pack a few things.'

I shook my head. 'I'll do it.' But nothing was registering. I was in shock, unable to think straight about anything.

A few minutes later, I was still sitting at the table. Ellie took my hand. 'I'll get some of your things together.' This time I didn't argue, just listened to my friend go upstairs. When she came down again, I watched her eyes flicker towards the vase of red roses on the kitchen table. 'They were here when I got in earlier.' My voice was hoarse as I looked at them. A dozen of the most beautiful, red velvet roses. Flowers of love.

57

January

In my bedroom, up in the eaves, I pack my bags and my suitcase, but there is one more thing I have to do before I leave.

Outside, rain falls heavily as I let the last bottled-up memories claw their way to the surface. They're of soft, red, velvety rose petals, the letter you left, my sense of shock multiplied by grief, the jagged sound of my life shattering; the reasons I haven't spoken to Gina, all of them holding me back.

Gina had known Ben struggled. But when she came round to Ellie's after Ben died, I couldn't listen to her. What she told me was too painful, about truths I didn't want to believe. So since, I've blocked them out – and I've blamed her. For her complicity in keeping Ben's secret. For not sharing it with me, when I was the person who should have known.

58

January, last year

After Ben's body had been taken away, Ellie packed a few of my things, then after coming downstairs, coaxed me out to her car. The next thing I was aware of was sitting on her sofa.

Nothing had prepared me for the flipside of giving my heart; trusting unreservedly. But when I fell in love, I'd believed that Ben was my destiny and that, together, we'd take on the world – a world I never expected to be savagely ripped away from me.

At some point, Gina called. Seeing her name flash up on my mobile, I let it ring.

'Would you like me to talk to her?' Ellie held out her hand for my phone.

But it didn't matter. Nothing did. As the phone stopped ringing, seconds later it pinged with a missed call alert.

Going out to her kitchen, Ellie came back and pressed a glass into my hand. 'Drink it.'

As my phone rang again, this time, Ellie didn't ask. Picking it up, she went back to the kitchen while I sat, catatonic, on her sofa. If only I'd taken the day off work, spent it with Ben... Seen how unwell he was... Got him to the doctor... Just then, Ellie came back in from the kitchen. 'I should have been there.' My face was wet with tears as I stared at her, utterly distraught. 'It wouldn't have happened if I'd been there.'

'Oh, Casey...' Her voice was desperately sad. 'What about the next day? Or some other day in the future? Short of being with him 24/7, you couldn't have changed anything.'

'But he must have been so frightened,' I cried. 'He was alone. He shouldn't have been alone...' My voice wavering, I collapsed into sobs, because Ellie was wrong. I'd failed him.

* * *

After taking two more calls in her kitchen, Ellie came and sat next to me. 'That was your dad. They're on their way but there was an accident on the motorway and the traffic hasn't moved for two hours. They're going to stop and find a hotel for tonight, then set off again first thing tomorrow.

Tomorrow? I stared at her. How was I going to do tomorrow?

'I'm taking the day off work,' she said quietly. 'Gina called again, too. She wants to see you. I said I'd call her tomorrow and fix a time.' Ellie hesitated. 'I told her where Ben had been taken. She obviously needed to know.'

I nodded. Gina had brought him into the world. This was as wrong for her as it was for me.

Unable to sleep that night, I stared at the ceiling in Ellie's room, aware of her sleeping next to me, as the questions kept coming, tears pouring constantly from my eyes. Why had this happened? When Ben had been one of the most kind, compassionate, good-hearted people, why him? Torturing myself with thoughts about what his last minutes had been like. Were you in pain, Ben? Had it hurt when your heart stopped?

A memory of last weekend came to me. Ben and I laughing, because it was a year to the day of the fated holiday with Ellie when I'd left my passport at home. The day I'd met Ben and my life had changed forever. And now a year later, it had changed again. What had been the point of us?

Why aren't you with me, Ben? Your face next to mine, your breathing regular because you always fell asleep before I did. I'd never touch him again. Never kiss him, feel his warmth. Lying there, I willed my own heart to stop. For this pain to be over, so that I could follow Ben. Be wherever he had gone.

As the room started to lighten, beside me I felt Ellie stir. Coming to, as she turned and saw me there, I watched the memory of yesterday wash across her face, her eyes filling with tears. Reaching out, she put her arms around me.

* * *

Gina arrived first. Overnight, grief had added twenty years, etched into her eyes, her skin, her air of defeat. She took both of my hands in hers. 'I don't know what to say.' Her voice was husky. 'I know he loved you. So much.'

'It must have been his heart.' I was still trying to make sense of it. 'What else could it have been?'

Ellie interrupted. 'Can I make you a cup of tea, Gina?'

'No thank you.' As Gina sat on Ellie's sofa, I sat next to her.

'Casey...' She sighed. 'I'm so sorry. I think we both know...'

'Know what?' My body turned to ice.

'Oh, sweetheart. We both know it wasn't his heart that killed him. He...'

'How dare you?' I snatched my hands away. 'You weren't there. You didn't see him.' Hating the anger in my voice, hating myself, when I knew how much she was hurting too.

'Casey, I know you're upset. We both are...' Her eyes were pleading

with me to let her speak. 'I thought when you were getting married, it meant he was better... I'm so sorry, we should have talked about it...'

Through the fog in my brain, I latched on to her last words. 'Sorry.' I frowned. 'You said better. You knew he'd been ill? Before?'

For a moment, she couldn't look at me. 'He always said that if he met someone important, he'd explain about his problems.'

'Wait.' My mind was all over the place as I tried to take in what she was saying. 'He said he'd been up and down in the past, but no more than that. What happened?'

Gina's sigh seemed to empty the air out of her. 'It was eight years ago.' Her voice was tight. 'He had a really bad time. He was between jobs and overnight, the stress of it seemed to catch up with him. In a big way.' Glancing at me, she swallowed. 'I suppose when he was a child, there were warning signs. I put them down to hormones and mood swings.' A lone tear traced its way down her cheek. 'They seemed to disappear. But one evening, he took an overdose.' Her voice dropped to a whisper. 'Fortunately, I realised and called an ambulance.'

I sat there, dumbstruck. 'You should have told me.' Suddenly I was furious. 'Ben should have told me. I could have made sure we'd found proper help from somewhere.' Getting up, I paced over to the window, unable to take this in.

'Casey, don't,' Ellie pleaded.

'Don't what? Be angry?' I flashed back at her. 'My husband is dead and I'm not allowed to be fucking angry?'

'It's OK.' Behind me, Gina's voice was tearful. 'I should have told you. But I thought he was over it.'

'Over depression?' I looked at her sadly. 'If only it worked like that.' I started walking towards Ellie's bedroom, pulling the door closed before collapsing onto her bed, burying my face in one of her pillows, as more sobs erupted from me. Oh, God... Why was this happening? What was I supposed to do now?

But my anger wasn't directed at Gina. It was at myself, for denying the truth. At the medical profession for not helping him. At the whole frigging world for the stigma around mental health issues. At Ben, too. And therein lay the dichotomy of what I was feeling. Anger at him for taking his own life, yet anger at myself for not being able to help him.

I'm not sure how much later my parents arrived. My mum wearing black, tearful as she hugged me briefly. As my dad held out his arms, I fell into them. 'I'm so sorry, love.'

That my parents had come, made it horribly, devastatingly real. But in the depths of my misery, I couldn't bring myself to even care about Gina. I knew she'd lost her son, but she still had Mick, while I had lost everything.

59

February

As I think about a mother losing her son, a different kind of grief catches up with me. A howling storm of it, crashing over me, not just for her, but for every woman whose child has been taken away from her.

It's one of my survival strategies that I haven't even been able to look at the white envelope on which my name is written in Gina's neat, curly handwriting. It arrived a couple of weeks after Ben's funeral, nearly a year ago. Going upstairs, I find it buried in the bottom of one of my bags. Perching myself on the bed, I open the letter for the first time.

> *Dearest Casey*
>
> *I truly understand why you don't want to talk to me. You feel I've let you down and you're right. I have. I should have talked to*

you about Ben's problems a long time ago, but I suppose I
wanted to believe that things had changed.

As a mother, nothing is more important than your child's
happiness. I thought, with you, Ben had found that. I hoped your
brightness countered his darkness and that the love you shared
was strong enough to overcome what he struggled with. After
the women who let him down, I thought my funny little boy with
his earnest ways and endearing smile had finally found a woman
who understood him.

I didn't know he was keeping secrets from you. He told me
you knew everything, and when I saw how happy you were, I
didn't want to pry. But as it turns out he lied – to both of us. But
he would never have intended to hurt us. He thought he could
cope, and he did, with fortitude and courage, until he reached
the point he couldn't.

Ben's depression was every bit as real as appendicitis or a
broken leg, just easier to hide. And he hid it so well. The day he
died, a part of me died with him. I will miss him for the rest of my
life. But we were lucky, both of us, to have him in our lives, even
if it wasn't for long enough.

With love, always
Gina

Tears stream down my face. At the time, I hadn't wanted to
listen to her. I was too angry with her for keeping quiet about Ben's
problems; wanting someone to blame, anything rather than face
the truth. Then afterwards, I'd blocked it out. Suddenly I'm filled
with shame, and regret, that I could have done that to her, when she
was hurting as much as I was.

My hands are shaking, more tears pouring down my face as I
scrabble for my phone. I can't think what I'm going to say to Gina.
When I've been so rude and insensitive, I don't even know if she'll

pick up when she sees my number. But after two rings, I hear her voice.

'Casey, dear,' she says gently. 'How are you?'

'*I'm sorry,*' I cry, unable to stop the emotions ripping out of me. 'I'm so sorry, Gina. I've been so awful to you.'

'Oh, Casey.' Her voice sounds choked. 'You really haven't. You're still grieving.'

'But so are you…' I sob. 'You lost your son. I'm so sorry…' Words, grief, pour out of me. 'I've been so wrapped up in myself. Will you forgive me?'

'There really is nothing to forgive,' she says tearfully.

'But I scattered his ashes without telling you,' I howl. 'He doesn't even have a grave to remember him by.'

'Casey, Ben doesn't need a grave for us to remember him.' Her voice is husky. 'You did what you felt was right. Tell me – how are you? Are you still in France?'

'Yes.' I wipe my face. 'I'm sorry I haven't kept everything – from the house…' My voice breaks again.

'It's not important.' She's silent for a moment. 'I'm pleased Ellie's got some of your things. I think Ben would've liked that.'

Her words trigger another torrent of tears. 'You don't think he'd mind?'

'No.' She says it quietly.

'I should have called you ages ago,' I sob. 'I should have been there for you.'

'No,' she says gently. 'After everything that's happened, you've needed to think of yourself.' Her voice unsteady, she pauses for a moment. 'You mentioned forgiveness.' Her voice wavers. 'And I've been thinking so much these last few months.'

'So have I,' I whisper.

'Well, I think apart from loving my son to the moon and back…' Her voice trembles again. 'We have something else in common.'

She hesitates. 'I think we both blame ourselves for what happened. I know I do. And I blame myself for keeping quiet.'

'He hated the idea of taking pills. It made him feel he was weak.' My voice shakes as I remember.

'Did Ben ever tell you that when he was younger, he wanted to join the army? He thought he'd follow in his dad's footsteps... but he didn't get in. It was his medical history. Afterwards, he never talked about it, but I think that was when he first saw himself as a failure. It was after that he went into advertising.'

Another shock hits me, more tears filling my eyes. 'I didn't know,' I whisper. 'Poor Ben... I wish he'd told me...'

'I don't know why he didn't. You two were so close...' Gina sounds upset. 'Maybe not getting into the army didn't help how he felt, but his problems started long before that. It's difficult to accept that there was nothing either of us could have done, but I think we have to – and start forgiving ourselves. It was out of our hands. There is one thing I have learned; it's that you can be there for someone, support them, love them, try to understand, but you can't change what they do and how they feel. The only person who can do that is them.'

'I know.' More tears stream down my cheeks. 'But it's the worst thing, that someone you love would take their own life.'

'Yes.' Her voice is tight. 'But we both know he'd never have wanted to hurt us.'

60

February, last year

After the funeral, when I picked up Ben's ashes, I'd thought about where I might scatter them, but until I decided where, I was hanging on to them.

Placing the urn in the sitting room for a few days, I talked and cried to it, until one night, after too much wine, I got mad as hell with it. 'So noble,' I shouted through my sobs, my face wet with tears. 'So fucking noble, Ben, to just sign out and leave me here on this fucking planet without you...' Knocking back my wine, I poured another, then another.

As well as the grief raging through me, Ben's death left too many questions – about why, and what next, and about where the hell was the sense in any of it.

'Oh, Ben,' I sobbed in my quieter moments. 'I can't bear living without you.'

As yet undecided about what to do with his ashes, one Sunday morning I woke up early. Pulling on layers of clothes, by the time I reached the Downs, dawn was breaking. With the urn safely in my ruck-sack, there'd been comfort in knowing Ben was with me.

Reaching the top, I found a place to sit. Scanning the easternmost vista, I watched the top of the sun creep above the horizon, bathing the fields in golden light.

In the silence, I felt the whisper of a breeze around me, its softness touching my face, an aching yearning for my husband, filling me. I wasn't ready to say goodbye.

Sliding my rucksack off, I got the urn out and opened it, and from it lifted the bag containing Ben's ashes. Then I picked up a handful, and closed my eyes. 'I guess I'll be seeing you, Ben,' I whispered. 'In the wind, the rain, the sun...'

Throwing them to the wind, I watched them swirl in the air as they were carried away, before doing it again. Repeating it over and over, as the breeze picked up, until the bag was empty, turning it inside out to free the last of them.

It seemed fitting that his ashes would be scattered by the elements, becoming part of the landscape he loved. But suddenly I was stricken. Was it a mistake, that there was nowhere to come to remember Ben? In my grief, I hadn't thought about other people. Would Ben's parents, my own, be upset that there was nowhere to take flowers, or sit quietly and spend time just remembering him? While Gina tried not to show it, my guilt knew no bounds. But nothing was right. As far as I could see, it never would be.

* * *

After the cards and flowers stopped coming, after everyone else's lives got back to normal, unable to face work, I'd written my letter of resignation. It wouldn't have been appropriate to go back to the school. Children didn't need the shadow of grief hanging over them.

It left me alone in our house surrounded by memories. Beautiful, sparkling, cut glass ones of falling in love and our wedding; the plans for the future we'd made. So much love had been condensed into just one year. A year that would have to last me a lifetime.

One morning I wandered over to the window and gazed out across the back garden, just as an orange ball came flying over the fence. Going to the door, I pulled on my shoes and went outside, picking up the ball just as I saw our neighbours' daughter peering over.

'Hello.' I took the ball over to her. 'I found this.' I tried to summon some humour. 'Do you know who it belongs to?'

Her face crinkled into a toothy grin. 'It's mine!' Then as she stood there, she looked sad. 'Mummy says Ben's died. She said he's gone to heaven.'

'Yes.' My voice sounded choked.

'Is he really in heaven?'

'You betcha.' I'd never believed in God and heaven less than I did right now, but I wasn't putting that one on an innocent five-year-old. 'Here.' I lobbed the ball over the fence, before going inside.

* * *

As more time passed, I still wasn't functioning. The independent woman with her busy life and defence mechanisms I had before I met Ben, no longer existed. I'd let love into my life, let it change me, and now my heart was broken.

Restlessly pacing rooms that still held the echo of Ben's last moments, I was unable to eat, the weight falling off me, despite well-meaning friends coming round with takeaways and wine. One night, glancing at the clock, I wondered whose turn it would be. A few minutes later, when the doorbell rang, it was Ellie.

'Hi.' Her cheek was cold as she kissed me. 'It's time it warmed up out there. I got Chinese.'

Suki had arrived with Chinese the previous night, but it was irrelevant. 'Come and have some wine. I want to get hammered,' I said bitterly. It hadn't been a good day, but they never were.

In the kitchen, Ellie switched on the oven, then got out the foil trays from the bag she was carrying. 'They need warming. I got held up on the way here.' She paused, frowning. 'I'll pour us some wine.'

Sensing a conspiracy I didn't know about, I looked at her suspiciously as I took the glass she offered, pulling out one of the chairs as she sat on another. But she didn't elaborate.

61

February

After speaking to Gina, I go outside. I wish you'd told me about wanting to join the army. I've tried, but I can't imagine you doing that. When we were so open with each other, there can only be one reason you didn't. The same reason you kept your depression from me. Shame.

It would have changed nothing, Ben. And it was no reason to feel ashamed. I loved you, remember? No matter what.

But there is still too much stigma about men showing their vulnerability. Since coming to France, I've googled the hell out of depression and tried to understand more. Not just the depths of blackness that engulf some people, but the guilt, the feelings of powerlessness and the sense of shame they feel, believing they're an inconvenience to everyone, while taking medication feels an admission of weakness. So many manifestations of an illness that's so difficult to treat.

I've read about people describing the depths as without colour, a monochromatic world without light, stretching interminably ahead, leaving no corner of your life untouched. A place that for anyone else is impossible to imagine, because unless you've been there yourself, how can you? And as Gina said, it's every bit as real as a broken leg or appendicitis. If only it was as easy to fix.

You were destined for something great in this world, Ben. But I don't blame you for checking out early. My biggest sorrow will always be that I couldn't help you.

You did help me, babe. And maybe in the strangest way, good will come of this. If I've left something behind that's made at least one other person think, that's how it starts. A few words that stick with someone, then ripple out to more people. And so it goes on.

I know you still think it was me who had a role to play. But it was always you. Look at how you spoke at my funeral. I was the catalyst that shocked you out of your predictable, material world! And we're not talking ripples, this is about tidal waves, babe. The irrepressible force of Casey Cassidy unleashed. You just wait.

Unsettled, I'm reminded of what Kevin said, which doesn't make sense because I've always believed I was destined for a quiet life – with a husband, my teaching job, a couple of kids.

Hasn't quite worked out that way, has it? Maybe you should ask yourself why.

Going to my laptop, I open the blog I've started. As I look at what I've written, something inside me clicks into place. It's as though I'm taking on the messages of the millions of people seeking change in the world, all of them wanting to be heard.

As a teacher, I can find a way to bring these harshest of truths to schools too, in a way for children to take on board. My heart starts to race. I can research, put material together, from anywhere. Then when I'm ready, I'll begin with the school where I used to work.

* * *

As I lie in bed, my head is buzzing. There are all these ways to further what Ben started, yet use my own skills, too. *And stay free.* Freedom matters more than anything.

On waking, a splash of colour beside the terrace catches my eye – a vivid unseasonal rose on the bush Kevin planted for Julia – just as, in one of those unpredictable twists the universe sends, my mobile buzzes with a message. It's from the eco-retreat in Sierra Nevada, where you were going for your Christmas present. After being closed to guests because of storm damage, they've reopened. The voucher I bought you is still valid.

As I start typing my reply, I hear your voice.

You go. I think, even as far back as last Christmas, it was always meant to be you going.

Starting again, I enquire about dates, because maybe I should go. Unforeseen things happen. Life changes track. And sometimes, in seemingly mysterious ways, when the time is right, what's meant to be will find you.

62

February, last year

One evening after the funeral, I'd opened my front door to find Kevin standing there. 'Is this a good time?'

I shook my head. There wasn't, never would be, a good time for anything. As I stood back, he winced.

'I didn't mean it like that.'

I shrugged. 'You'd be amazed how the most innocent phrases take on new significance.'

'I bear gifts.' Kevin held out a bottle of brandy and a house brick of chocolate.

Closing the door behind us, I headed for the kitchen, Kevin behind me. When we got there, he peeled his jacket off. 'You've lost weight, Cassidy,' he said quietly. 'You need to eat.'

'I don't have an appetite.' I watched him go to one of the cupboards, collecting two glasses and putting them on the table before unscrewing the bottle he'd brought with him.

'This is good stuff.' He glanced at me. 'Obviously not top end, but still good.'

I took the glass he pushed towards me as, without saying anything, he picked up his and chinked it against mine.

It was good. Smooth, rich and gloriously strong. 'Everything is shit, Kev.' My voice was husky with sadness, bitterness, grief. 'So shit.'

'I know.' Leaning forward, he put his glass down. 'The worst ever kind of shit.' Kevin was quiet for a moment. 'Eat this.' He shoved a wedge of chocolate at me. 'Or you're not getting any more brandy.'

Breaking off another chunk, he went on. 'Actually, I've something to run by you.'

My heart sank. I was sick to death of well-intentioned suggestions.

'I know the last thing you want right now is someone like me trying to help, but hear me out. There's this house. In France. It belongs to a friend and it's been empty for a while. It's nothing special. I mean it's nice – just not fancy. Anyway, it's yours for a while if you want it.'

'I don't want to go to France.' I gazed miserably at my glass.

'I know you don't.' Kevin was silent for a moment. 'Right now, you don't want to go anywhere. But it would get you away from here.'

I was silent.

'It is a thing, you know,' he went on. 'Putting distance between you and whatever is breaking your heart. It won't change what's happened. Nothing can,' he said gently. 'I just thought, you have nothing to lose giving it a go. I thought you might be fed up with people turning up at your door bearing brandy and chocolate. It's a pretty safe bet you'd be left alone.'

I thought about it, weighing up the effort it would take versus the security of staying where I was. Security winning out, until I remembered the endless monotony of the days, the unstoppable onslaught of memories. 'Who owns the house?'

'A friend. Her name's Antigua. Rich hippie chick who's perfectly happy with her city life. She hardly ever goes there.'

Even in my unhappiness, the thought of getting away had lodged in my brain. 'Can I think about it?'

'Sure.' Fishing in his pocket, Kevin put a small zip seal bag on the table. 'I brought you something else... It'll make you high and knock you out for a bit. There might be a few colours along the way...'

I shook my head. 'I'll stick with the brandy.' My brain was struggling enough as it was without hallucinogens. Grabbing the bottle, I topped up my glass.

'Sure.' He put it back in his pocket. 'Hey, take it easy.'

Maybe I should have heeded his warning. On an empty stomach, the third glass of brandy was enough to knock me out. Making it into the sitting room, I collapsed onto the sofa.

Somewhere during the night, I was vaguely aware of Kevin covering me with a blanket, while I thought I heard his voice softly whispering.

'One day, Casey Cassidy. This will pass.'

* * *

When I mentioned the house in France to Ellie, it was clear Kevin had got to her first.

'I had a call from him the other night, when I was on my way round to you.'

'He told you about the house?' I said angrily. I was sick to death with the way that being bereaved made me everyone else's business; that even Ellie was going behind my back. 'And you didn't mention it to me?'

Ellie shook her head. 'He didn't mention the house specifically.'

'I've told him I'll think about it.' I said crossly. 'Why can't he butt out and leave me alone?'

'He's being a friend,' Ellie said tactfully. 'So. Have you? Thought about it?'

I couldn't believe she was even asking. It's only a few weeks since Ben died. Wasn't I allowed to grieve for Christ's sake?

Seeing the look on my face, she went on, slowly, gently, patiently, the *way Ellie is.* 'It isn't just Kev. We're all worried about you, Case. I mean, it's understandable that you're not up to doing anything, but maybe—'

'Maybe what?' I demanded. 'Snap myself out of it, get back to work and act like nothing's happened?' Seeing her face, I was mortified. 'Oh God. Ellie... I'm so sorry. You've done so much to help me. You didn't deserve that.'

'No.' She was quiet for a moment, before looking at me again. 'Do I dare say what I think?'

'I'm sorry. Please do.' I stared at her.

'This house is filled with memories. And you're sleeping in the bed where Ben died. Don't you think a change of scene would be good? Even if it's only for a week or two?'

I looked at her, aghast. 'I can't believe you're suggesting I go on holiday.'

'I'm not.' Ellie was shaking her head. 'I'd been thinking more along the lines of a retreat. Not an organised one, just somewhere away from here, that's really peaceful. I don't know. Kevin might be onto something with this offer of the house. And if it all goes wrong, you just come back.' Her eyes were troubled. 'But I don't like the idea of you being alone.'

'But I am, aren't I?' I said more calmly. 'I can't go on leaning on you and everyone else. Like I said to Kevin, I'll think about it.'

* * *

The clincher came when I told my parents. 'It belongs to a friend of a friend. No one uses it.'

'You can't possibly go driving across France on your own.' My mother sounded horrified. 'You don't even speak French. What if you're ill? It makes far more sense for you to move back here. Now, I was thinking perhaps we'll come over the day after tomorrow...'

As usual, she had it all mapped out. But even the thought was too much for me. 'Mum, I wasn't calling you to discuss it. I've already decided. I'm taking the house.'

63

AFTER

February

Out of the blue, Kevin calls me.

'How are you, Cassidy?'

'I'm OK – I think.' I pause. 'I'm going to head for the Sierra Nevada – to an eco-retreat. But it's all got a bit weird.'

'That's great you have a plan.' He doesn't ask what's weird. 'Have you thought any more about how long you want to stay?'

'I've started packing,' I tell him. 'I started packing last month. But for some reason, I haven't finished.'

'So, you're going but you're not.' Kevin's voice is amiable. 'What's stopping you?'

Pausing, I sigh. 'Stuff I don't particularly want to take with me.' I take a deep breath. 'I got here mid-March last year, right? OK.' I'm not sure where it comes from as I tell Kevin that I'm moving out exactly a year after I arrived here. But it feels right.

'You're sure?' He sounds doubtful.

'No,' I say firmly. 'I've needed to make a decision. And now I have.'

'Cool.' He hesitates. 'Let me know when you hit the road?'

'Sure.'

As he ends the call, suddenly I realise I didn't ask him where he is. Hurriedly I text him.

Sorry for being so horribly self-obsessed. I didn't ask you where you are Kev, or how you are. x

An hour or so later, his reply is brief.

I'm good! Look after yourself, Cassidy x

A thought comes to me. If Ben was a catalyst in my life, in some unknown way, is Kevin another? With Christmas and everything else, I've never finished reading his diary. Hunting around, finding it under a cushion, I leaf through it to find the final entry.

30th December

So, here we are again. Another year almost over, a few more war wounds and a whole lot of miles behind me. OK, so there have been low points – Julia being the lowest. But it's clarified something in my mind. Something I've been deluding myself about. My big secret, folks, one I've been hiding from myself. You see, it's this girl – the sassy one I've mentioned before. What I've realised is, all along, I've been in love with her.

I stare at the diary, trying to think who she is. Then as the cogs of my mind turn, I think of the party where I first introduced him to Ben. *She doesn't know it yet, but this is the woman I'm going to marry.* The way he found this house; his kindness, as the realisation slowly comes to me. I know who this woman is, why Kevin set all this up. It's me.

Slightly dazed, I carry on reading.

Anyway, moving on. As for the high points... Well, where do I start? And more to the point, what have I learned?

That solitude and loneliness are addictive. That the more you know how peacefulness feels, the more you crave it. Those things in life which aim to break you make you stronger. That the greatest magic happens in the darkest times, and that endings lead to new beginnings. How, if you listen to the silence, the universe whispers to you. As for grief, hopelessness and unhappiness, they can knock you off track, but they can never put out the fire inside you.

What I've discovered is there's beauty all around us – from the widest, clearest sky, to the deep quiet of the forests; from the motion of the tides, to the most delicate flower and tiniest butterfly – and there's beauty in grief, too, because it means you loved. And that, folks, is what this thing called life is all about. Going about each day with love in your heart – for other people, for this incredible planet, for yourself. It's the only thing that's going to change the world. I think that's about it. So, I'm signing out. I've got a flight to catch, a party to go to. And if this girl is there, who knows...

Emotion wells up inside me. Here on this page is the really important stuff – none of the rest matters. Suddenly I have to speak to him. Picking up my phone, I call Kevin.

He answers straight away. 'Yo, Cassidy. Twice in one day? Are you OK?'

'I'm good.' I pause. 'Really good. I had to talk to you. I guess you could say things are shifting – and a lot of that is thanks to you.'

'Me?' He laughs loudly. 'And how is that?'

I hesitate. 'I finished reading the diary. Just now.'

'Oh.'

It's the first time I've known Kevin lost for words. 'I don't know how to describe it. That last part... It's all there.' My words tail off. 'Thank you for letting me read it.'

'You've kind of surprised me, Cassidy. I wasn't expecting that. Anyway, I'm glad you liked it.' But from his silence, I can tell he knows – that I know it was me he was in love with. Suddenly, I'm regretting calling him. He's one of my best friends and I can't bear to think I may have jeopardised that.

'Kev...'

But he interrupts. 'You don't need to say anything. Just keep shifting, OK? Hey, I've got to go.' His voice is bright. 'Look after yourself. I'll see you around.'

As he ends the call, I stand there, uncertain. But I'll talk to him another time. Then I take a deep breath, because at last, I'm ready. It's time to face what I've been putting off, because however hard, it's the only way through, and because I have to believe that on the other side, there will be a light.

64

BEFORE

January, last year

That day you died... In shock, I barely noticed when the policeman came downstairs. He stood at the doorway into the kitchen. 'Excuse me. I'm so sorry to interrupt you. But could I have a word?'

Ellie glanced at me. 'It won't take long, will it?'

'No.' Coming in, he looked at me. 'Mrs Summer, there was an empty bottle of sleeping pills on the bedside table. Were you aware that your husband was taking them?'

I shook my head. 'Ben doesn't take sleeping pills. He hates taking anything.'

'There's a label on the bottle. He must have got them on prescription.' The policeman hesitated. 'Was he taking anything else that you were aware of?'

'Antidepressants.' Numb, it was as though my feelings had shut down. 'But he'd stopped them.' Then I took in what he was suggesting. 'Ben wouldn't have taken anything.'

He didn't reply. Then his eyes flickered towards the vase of red roses.

'They were there when I came in from work.' My voice was toneless. 'He must have put them in water before going upstairs.'

I felt Ellie's hand clasp mine. 'You should tell him Ben left a note,' she said quietly.

'Where?' The policeman's voice was sharp.

'On the table. Casey hasn't read it yet.'

There had been a note leaning against the vase of flowers. But we often wrote each other notes. It didn't mean any more than that. I looked at Ellie. 'Can you open it?'

Reaching for it, Ellie pulled the flap from the envelope before handing it to me. 'I don't think I should read it, Casey. Ben wrote it for you.'

Unfolding the sheet of paper, I read the first line.

Dearest Casey,
    It's important you understand...

My hands were shaking. 'I can't.'

Ellie looked troubled. 'I think the police are going to need to take it. Are you sure you don't want to read it first?'

'I don't want them to have it,' I said hysterically. 'You said it was mine. Ben wrote it for me.'

'We'll return it, Mrs Summer. I'll see to it myself.'

'Before you take it...' Hesitating, Ellie picked up my phone. 'Casey? Can you unlock it?'

I punched in the code which was a play on the date of our wedding, then watched as she photographed the letter. 'It doesn't mean you have to read it,' she said quietly, handing back my phone. 'But it's there in case you change your mind.' Slipping the letter back into its envelope, she handed it over.

'Can I make a note of your contact details? Both of you?' As Ellie rattled them off, he made a note.

'That will be all I think.' He backed towards the door. 'I'm very sorry for your loss.' He nodded towards me. 'I'll let myself out.'

65

February

I hold the envelope the police returned. I don't think I will ever be ready to read your last words to me.

You can do this, my inner voice whispers to me. Or is it your voice? It's getting increasingly hard to tell.

Taking a deep breath, I slide the letter out. Then I start to read it.

Dearest Casey...

It's important you understand, this was never about you. How could it have been? Ours was the greatest love story. And believe me, I never meant to deceive you. When I met you, I thought my problems were behind me. And for the first few months, they were.

I remember seeing you that first time in the airport. As I watched you looking for your passport, I had a sixth sense about you. And I was right. You changed my life, Casey, in so many ways. Breezing in with your chaos, which I needed as much as your love. You brought light into my world. Vivid colour that had long been missing – I'm not sure you know what that meant. It was beyond my wildest dreams when we fell in love.

I've believed since that we were destined to meet. We changed each other's lives, didn't we? I know you wanted to help me, but depression made me feel like the world had closed in, a world no-one else could enter. I hated the way I shut you out. And I know it hurt you, but I couldn't stop myself.

For me, it was a hopeless, dark world there was no way out of. But you are starlight. Sunlight. A thousand kisses. Blazing fire. You don't know it yet, but it's you this world needs: your compassion and energy, optimism, strength. Your dazzling light in the darkness – don't I know that better than anyone.

You were part of my story as much as I was part of yours. And yours isn't over yet, but how it unfolds is up to you.

So don't remember how it ended. Find me in the passion we both shared for a kinder world, on the quiet hills, in the early morning as the sun rises, in the wildest storm, the transient peace, and in the widest night sky in which you are and always will be my brightest shining star, Casey Cassidy. Go blaze your trail, for both of us.

With all my love forever
Ben

After reading your letter, grief engulfs me, but this time, I don't resist it. Instead, I surrender, letting it take me over as each of its elements rages through me. As the full force of it hits me, I feel myself dragged into a place of swirling blackness. In that bleak, most hopeless of places, I finally have a window into your world, one filled with pain, that there was no way out of. But there is no anger. Just the deepest, indescribable sadness, because I understand, Ben, how you couldn't live with this. All I can think is how extraordinary you were, that for so long, you kept going.

I'm one of the lucky ones. Unlike you, when morning comes, the darkness passes and a healing starts. Like I knew it would; as the sun rises, the rain-washed sky is streaked with light.

February, last year

Strange weeks followed. After the coroner's report and confirmation that Ben took an overdose, only then did I begin to realise how much he'd kept from me. On talking to his GP, I learned the meaning of the words I'd never heard of. Depression, eco-grief and solastalgia, and their potential impact on anyone, let alone highly sensitive, empathic people such as Ben was.

I learned that the anguish felt in this changing world is very real; that there are many people who are desperate about the global scale of devastation and destruction. And I hadn't understood how insidious depression was. The effort it takes just to get out of bed, the knife-edge they walk between wanting to stay alive and the escape from pain that only death brings.

In short, the destruction of our planet was what killed Ben, as well as the blindness and complicity of those in power. He simply couldn't bear any more of man's inhumanity to man. The inherent selfishness in our possession and exploitation of the natural world. The pain too much for him, he bowed out.

* * *

With the date of my departure fast approaching, the night before I left, Kevin called in. 'Hey.' His eyes were sombre as I opened the door. 'How's it going?'

'Shit.' I told him.

'I guessed as much.' He paused. 'But you're going to France?'

I nodded. 'I won't be there for long. A week, maybe two... but it will be good to get away.'

'Stay as long as you like. Like I told you, it isn't fancy, but it's a nice place.' His eyes lingered on me. 'You're going through a lot just now. Maybe the quiet and space will be good.'

I seriously doubted it. 'Maybe.' I shrugged. 'But thanks – for organising it.'

'You're welcome.' He paused. 'I hope it helps.'

* * *

After he'd gone, I went to the kitchen and opened the one remaining bottle of wine, just as my mobile buzzed with a text from Polly that was brief and to the point.

Good luck little sis. Hope it's a smooth crossing. Don't think too much. Just do it.

67

AFTER

February

The way I see it, I can tell my story two ways. One that's come to an end, or one that's just beginning, with the knowledge that sadness is part of life and like everything always does, will come to pass.

After tidying the house, I carry on packing. A few more boxes done, I go outside. Sitting in the quiet of the garden, my mind fills with a thousand images of you. We have the best memories, Ben Summer. Rainbow-coloured, glittering, psychedelic frigging memories of the most joyous dazzling days and the depths of sadness. The entire scope of human emotion condensed into just twelve months, wrapped in a ribbon-bedecked parcel of us.

That's something, isn't it? Your voice is back. *To be lucky enough to know how all that feels? In a whole lifetime, not everyone gets that.*

But it wasn't supposed to break my heart.

It's part of being in love, babe. The highs and lows – unless you plod along in an almost straight line, barely registering anything. But what's the point of that?

I watch the sun sink lower, painting the sky orange and illuminating the mountains, as suddenly I realise everything is connected; this gnarled old house with all its stories, the trees whose roots are entwined and whose branches interweave overhead, the soft breeze, the damp earth – even me, because I'm part of it, as I feel myself drawn into the next chapter.

68

March

The rising sun lights my bedroom as I pack the last of my things before taking them out to the car. Then I call my parents to tell them I'm leaving and that I'll let them know where I end up. There are no recriminations from my mother – a hint of reluctance to share my excitement maybe, but to my mind, that's progress.

Standing in the kitchen one last time, I whisper a thank you to the empty rooms. Then, putting my car keys in my pocket, I pick up the diary.

Closing the door behind me, I leave the house key under the mat. As I walk to my car, I turn to take one last look at the old stone house that's been my haven this last year, grateful that for a while, I could be here.

Half an hour down the road, when I stop to buy petrol, I text Ellie.

I'm on my way Ell! Heading south!

Then I text Kevin.

Yo, dude. I've found my wings! I'm on the road. Destination as yet unknown. xx

Straightaway, he texts me back.

Come to Jávea, Cassidy. Little bar called Bambudda. Great place by the sea. I'll buy you a beer x

Thanks, but I'm headed further south.

Yeah? Shame, I think you'd really like it here. But I get it. Let me know where you end up. Safe travels x

Then a few minutes later, Ellie replies.

Yay!!! Keep me posted! XXX

And so I head south towards the Pyrenees, the strangest feeling staying with me, my head filling with images. A dazzling, rising sun. Pink-splashed mountain peaks. Small waves lapping on pale sand. A vivid, tangerine dream of a sunset. Your face. But your face will always be there.

It's like you said. In the short time we were together, you changed my life. Since losing you, it's changed again. We had only a year – nowhere near long enough. But some people don't need long. They burst fleetingly into our lives, opening our eyes to new horizons, changing them and us forever.

Hey! It's so great you're rediscovering life again, babe. Different now, isn't it?

It is different. Brighter for knowing the darkness, moments of joy more precious when you've known the pain of heartbreak. This amazing life that goes on, changing with each twist of the path, each glorious high point, with each loss; that will go on changing, as I whisper to you, thank you...

As the afternoon passes, France falls behind me and as it does, I let you go. But even though your voice has faded, you're where you'll always be, in my heart. Reaching the sign saying *Espagne* suspended across the motorway, as the road opens up ahead of me, a sense of freedom fills me.

After the eco-retreat in Sierra Nevada, maybe I'll go and find Sylvie. Then, who knows? A little house in the *campo* where I can write from, maybe. But I can work out where nearer the time.

As Valencia grows closer, I pull over at the roadside. Getting out, I gaze across the sea at the twinkling lights of a ferry. Beyond are the Balearic Islands. Even Morocco isn't much further south – my mind flashes back to the holiday with Ellie, the day fate brought Ben and me together. How different my life would be now if I hadn't left my passport at home that day. By the time he'd walked past departures, I would have been long gone. I might have hooked up with that hot guy in Morocco who'd seemed to follow me and Ellie everywhere, then come home, life going on, unchanged.

Or maybe fate would have found some other way to bring us together. Isn't that what's supposed to happen to soul-mates? That's how I've always seen us. Still gazing out to sea, as the breeze flickers across my face, I smooth my hair back, wishing he was with me. I will never stop wishing he was with me.

The sky is alight with brilliant shades of pink as I get back in my car. Switching on the radio, I find a chill-out station, turning it up loud as I start the engine. Then as I set off, a track I haven't heard in ages starts to play.

It's the perfect song for this moment. Turning it up loud, I listen to the lyrics of Lola's Theme, feeling my heart swell, knowing I've found the soundtrack to this new chapter of my life. I don't know where the whisper comes from.

This is about you now, Casey. Still shades of the girl you used to be, but stronger, softer, kinder, wiser. If you hadn't loved him and lost him, you wouldn't be this person. Trying to find answers. Embracing change.

Embracing? But however broken I was when all of this started, I realise I am embracing every beautiful second of this, whole-heartedly.

Lighter than I can ever remember feeling, the open road ahead seems filled with promise. So, with my destiny held firmly within my hands, my passport on the seat next to me – I've checked, more than once – I segue, if not exactly seamlessly, I like to think, fear-lessly, into the next part of this great adventure that life is.

POSTSCRIPT

As I keep driving, I pass the road sign indicating the next turn off. Glancing at the time, on impulse, I take it, following more signs to the city centre, keeping going until I reach the sea.

After eight and a half hours of driving, I should be exhausted, but it's only a few more minutes before I park my car at the road-side. Getting out, I take in a quiet buzz that seems to energise me. Looking up at the sign above the bar, I read the name. Bambudda. Picking up Kevin's diary, I cross the road.

As I go inside, the bar is dimly lit, but one figure is unmistakable. When he sees me, a look of surprise crosses his face, swiftly followed by one of delight.

Standing in front of me, there's the broadest of grins on his face. 'Casey Cassidy. What the devil are you doing here?'

I hesitate. 'It just so happens I was passing. And I thought I'd better give you this.' I wave the diary at him. 'You wouldn't want it getting into the wrong hands.'

He looks guarded for a moment. 'You really read it?'

'All of it.' My eyes gaze into his. 'And you did say something about buying me a beer. I'm parched. I've been driving for hours,

Kev... Eight and a half frigging hours, to be precise... But I have all these plans for what I'm going to do next and I'd love to tell you about them – if you have time. And then...' I pause. 'I thought maybe you could tell me about Julia.'

'I can't believe you're here.' Slowly shaking his head, he takes my hand. 'I have so much time. Come on – let's get you that beer.' His eyes hold mine as he smiles at me. 'Frigging awesome wings, Cassidy. Did you see the mountains tonight? Weren't they spectacular?'

Still holding my hand, as he carries on talking, I know that everything is just the way it's meant to be.

Some people come into our lives when we need them most. We might not know it at the time, but they leave their footprints in our hearts, changing us with the richness they bring, with their own unique way of looking at this beautiful world, the multi-coloured layers of their rainbow dreams. They are the gems and shining lights and they fill our lives with love. Ben was one of them and who knows, just maybe, Kevin is another.

But none of us knows what the future holds. For us all, it's about the dance between dark and light, death and life, and if we're lucky, love, wherever that takes us, whatever happens along the way.

NOTE

Depression is a devastating illness to live with. Unlike many other conditions, it can be invisible, and like many mental health issues, unfairly subject to a lack of understanding, even stigma. Depression removes the light and joy from life, affecting every hour of the day and every aspect of it – from close relationships, to work, to even the simplest things that become impossible.

There are many manifestations but in common is the sense of the world being a dark, joyless place, and feelings of worthlessness. Then there's pain – of bearing this terrible weight, of seeing its effect not only on yourself, but on your loved ones. Of not having hope that it will ever change.

Suicide isn't an act of selfishness. It comes from desperation and illness, an inability to see any solutions. But it isn't the answer.

If these issues affect you or a loved one, Samaritans.org, mind.org.uk, thecalmzone.net and many other organisations are there to listen.

ACKNOWLEDGMENTS

This is my first women's fiction book to be published by Boldwood and for it to be out in the world is the best feeling! I'm so grateful to my superstar agent, Juliet Mushens, for believing in it and for all her work before it went on submission to publishers, and to the truly awesome team at Mushens Entertainment – you all rock!

Knowing this book had found an editor who loves it was a magical moment. Thank you so much Tara Loder, for your brilliant and insightful editing. It's a joy to be working with you. Thank you also to Caroline Ridding, to Dushi Horti for meticulous copyediting, to Trish Bellamy for proofreading, and to everyone who's part of the wonderful and dedicated team at Boldwood.

I was inspired by many things when I was writing this book – love, friendship, untimely loss and the grief it leaves us with. It's set between Sussex and the beautiful landscape of rural France, where I've spent a large part of the last three years – and where there are mountains, forests, vast skies and a sense of solitude I've tried to put into words.

This book also looks at the mental health issues so many people live with – and there are other themes relating to the concerns that many, if not most, of us have, about the way we live on this planet. I hope it starts conversations that continue on social media and on my blog. If these affect you in any way, please do get in touch. I'd love to hear from you.

I wrote this book in a tiny village in a part of south-western France with mountain views, in the loveliest of old houses, L'Arpent, which belongs to Nik and Judy Scopes. This story flowed onto my laptop as I sat at your kitchen table! No doubt helped along by being in such a peaceful, inspiring setting. Thank you so much to you both for our time there.

More thanks and much love to my dad, my sisters, and my amazingly supportive network of friends. To Georgie and Tom, my brilliant, wonderful children. You inspire me every day. I love you to the moon and back.

To Martin for sharing this road trip that keeps on going – also for redesigning my website, and to you and Richard Henson for the photos. (No mean feat, as you know!)

Finally, to you, my readers. Thank you for buying this book. It comes from my heart to yours, with love. I hope so much you enjoy reading it. X

MORE FROM DEBBIE HOWELLS

We hope you enjoyed reading *The Life You Left Behind*. If you did, please leave a review.

If you'd like to gift a copy, this book is also available as an ebook, digital audio download and audiobook CD.

Sign up to Debbie Howells' mailing list for news, competitions and updates on future books.

https://bit.ly/DebbieHowellsnews

ABOUT THE AUTHOR

Debbie Howells' first novel, a psychological thriller, *The Bones of You*, was a Sunday Times bestseller for Macmillan. Four more bestsellers followed, including most recently *The Vow*, published by Avon. Fulfilling her dream of writing women's fiction she has found a home with Boldwood.

Visit Debbie's Website:

https://www.debbiehowells.co.uk

Follow Debbie on social media:

twitter.com/debbie__howells

facebook.com/debbie.howells.37

instagram.com/_debbiehowells

bookbub.com/authors/debbie-howells

ABOUT BOLDWOOD BOOKS

Boldwood Books is a fiction publishing company seeking out the best stories from around the world.

Find out more at www.boldwoodbooks.com

Sign up to the Book and Tonic newsletter for news, offers and competitions from Boldwood Books!

http://www.bit.ly/bookandtonic

We'd love to hear from you, follow us on social media:

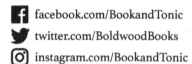

facebook.com/BookandTonic

twitter.com/BoldwoodBooks

instagram.com/BookandTonic

9 781804 150344